"Ford captures the Roman first century B.C. from a novel perspective . . . Battle scenes are described with great skill . . . a mastery of military history."

—*Publishers Weekly*

"Michael Curtis Ford's love for the ancient world emanates from every page: in his magical settings and spectacular re-creation of monuments and landscapes, in his bold portraits of the protagonists, and in his intriguing and swiftly moving plot."

—Valerio Massimo Manfredi,
author of the *Alexander Trilogy* and *Spartan*

"A swift and exciting story . . . Brutal, straightforward, exciting and informative . . . a hair-trigger ride on ancient sands and hills. This is Ford's best so far, and only those who have read his first two know just how good that makes this book."

—*The Statesman Journal* (Salem, Oregon)

"Powerful telling of historical drama. Michael Curtis Ford brings the Roman Empire to life. *The Last King* is complete with battle scenes and powerful storytelling about one of history's most feared warriors."

—*The Oregonian*

GODS AND LEGIONS

"Thanks to the author's excellent research of both his subject and era, the reader experiences this great man's transformation step by determined step. Highly recommended."

—*The Historical Novels Review*

"Powerful and passionate. A truly compelling story—one not just of gods and legions but of men."

—Library Journal (starred review)

"Stirring and adventurous tragedy of the first rank, written with all of the gusto of a master."

—Kirkus Reviews

THE TEN THOUSAND

"A worthy successor to Steven Pressfield's *Gates of Fire*."

—Library Journal (starred review)

"Thrilling, eloquent, illuminated by scholarship, comes this retelling of the epic running battle of the Ten Thousand from Babylon to the sea."

—James Brady,
author of the bestseller *The Marine*

"Michael Curtis Ford's moving account of the fighting and dying of these heroic Greek mercenaries is not only historically sound, but very human, in making Xenophon's tale come alive in a way that no ancient historian or classicist has yet accomplished."

—Professor Victor Davis Hanson,
author of *The Soul of Battle*

St. Martin's Paperbacks Titles
by Michael Curtis Ford

The Ten Thousand: A Novel of Ancient Greece
Gods and Legions: A Novel of the Roman Empire
The Last King: Rome's Greatest Enemy

THE
SWORD
OF ATTILA

A Novel of the Last Years of Rome

MICHAEL CURTIS FORD

St. Martin's Paperbacks

THE SWORD OF ATTILA

Copyright © 2005 by Michael Curtis Ford.

Maps by Jackie Aher

ISBN: 0-312-93915-9
EAN: 9780312-93915-1

Printed in the United States of America

St. Martin's hardcover edition / March 2005
St. Martin's Paperbacks edition / April 2006

St. Martin's Paperbacks are published by St. Martin's Press, 175 Fifth Avenue, New York, NY 10010.

10 9 8 7 6 5 4 3 2

For Eamon, Isabel, and Marie-Amandine

HISTORICAL NOTE

Rome survived some twelve hundred years, and its ultimate collapse was not a fast one—indeed, it was decades, if not centuries, in the making. By the fourth century of our era, the administration of the Roman Empire had been divided into two halves, more or less following the cultural division between the Hellenized eastern Mediterranean and the Celtic regions of western Europe. The emperors of both sides were generally related by blood or marriage and over the years cooperated with each other to a greater or lesser extent in their policies. Both sides considered themselves to be full cultural and intellectual descendants of the original, unified Rome. The eastern half, based at Constantinople, survived as late as 1453 in the form of the Byzantine Empire; the West, however, whose capital was variously Rome, Milan, and Ravenna, fell under a Germanic invasion led by the half-Hunnish chieftain Odoacer in 476, scarcely twenty-five years after the principal events of this book.

Dates and statistics, however, do little to explain the extent of the disarray that existed in the Western Empire for the hundred years or so preceding its fall. For decades, Rome's eastern borders had been under pressure from massive influxes of Germanic tribes along the Rhine and Danube Rivers. Rome made valiant efforts to defend its lines, bolstering its border garrisons, engaging in diplomatic maneuvering, even periodically permitting passage into the empire of carefully selected tribes. Still, however, the problem continued to build. It was not as if the emperor could mount a massive military effort, as in centuries past, to seize territory and drive the Germanic tribes off the land. Rome was simply too weak, and the tribes too numerous. More critically, there was nowhere the tribes could be driven *to,* for they themselves were being pushed west, to the brink of starvation and desperation, by a mysterious and terrifying new force that had recently arrived from the East: the Huns.

Nor was the empire's internal situation any more stable. By this time in its history, the Roman Senate had become toothless, more a country club for old men than a true governing body. Supreme power in the Western Empire had devolved upon the emperor and his court, which was racked by political infighting, nepotism, and decadence. The legions themselves were weak and disorganized, manned largely by foreign auxiliary units and mercenaries, and even commanded by non-Roman generals; and vast swaths of territory, such as Britain, North Africa, and Pannonia, which had previously comprised valuable parts of the empire, had fallen away from the emperor's direct control and were now under the command of indigenous leaders or invading tribes.

It was during this period of chaos and upheaval that two men were born on opposite sides of the known world whose destinies would pair and clash in a way rarely seen in human history. Both were giants in their way, whose sheer force of personality and will brought them to the pinnacles of leadership of their respective nations. And though they admired each other and indeed at one time were even friends, each found his ambitions stymied by the other—and they concluded, no doubt reluctantly, that the world was too small a place for both to exist.

Thus the stage was set for the Battle of Campi Catalaunici (usually known by its modern French name of

Châlons), one of the most crucial and cataclysmic battles in all of history—not only in terms of the enormous quantities of men and weaponry brought to bear, not merely in terms of the vast territories (all of Europe!) whose control was in play, but most important in terms of what we now know as Western civilization, whose very survival depended upon the battle's outcome. For though Rome did indeed fall twenty-five years later, it nevertheless experienced a "soft landing," in which political structures, culture and habits, buildings, religious institutions, and laws largely survived to form the basis for the Middle Ages and eventually our modern times. Had the outcome of Châlons been different, however, one can plausibly argue that all of that ancient patrimony would have been lost, indeed destroyed and scattered with a viciousness unprecedented in human history. And our lives today would be immeasurably different, and poorer, for it.

This, then, is the story of the Battle of Châlons.

The Roman and Hunnish Empires A.D. 451

Atlantic Ocean

BRITONS

SAXONS

SAXONS

THURINGIANS

SLAVS

RHINE R.

FRANKS

Paris (Lutetia)

Orleans (Aurelia)

BURGUNDIANS (SAPAUDIA)

ALAMANNI

ROMAN EMPIRE

Milan

Aquileia

VISIGOTHS

WESTERN

OSTROGOTHS

Arles (Arleta)

Ravenna

Toulouse (Tolosa)

Rome

Narbonne (Narbo)

Naples (Neapolis)

Carthage (Cartago)

VANDALS

Mediterranea

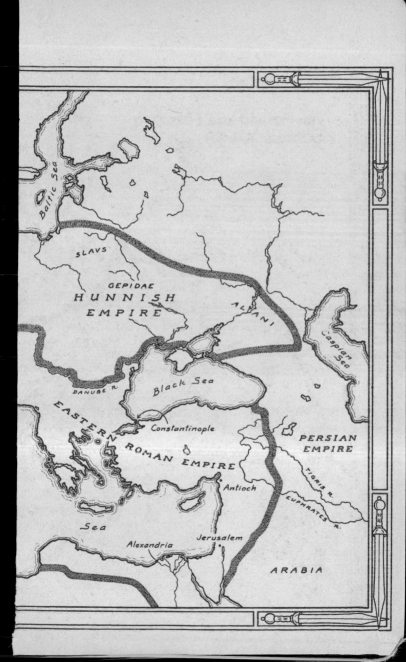

Quae potest digna causa tantorum motibus inveniri? Aut quod odium in se cunctos animavit armari? Probatum est humanum genus regibus vivere, quando unius mentis insano impetu strages sit facta populorum, et arbitrio superbi regis, momento defecerit quod tot saeculis natura progenuit.

What good reason can there be for the mobilization of so many nations? What hatred inspired them to take up arms against one another? It is proof that human beings live for their kings, for it is at the mad impulse of one mind that a slaughter of nations ensues, and at the whim of a proud ruler that what nature has taken ages to produce perishes in a moment.

—JORDANES

THE
SWORD
OF ATTILA

PART I

ONE

Campi Catalaunici, Gaul, June 20, A.D. 451

The blackness of the heavens melded with the dark of the surrounding fields and woods, and the rain poured down on a scene of collective misery, the likes of which the world has rarely seen. It was as if even the gods were weeping for the fallen greatness of the empire, and for themselves.

A quarter of a million soldiers staggered in ragged formation along a dirt road whose ruts had long since turned into a quagmire. Each man's world was reduced to the tiny space around his own body—the tramping of hobnailed sandals, the dripping of water from helmet into eyes, the cold armor of the soldier in front of him, which he touched with his hand for reassurance that he was still following the right path in the darkness. As often as a soldier may train and drill with his legion, as far as he may march in close formation with a thousand comrades, as fiercely as he may fight as part of a vast body of troops, in the end, his survival depends not on his fellows or his enemies but on himself alone. No other man can endure for him the cold rain trickling down his back, the stabbing pain in his thigh where the spear point remains embedded, or the deep fear in his gut that this night, this night of agony and exhaustion, this last night, might not yield to dawn.

No light penetrated the sky, though in the distance, on

the near horizon where lay the enemy camp, the sparks of
a hundred thousand fires pierced the blackness like earth-
bound stars, as if the positions of Heaven and Earth had
been reversed. Close at hand, however, the only light was
that which shone from the occasional pine-pitch torch
stuck into the sodden earth of the ditch, or the lingering
fire of an incendiary missile slowly guttering in a puddle
of oily liquid. The dwindling flames seemed only to ex-
aggerate the darkness by their infrequency, and as the
column snaked slowly past, they cast quivering shadows
on bloodied faces, on expressions constricted in grief and
pain.

    It was not the pain of physical injury, for a legionary
is inured to that. A man who serves Rome by strength
of his arms becomes resigned to leaving a part of himself behind in each campaign—a finger here, lopped off
by a Germanic sword or a clumsy colleague's kindling
hatchet; a slice of shoulder there, taken by an enemy
catapult bolt or the teeth of a recalcitrant cavalry horse;
an eye, the straightness of a nose, superfluous teeth, lost
to brawling, or to rot, or to the ill-favored gift of a
syphilitic prostitute. Yet perhaps this is only fair, to
leave something behind, something personal, in exchange for the lives and treasure a soldier takes away in
return. Veterans soon learn the tricks to remaining intact, for a soldier cannot survive a twenty-year hitch in
the legions and continue to lose a critical appendage
every year—there would be little left of a man to enjoy
his meager pension if that were the case. After a few
years of experience, a man learns to temper his bravery.
Not to shirk his duty, of course, but to not take needless
chances, either—to volunteer for safer guard postings,
to lag a fraction of a moment behind the front line in a
charge, to keep a weather eye out for snipers on the
flanks rather than focusing solely on the enemy directly

in front of him. *Eyes to the East!* the inner voice of experience cries—for in direct, man-to-man combat, a Roman can dispatch any foe by using superior skill and technique, and even an Alaman's greater strength is actually diminished by his very blood rage; but a cool, calculating sniper aiming from behind a tree can only be avoided by experience. After a man loses two or three fondly remembered body parts, second sight becomes second nature.

Yet the pain these faces expressed went far beyond the usual degree of physical suffering. The armor was blood-spattered and dented. Limbs were bandaged, or missing, or hanging at odd angles. There was no talking or singing, not even the usual litany of complaints of an army on the march.

Only the incessant tramping and squelching of half a million feet wending their way along the vast river of mud.

This very silence was a conundrum rarely encountered. Silence among Romans, a Roman silence, is a contradiction in terms, a condition that, like bare dirt in a lush forest, or a beautiful woman traveling alone, is unstable by the very laws of nature—a vacuum begs to be filled. And as if Stentor, that forgotten God of Clamor and Din, had blearily wakened for a moment and realized his inexplicable lapse, a sound of determined voices rose suddenly to the fore. The weary troops stumbled and hesitated in their sticky trudging, wanting to stop and listen, to experience the relief of knowing life existed beyond their own individual circles of darkness and damp, but each unwilling to lose contact with the shoulder in front of him or be pushed into the mud and trampled by the unseen column of shades marching behind.

The clamorous voices became clearer, punctuated by oaths and the lusty braying of mules unhappy at the conditions under which they were being driven. A column of wooden wagons struggled along in the opposite direction from the troops, forcing its way through the weary wounded. Silently and grudgingly, by touch and by sound rather than by sight, the men stumbled into the ditch at the roadside and stood shivering in the rivulet of muddy water as the wagons passed by. Each vehicle was drawn by a pair of mules, their way lit by a field lantern mounted on a long pole arching over the animals' backs. The yellow lights glimmed weak and sickly on the faces of the auxiliaries walking beside the mules and the wagon wheels. They were young and green-looking— mere boys, hastily conscripted from a local village a few days before, lacking even the rudiments of armor and weaponry—and they stared at the exhausted soldiers they passed in wide-eyed amazement.

The leader of the wagon squadron, a burly centurion, stalked along the side of the road, whipping mules, wagon boys, and the surrounding troops indiscriminately as he worked to clear a path for his train. The weary legions, who only hours before had stood their ground against the fiercest enemies Rome had ever faced, now shrank into the darkness to avoid the sting of the leather mule strap wielded by one of their own. Every man has his job, and these troops had completed theirs. Driving a wagon train was this centurion's, and officers and common troops alike deferred to him and to his snarling whip.

As he passed, the centurion strode up and down his line of rumbling wagons shouting instructions in a clipped, military monotone.

"The truce will hold until sunrise, men! Ignore any Huns on the field—they're looking to their own wounded. And remember the general's warning—no looting! Any man I catch looting the dead, even dead Huns, will be flogged!"

With excruciating slowness the mule column strained up the short hill looming before them in the darkness. The tide of legionaries parted before them and re-formed behind them, in orderly, Roman formation. The only sounds were the exhausted veterans' soft cursing as they were forced to halt their painful progress to stand in the ditch, and the centurion's monotonous harangue.

"Just over this last hill, men. The truce will hold until sunrise. Eight hours to collect the wounded. Get those mules up to this crest. Almost there. . . . *Good God!*"

The centurion stopped as he arrived at the top of the rise and peered over it at the battlefield. He subconsciously made the sign of the cross as the column of wagons behind him slowly ground to a halt.

Below him was a scene of appalling carnage. In the dying light of the sputtering puddles left by missiles, the vast plain was littered with the black, quavering shadows of bodies. Not thousands or tens of thousands but hundreds of thousands of men and horses, lying half-sunken in the churned-up mud, rain pelting their prone forms, turning everything—mud, bodies, the very darkness itself—into a thick soup, the ground barely distinguishable from the bodies and the bodies from the darkness.

After staring for a moment, he began to perceive the individual elements of the scene. The field was not still—rather, it was a vast, writhing quagmire, slowly churning and rippling like the surface of a Saxon bog. Some of the forms crawled weakly or dragged themselves; others lifted a feeble limb as if beckoning to one another; most lay perfectly still. Wild dogs and pigs scurried stealthily among the bodies, and other groups of wagons and stretcher bearers were already hard at work, carrying the wounded and stacking the dead.

In silent horror, the young soldiers of the wagon train gathered behind the centurion and peered over his shoulder. It was a hellish sight, and the young crew froze in shock. The centurion, however, was not one for long pondering.

"Get to work! At daybreak the truce is off. I want all the wounded in by then. *All of them!* The dead we'll burn later."

With a crack of his whip and more curses from the marching legionaries forced into the ditch, the wagon train lurched forward over the crest and began its slow, careful descent down the muddy hill to the edge of the field, where the vehicles fanned out to the largest clusters of dark shapes littering the plain.

Two young Gauls, pressed into service with the Roman ambulance crew only three weeks before, picked their way slowly through the mud and moaning bodies.

"I didn't enlist with the legions to be dragging Romans out of the mud."

"Shut up. You didn't enlist at all. Father ordered us to go because the prefect ordered him to send us. What'd you expect—to get conscripted as a general?"

"No, but at least to do some fighting, kill a Hun or two. . . ."

"Shut up, I said. Help me turn this one over—"

The brothers stooped and grunted as they lifted a prone soldier to flip him onto his back. The mud grudgingly yielded its grip on the man's body with a wet, squelching sound.

"Dead. Leave him. Let's get this one over here. I saw his leg move."

Heaving the injured man onto the filthy stretcher, they trundled the load to their wagon, where the mules stood stoically in the driving rain. The wounded Roman moaned softly with the swaying of the stretcher, and the two Gauls, cursing as they tripped and stumbled through the darkness, did little to smooth his ride.

"Watch it, idiot. Can't you see his arm's almost falling off?"

"Tie it across his chest so it doesn't dangle. Do I have to do everything in this outfit?"

Laying the stretcher on the wagon's lowered tailgate, they slowly slid him off the blood-soaked canvas and onto the floorboards, settling him tightly between two others they had already picked up.

"Room for two more. Get going."

"How about that one? He's moving. . . ."

The brothers approached with their stretcher and bent down to peer at the injured man's face in the dim light.

"Nah—he's a Hun. Yellow as a sunflower, if it weren't for the mud. Half-naked, too. Huns don't even have enough sense to wear metal."

"I don't see as you have any armor yourself."

"Shut up—there's some Huns now!"

The Gauls stopped in mid-squat and stared. Several yards away, two figures strode through the field, their dark leather cuirasses gleaming wetly in the light of the scattered fires. Each bore a six-foot spear, though no other weapons that could be seen, and they, too, bent here and there to examine a prone figure in the mud.

"Are they doing the same thing as we are?"

"Picking up wounded? Why not?"

"How're they going to carry them? They've got no stretcher or wagon."

As the Gauls watched, the Huns toed a shadowy figure on the ground to turn him over. The injured man weakly twitched an arm. One of the Huns, apparently the more senior, growled something to the other in a guttural tongue and then stalked on to investigate more movement several yards away. The other paused a moment, as if waiting for his leader to step away, then placed the tip of his pike carefully on the throat of the injured man lying at his feet, and leaned heavily onto the shaft. The injured man's arm jerked up suddenly, once, then flopped lifelessly into the mud. The Hun seized his shaft and pulled it out. He then glanced up and saw the two Gauls observing him. For a moment he stood motionless, leaning on his pike as if deep in thought, while the brothers gingerly fingered their belts, hoping they had remembered to attach their sheath knives. Then, with a grin that gleamed yellow in the firelight, the Hun nodded slightly and strode on to join his comrade, who was pointing out another injured soldier.

"Almighty God in Heaven! Did you see that? They're murderers, of their own men! Should we kill them?"

"*Kill them?* Look at their weapons, man; look at their armor—those men aren't conscripts like us; they're real soldiers."

"But . . ."

"Don't get any ideas. The centurion said no contact with the Huns. They're doing their business, and we're doing ours. Let's just get on with it."

Behind them, one of the mules snorted, and both men jumped.

"Not much more room in the wagon bed. Time we picked up a couple more and got back to camp."

As the two men again began slowly making their way through the carnage, a thin voice rose out of the darkness.

"Romans! . . . Ah, for God's sake, over here. . . ."

An arm gestured weakly from a mound of cadavers the Gauls had purposely avoided thus far, being many yards from the nearest fire, its gory details shrouded in darkness.

"There's a live one in there. Hurry . . ."

The two soldiers rushed over, seized the arm, and tugged the wounded man free of the cadavers on top of him, laying him in the mud on his back.

"I can't see a damned thing. Drag him over here."

Cursing softly as they slipped in the mud, the two bent and lifted the wounded man onto the stretcher, then slowly began carrying him away. As they passed in front of a sputtering fire, however, the elder of the two suddenly swore and dropped his burden. His brother, caught off-guard by the sudden shift, staggered backward, then released his own grip on the two poles.

"Idiot! What'd you drop him for?"

"Look at him! He's a Hun!"

The two peered at him closely in the dim light. The wounded man wore a Roman battle helmet but no armor, only a woolen camp tunic and cavalry boots.

"You're right—an old Hun, and an ugly one at that. Looted a Roman helmet from somewhere. Get him off the stretcher."

"Wait. He called out to us in Latin."

The injured man interrupted the bickering above him with a wet cough, weakly struggling to sit up between the two poles of the stretcher on which he lay.

"Romans, please . . . wait!" he gasped, in rough camp Latin. "I have information for you. . . ."

The Gauls squatted in front of him. "Information? Well, you're taking up space a Roman boy could use. Spit it out, old man, and be done with it."

"My information is for your general alone."

The Gauls stared at him incredulously.

"You expect us to take you to General Flavius Aetius? Just like that? Every Hun here would ask for the same thing."

"Huh! Beats being skewered in the throat by their own men, don't it?"

The Gauls laughed, but the wounded Hun coughed again and gripped the stretcher poles tightly with his hands to keep from being tipped out.

"Please . . . take my purse. It's on a string at my belt . . ."

One of the Gauls looked around carefully to see whether anyone was watching, then bent, groped the Hun's thin waist, and tore away a leather purse. He stood back up, stealthily peering inside.

"The centurion told us there was to be no looting."

"But the old man's got money—gold!"

"Probably looted it along with the helmet, before he took a sword in the gut himself."

The Hun spoke up again.

"Please . . . there isn't much time."

The soldiers glanced at each other and nodded. Then they bent to the stretcher, staggered back to the wagon, and roughly heaved him in. After adjusting the cargo for a moment, they stood back to appraise their work.

"What do you think—room for one more?"

"Yes—come on."

The Gauls moved off slowly to seek one more wounded Roman soldier but after several paces stopped suddenly in their tracks, listening.

Hoofbeats and baying dogs—riders were rapidly approaching. In the darkness and rain, all sense of direction was lost—the commotion could have been coming from anywhere. The two turned slowly where they stood, bewildered. They were no strangers to the sound of hoofbeats, but the baying was not that of a normal hound—it was deeper and throatier, mingled with a vicious snarling. The soldiers tensed, and again began nervously fingering their belts. Suddenly, a trio of huge northern wolves, long neck fur flaring out like manes, raced past a nearby fire, tugging at the ropes of the Hunnish handlers behind them. The Gauls stared in astonishment.

"Did you see? Are those . . . ?"

"I'd heard the Huns kept wolves, like General Aetius, but I didn't believe it. . . ."

The huge beasts leaped over bodies on the ground and then stopped, growling, at the pile of corpses from which the old Hun had just been pulled. Snorting and snuffling, they milled about angrily, confused.

A new torrent of rain burst from the sky, and just as

the Gauls ducked their heads for cover, a dozen Hunnish horsemen, shouting in their harsh language, thundered out of the darkness, surrounding them with their snorting, pawing horses. Their leader, a commanding figure, loomed over the terrified boys. He wore no metal but only the grimy, worn leather battle gear they had seen on the other Hunnish soldiers. His only distinction of rank was the matted fur trim around the collar and sleeves of his tunic. He was broad-shouldered and muscular, with a controlled physical strength that belied the fury in his face. He glared down at the two cowering Gauls, eyes glittering in the torchlight, avid as a lion's when staring down at its quarry from a low branch.

The leader nodded to one of his mounted comrades, and the two of them suddenly maneuvered their animals behind the Gauls, bent down from their horses, and pressed long knives to the soldiers' necks. The conscripts froze in terror; a sudden shift by a horse, and their throats could be slashed. They stared up, motionless, the rain coursing down their faces. The commander leered as he jerked the younger Gaul's chin up and brandished his weapon before the frightened man's eyes. It was a steel blade with a finely wrought serrated edge such as the Gaul had never before seen. It reminded him of an animal's teeth, and he shuddered.

"Look lively, Roman jackals!" the leader snarled at them in perfectly accented Latin. "Did you see an old Hun pass this way earlier?"

The Gauls could barely stand on their feet for fear. The younger one opened his mouth to speak—*Give away the goods; save your skin!* his inner voice cried. But before he could croak a word, the lead horseman interrupted him.

"If I find you Romans have sheltered this man in any

way, then the night truce is over. Your heads will decorate my tent poles. Search their wagon."

The Huns released their grip and the two Gauls sank to their knees, weak with terror. Two other Huns in the party dismounted and began walking toward the wagon with a lit torch. Just as they approached it, an Ostrogoth horseman thundered up breathlessly out of the darkness.

"Great King!" he exclaimed breathlessly. "The wolves are baying at a fresh scent! If we hurry, we may still be able to find the old man alive!"

The two Gauls glanced at each other wide-eyed. The elder whispered to his brother out of the corner of his mouth.

" 'Great King'? It's Attila himself!"

The Hunnish commander wheeled his horse about and shouted an order in his strange tongue. The other horsemen galloped off, and the two Huns who were moving to inspect the wagon quickly remounted and raced away after them. The leader lingered a moment longer, glaring down at the two brothers, fingering his serrated blade as if in thought. Then viciously whipping his horse, he thundered off after his men.

The two overwhelmed Gauls staggered back to the wagon. There they stared at the injured old Hun, who peered back at them with rheumy eyes, as he passed in and out of consciousness. A trickle of blood glittered in the dim light as it flowed down the corner of his mouth. The soldiers stood up straighter and tried to recover their former bravado. The elder slapped the old Hun on the foot.

"Well, with all the trouble you've caused, we've got to take you back to camp now. You'd better be worth it."

One body short, they turned the mules around and began the long trek back down the road from which they had come.

*   *   *

Neat rows of canvas tents, each fronted by a smoldering cooking fire for the ten men who slept inside, flanked a narrow dirt path that had deteriorated into a deep-rutted river of mud. Smoke hovered low on the ground, as if pressed down by the rain, and as the weary legionaries trudged into camp and dispersed to their units their exhausted faces were lit fleetingly by the fires and torchlight. A column of wooden wagons was lined up before a large tent, the camp's field hospital, and men moved frantically around the placid mules, shouting orders and rushing up with medical supplies. They methodically unloaded the carts of their grim burdens, and the open space in front of the hospital tent became ever more thickly filled with moaning bodies. The prone men were packed so closely that orderlies were forced to roll them onto their sides, regardless of the location of their injuries, spooning them against one another to allow room for the endless quantities of new wounded who continued to arrive. The suffering men were not even sheltered from the rain. Many were unconscious, but those who were awake groaned feebly, calling for blankets, for food, for their wives, for their mothers.

At the unloading station, the two Gauls stood arguing with their commanding centurion, who was apoplectic with rage.

"Damn you two lunkheads by all the bloody gods of Gaul! General Aetius has lost a hundred thousand men or more this day. *A hundred fucking thousand men!* And you want me to bring him a half-dead old Hun because he speaks a bit of Latin? My stable boy speaks better Latin than this old hound, and I wouldn't bring him to meet Aetius!"

The two soldiers quailed, but the elder spoke up meekly.

"I swear, sir, it was Attila himself, hunting him down! He must know something. . . ."

The centurion cursed in exasperation, at the thickhead-edness of the Gauls, at the freezing rain that was pouring down his back, at the overwhelming fatigue he felt after fighting in the lines all day and now working in the dead wagons all night.

"Attila. Right. You've been hitting the grape juice again, boy. Get your sorry ass back to work. We've still got half the night left. I'll deal with the Hun now, and you two later."

The soldiers shrugged, slapped the mules, and began the hike back out to the field with the empty wagon to pick up more wounded. As they waded away, the centurion watched them with disgust, then looked down at the unconscious Hun with an expression of equal distaste.

"So what the hell am I supposed to do with you, eh?"

Bending down, he slapped both sides of the Hun's face lightly several times in an attempt to waken him.

"Speak up, Hun. I can't hear you. Ah hell."

The centurion picked up the old man as easily as if he were a sack of barley, threw him over his shoulder, and trudged off.

The tent was large, airy, and well lit, roomy and com-fortable by military standards, though by any standards other than military it was slovenly and cramped. Maps and documents were strewn on a table and spilled onto the rough plank flooring, and aides bustled in and out, shaking off water and scraping muddy boots. Rain ham-mered on the sodden canvas, and the wind shook the fabric so that it seemed to vibrate like the skin of a drum, forcing all inside to raise their voices to be heard. Furniture and papers had been hastily stacked in mounds, away from the seams of the fabric—for under these, at the needle holes, even liberal application of lard and wax had failed to stem the effects of the down-pour, and long strings of water beads formed on every edge where two pieces of fabric were joined. A gust of wind that swelled the tent, or a clumsy shoulder brushing against the canvas wall, would send a row of cold droplets onto the heads of those sitting below, and the sound of the driving rain outside was periodically accompanied by angry curses within.

At a table and bench in the middle of the tent, General Flavius Aetius sat conferring with half a dozen of his officers. All were dressed still in the field armor they had been wearing for the past sixteen hours, and all were soaked and filthy—none had bathed or eaten since their own return from the battlefield hours before.

Their faces were grim and exhausted, but Aetius remained calm and unflappable. A tall, lean man, he had a highbred look and patrician bearing, though without the vacant stare or excess of emotion of those who come by their position undeservedly. He exuded quiet confidence and competence, and his officers sat before him tensely as he questioned them about the army's current situation.

"What's the casualty count?"

Pellus, a veteran tribune from Dacia, squinted at a torn scrap of parchment he held in his hand, struggling to make sense of the figures he had scrawled a few moments before from the reports of his field centurions.

"General Aetius—our preliminary estimate, before darkness fell, was three hundred thousand casualties on the field. No idea how many are Huns, how many are ours. . . ."

There was a collective sucking of breath from the men present. Though every one of them was a hardened veteran, accustomed to witnessing death and sending his troops into the maw of combat, these figures were unheard of. Three hundred *thousand*? Never in history had a single battle destroyed so many lives.

A second tribune, Antony, cleared his throat and continued the summary.

"The ambulance squads are out now, sir, picking up survivors. After they return we'll have a more accurate count."

Pellus resumed the thread of his report.

"The worst of it is, sir, reports say that King Theodoric was found beneath a mound of dead Huns."

At this news, Aetius looked up in shock.

"Theodoric? What was his condition, Tribune?"

"Dead," Pellus rejoined. "Witnesses say he took an Ostrogoth javelin that knocked him off his horse. He got up fighting but in the end was overwhelmed. Wounds in all the proper places. He died bravely, that one, battling like a *primus pilus*."

Aetius shook his head in dismay. "The idiot. I have plenty of men to fight like centurions. I needed him to command like a king."

He paused for a moment, considering this latest turn.

"The Visigoths are our largest ally—that leaves them with no commander."

Antony leaned forward, dropping his voice.

"Correct, sir—all two hundred thousand of them. Even now, word is spreading through the camp. The Visigoths are confused, leaderless. Some vow vengeance under his eldest son, Thorismund, while others say they'll return to Tolosa, to prepare his funeral."

Aetius remained calm and silent, thinking. The others bore shocked expressions, the look of men who had lost everything. Finally, Pellus cleared his throat.

"General Aetius, a decision is needed," he said hesitantly. "The Visigoth king is dead. His two hundred thousand men may not fight. We have lost—"

"I heard you perfectly well the first time," Aetius stopped him. "We have lost nothing."

Sudden shouts from outside interrupted the conversation. The men pricked up their ears at the commotion and stood to investigate.

"You men are dismissed," Aetius growled as he stood up. "Antony, get a more accurate casualty count and check in again at the next watch." He shouldered past them toward the tent opening, muttering in annoyance at this new disruption. "What the hell is going on now?"

Lifting the door flap, he strode out into the rain.

In the river of mud fronting the tent, a centurion stood arguing with two of Aetius' guards, who had prevented him from approaching the general's field headquarters. The old Hun lay on the ground at the centurion's feet, wrapped in a sodden blanket, eyes half-open, shivering and gazing around in befuddlement. Aetius approached and pushed through, confronting the men in irritation.

"Centurion—what's the meaning of this? Have you nothing better to do on such a night?"

The centurion snapped to surprised attention at the appearance of the high commander himself.

"General Flavius Aetius! Greetings to you sir, from the Tenth Legion, and all due respect. My ambulance crew encountered this Hun—" he toed the half-conscious old man, eliciting a moan of pain—"who insists on talking to you. Claims to have vital information. Sir."

Aetius glanced down curiously at the Hun, but his face registered no emotion. The injured man stared up at him, his eyes gradually focusing and widening in recognition. With difficulty, he removed his hand from the folds of the bloody, rain-soaked blanket that enveloped him like a shroud, and extended his closed fist to Aetius.

Aetius bent down and held out his own hand, and the Hun dropped something into it. The general stood and held the object to the torchlight for examination. It was a polished, yellowed fang, dangling from a plain leather thong, a common-enough talisman among the Huns. And yet it bore a *tamga,* a property mark—unusual for such a valueless thing as this. He held it closer to the light.

There, he could barely make it out—a crudely carved letter "A."

The general started in surprise and stared back down at the Hun. The face—at first he had not recognized it, but now there was no mistake. That broken nose, which had healed so badly . . .

"Centurion, bring this man into the tent immediately. Guard—call a physician."

The guard sprinted away. The centurion bent and heaved the Hun again onto his shoulder, striding toward the tent opening. Aetius followed close behind.

Ducking inside the tent, the centurion deposited the Hun onto the general's cot with a grunt, then stood and saluted smartly with upraised hand. Aetius nodded to him absentmindedly and stepped toward the cot, but the centurion remained standing. The general turned to look at him a moment, at this burly veteran covered with mud and soaked to the skin, his tunic and armor streaked with blood from the wounded man he had been carrying. The centurion remained at stiff attention, eyes expressionless, staring straight ahead.

"At ease, man. What are you waiting for, a medal?"

The trooper flinched slightly, dropped his upraised hand, but remained motionless, and suddenly it dawned on Aetius why. For the first time in hours the man was out of the rain, and he was reluctant to venture back to the field again so soon.

The general's expression softened slightly. "To the guard shack with you. Tell the armorer I sent you for a cup of hot wine. I know he keeps it behind the forge."

"For the prisoner, sir?" the centurion inquired.

Aetius turned away. "The prisoner? He's barely conscious, soldier. Drink it yourself, and back out to the field!"

The centurion nodded, still expressionless, and then

strode impassively out the door flap. Aetius stood for a moment listening to the splashing footsteps fade away outside. Then sighing deeply, he seized a nearby oil lamp and bent over the Hun. Though the lamplight shone close, the injured man's eyes did not even flicker.

Aetius examined the face closely, taking in the features, so familiar yet so changed with the years. Could he himself have changed as much? A man's face and body mature, then decay, becoming almost unrecognizable over time. But does his core remain fixed, as when one takes an ax, swings it at a tree, and bites all the way to a sapling that witnessed the march of Julius Caesar? This old man in front of him—was he the same man Aetius had known? Was he here out of friendship? Or something else?

A deafening burst of rain pounded on the tent canvas, like a volley of arrows striking a shield. Aetius pulled a camp stool up to the cot and sat down. He had barely settled into position when the door flap opened again, sending a spray of water into the tent.

A miserable-looking civilian stumbled in, nearly tripping over an enormous ball of fur curled up on a woven mat in the middle of the floor. The fur ball twitched in irritation, looked up with gleaming yellow eyes, and emitted a menacing growl.

"Lucilla! Hush!" Aetius ordered.

"Greetings, General Aetius," the man mumbled anxiously. "You called for a physician? With all due respect, sir, that wolf makes me nervous."

"She's tame. She hasn't eaten a doctor in days."

The man's eyes opened wide and he edged carefully around the glowering animal, who fixed a hungry stare on him. Finally putting Aetius between himself and the beast, the physician sidled over to the brazier in the middle of the tent with slow and deliberate movements, as if reestablishing his wounded dignity. He removed his felted woolen cloak, on which the droplets had settled like tiny pearls, and stretched it over the back of a chair. He then calmly removed his felt cap and ran a hand through his hair, allowing more droplets to fall onto the hot metal at the edge of the brazier, where they jumped and spat. Finally, glancing at Aetius, who eyed him coldly, he nodded his readiness and strode to the cot to venture his first look at the patient he had been called to examine. His face immediately registered distaste.

"General Aetius—this man is a Hun!"

Aetius sighed deeply. "This is news to me?"

The physician blinked in surprise, then averted his gaze. Between the yellow eyes of the wolf and the impassive stare of the general, he felt as if stage lanterns were being trained on his face. He bent down self-consciously to rummage through his medical kit, grunting and mumbling to himself, then grudgingly set to work, unwrapping the Hun's sodden blanket and cutting away the woolen tunic. As he carefully lifted away the fabric, snipping the fibers where dried blood had adhered to the man's skin, he glanced at Aetius and shook his head in dismay.

The general leaned over the physician's shoulder to see for himself and winced. He stepped back for a moment, staring at the low ceiling as if composing his thoughts. Then, edging around the hunched form of the physician, he bent down, seized the Hun's face with his hand, and turned it toward him.

"What is it? Why are you here?"

The wounded Hun started at the sound of the general's voice and his eyelids fluttered open. His eyes, however, remained unfocused and distant, and his mouth worked laboriously.

"Must tell Flavius. . . . Must . . . tell Flavius!"

"Tell me what? Old man, why have you come?!"

The physician sat back and gently removed Aetius' hand from the patient's face, respectfully but firmly shouldering him aside. The general stepped back slightly, though his eyes never left those of the old Hun. As the physician carefully adjusted a bent flange on a set of metal tongs, he conversed with Aetius, seeking both to inform him and to distract him.

"The man won't last another day, General. I would be surprised if he survived the night. If I may ask: Who is he?"

Aetius paused for a moment before responding.

"This man . . ."

At a sudden loss for words, he looked across the room, staring into space.

"This man," he continued, "he used to be a Hun."

The physician scoffed.

" 'Used to be'? They don't get more Hunnish than this specimen. So what is he now?"

Aetius looked down sadly at the dying man and held his silence. The physician observed him for a long moment, and then, fearing that his question had been forgotten or ignored, he screwed up his courage to interrupt the general's thoughts.

"General Aetius, as a matter of professional interest and . . . personal curiosity—what is this man now?"

Aetius sighed and stood up straight. Composing his face, he fixed his gaze firmly on the physician.

"Thirty years, it's been. Thirty years and more. No, physician, this man is no mere Hun."

"Ah. You know him then? A captured enemy officer, perhaps?"

Aetius shook his head. "No, not just an officer, though he is that, too. Keep him alive, physician, alive at all costs."

The physician's eyes gleamed at the trust the great man had placed in him.

"So this Hun, he is of quite some importance then?"

Aetius nodded and once again bent to examine the wounded man's face.

"Physician," he said, "at this moment, he may be the most important man in the Roman Empire."

TWO

Ravenna, A.D. *409*

I

It was not the largest *triclinium* in the palace, but it was by far the most lavish. The emperor's private banquet hall, here in his capital city of Ravenna, was decorated with the costliest and most glittering of materials, as befitted the tastes of the sovereign of the Western Roman Empire. The walls glowed with the warm red and orange hues of the nymph and satyr mosaics, and wherever one looked the subtle yet pleasantly surprising glint of an inlaid or bejeweled detail caught one's eye—the gleaming, gold-plated hem of a nymph's short tunic as she laughingly let it slip to the ground; the wicked lapis lazuli gleam of a man-goat's eye as he leered at a group of maidens frolicking in a spring; the flashing garnet set into the nipple of an enraptured wood sprite, arching her back over the caprine legs of a slyly grinning Pan. Light gleamed from a hundred lamps scattered about the room, from hanging chandeliers, from costly beeswax candles placed on the tables, and from gilded lantern sconces carefully set into the walls and painted with optical tricks that made them seem to be grasped by the hands of the very creatures who pranced across the wall mosaic. Everywhere there was light, and the heat from the flames, the scent of the smoke, and the stench of the perspiring bodies rendered the air heady and thick. The perfumed haze made the life-size figures in the mosaics seem almost to move and come alive in all their intoxicating, priapic glory.

Scattered about the room, half a hundred senators and sycophants reclined comfortably on gilded couches and Indian silk carpets, laughing drunkenly as they swilled century-old wine from precious Saracen goblets and munched nuts and fig bread. Lovely attendants, dressed in short, diaphanous silk tunics and coiffed to match the languid wood nymphs displayed on the wall, refilled the goblets and supplied neck rubs between bites of delicacies.

At the front of the room, a quartet of musicians furiously tripped their way through airs from the latest Greek musical follies filling Ravenna's amphitheaters; and swirling among the couches, Syrian dancing girls swayed and flirted in scanty half costumes, oiled breasts set with flashing jewels bobbing and gleaming in the lamplight. From his padded throne of polished wood, the Emperor Honorius surveyed the festivities with an expression of pride and satisfaction, and well he might: At only twenty-six years of age, he was already famous throughout the empire for the lavishness of his entertainments and the artistry of the dramaturges, musicians, and rhetoricians he kept on hand as his chief advisors. He was even more famous for the quality of the chickens he bred, descendants of an ancient thoroughbred line introduced from Persia years before, which he raised in luxurious quarters in a converted courtyard behind the palace baths.

This night he was hosting one of the weekly dinner parties for which he was so well known. Yet despite his exquisite taste in the way of dress and furnishings, his preferences in matters of love were distinctly low-caste. Even now, observant guests noted, the most powerful man in the empire was lustily eyeing a young, plainly dressed serving wench who, noticing his interest, blanched and sidled cautiously out of his reach.

With a sudden burst of drums and flutes from the musicians, a line of servants filed in, bearing huge platters and boards on which the main course of the feast was arranged: a whole roast boar, propped with metal rods into a running position, topped by a small saddle confected of artfully molded bread. This, in turn, was straddled by a live African monkey who rode gleefully into the room on his mount, acknowledging the diners' cheers of delight, and then leaped onto the nearest chandelier. From there, screaming and scolding, he scurried into the rafters. The horse-boar on the platter was surrounded by the honey-glazed carcasses of four roast swans, heads and necks propped as if still swimming, each bird set into a tray of blue-dyed aspic filled with carefully peeled apples, peaches, and pears carved to resemble tiny fish swimming in water. Other plates contained enormous mounds of succulent braised vegetables, fruits, pectins chilling on ice laboriously carted from the southern Alps the previous spring, sweetmeats, and honey drops. The diners' eyes grew wide as the food was produced—such a display could only enhance the emperor's already formidable reputation.

As heaped plates were distributed by the servants, Honorius clinked his goblet with his knife and called out above the rising conversation and compliments.

"Court poet! A poem, if you please, to commemorate this delightful occasion!"

In the corner, a morose and shoddily dressed individual rose slowly to his feet, looking around bleary-eyed at the other guests. Though apparently dining alone, lacking even the company of one of the massage girls, he had been drinking heavily, and was already deep in his cups. Swaying slightly, he raised his goblet in toast to the emperor. The room quieted but did not become completely silent. Scattered insults were whispered here and there, and the poet glared about himself fiercely, attempting to locate the source of the mockery he could only half-hear.

"A poem," he slurred, raising his chin and donning a dignified demeanor. "A masterpiece, a veritable work of art, to be handed down over the ages, to outshine even Catullus and Virgil, yet composed before your very eyes . . ."

Scattered tittering could be heard, and then a rude interruption from a group of diners sitting across from the poet.

". . . and under your very noses!"

There was a burst of unrestrained flatulence, accompanied by groans of dismay from those in the vicinity and hearty laughter from those farther distant. The poet, however, merely blinked in confusion and then forged ahead, determined to ignore the catcalls and commotion.

"A toast to our beloved patron, the divine Emperor Honorius!"

The poet screwed up his face in concentration and declaimed slowly. Though halting at first, he soon warmed to his theme, and became more confident as he progressed.

> *"To our Emperor Honorius,*
> *Commander ever glorious:*
> *His dinners are uproarious;*
> *He leaves the girls . . ."*

Here the poet hesitated in thought and every guest and servant in the room looked pointedly from him to the emperor, who, just at that moment, was taking advantage of the seeming distraction of the poetry recital to slide his hand stealthily up the thigh of the nervous servant girl. Seeing the entire party turn to watch him, the emperor blushed and dropped his hand quickly, pretending he had merely been brushing a bit of splatter off the girl's lap. The poet smiled as a flash of inspiration crossed his face.

". . . He leaves the girls euphorious!!"

A roar of laughter and cheers erupted, and the party resumed as everyone tucked eagerly into the food. The servant girl scampered away in the commotion, and the emperor discreetly beckoned his chancellor, Didymus, to approach.

"Yes, Augustus?"

The elderly eunuch, who was never without his impeccable silken robes, nor an unctuous, condescending smile, bent low over his master's shoulder.

"Take a note, please, Didymus. . . . We must replace that dreadful court poet. He is an embarrassment."

Didymus drummed his long, slender fingers on the table for a moment in thought, then nodded obediently and glided away.

Honorius again called the diners' attention.

"Senators and honored guests, we do have one small piece of business to attend to before the real festivities begin. Our *magister equitum*, Chief Cavalry Officer of the Legions, General Gaudentius Aetius . . ."

At these words a tall man of middle age stepped forward from a side door, straight-backed and poker-faced. He appeared Germanic in origin—tall, light-haired, and imposing. His ceremonial armor and dress and his severe demeanor identified him as a high-ranking military officer, and his posture and expression showed his discomfort with the frivolity he was witnessing. He seemed to be a man who wished only to report his news and then be quickly on his way.

"Augustus," the man said, in crisp tones, "the Hunnish king Rugila has agreed to the terms of an alliance."

The emperor smiled and glanced around the room, taking in the reaction to this news among his guests. A hubbub ensued at mention of the Huns, and after a moment several voices rose drunkenly above the commotion, competing with one another for the attention of the other guests.

"The Huns! I thought we only signed treaties with humans!"

"Did you see them in the Triumph last year to celebrate our victory over the Slavs? Who arranged for the order of marching in the parade? Was it you, Didymus? Those magnificent Visigoths with their beards and chain mail—six feet tall, every one of them—marching just behind that bowlegged little bastard Uldin and his grubby Hunnish cavalry."

"Haw! Flat-nosed, slit-eyed little devils, yellow faces—looked like they'd just crawled out of the emperor's *bestiarium* on Capri and needed to be put back in their cages."

"Nice contrast with the Visigoths, Didymus—you have a real eye for decorating!"

Didymus preened with pleasure while glancing sidelong at the emperor.

Honorius, in turn, smiled indulgently at his steward, but the emperor's eyes were vacant and his face distracted. The servant girl had again ventured close to him as she bent to remove an empty platter, and he craned his neck to peer down her tunic. Seeing his intent, the girl straightened up nervously, the platter in her hand trembling. Disappointed, the emperor turned back to the military man, who stood stiff-backed and silent, observing his commander's actions with obvious contempt.

"So, Gaudentius, now we have a formal alliance with these creatures, these . . . Huns?"

"We do, sir, yes," the officer responded curtly.

"And . . . we consider it wise to be dealing so closely with these devils?"

Didymus chuckled again, more loudly this time, and interrupted the questioning in his high, cultured voice.

"Oh, the Huns themselves have a saying, Augustus: Better the jackal inside the tent pissing out than outside pissing in."

The room erupted in laughter, and the same drunken voices again clamored for attention.

"Or is it a camel? I heard the Huns ride camels into battle . . ."

"Makes them almost as tall as real men!"

The guests continued to laugh, and the emperor again showed traces of an indulgent smile. Gaudentius, however, displayed increasing annoyance as he listened to the conversation and catcalls. His face tightened and he shifted impatiently on his heels. It was not his place to interrupt—these types of events were often a trial, though he always managed to maintain his silence and his dignity—but this time he was determined to be heard. He stepped forward and raised his voice over the distracted chatter.

"I can assure you, Augustus, they do not ride camels."

Immediately one or two exasperated sighs were heard from the diners, but Gaudentius pressed on.

"They ride horses, though of a species that is rather ugly and stout by Roman standards. And they are the finest cavalry in the world. Bar none."

The emperor winked at the diners nearest him and then glanced up at the officer with an amused expression on his face.

"General Gaudentius," he intoned sarcastically, "would you care to join our meal, as you have joined our conversation? I'm sure a couch can be found for a knowledgeable officer such as you."

The other diners tittered rudely, but Gaudentius seemed not to notice he was being mocked. He nodded politely to the emperor.

"Thank you, Augustus, but I must be on my way, as soon as—"

" 'Finest cavalry in the world,' eh?" the emperor interrupted. "That must look quite a sight, such skilled horsemen riding fat-bellied, short-legged beasts such as those. Bit like a senator riding a sway-backed old mule, eh? Ah, that gives me an idea for the next festival!"

The emperor nudged his neighbor, and the senator blushed deeply, to general laughter.

"Augustus," the learned eunuch Didymus broke in, "the Hunnish horses are bred to that anatomy. The Huns prefer them to be built like . . . er, *sheep,* actually, rather than horses. They have broad backs, because their riders never dismount. They do everything on them—sleep, cook, even copulate!"

At this, the room fell silent and the emperor's eyes lit up at this first interesting thing he had heard all evening.

"Fascinating!" the emperor rejoined languidly. "Didymus, did you say they even . . . er . . . *cook?* Now, copulating on a horse, that I can imagine, and perhaps even endorse. But . . . cooking, did you say?"

"Indeed, Augustus, in a manner of speaking," the eunuch replied. "You see, they take a slab of raw meat—usually horsemeat, I am told—"

"From a beast that was too skinny to screw on!" broke in a besotted diner from the back of the room.

The eunuch ignored the interruption. "As I was saying, they take a slab of raw meat and place it under their thighs, against the horse's sweaty back, something like a saddle pad. Then they ride on it all day."

The emperor waited expectantly, as if for a punch line, then looked up at Didymus, puzzled.

"And, um, when precisely do they cook it, Didymus?"

Didymus smiled triumphantly. "That *is* their cooking, Augustus! The riding tenderizes it, salts it, and warms it. The Huns eat their meat just like that. Hunnish cuisine at its finest!"

Everyone stared at the eunuch, unsure whether he was joking. Gaudentius stepped forward, glaring at Didymus.

"That is utter nonsense. The meat is put there to heal sores on the horse's back caused by the saddle. The Huns may be greedy and cruel, but they are not stupid by any means. I might remind you, Augustus, that the Hunnish horsemen decimated our enemies last year at Florentia, which the Roman legions alone were unable to do. Had the Huns not intervened on our side, we might now be serving wine to a troop of yellow-bearded Ostrogoths, or worse."

The emperor's eyes narrowed at this reminder of the near disaster.

"And that is further nonsense, General. A bit of good fortune on the Huns' part. Barbarians on foot have stood up to charging cavalry before. There is no reason to think they could not have done it that time as well. . . ."

"No, Augustus, they could not have. Not against cavalry on stirrups. Not against thousands of Huns on horseback, charging shoulder to shoulder—and using stirrups to brace their weapons and strengthen their charge. No infantry force on earth can stand up to that."

The emperor raised his eyebrows and stared, though it was not clear whether he was surprised at the general's audacity or puzzled at the discussion of this new weapon, these *stirrups*. There was a palpable tension in the air as the room fell to a hush, which Honorius then broke with a sudden smirk.

"Thank you for enlightening us with that invaluable recollection, General."

Gaudentius nodded and cleared his throat, oblivious to the emperor's mounting irritation.

"Augustus—if I may return to the subject at hand. We have entered into a treaty with the Huns, and hostages will be required, to guarantee compliance by both sides. King Rugila has offered to send Rome his young nephew, eldest son of Mundzuk, the former Hunnish king. We must identify an appropriate counterpart from our side."

The room fell silent as everyone now avoided the emperor's gaze. Not a man relished the idea of being sent to live for years in the Hunnish camp or having one's relatives assigned. The emperor gazed about, thinking.

"This is indeed a problem," he finally sighed. "We have entered into so many alliances in recent years, to keep the peace on the frontier, that it becomes difficult to find suitable candidates for these little exchanges of goodwill."

He thought a moment longer, smiling slyly.

"My dear Gaudentius—you have a young son, do you not? A lad of thirteen or fourteen, if I recall?"

Gaudentius stared at the emperor coldly.

"Flavius is fourteen years old, Augustus."

Honorius held the officer's stare remorselessly.

"I am honored, Gaudentius, to accept your kind offer to present your son as hostage to the Huns. Tell me, General: Does young Flavius Aetius suffer from the same inability to show proper deference to his betters as you do?"

Gaudentius paused, carefully considering how to answer. Though Honorius was not as vicious as many past Roman emperors, an ill-considered response could still cost him his career—or his life.

"My son does indeed have little patience with pointless flattery."

This time it was the emperor who paused, as if carefully weighing how to reply to this implicit accusation.

"That is not precisely what I meant, but no matter"—

he smiled around the table—"it is a fine evening and my own patience is quite expansive tonight."

He turned back to Gaudentius and glared.

"You might wish to discuss with your son the rudiments of politeness and protocol, General—or perhaps you are the wrong person to be giving such lessons. Crudeness of manners may be quite the asset in the Hunnish camp, but I can assure you that such behavior will not lead to a long career, or a long life, here in Ravenna."

Gaudentius nodded crisply, spun on his heel, and began striding out of the room.

"Oh, and one more thing, General," the emperor called after him.

Gaudentius stopped and turned, his face a neutral mask, giving away nothing.

"Your Flavius will not leave immediately," the emperor continued. "I want him to be a companion to the young Hun here for a few months. Make him feel at home, get him settled in. Our hostages are not *prisoners*—we must do all we can to make them feel welcome."

"As you command, Augustus," Gaudentius replied acidly.

The emperor eyed him in silence for a moment. "General Aetius: Our relationship with the Huns is of no small consequence to the future of Rome. Let us see if we can teach this boy to be not so . . . Hunnish." He wrinkled his nose in distaste.

"Indeed, Augustus. And would you care to know the name of this young Hun, who will be living here in the palace?"

The emperor nodded and glanced at Didymus, who was scanning a copy of the treaty. After a moment, the steward looked up with satisfaction, his finger marking the spot on the parchment.

"Aha!" Didymus announced. "It says here the prince's name is Bleda."

Gaudentius nodded. "Bleda. My son Flavius for Bleda. So be it."

He nodded curtly to the emperor, turned, and left the dining hall without another word. The conversation and laughter resumed.

II

The Hunnish horsemen clattered down the cobbled Ravenna street, looking so fierce and exotic with their greasy leather gear, topknots, and squat horses that they could have been creatures of another species to the wonder-struck passersby. They were a *zuun*, a squadron of a hundred Hunnish cavalry, accompanied by a century of horse-mounted Roman praetorian guards, who were themselves garbed in armor polished to a blinding sheen, their immaculate crimson cloaks fluttering elegantly behind them. An *aquilifer* carrying the Roman eagle led the stately procession, his booming voice carrying out over the haggling of merchants and the rattling of carts and wagons.

"*Cedite!* Way for the emperor's guests! *Cedite!* Way for the Huns!"

The people of Ravenna stood aside and stared. The party turned into the palace courtyard, and the Hunnish guards dismounted and squatted nonchalantly at the side of their horses, leaving only the officers mounted. Their demeanor seemed relaxed, but their eyes flitted about watchfully, and their hands remained tense and never far from the hilts of their blades. In turn, the foreigners were observed carefully and distastefully by the Roman troops, who remained sitting stiffly on their restless mounts. No one said a word.

In a moment, the double gates to the palace were thrown open, and with a shouted greeting the eunuch

Didymus strode through, carefully coiffed and arrayed in fine Oriental silks and bearing a broad, welcoming smile for the occasion. He was accompanied by a number of teenage boys, of all colors and dress: a black Numidian youth in the royal leopard-hide cape of his distant tribe; a silver-haired and pink-skinned Slav blinking uncomfortably in the bright sunlight; several Arabs and Berbers in flowing robes; and a pair of gangly redheaded Celts smirking and elbowing each other. Gaudentius, too, was present, as was his son Flavius, a lean but broad-shouldered lad standing somewhat apart from the other boys. In contrast to the foreign princes dressed in their colorful native finery, he wore a simple white tunic of fine wool, eschewing any jewelry or embroidery. Like his father, he combed his auburn hair straight back off his forehead, unadorned, and his dark eyes were set off by the olive complexion he had inherited from his mother, a Milanese noblewoman.

As Didymus approached, a short, muscular lad in the front of the Hunnish squadron gracefully dismounted, landing catlike on the paving stone in his soft doeskin riding boots. He stepped forward with the confidence of one accustomed to being observed and admired, though his grimy leather riding kit was indistinguishable from those of his bodyguards. The boy's thick black hair hung to his waist and was tied back with a simple leather thong. Only the richly jeweled dagger at his belt and the confident spring in his step set him apart from his guard as a member of the royal family of his vast tribe. His skin was dust-streaked and deeply tanned, with high cheekbones studded with a striped pattern of decorative scars, and his broad nose was so flat that it scarcely extended out beyond the ridge of his eyebrows. Most striking of all to the closely watching boys in the courtyard were his eyes—slits so narrow they seemed almost to be closed, yet without the creasing of a squint. Only the occasional obsidian glint of the black irises, flashing alertness and intelligence, indicated his watchfulness.

Gaudentius was familiar with such eyes from his many previous dealings with the Huns, and he often envied their advantages. With eyes such as these, it was impossible to tell what a man was thinking or feeling. The only way one could negotiate with such a man was by counting on his words alone. It was a method Gaudentius heartily mistrusted, though trusting a Hun's words generally posed fewer dangers than trusting those of certain other peoples—including, he felt, many Romans.

The boy stepped forward smartly, appraised Didymus for a moment, and then bowed long and low, though never taking his eyes off the eunuch. The other hostage princes stared at him, silent and unmoving, their mouths slightly agape at this scion of royalty who had arrived in Ravenna, the center of the world's power, not in a silk-curtained sedan chair as had they, but on a sweaty and dirt-caked pony; garbed not in purple robes, but in sheep's wool and leather; and surrounded not by an honor guard, but by a squadron of glaring warriors.

Undeterred by the horsemen's bizarre appearance and the youth's mute bow, Didymus fluttered forward to greet the company, clasping his hands in front of him in delight.

"Welcome, foreign friends, welcome to all! Ah! The latest addition to our menagerie of guest princes from allied nations! A member of the Hunnish royal family, no less! Young prince: You may officially present your credentials at a later time, but for the moment, allow me to informally present a few of your future comrades. Prince Vortigern of the Londinium Celts—"

The taller of the two lanky redheads offered a sly, gap-toothed grin and produced a low bow, a mocking reference to the Hunnish boy's own.

"—Prince Gundioc of the Burgundians; Flavius Aetius, who will soon be departing for your own homeland; and the rest of these royal scoundrels, with whom you will, of course, become better acquainted before long, I shouldn't wager. Ah, this is the baby of our little family, Prince Theodoric, son of the Visigoth king, Alaric."

Reaching into the crowd of boys, Didymus seized the tunic collar of a small dark-haired urchin and affectionately ruffled his hair. At twelve years of age, Theodoric was younger than his comrades, and small for his size at that.

Didymus smiled. "Alaric keeps threatening to seize Rome. Fortunately, our young friend here should help keep the empire safe." The lad shook his head in annoyance and glared at Didymus, which the eunuch ignored.

"Boys," he said, turning to the gawking group gathered expectantly behind him, "may I introduce . . . the Hunnish prince Bleda!"

At these words, the squadron of horsemen froze, and the young Hun stiffened suddenly, his eyes flickering in consternation between Didymus and Gaudentius. After a moment, one of the lead riders, a stocky, athletic officer in his mid-forties, dismounted and calmly strode forward. Without ceremony, he stepped in front of the abashed prince and began speaking softly to Didymus and Gaudentius, in a voice only they could hear. Didymus' reaction to his words, however, fell harshly on the ears of all present.

"*Not* Prince Bleda?" he hissed. "Sir—we had an agreement! General Gaudentius, did we not have an agreement as to the rank and position of the hostage?"

Gaudentius nodded and addressed the Hunnish officer sternly. "Indeed we did. So therefore have the Huns violated the hostage agreement before it has even been implemented?"

The officer did not flinch or even blink but rather stood erect, chest thrust forward and head back, looking directly into Gaudentius' face. He turned a blind eye to Didymus' hand-wringing and raised his own voice to a level equal to that of the general.

"We agreed to exchange hostages of equal value," the Hun said, in labored, measured Latin. "At the time, we did not know your Emperor Honorius had no sons, and so could not send us a hostage of value equal to Bleda, who is next in line to our throne. But as a sign of good-will to Rome, King Rugila sends Bleda's younger brother, Attila."

Gaudentius glared at him. "And who might you be, who know so well the king's intent?"

The Hun was unfazed and dipped his head slightly in a formal bow. "Captain Turgrid of the king's personal cavalry guard, late of the Roman auxiliary legions on the Danuvius, honorably discharged after completing a full tour of duty under your emperor's command. At your service."

Gaudentius continued to stare until Didymus broke the awkward silence.

"We shall settle this confusion later," he stammered, "though in the meantime, since you have come all this way, I see no alternative but to accept the hostage your good king has seen fit to send us. Now, Prince . . . Attila, did you say your name is? You must be tired and hungry from your journey. Please enter our humble palace."

At these words, Vortigern stepped forward, affecting another gallant bow. "Hungry, is he?" he exclaimed in his Celt-inflected Latin. "I'll get him something to eat!"

Didymus started and looked at the boy with an expression of slight alarm. "Thank you, Vortigern; that will not be necessary. . . ."

But the young Celt had already run off, snickering.

Didymus shrugged resignedly and perhaps with some relief.

"Meanwhile—I shall leave you boys to become acquainted. General Gaudentius—a word with you, if you please, to arrange lodging for our, er, gentle horsemen here . . . ?"

The eunuch and the general stepped aside, and the boys walked off as a group, chatting spiritedly, with Attila lagging behind, glancing once or twice over his shoulder as if hoping someone would ask him to carry his own baggage or otherwise assign him something to engage his hands. It was an inauspicious start—scarcely off his horse, and already his credibility and value had been called into question, even in such a shameful role as a hostage. For days, the previous spring, Attila had argued with his uncle the king about the indignity of being sent to a foreign nation under such circumstances—he, the finest bowman and wrestler of his clan, the canniest huntsman, the swiftest rider. He, the closest of his father's sons to the king, for though the crown would be passed to Bleda by law and tradition, it was known to all that the king's wisdom and blessing would go to Attila. But King Rugila had merely smiled at Attila's protests.

"Young Bleda will remain here with me," the king had told him. "He is weak and unfit for travel, or for life in Ravenna. Only you are worthy of this honor, for of the two, only you could make me proud before the Romans."

That day, for the first time, Attila had cursed his uncle, though he waited until he was alone with his horse, on the plain, to do so. Now, however, after the shame he had just experienced at the hands of this know-nothing Roman eunuch, he cursed him again.

Theodoric trotted beside the longer-legged Flavius Aetius, observing the strange new arrival from the corner of his eye.

"A Hun!" the young boy whispered excitedly. "Do you think he even speaks Latin?"

"No idea." Flavius shrugged. "Try him out, Theodoric."

The younger boy approached Attila with a friendly smile, but just as he was starting to speak, an object fell from above their heads and spattered wetly at Attila's feet. The crowd of boys stopped short, staring wide-eyed at the slab of raw, bloody meat on the marble-tiled floor. Vortigern and his friend stood on a low balcony above them, laughing.

"Here's your lunch, Hun," Vortigern cried mockingly. "Hope you feel at home!"

Attila glared as the two Celts ran away, laughing, and a flush rose up his face. The other boys stood silent and un-moving, eyes darting from the meat to Attila's expression, until Theodoric could contain himself no longer. He broke the silence with a snort of suppressed laughter. It was all the catalyst needed for the other boys to do the same, in a spontaneous burst of guffaws. In a rage, Attila stalked over to the young Visigoth and pushed him hard. The smaller boy staggered back in surprise, recovered, and then launched himself at Attila in return, head-butting him in the chest and slamming the Hun back against the wall of the corridor. Attila shoved him away furiously.

"You think that funny?" he shouted in serviceable camp Latin. "You think that funny? I show funny, you lit-tle white-faced monkey. . . ."

With that, Attila rushed at the fierce Theodoric, who despite his smaller size was prepared to hold his ground. The Hun's charge was stopped short, however, as Flavius stepped between the two. Theodoric protested with a string of mule-driver obscenities aimed at both older boys, but Flavius ignored him as he attempted to calm their tempers.

"Vortigern threw the meat, Hun; Theo here had nothing to do with it. Fight someone your own—"

Before he could even finish, Attila landed Flavius a lightning jab to the face with his fist, dropping the bigger boy to the floor like a sack of grain. The Roman peered up in astonishment, his eye already beginning to swell, as Attila glowered down at him.

"My own size," the Hun sneered. "Like you?"

Flavius leaped to his feet and dove at his assailant, but though he was strong and nimble, by far the best wrestler in his *contuburnium,* the Hun easily sidestepped the maneuver. Flavius quickly recovered, but accustomed to the steady and well-regulated rhythms of the wrestling ring, he was not prepared for the speed and intensity of the attack he now faced. Attila had become a whirl of motion, feinting here, lunging there, leaping and lashing out with his boot-clad feet, jabbing ferociously with his fists, diving at the Roman's knees, and tripping him up so thoroughly he tumbled to the ground, empty-handed, with his head spinning.

Flavius was bewildered. The pancratic techniques he had learned from his Greek drill instructors were all about grappling—he could break an opponent's fingers in a heartbeat, double him over with a knee to the groin, strangle him quickly or slowly, as he saw fit. But what could he do if he could barely *see* his opponent for all his spinning and leaping, much less seize him and throttle him? Attila was like a one-man legion, swarming over his rival from all sides, pummeling and bruising him with swift kicks to the ribs and hard knuckles to the jaw. Yet though his head ached and his vision was beginning to blur from the blows he was taking, Flavius fought stubbornly on. The other boys formed a circle around them and hollered for blood.

"Come on, Flavius—you can do better than that!"

"Take him out with your fist, Flavius! You've got the reach!"

"Flavius! Hold him tight! You're stronger than the Hun!"

Flavius took a last clumsy swing, a roundhouse that even a novice could have seen coming from afar, and Attila unleashed a killer feint, throwing him far off-balance. The Hunnish boy then ducked behind him, leaped onto his back, and put a hammerlock around his throat, squeezing hard with his forearm.

"Surrender, Roman!" Attila shouted.

Flavius gagged and slammed himself backward against the stone wall to shake his tormenter loose. "I . . . will . . . not!"

Attila grunted in pain at the impact of the wall but squeezed Flavius' throat all the harder. "Surrender, I said!"

But the Hun's domination over his larger rival was too much for Theodoric to bear. Seeing Flavius in trouble, the young Visigoth stormed back into the fray, leaping onto Attila's back and applying the same hammerlock to him: The three of them staggered about the hall, one atop the other, each as red in the face as a Gaul in the African sun.

"Surrender, Hun!" Theodoric screamed in Attila's ear.

The Hun grunted, and tried to twist himself around to shake off the fierce little fighter, all the while wrapping his own arms and legs more tightly around Flavius. Just then, Gaudentius and Didymus, hearing the commotion, arrived running on the scene, shouting for the combatants to break up the fight.

"What's going on here! Who started this?" Gaudentius roared, while Didymus hopped about like a frightened peacock, wringing his hands at the unprecedented display of barbarism he was witnessing in the very heart of the palace.

Sprawled gasping on the floor on opposite sides of the corridor where they had been flung when Gaudentius forced the boys apart, Flavius looked at Attila and Attila glared back at him, waiting for his adversary to denounce him to his father, and to hear his punishment. He had not even been in Ravenna for an hour—how could things have gone so badly so quickly?

"I'm waiting! Who started this?"

Flavius lifted his head, as the other boys eyed him eagerly.

"No one, Father," he lied. "We were just . . . wrestling. The Hun was showing me some moves."

"Wrestling, eh? You three looked fit to kill one another. Enough of that. Now shake hands and move out of here."

The boys staggered to their feet and glared, arms held stiffly at their sides.

"I could have whipped you," Attila muttered under his breath, eyes flashing defiance.

Flavius scoffed. "Not without your bodyguards," he retorted, in an equally low tone.

"I said shake hands!" Gaudentius repeated sharply.

Flavius peered through his one good eye and reluctantly stretched out his hand.

"You fight well, Hun," he muttered through split lips. "I wouldn't mind learning such moves."

Attila appraised him coolly, raising a curious eyebrow. "A Roman, fight like a Hun?"

Flavius thrust out his jaw and nodded, and Attila, after a pause, grudgingly grasped the Roman boy's hand. With congratulations all around, the crowd of boys resumed their chatter and continued their walk down the corridor.

Suddenly Flavius broke away from his friends and trotted back to the scene of the fight of a few moments before. Gaudentius and Didymus had already returned to the courtyard, where they were making arrangements for the Hunnish squad's lodgings. Finding the place where the scuffle had occurred, Flavius stopped and looked about for a moment, then spied the object he was seeking, where it had been kicked into a corner by the wall.

The bloody slab of meat that had started the whole business.

He picked it up between two fingers and sprinted after his noisy comrades.

III

An hour after the palace skirmish, Attila was being toweled dry by a young bath attendant who was doing her best to wipe gently at the scrapes and bruises on his back. This treatment he stoically endured, but he winced as another slave, a boy who assisted Didymus' hairdresser, attempted to dab at him with a perfumed sponge. Theodoric and Flavius reclined nearby on lounging chairs, grinning in amusement, although Flavius occasionally winced as well, as he shifted the position of the meat he gingerly held to his face.

"If you hold such meat on your eye," Attila remarked in his monotone, belabored Latin, "you be glad that Celt not put spices on it first."

"Hmm," Flavius grunted, removing the meat for a moment and inspecting it critically. "The Celt wouldn't have enough brains to think of that. Or else he figured you Huns *like* your raw meat this way."

Attila wrinkled his nose at the suggestion. "Very ignorant. We put many spices on meat—eastern pepper, cumin, of course salt . . ."

"How do you cook it?" Theodoric asked slyly.

Attila responded with a disdainful glance. "You think we cook on horse's back, beneath our legs?"

Theodoric dropped his gaze guiltily. "That's what they say."

"Well, they right," Attila answered, then whirled and darted a punch at the perfume-wielding attendant edging toward him from another angle, clipping him on the ear. "That sponge boy come at me again, I shove it up his ass."

The bath attendant yelped in pain and dodged back to a safe corner while Flavius shook with silent laughter.

"Prince Attila—we'll show you around the city," he said, changing the subject. "The most backward place you ever heard of. You saw all the marshes when you arrived, and the connecting causeway you crossed over? Ravenna sits on the sea, so it can't be attacked by land— that's why we don't even need defenses on that side, except on the causeway. They call it the city where the walls are low and the waters high, where towers float and the ships are seated."

"And where frogs and mosquitoes are the leading citizens!" Theodoric laughed.

"And where the patron goddesses are Febris and Scabies!" rejoined Flavius.

Attila paused, puzzled at the deities' names. "Fever and Itch? Truly, is this such a swamp?"

"It used to be," Flavius conceded. "There's an ancient altar to those goddesses in the forum—"

"Wait till you see the forum!" Theodoric interrupted. "It's the biggest open space in the world!"

Attila shot a glare at the sponge slave, who froze as if pinned to the wall by the force of the Hun's stare.

"And you, Theodoric," the Hun said suspiciously, "your father is Alaric, a Roman enemy. Yet you are allowed to walk in streets?"

Flavius laughed again. " 'Allowed' is not a word Theodoric knows. Didymus' arm became too tired from beating him every time he escaped, so now the eunuchs pretend not to see him when he sneaks out of the palace. Once he's in the street, he fits right in, like every other nobleman's bastard looking for trouble. You will, too."

Attila snorted, fingering the scars on his cheek. "I think Romans have seen few Huns."

"They'll get used to you," Flavius said laconically, standing up and adjusting his tunic. "Let's go. What's taking so long?"

Attila jerked his head at the bath girl who had finished carefully drying the prince's long hair and was attempting to sort through the weeks-old tangles with a narrow-toothed tortoise shell comb.

"Drusilla!" Flavius scolded. "Leave him alone!"

Attila nodded in relief and hurriedly slipped into the clean Roman tunic that had been laid out for him on the dressing rail.

Half an hour later, the boys stood in the middle of the magnificent Ravenna forum. Flavius pointed out Trajan's aqueduct to one side, the lavish Porta Aurea gateway to the other, and in the distance the deepwater port, filled with ships from every corner of the earth, with as many again hauled up into dry dock for repairs at the massive ship works. The air was filled with the sounds of vendors hawking their wares, and the boys dodged through an obstacle course of pushcarts loaded with salted anchovies and pickled shellfish, merchant slaves carrying on their heads stacks of cunningly fitted tin cookware that clanked with every step, and wheeled trolleys bearing charcoal braziers on which joints of rabbit and game fowl from the countryside were grilling, emitting delectable odors. Jugglers and acrobats weaved through the crowds, shouting for attention, and soothsayers vied for people's palms and coins. On one side, a pair of nut-brown men in turbans sat cross-legged on a rug, eyes closed and voices emitting a strange humming chant as a snake writhed hypnotically to the wail of a pipe. On another, African dancers leaped and rolled to the frantic rhythm of drums, while an ancient magician tottered un-scathed through their midst, blind eyes rolled back in his head, offering his services to concoct love philters, re-store lost virility, or pull teeth.

In the covered galleries on all sides of the plaza stood permanent shops and eating establishments, with touts outside the doorways praising the virtues of the prod-ucts, each man's claim shouted more loudly and boast-fully than the next's. On the side nearest the port, a group of enterprising Ephesian prostitutes had set up a brothel of sorts against a shady wall that was part of the immense basilica. They swayed their hips lasciviously at the boys as they passed, beckoning toward the colony of small, wood-framed cubicles they had erected, walled with canvas tarps, each barely larger than the single cot inside.

"It's the center of Ravenna—the center of civiliza-tion!" Flavius explained proudly, with a dramatic gesture that took in the whole enormous space. "Even bigger than Rome's forum. The whole world meets here. Come on!"

Attila lingered on, however, looking about him in surprise.

" 'Center of civilization'?" He chuckled quietly. "Yes, a good space, this 'forum.' In my country, we have a forum, an open space, too. You will see when you go, Flavius."

"Let's go," Theodoric broke in. "I'll show you two something you haven't seen."

The young Visigoth quickly began making his way down the *cardo maximus*, the major thoroughfare in the center of Ravenna, which was laid out in a straight north–south direction. "There are the factories," he an-nounced matter-of-factly to Attila, pointing down a side street to his left. "And there are some more markets down there." He needn't have bothered with the explanations, however, for Attila could immediately discern their location by his nose. As in all great cities, a tour by smell is the most vivid and perhaps most satisfying, and one can identify the specialty of each little lane that leads off the main avenue by its scent. One street reeked of rotting fruit and vegetables; another was heavy with the sour odor of hides being tanned. Some lanes stifled the senses with charcoal smoke from the forges of metalsmiths, while others were rank with the stench of live game, dormice and birds and turtles, confined in their small stick cages and waiting to be sold as food or pets.

Theodoric stepped up his pace, and the two older boys broke into a run to catch up with him. Despite his muscular physique, Attila was quick and agile, weaving like a nimble rabbit down crowded streets, under donkey carts loaded with vegetables and around bored praetorian guards patrolling the commercial quarters on horseback. His savage features and long, unruly hair startled passersby, and children stopped and pointed at the three boys as they ran. As they left the forum and ventured into the residential neighborhoods, however, Theodoric further increased his speed, cutting through courtyards and scaling garden walls like a monkey. Flavius and Attila doggedly tried to keep up but in the confusion of the throngs soon lost contact with the young Visigoth and then with each other. Stopping short in a crowded alley, Flavius stood on his toes and peered ahead in puzzlement, straining to see over the stalls and awnings festooning the walkway for several blocks ahead of him.

"Attila?" he shouted out loud. Then looking down a side street, he muttered, "Where did he go?"

"I can't find him, either!" exclaimed Theodoric, who wormed his way out of a crowd of young men shouting and betting at a dice table set up in a corner away from the watchful gaze of the praetorians. "I lost him back at that last street."

Flavius looked about worriedly. "Father'll kill me if we go back without him—I was specifically told to watch out for the Hun. He's never been to a Roman city before. . . ."

Just then he lurched forward in surprise at the impact of a blow on the back of his head, and as he raised his hand to his scalp his eyes opened wide upon finding the remains of a soft, rotten pear, which had left a mass of pulpy fruit in his hair. He whirled to find a grinning Attila standing a mere three paces behind, just where he least expected him, nonchalantly munching a less mangled specimen of the same fruit.

"Eyes to the East!" He grinned. "Your Roman fruit is defective."

Flavius scowled as he squatted and began wiping his head on the hem of Theodoric's tunic. The younger boy protested loudly and attempted to pull away, but Flavius pinned his arm behind his back until he had finished.

" 'Eyes to the East'?" he muttered menacingly. "What's that supposed to mean?"

Attila smiled. "Just an old Hunnish saying. . . ."

Flavius suddenly let go of Theodoric and lunged for Attila, but the quicker Hunnish boy was expecting the maneuver and deftly sidestepped it. Laughing once again, the three continued their leaping, dodging run until Theodoric led them to a plain gate piercing the city's massive southern walls. Here they scarcely paused to take their bearings before diving into the farm crowds streaming against them into the city. They pushed and dodged their way through the throngs of carts and barrows trundling toward the market. Forcing their way through the funnel-like gates and past the bored guards, they emerged finally into the clear, outside the walls. Here Flavius hoped they could pause to enjoy the warm morning sunshine and the fresh air free of the stench of the city behind them, but instead they stopped short, Theodoric with an oddly triumphant expression on his face and Attila with a sharp intake of breath. Flavius looked ahead of him in wonder.

Mounted along both sides of the dusty road leading to the gates were row upon row of hanged bodies, dozens of them, each spaced several yards apart from its neighbors, all twisting slowly in the wind on the ends of creaking hemp ropes. Their desiccated features had dried and decayed into exaggerated grimaces, silent screams, even ironic grins, caricatures of the expressions they had once borne in life. The victims had met their ends quite some time ago, and indeed the other travelers and merchants on the road, many of whom came this way every day, took scarcely any notice of the grisly sight, despite passing by so close they could almost reach out and touch the dead men's feet. The living had become so accustomed to the grim presence of the dead that they paid them no more attention than if the row of gallows were merely a hedge of withered juniper bushes. Attila stared in shock.

"Who are they?" he asked hoarsely after contemplating the scene for a moment or two.

"Deserters," Flavius replied. "We used to crucify them, but Constantine abolished that practice nearly a century ago."

At this, Theodoric cut in enthusiastically. "Now we just hang them!"

Attila winced and approached the nearest body cautiously. The executed deserter faced away from the road, his face almost snug against the vertical timber of the crudely fashioned gallows, as if even in death hiding his eyes from curious passersby, a dunce in the classroom of the dead, ordered to stand in the corner in shame. Attila gingerly touched the man's foot, with its dirty, scaly skin and black toenails, and the body slowly swung around so that its empty, crow-pecked eye sockets gazed down lifelessly at the source of its disturbance. The boy stared intently into the face, then gasped in surprise.

"But look at the face—the scars on the cheeks—this one is a Hun! Why do you hang my people?"

Flavius contemplated the hanged prisoner silently for a moment, then looked back down at Attila in puzzlement.

"He *used* to be a Hun, but he enlisted with the legions. A soldier of Rome is a soldier of Rome. Look—by his clothing, that one there was a Goth, and the one beyond him a Frank."

"Were they slaves in your army?"

Flavius frowned. "Not these. Huns and Goths serve as mercenaries, and receive Roman pay. But if they run, they're treated as Roman deserters."

Attila walked down the road several yards along the row of gallows, carefully inspecting each body.

"They're all foreigners. I see no Romans here."

"Well, there aren't many," Flavius patiently replied. "Romans mostly don't serve in the army anymore. My own father's Pannonian, you know, and he's senior general of the cavalry. Stilicho, the commander of all the legions until he was killed last year, was a Vandal."

"This I do not understand. Why do Romans not serve? How can a man not serve in the army of his own homeland?"

Flavius shrugged. "I suppose the empire has enough barbarians to do the job."

Attila looked up abruptly at the word "barbarians," his expression registering offense. Flavius, however, threw him a disarming wink.

"Get used to it." Flavius smiled. "After all, on my father's side, I'm a barbarian, too."

Attila stared at him, without a smile.

"Come on, snails!" the energetic Theodoric shouted.

"Flavius, let's show him the Circus. Chariot racing in two days! Maybe we can watch them training!"

Flavius and Theodoric trotted off, joining the lines of merchants and carts slowly funneling through the city gate. Before leaving, however, Attila respectfully touched the corpse's foot.

" 'He used to be a Hun,' " the boy whispered, repeating Flavius' explanation. "Now he's just dead."

IV

"By definition, a hostage must be an important personage in the subject nation," the emperor complained. "All our other hostages are first in line to their respective thrones."

Attila burned in anger. The presentation of credentials had not gone well. His Latin was too weak to allow him to argue his case or even adequately answer the questions put to him. Yet he understood the dispute perfectly.

"Huns are not subject nation!" he blurted. "And I am not mere hostage. I am Attila, son of Mundzuk, who was son of Turda, who was son of Scemen, who was son of Ethe, who was son of Opos. . . ."

Gaudentius elbowed him to keep quiet, then nodded respectfully to the emperor. "The boy is technically correct, Augustus," he said. "Since the Huns are not subject, and they see little to gain from alliance with us, they therefore have no reason to risk sending us a first-born prince."

Honorius eyed the boy coldly for a moment. "Insolent lad. And his litany of names is nonsense. How can a people without even a written language know who their ancestors are? His own name is nothing but a barbarity—"

"Attila means 'iron' in my tongue," the boy interrupted.

"And our little iron boy has manners to learn, as well as a bit of Roman humility," the emperor grunted. "Didymus is right—he is our burden now, though it's beyond me how he will guarantee his nation's good behavior if he has such little personal worth. Romanize him, Gaudentius, and perhaps he will serve us in good stead in the future when he returns to his people."

"I am a soldier, not a tutor, Augustus. Shall I leave command of the legions' cavalry to Romanize our Hun?"

The emperor's cold gaze now flitted to Gaudentius and lingered there. "No, you shall not leave the legions," Honorius replied evenly. "He shall live with your family, in your house, but shall learn rhetoric, law, and mathematics under the palace tutors."

"I shall enroll him, then, with my son, in the first section."

"No," the emperor said after a pause. "I believe the second section will be quite sufficient for one of his rank."

With that, Gaudentius and the boy turned and strode out of the receiving hall without further word. The official presentation of credentials had been accomplished, and Attila breathed a sigh of relief as they stepped into the fresh air of the courtyard.

"Do not think it's over," Gaudentius told him gruffly as they walked across the smooth flagstones toward the other side of the palace where his family kept quarters while he was in the city.

"This second section, first section . . . I do not understand. . . ."

"You will soon enough." And when Attila looked up at the older man's face, he saw the jaw clenched in fury.

The palace educational system, like many such institutions in the world's great courts, was divided into two distinct levels. The first was for the sons of the imperial family, though since Honorius had none himself, it was opened to more distant relations as well—cousins, sons of the most senior military officers, and, most numerously, the emperor's various princely hostages. Some thirty or forty youths of various ages were enrolled in the first section. It was staffed by the most renowned tutors of the world and allocated the finest scientific equipment and the most exquisite instruments of music and art. From this section emerged future emperors and kings.

The second section was the level afforded to the children of other palace retainers—couriers, stewards, advisors, experts in various fields and disciplines who, because of the emperor's perceived need for their proximity, lived in the palace with their families. This section, too, received great resources—not as vast as the first section's but of the highest quality nonetheless. What it lacked, however, was the confidence among its students and tutors that they were *worthy* of such resources. For as long as those students in the second section could recall, they had been regarded as fortunate but inferior, endowed but ungifted. They were "second section" and . . . second-rate. Most of the students and their parents simply accepted this as their station in life and indeed were thankful to the emperor for the opportunity to study under tutors who were, in fact, the second-finest in the empire.

Yet Attila took it as the most mortal of insults.

On the first day, as he walked with Flavius from his house across the palace grounds, he was stunned when Didymus appeared and directed him to split off to enter the courtyard at which the second-section tutor was preparing to lecture. When he found he was to be isolated from the other princely hostages and educated with the sons of the palace astrologer, he was furious.

So furious, indeed, that on the second day he refused to emerge from his room.

To be sure, Gaudentius had known from the beginning that a lad as proud and hardheaded as Attila would never accept relegation to a lower status. In the end, unable to make the emperor understand the humiliating position into which Attila had been thrown, Gaudentius simply took matters into his own hands. He prepared the necessary transfer order, signed it himself as the palace's senior military officer, and presented it to Didymus, who administered both sets of tutors. The eunuch accepted the paper distastefully, as if it had been drawn up by a leper, yet he had not the rank to challenge Gaudentius, nor the temerity to complain to Honorius. Two weeks after arriving in Ravenna, Attila began attending the lectures of the first-section tutors.

Nevertheless, the damage had been done. Insult was compounded upon insult, and the difficulties did not end with the Hun's admittance. Attila's Latin was leaden and clumsy; he knew no Greek, the language in which many of the lectures were conducted; and indeed he was unpracticed even in basic reading and writing, not to mention the classics of literature and philosophy with which his classmates had been imbued since their earliest years. His flat face, dark complexion, and long hair did nothing to endear himself further to them or his instructors, and his lack of European noble blood made it difficult for him to demand treatment on equal terms with the other boys.

Flavius alone treated him civilly, and indeed as a brother, at first out of pity and then out of sincere admiration and friendship. The two boys spent long evenings in the dining room of the Aetius family compound as Flavius untiringly instructed his friend in the rudiments of Roman education. Attila returned the favor in their early-morning exercises, before dawn, teaching his friend certain of the crafty fighting techniques that had so baffled Flavius in their initial encounter. The Roman was a quick study in the martial arts and within several weeks had managed even to approach Attila's skill in certain maneuvers.

Yet the progress was not reciprocal. The Hun's impatience with bookwork and the limited time Flavius had available from his own studies and court responsibilities conspired only to frustrate Attila's efforts to catch up with his classmates. Indeed, Gaudentius soon concluded that he had no recourse but to engage a supplemental afternoon tutor for his Hunnish ward, at considerable personal expense to himself. This he did, and Attila's seething resentment grew with every new hour he was forced to labor indoors, spine curved, over the unintelligible rhetorical and grammatical exercises the wizened old Greek instructor assigned him. Even Flavius' patient friendship could do little to mitigate Attila's academic difficulties and anger. The Hunnish prince had to grit his teeth to attend the lectures every morning with his comrade, enduring the raps on his knuckles from the instructors impatient at his clumsy speech, silently tolerating the whispered jibes and jokes about his hair and clothing from the other boys. It was a wretched way to spend one's life, and Attila seethed whenever he thought of the vast grassy plains of his homeland and gazed about at the close and smoky walls of this incomprehensible eunuch-run palace. His only friend was Flavius, his only father Gaudentius.

Yet Flavius' time was growing short; the Hunnish guards who had brought Attila were demanding to begin their return trip home with their Roman hostage before the rivers swelled with the autumn rains. It was time for Flavius to prepare to make his own journey east.

Six weeks after the Hun's arrival, Flavius, in newly fitted and polished Roman armor and with a freshly dyed woolen officer's cloak, awkwardly mounted Attila's war pony as the same squadron of fierce Hunnish troopers who had escorted Attila now surrounded him. He strove to keep his features dignified and expressionless, but the very lack of expression on his normally smiling and open face betrayed his nervousness. Several yards away, a small knot of well-wishers stood watching, and his mother, beautiful and elegant in her palace gown and finery, suddenly lost her composure. She collapsed in sobs into her husband's arms, while Gaudentius remained standing in stoic silence, one arm draped stiffly over his wife's shaking shoulders.

Flavius opened his mouth to say something, but in his roiling emotions—sadness, fear, anticipation, excitement, all surging through him simultaneously in a disconcerting flood—he was at an utter loss. Gaudentius saw the boy's quandary and understood. Nodding a swift and silent farewell, he turned and led his weeping wife into the palace without a backward glance.

Flavius looked at Captain Turgrid, the lead rider of his Hunnish escort, and nodded. In silent and meticulous formation, the horsemen wheeled as one, like a flock of starlings that had suddenly encountered an obstacle, and without a single verbal command, the horses clattered down the street.

Standing alone, beyond the group of onlookers, Attila listened resignedly to the group of jostling, unruly barbarian princes he would be expected to join—for how long?

For as long as his king, and the Romans, required him to stay.

"Come on, Hun! Let's go eat some meat!" The Celt's lilting accent and hoarse laughter were unmistakable, and Didymus chuckled in amusement.

"Silence, Vortigern!" the eunuch scolded mildly. "We all have our favorite foods—even Huns!"

Attila clenched his fists but remained expressionless, staring at the leather-clad backs of the *zuun* as they receded and finally disappeared beyond the far corner of the palace wall. Glancing at the mocking expressions of his tormenters, his anger flared. The time would come when he would teach these foreigners—all of them, Romans included!—who were the true barbarians.

Yet the time was not now. He swallowed his rage, turned, and walked slowly past the other princes and into the palace.

V

The last Roman community of any size Flavius rode through was Viminacium, on the muddy banks of the Danuvius, the rough border between the farthest outposts of the Roman Empire and the domain of the Huns. That now-distant city—which Turgrid had described tersely as a river trading post—had shocked him for its poverty and lethargy. Indeed, he had at first mistaken the line of precarious stick-and-wattle huts along the edge of the river for animal pens. He only realized their true function as dwellings when the Hunnish riders admiringly pointed out how they hung over the water on stilts. He failed to understand the advantage of this novel architecture, however, until he witnessed the inhabitants fishing with strings from inside and economizing on space by pulling their catch through the same floor holes as they used to void their personal waste. Flavius immediately resolved not to sample any village cooking involving river fish.

Although the site was nominally under Roman control, it had so often been plundered by invaders from both sides of the river that any desires among the locals to improve their lot through building or investment had quickly faded. The street gutters overflowed with offal, the baths were in crumbling ruins, and half-wild dogs ran rampant through the ramshackle galleries of the pub-

lic market. Young people moved away as soon as they
were able, and the town was largely populated by the old,
the feeble-minded, and those simply wishing to earn a
quick coin or two by swindling passing travelers. The
race of the inhabitants was indefinable—they were a
mixed population, a town of mongrels, whose features
and bodies bore traces of Hunnish and Ostrogoth ances-
try, as well as that of a dozen other nations. Conversa-
tions that Flavius heard in the street were sprinkled with
the rusty Latin of long-retired Roman legionary veterans, some of whom had taken advantage of the cheap
land to settle with their pensions, their silent wives, and
their wild-haired children in this last bastion against the
barbarians.

Upon arriving, Flavius and the guards spread their
bedrolls in the center of the muddy forum to await the
next morning's weekly market and to haggle for supplies.

"This place is like the end of the world," Flavius com-
mented to Turgrid.

"It is," the Hun grunted in reply. "The end of *your*
world."

The river crossing was managed by Hunnish boatmen,
whose duties were not only to ferry travelers across the
broad, yellowish expanse of the Danuvius but also to prevent those from the northern side, Huns and their allies,
from crossing without authorization into Roman territory in the south. The boatmen used dugout canoes they
called by the Greek word *monoxyli* to transport passen-
gers, while horses and gear were sculled to the far bank
using rickety rafts of loosely tied logs through which the
waters splashed, soaking baggage and terrified animals
alike. Flavius queasily endured the ordeal, during which
he lost all of the poorly cooked breakfast he had choked
down that morning. He comforted himself with the
thought that if he had to be a hostage, it was good he was
being sent to a land-dwelling nation like that of the

Huns. Had he been assigned to a seafaring people, he never would have survived the initial voyage. It was with genuine relief, then, that Flavius took his first strides on the foreign shore.

Nevertheless, he had little time to savor his small victory, for his escort, silently rejoicing at their arrival on home territory, now picked up their traveling pace considerably. Advancing away from the river, on the well-worn road to the Hunnish capital, he was first amazed and then puzzled by the countryside—a landscape endlessly broad, impossibly vast, of undulating grasslands as far as the eye could see in all directions. From his readings of the geographers Flavius knew that this land, though now starkly beautiful in the summer, could be terrible and bleak in the winter and that the harshness of its climate brought out the hardness and the silence of both the men and the animals that inhabited it.

On the night of their first camp beyond the river, Flavius stepped briefly out of earshot of his comrades, and for the first time in his life he heard nothing, he saw nothing, he smelled and tasted nothing. All around him was darkness, without doorlamp or glowing horizon, without human voice or odor of animal, without taste of dust in the wind. Often, as a child, he had closed his eyes or blocked his nose or ears, depriving himself of a stimulus, of a sense or two, merely for the novelty of it; but to be deprived of four senses simultaneously, and not by his own actions but by the very *lack* of stimuli around him, was deeply disturbing. When he realized what had happened, it was as if he had lost his footing—or rather, his footing was the only thing left to him, his only contact with the earth and the physical world. He dropped to his knees, palpating the ground with his hands and lifting clods of dirt to his face for the scent of fresh earth. And then after a moment there came to his ears the hollow cooing of a ground bird nesting nearby with her young; and a light breeze sprang up that hissed softly through the high grasses; and a mild tang of pollen rose to his nose and lips; and he realized his senses had returned and all was well again.

The next morning, as they broke camp, Turgrid called him over. In his arms he held a long bundle, wrapped in an oiled canvas, which he laid silently in the boy's hands.

"What is this?" Flavius asked, puzzled.

"You are in Hunnia now," the captain replied tersely. "You will be brought up in the royal court. This is the gift our boys receive at ten years of age. You are late, but you will catch up. The king sends it to you as a welcoming gift, and I have been carrying it since we first left Hunnia months ago."

Flavius squatted on the ground, laid the bundle down, and carefully unfolded the fabric. An ash-shafted spear with a gleaming bone warhead; a long loop of rope fashioned of strips of braided cloth; and a magnificent polished bow, of a kind he had seen slung from the backs of the soldiers escorting him, but which he had never had an opportunity to examine close at hand. Delighted, he picked up the weapon and carefully turned it over in his hands.

"This is for me? From the king? I've never seen a bow like it . . ."

"It is a war bow," Turgrid replied, "fashioned by our greatest craftsmen. It took ten years to make."

"Ten years!"

"Ten years, to select the finest pieces of wood, horn, and bone, properly season the materials, cut them into the right shape, mold the caribou sinews for the back, and identify the correct proportions between the flexible and rigid parts of the weapon. It is not a simple task."

This was the greatest number of consecutive words Turgrid had spoken since leaving Ravenna, and Flavius looked up with surprise at the transported expression on the officer's face as he gazed at the extraordinary weapon.

"Look," Turgrid continued, taking it from Flavius'

hands. "It is a reflex bow—when you string it, it reverses its curve. The core is ashwood, stiff and durable. It is backed by sinew for flexibility, and bellied by deer horn for springiness. It has a range of two hundred fifty paces."

"Two hundred fifty! But that's . . ."—Flavius quickly calculated in his head—"that's nearly twice the range of a Roman bow!" He gazed at the weapon in awe.

"It is the unity of the materials that lends it its power. The patience and durability of wood, the speed and cleverness of the buck, the lethal strength of the great horned caribou . . ."

"Yes, I've seen compound bows before."

"Ah, but not like this one. See here, the seven bone plaques on each end that stiffen the ears to make a more rigid base for the string. The two limbs are uneven—this lends greater power to the arrow, and greater ease of movement to the bowman when riding."

"When riding? I'll be shooting when riding? But I'm only a hostage! How will I learn—"

"You will learn the way our other boys learn," Turgrid replied. "There are no idle guests among the Huns, even hostages. You will not sit in your room and complain about the status of your classmates. All men earn their meat by serving with their comrades."

Flavius nodded self-importantly. "Excellent. Shall we begin now?"

Turgrid eyed him skeptically. "Now?"

Flavius snatched the bow and began pulling back on the string. "Now. We're riding today—we can practice shooting as we go."

Turgrid took the weapon back and returned it to the cloth wrapping. "You are holding it upside down. We will start with the simpler weapons first. Pick up the spear. You are a Roman—surely you know how to throw a *pilum*?"

Flavius smiled. Like every Roman boy, he had been

throwing spears since he was old enough to walk. He glanced around and spied a goatskin water bag, the size of a man's torso, hanging from a tripod improvised of three cavalry lances thirty paces away.

"Watch," he announced, and picking up the spear at his feet, he hefted it once or twice in the palm of his hand, feeling its weight and searching for its balance point. Then, satisfied with his grip, he turned toward the bag. He paused long in concentration, like an Olympic athlete preparing to throw the javelin, and he carefully aimed, aligning his feet in the precise stance and form taught him by his gymnastic instructors. Timing his breathing, he slowly drew back his right arm, lifting his left hand before him as a counterbalance, and then, with a forceful grunt, he hurled the spear.

The weapon flew quickly and powerfully. Glancing off one of the lances with a splintering crack, it sheered into an upper corner of the bag, slicing through the leather and causing water to spurt out the top.

Flavius whooped with excitement. "Did you see that? Got him in the shoulder! Blood spurting out and everything. That soldier won't be fighting much longer!"

Turgrid stared, expressionless, at the damaged goatskin. He then stalked over to the tripod, hung his leather skullcap head-high on a burr, seized the spear where it had stuck into the ground, and gave a short whistle.

From the herd of horses grazing in the long grass nearby Turgrid's mare lifted her head, gave a whinny in reply, and trotted over, nosing her master in the chest. He quickly hoisted himself onto the saddle blanket and fitted his feet into the stirrups. Flavius watched in puzzlement. During this entire time, Turgrid said not a word.

Making a soft smacking sound with his lips, the officer turned and trotted out of the camp. After two hundred

paces he stopped, wheeled, and without pausing even to
gain his bearings, he dug his heels into the horse's loins
and lunged forward.

Leaning low over the animal's neck, creating a profile
scarcely higher than her head, Turgrid raced toward the
tripod at breakneck speed. Men stepped aside and
glanced at him in curiosity as he surged past. At sixty
paces distant, he suddenly released the reins and stood
straight up in his stirrups as the horse continued to sprint
beneath him. With a single quick, fluid motion, he drew
back his arm and hurled the spear.

With the combined speed of the horse's furious dash
and the strength of the Hun's throw, the spear became almost invisible. It hissed past the astonished Flavius and
into the middle of the tiny cap, flew through the close-
leaning lances of the tripod without touching one, and
slammed into a grassy hummock some distance beyond,
burying both warhead and cap in the soft earth.

Flavius, however, had no time to thrill at the astonishing throw, for just as Turgrid thundered past him on his
mount, the boy's arms were suddenly pinned to his sides
and he was lifted bodily into the air. Landing heavily on
his shoulder, the wind knocked out of his lungs, he found
himself being dragged at breakneck speed through the
long grass. Dirt and tufts of weeds filled his mouth and
eyes, and through a haze of pain and confusion he
glimpsed the goatskin leggings of the soldiers as he tumbled past and through the roaring in his ears heard their
scattered shouts and hoots of laughter.

After what seemed an eternity, his skidding and
bouncing progress through the grassy field slowed and
came to a halt. He lay stunned and gasping, feeling the
scrapes from the dragging beginning to burn on his hip
and shoulder. Instantly hands reached down to lift him
back to his feet. In confusion he saw Turgrid looming
over him on his horse, lifting a noose up over his head

from where it had been dropped down upon him a moment before. It was of the same braided cloth as the specimen that had been included in the assortment of weapons given him by the king.

"A war noose, lad," Turgrid pronounced cheerfully, unfazed at the bruised and confused condition of his ward. "The *pilum* is not a bad weapon, of course, but if you merely wound a man in the shoulder, he will still gut you with his sword. For close-in fighting on a horse, there are few things more effective than a war noose."

As Flavius gained his breath, so, too, did his anger rise. "You could have killed me! What kind of madman are you?"

"Romans do not have nooses. Goths do not have them, nor the Gepidae, nor the Alani. We use the nooses to capture and break wild horses, which few other peoples do. We also use them against enemies. If I had meant to kill you, I would have notched it from the tip of my cavalry lance, for greater reach and leverage. And I would not have dropped the loop around your arms and chest. It would have been around your neck."

Flavius stared at him in dismay. Finally, he found words to speak.

"And the bow? When will I learn the bow?"

"In good time," Turgrid replied, turning away. "You will learn the spear and the noose first. Like our boys. Come, it is time we were riding."

Flavius gathered his bundle of weapons and tied it to the saddle of his horse, then painfully mounted the animal. In Ravenna, he had been considered the most accomplished in weaponry of all his comrades and had often been praised by his drill instructors. But what manner of men were these Huns, who twice now had thrown him helpless to the ground before he even realized his disadvantage and who laughed off his efforts as if he were nothing more than a fly they were swatting away?

He pondered with dismay the rising pain in his shoulder and hip where the layers of skin had been scraped away in his dragging, and he wondered at the skills he would need to learn before he would be able to even hold his own in this society.

And with even more dismay he considered the two weeks of riding that still remained before he would even arrive.

But the time passed quickly, and since the day he had left that pestilential trading post on the banks of the Danuvius Flavius had seen scarcely any signs of habitation in this vast land—until this day, when at last they had come in sight of the capital.

Tired, dirty, and sore to the bone, he sat his horse on a small rise overlooking the plain. Turgrid brusquely pointed into the distance. Flavius looked with astonishment at the rambling collection of wooden-slat buildings, tents, and felt-covered domes. Six weeks of hard riding through wilderness, forest and vast plain, and this city— if one could even dignify this sprawling camp by such a name—was the result?

In its homeliness and simplicity, it was scarcely more than an overgrown shepherds' village. Yet it lacked the sometimes rustic charm of those rude settlements. Indeed, while retaining the poverty and dirt of the rural hamlet that had surely been its origin, it had taken on the worst features of a benighted refugee camp, most particularly, from what Flavius could make out, a sense of unparalleled squalor. He stared in disappointment and tried not to think about the number of years he would be forced to live here, away from the liveliness and color of Ravenna.

Suddenly, however, an odd question came to him.

"Captain," he called to Turgrid, who slackened his

pace slightly to allow the Roman's horse to catch up to him. "We've almost arrived, and yet I don't even know the name of your capital. What do you call this place?"

Indeed, whenever anyone spoke of the Hunnish capital—whether his father, or other Roman officials in Ravenna, or even Attila himself—they referred to it as merely that: the Hunnish capital. In response to the question, Turgrid did not even deign to look at his ward but simply set heel to his horse.

"The Hunnish capital," he growled roughly. "It has no name. It is here today, now, because the winter season is beginning, the herds are gathered together, and the king is holding court. Next season it will be gone."

"Gone?! How can a city be 'gone'?"

Turgrid shrugged. "Gone. Most of the people will take their herds to the steppe to graze. Rugila and the army will ride on. A few slave farmers will stay to till fields. No need for a city."

"And they will come back next year?"

"Maybe next year, maybe not. Maybe here, maybe upriver. Or downriver. Why name such a city? Do the Romans name every camp where the legions sleep?"

"No, but . . ."

"Just so." And no further information could Flavius extract.

Only moments later, it seemed, hardly time to adjust to the idea of the rabble of huts to which he had arrived, Flavius and the soldiers were riding through the streets. The experience only added to his amazement and dismay. His armor and cloak set him off as distinctly here as did the troopers' grubby leather gear when they had ridden through the streets of Ravenna. Here, too, as in his home city, people stopped to stare, but this time at him, rather than at the fierce and impassive faces of his bodyguards. The principal boulevard through the capital was barely more than a garbage-strewn dirt track, claustrophobic and squalid. It ran bursting with mangy dogs, half-wild poultry, and filthy street urchins swarming about the feet of the horses. Hastily erected wooden structures leaned in precariously from the sides. After weeks of riding through forests and plains with the silent horsemen, the cacophony of the street was deafening—his senses were overwhelmed at the sounds of the vendors hawking their primitive and filthy wares, women shouting shrilly at one another, and barnyard animals standing in the very doorways of the buildings.

Flavius leaned forward to shout again at his escort riding nearby.

"Turgrid! Where is the forum?"

The Hun stared at him, uncomprehending, and thinking Turgrid had not heard his words, Flavius repeated his question, enunciating slowly.

"The forum, I said! You know . . . the big open space!"

Turgrid merely shrugged and pointed ahead.

"We go to king's palace now."

Flavius shook his head in amazement and frustration. A capital with no name? A city with no forum?

The squadron trotted through a heavily guarded stockade where the sentries nodded in silent deference, and up to a set of splintering wooden steps, above which was constructed a modest wood-plank building, with roughly planed window cutouts and chimneys. The structure was terribly crude by Roman standards—the prefect's quarters of even the most insignificant provincial capital were grander than this unpolished affair—but it was by far the largest and finest structure in the city. The strength of its construction was apparent from the outset, for the numerous wooden pegs in the joints, and the bracings beneath the decorative eaves, were luxuries absent in most of the other structures.

The building was also far larger than the others he

passed, though by Roman standards still curiously small. Flavius estimated that it contained possibly six rooms, while few other structures could have contained more than one or two. In this, as he later found out, he was both right and wrong, for the palace did indeed contain *space* for six rooms, though in reality it was merely one room with movable dividers made of tapestry screens. Despite the palace's size, however, it was as portable as every other structure in the city. As Flavius would see with the coming of the spring, it could be dismantled, transported on a half-dozen ox-drawn wagons, and reassembled in roughly its current layout. For years, the ancient boards had been repeatedly stacked and pounded and structured to produce a "palace" fit for the king of the Huns. For so many years, in fact, that even here in the courtyard, the oppressive smell of mildew that emanated from the old, rotting wood was almost overpowering, permeating the air as it wafted out the windows. Here and there, where the crumbling old wood of the walls had finally been replaced, new patched-in pieces could be easily identified by the fresh budded beads of pitch that sprang from the green wood and gleamed in the sunlight like jewels.

Flavius snorted in distaste. "Didn't even see the forum!" he muttered. "Attila said there was a big open space . . ."

At the foot of the stairs he began to dismount but was stopped by a sharp hiss from Turgrid. Looking up, Flavius saw the party of horsemen remained mounted still as they prodded their horses up the steep wooden steps.

"We dismount only at the king's pleasure," Turgrid muttered.

At the top of the steps Flavius stopped and turned to look behind him. The palace, he saw, was on the edge of the city, and from this vantage point he could peer out past the palisades, beyond the teeming streets—to the vast, empty plain beyond, grasslands stretching to the horizon, the steppe. Suddenly he recalled Attila's words—*a big open space*—and smiled to himself.

Seated on horseback at the top of the stairs, at the entrance to the palace, was an older man, perhaps fifty years of age, but with the same athletic bearing and weathered face as the veteran soldiers in his escort. This man was different, however—his thin beard, white with streaks of dark gray, stood out from the plucked chins and scarred cheeks of the guards who surrounded him, and his open, friendly expression was in sharp contrast to the soldiers' impassive stares. It was a *lively* face, Flavius thought, and he was struck at how much vitality he saw reflected in it. Indeed, the man was even *smiling*, and Flavius felt an almost physical relief well up inside him. A smile—it was the first sign of human warmth he had seen since leaving Ravenna. King Rugila edged his mount to Flavius' side and seized the boy's forearm warmly.

"Welcome. Welcome, Prince Flavius Aetius!"

Flavius stared at him, thunderstruck at both the sincere kindness the man radiated and the title he himself had now unexpectedly acquired. *Prince . . . ?* Before he could respond, however, the king nodded, and a group of musicians stepped forward from where they had gathered behind the king, launching into a wild refrain of what Flavius could only assume was welcome music. Fiddles carved with the likeness of horse heads screeched a plaintive wail, a pair of wooden flutes skirled, and a man with a small, tambourinelike drum slung over his neck began thumping rapid riffs with his fingers, seemingly independently of the cadence and rhythms of the other musicians. The king smiled happily, patiently awaiting some greeting in return, and Flavius stammered out the first words that came to mind.

"Thank you, my lord. But I'm not a prince! My father is a Pannonian general in the service of the emperor—"

But his last words were drowned by the music, and the king waved off the boy's concerns, seemingly unruffled by his lack of royal blood. Just as Flavius was gathering his wits and breath for another attempt at clarification, an elderly woman, also smiling, stepped forward and respectfully touched his foot. The king shouted something to Flavius in broken Latin that sounded something like "Queen Mother" but then was interrupted again as two young women who followed the dowager glided gracefully in between the two horses and lifted a small silver table above their heads, to a height convenient to the two riders. Smiling broadly, the king picked up one of the two goblets and handed it to Flavius.

"The Queen Mother invites you to share the hospitality of our royal household, and begs you to taste her wine and meat, which she prepared with her own hands."

Flavius watched the Hunnish king closely and following his lead picked up a morsel of dried meat from a bowl on the small table. Swallowing it quickly, Flavius then downed the entire goblet of wine in a gulp. Around them, happy shouts and cheers arose from the onlookers, and even the normally silent cavalry riders grunted their approval.

The king winked. "This wine—a fine custom we have learned from our western friends," he pronounced. "In my father's day we had only *airag*—fermented mare's milk—with which to honor our guests. But now we have become much more sophisticated."

Smacking his lips in satisfaction, the king set down his goblet, swung his leg over his horse's neck, and dropped to the ground, agile as a boy.

As Flavius did the same, a crowd of young women gathered about, chattering and calling to the young Roman and staring at him curiously. The king glanced at the musicians, who had begun playing even more raucously to make themselves heard over the gay voices of the women, and then gestured to the players to be silent, before turning back to his guest.

"My wives," he fondly announced to Flavius. "Some of them! And this—this is my nephew Bleda, elder brother of Attila. Bleda, present yourself, boy!"

From behind the king a frail, timid figure peered, and then cautiously stepped forward, leaning heavily on a wooden crutch that was so short for him he had to bend to gain its support under his armpit. Clearly this was no temporary injury from which the boy was suffering, such as from a fall off a horse. The crutch was worn and long-used, and the light wood of the grip gleamed like smooth, polished bone. The boy's expression was hesitant but intelligent and curious, and he limped up to Flavius on crooked legs and gave him an equally crooked grin. Flavius now understood why sturdy Attila had been sent as a hostage rather than his sickly brother.

The king gazed at the boy proudly. "Bleda may never be a great rider or warrior," he said, "but he is of good counsel, and will make a wise king!" Bleda blinked and smiled and then stepped back to his former position.

Behind the wives, dozens of small children who could no longer restrain themselves rushed forward, standing on tiptoes and climbing onto one another's backs in an effort to catch a closer glimpse of the tall, odd-looking foreigner. The boys were shaved bald, their smooth pates oiled and glistening in the bright sunshine. Two columns of older girls paraded solemnly out to the king's side, garbed in shimmering silk gowns like those worn by the Persian ambassador Flavius had once seen in Ravenna. Their hair was arranged in artfully braided tresses that reached nearly to the ground. Each girl grasped in her hand the hem of a long white sheet of linen, and when they arrived at the king's side they raised the fabric to form a tunnel-like canopy fluttering over their heads and leading to the entrance to the palace.

". . . And my children!" the king continued. "Welcome, Prince Flavius. You will live here with us, in the palace, which, as you can see, has been built by the finest Gothic carpenters. You needn't hide your astonishment. And since Attila, my beloved nephew, was like my own *oylan,* my own son, so, too, will you be considered part of my family. All that I have"—he gestured expansively around him at the ramshackle palace and his enormous family—"is yours. Captain!"

At this shouted command, the king clapped loudly.

"Captain of the Guard! Turgrid!"

Turgrid stepped forward, carefully picking his way through the teeming urchins and women. He moved quickly and efficiently, with an athletic grace and confidence that clearly identified him as an important personage in Rugila's court.

"Ah, there you are," the king continued. "I am pleased you have returned safely from your journey."

Rugila turned back to Flavius. "Turgrid will show you to your quarters and attend to all your needs. Again, young prince—welcome!"

Flavius walked into the palace at Turgrid's side, followed by the throng of women and children and the prancing musicians. He could only wonder at the strange turns of fate that had brought him to a nation without a capital, a city without a name or even a forum, a palace that was scarcely more than a wooden barn—yet a king with fifty young wives, a hundred children, and the impression that every guest was a prince. Ravenna suddenly seemed impossibly distant, as if he had departed the palace a lifetime ago.

His thoughts turned to his father, and yet inexplicably, the memory of Gaudentius' face began to drift and blur.

In consternation, Flavius snapped his mind back to the present. There would be time for reflection later.

For now, his task was to endure his service as a hostage in this foreign land. It was this that he had been assigned by his emperor. And it was this that would bring honor to his father, and to Rome.

THREE

Hunnia, A.D. 409–425

I

The riders raced their ponies across the limitless grassy plain, like warriors attacking an enemy column, the crisp spring air clearing their brains of the heavy, woody atmosphere of the palace. They were accompanied by a pair of huge Hunnish hunting wolves, which loped easily behind them at a steady pace, catching up with the charging horses between sprints. A single, watchful outrider traveled on their flank, somewhat apart from the group. He was larger and older, with a veteran's easy slouch and a thick bundle of arrows bristling from the quiver on his back. From a distance the group might have been mistaken for a roving squadron of scouts or perhaps a band of mounted guards who had ventured away from the wandering herds of the king's horses to which they had been assigned. Close at hand, however, their identity was even more puzzling: But for the older warrior, they bore no armor, as scouts or guards would be expected to wear; and indeed one of them, a tall, slender youth, even sported a faded Roman military tunic, in contrast to the embroidered woolen shirts usually favored by Hunnish riders. The youths carried no weapons, for in fact, this was not a war party or a band of guards.

Flavius and the young princes of the court continued their sprint across the empty plain for a long while before finally stopping for water at a small, reedy marsh, their horses breathless and foaming. The marsh was thronging with wading birds, and as the riders approached, a flock of them lifted off in flight, their great wings flapping so close the boys could feel the wind from their feathers. Flavius looked down in satisfaction at his mount—a steppe warhorse, bred from the royal family's private herd. It was the unlikeliest beast he had ever ridden, and one that would have made him a laughing stock had he been seen riding it in Ravenna. Its great hooked head, bulbous eyes, and broad jaws reminded him of a mule from the shoulders up, while the overlarge ribs, curved back, and wide-spreading hooves were almost sheeplike. Most extraordinary of all was the shaggy mane, which hung off the horse's head down to its knees and was left unadorned but for light combing and braiding at the top to keep it out of the animal's eyes. Flavius leaned down and patted its neck, and it snorted with pleasure.

Despite its homeliness, he reflected, there was a practicality to this breed that could not be ignored. Unlike the delicate Roman warhorses to which he was accustomed, which required warm shelter every night to prevent catching one illness after another, the Hunnish horses required no stables or medical care. They were equally content with searing heat and freezing cold, camel-like in their adaptability, and could travel long distances without water or food, even when injured. Flavius had already resolved to purchase several such specimens during his stay in Hunnia, as a gift for his father when he returned. A horseman like Gaudentius, he knew, would be able to see past the animals' unsightly appearance and sense the beauty in their very ugliness.

Turgrid cantered up behind them and maneuvered his pony into the water alongside that of Flavius.

"It was a long ride," the boy said ruefully, rubbing the

back of his thigh where the edge of the crudely carved wooden saddle had rubbed. He feared he would never get accustomed to these primitive rock-hard devices, though his companions had assured him that a firm platform was the most comfortable seat for a long journey. His sit bones remained unconvinced.

"A long ride? It was nothing," Turgrid grunted in his heavily inflected Latin. He slid off the side of his horse, landing with a slight splash, and strode through the marsh to a clump of sedge supporting a large nest. Reaching in with both hands, he removed four round, speckled eggs, and tossed two of them up to Flavius on his horse.

Flavius caught them and examined them critically. "Fifteen miles at a gallop is nothing?"

Turgrid neatly sheared off the top of one of the eggs with his knife and slurped the contents, crunching the soft bones. "It is nothing. *Eighty* miles is nothing. Or it should be nothing. What good is it to ride all day if, when you arrive, you are so stiff and breathless you cannot defend yourself against the first man who charges you with a lance? He will kill you, and then your long ride will have been wasted."

Flavius' smile disappeared, and he looked down at his horse in dismay. Turgrid softened his tone.

"Where did you learn to ride?" he asked. "The stirrups are difficult to master, no?"

Flavius lopped the top off one of his eggs and looked up.

"I'd ridden Roman ponies at home, but I learned stirrups from watching you and the Hunnish troopers, on the journey here from Ravenna."

"That is not much time. Most of these boys learn to ride before they can walk. They are lashed to the horse as infants. You do quite well. For a Roman."

"I had good instructors."

"Hunnish cavalrymen are the best in the world."

Flavius tossed his head back and swallowed the contents of the shell. The corners of his mouth turned in with a wry grimace. "Perhaps."

Turgrid smiled. "You do not believe me?"

"I've had little experience to judge. When I was a child I used to sit on a fence and watch my father's horse troops train. They were very good, too. But I knew nothing then."

"You sat on a fence? Why?"

Flavius put the remaining egg in a pouch at his belt and pulled his horse back from the watering hole. It wouldn't do for the animal to drink too much. There was still the long run back to the city before nightfall, and a belly swollen with marsh water could send a horse into crippling spasms if it was run too hard. He glanced at Turgrid, puzzled at the question.

"Why sit on a fence? Because there was nothing else to sit on."

"No," said Turgrid, remounting his pony. "I mean— why was a fence there in the first place?"

"Why a fence?" Flavius asked. "To keep the horses from running away, of course!"

"And why would they run away? Where would they go?"

Flavius paused, at a loss for words, but Turgrid continued to prod him.

"We Huns use no fences. No paddocks. No barriers."

Flavius stared out across the steppe. Rolling waves of knee-length grass stretched treeless and flat to the horizon. Here and there black shadows appeared on the otherwise golden expanse of plain—the king's vast herds of horses, grazing for the summer months in the rich grasslands surrounding the Hunnish capital. The animals of other, lower-ranking officials, and the lesser herds of minor dignitaries and retired military officers, grazed in more distant regions. Those plains were equally fertile and golden but less desirable because they were beyond sight of the capital city, which Flavius could barely make out as a smudge on the horizon behind him, identified by a faint gray cloud of dung smoke wafting gently over the ramshackle buildings.

"Each clan brands its animals with its own *tamga,* of course, for identification. But beyond that, no other measures are needed. An animal, or a man, does not run unless he is lacking something—food, water, companionship. If a horse is given all it needs—and not merely food, for a horse requires love and respect as much as a man—it will not run away."

Flavius scoffed. "That's absurd. It may work for a horse, but not for a man. What about curiosity? What about ambition? There are things beyond mere food and companionship that drive a man to new pastures."

Turgrid eyed him closely. "Those are traits that separate man from beasts, and cause much unhappiness. That very Roman arrogance you are exhibiting now is another such trait."

"Arrogance? Is it arrogant to question a wrongheaded claim?"

"Not at all. What is arrogance is to insist that the world must be fenced without examining your own justifications for this belief."

"But these urges I mentioned," Flavius pressed, "don't they require force to be controlled? How else could Rome contain the Alamanni from attacking us at every opportunity, without threat of retaliation by our legions? How else could we keep our legions intact, without the threat of hanging for desertion? How else could we keep our own household servants from murdering us in the night, without threat of execution? Those threats are fences, are they not?"

"True," Turgrid agreed quietly, backing his own horse away from the water. "But even those urges can be satisfied, or at least controlled, by a wise leader. Take you, for instance."

"Me?"

"Certainly. You are here as a hostage, not as a prisoner, are you not? You can run if you desire. Huh! You do not have to run. You can walk away in broad daylight. You can take a pair of my cavalry horses with you, to speed your journey. I will even give you an extra blanket—my gift. No one will stop you. But there are fences that keep you here."

"Like curiosity?"

"Perhaps. Part of my duty is indeed to satisfy your curiosity, to keep you from straying or from falling into trouble. Part of my duty is to satisfy your ambition, to keep you from seeking greater challenges elsewhere."

"And what about honor? Even if I hated your land— even if I had no curiosity about it, or ambition to achieve things—I would still remain here, because my father and my emperor have ordered me to remain here, and I am honor-bound to obey."

Turgrid glanced at him skeptically. " 'Honor-bound'? And what is your reward for obeying?"

"My reward? Well, I suppose, a position of responsibility when I return, glory for my father, valuable contacts among the Huns—that sort of thing."

"Then is not 'honor' merely another word for ambition?" Turgrid asked. "No one does a deed merely for the sake of 'honor.' It is what comes attached to that honor that counts, is it not? Rank. Glory. Valuable contacts. You expect to make a mark on Rome when you return; you aspire to do great things—yes, I've seen ambition burning in you from the first day I met you. Yet you know that if you do not perform well here, you will reap nothing but shame for yourself and for your father. Is this not true?"

"It is," Flavius admitted.

"We all have our fences."

Confused, Flavius bit his lip and gazed forward. His young comrades had long finished watering their own mounts and were already well ahead of him, calling to him in the Hunnish language, which he was already beginning to understand well. Was "honor" truly just another form of wealth, something to be fought for, or lusted after, or traded, like gold or women or any other asset? Certainly not the way his father had taught him. And who was this Hun, this barbarian, to contradict Roman beliefs, the teachings he had learned from the great Roman and Greek tradition, of which he stood at the pinnacle? He opened his mouth to argue some more, but Turgrid had already turned, reaching into the bag attached to the back of the saddle, removing some meat he had brought for the hungry hunting wolves accompanying them. The Hunnish officer glanced up to see Flavius watching him.

"It wouldn't do for the wolves to go hungry when there is no living game on the steppe besides our horses." He smiled as he tossed the wolves two large chunks of deer flesh.

Flavius nodded and said nothing. Tired of conversation, he turned his head to the path beaten through the grassland by the other youths far ahead of him and urged his horse back into a gallop.

II

It was the day of the autumn equinox, the final day of the gathering of the western clans for the annual horse roundup, the "roping." Hundreds of families had trooped in, some walking and riding for many weeks from great distances. The air was thick with the low-hanging smoke of dung cooking fires and the rank, greasy wool of the sheep and goats that wandered among the felt tents in search of scraps. Though the roping itself and the contests around it were for men alone, it was the women who set the tone in the camp, and on a day like this, of fine, cool sunshine, they had dragged their household chores out of the tents and into the open air, laughing and chatting easily as they squatted in the paths, scouring cauldrons, weaving woolen mats, and scrubbing dirty floor rugs with urine to remove stains. Several had gathered their sheep together in a small communal herd and were happily milking the bleating ewes, while others poured the foamy milk into goatskin bags, to be fermented later into *airag* or fashioned into the small hard cheeses that would nourish a family through the winter when the udders went flat. A toothless old man nearby had seized a plump lamb, strung it on a tripod by the hind legs, and slit open the belly from breastbone to groin. Reaching into the cavity with a short, curved knife, he quickly lopped out the heart and held the steaming organ in his hand above his head, grinning as the blood dripped down his arm, while a troop of small children laughed and danced around him, clamoring for the warm delicacy. He sliced it into quarters and tossed them to the youngsters, who fell on it like famished dogs, the blood smearing their lips; then he cut out the other viscera, the liver and stomach, and gave those away, too, before turning to butcher the carcass.

There was a shout of men from the edge of the camp, and the barking of dogs, and the women all looked up briefly from their chores and smiled. It would not be long now—the contests were done and the menfolk would soon be returning, sweaty and battered and clamoring for *airag*. Time to put away the scouring stones and duck into the tents to dress their hair and begin preparing the thick soup. This night would be the final feast.

Beyond the camp, at the sand pit that had been hastily dug the night before, excitement still hovered in the air, though the awards ceremony had been completed and the bettors had long since finished their raucous arguments over the winnings. The final wrestling match had ended over an hour before, yet in the dressing area, a small, flat clearing ringed by brightly colored woolen rugs hung on lines, one youth still lingered. Not out of pain, for he was unhurt, nor out of despair, for he had been the victor, but rather out of sheer amazement at the turn of events in his life.

The young man stared at the brightly polished Gepid war shield he had been awarded by the king. It was a magnificent artifact, captured in battle a generation earlier and since then hung in the great hall of the palace and often admired by visiting warriors. So different from the small Hunnish wickerwork shields, designed for lightness and covered with hardened and stretched leather for durability. This prize could clearly have been wielded only by a warrior of the gigantic physical proportions of the Germanic tribes. Constructed of solid oak, layered with smooth iron plate, and crowned with a magnificent gorgon-headed *umbo*, the hollow boss of bronze that covered the aperture in the middle, the affair weighed as much as three Hunnish shields put together. And unlike the wickerwork specimens, which were meant for use on horseback, the Gepid design afforded protection from shoulder to knees, even for a warrior as tall as he.

It was a splendid prize, which he had duly earned as champion. After victories in two qualifying rounds of wrestling, in the final bout he had faced a formidable opponent, a cagey veteran nearly as tall as himself. The betting had been heavy and heavily against him, and the shouts of the frenzied crowd that had gathered around the improvised wrestling pit still rang in his ears. For nearly an hour the two champions had battled, testing muscle and sinew against each other, until finally his opponent had shown signs of fatigue. Deftly dodging the Hun's takedown and throwing him off-balance with a mighty cuff to the side of the head, he had hurled himself on top of his surprised adversary with all his weight, pinning him to the dirt with a shoulder in the throat until the Hun raised a finger in surrender. As the two battlers rose shakily to their feet, the crowd fell silent, contemplating this extraordinary man, who with his skills and determination had captured them, had taken them hostage, as surely as they had taken him.

For the wrestling was merely a small part of his accomplishments. Weaponry? He had been the only competing warrior to send his spear hurtling successfully into the impossibly distant target while standing in the stirrups. Not only had he struck the straw effigy where it swayed in the wind, but he had struck it in the very *throat*, pinning it to the post like a trophy to the wall, its head flopped down onto its shoulder. Horse breaking? He had raced his mount into the very midst of the herd of wild horses, which had been driven to a frenzy for the occasion by the release of a pair of hunting wolves snapping at their heels. Picking not a terrified mare or an ungainly colt, he had set his sight on the lead stallion, a ferocious animal of enormous size whose eyes blazed fire. The youth had deftly singled him out from the rest of the herd, slipped his noose over the animal's head, and then with his superior size and strength stopped the beast cold, flipping him to the ground with a twist of the line at the end of his lance and leaping upon him with the fury of a lion.

Horse racing? It was only in this event that the youth had fallen short, though not from want of effort or skill. It was simply that his larger size placed him at a disadvantage to smaller, more nimble Hunnish riders who, with ponies that could run forever with such light weights on their backs, had been able to outsprint him in the end. Still, he had come in third, a worthy outcome and one that had not endangered his ranking as overall winner.

When awarding the prizes, King Rugila had graciously complimented him but had saved most of his words for General Turgrid, who stood by the king's side throughout, introducing the clans' various champions as they passed by. When the shield was finally awarded, the king hefted it with a grunt, passed it to the youth, and then placed his hand on Turgrid's shoulder.

"You have done your work well," he told the officer quietly. "Never has an outsider been so much like one of us. It is as if he were my own son, my own *oylun*."

Turgrid nodded, expressionless as always. "His father is a great man himself, and a fine general. But his son will surpass him. I see it in him."

The shield was superb, a worthy prize for his efforts, though so unwieldy as to ensure it would never be used in actual warfare—at least not in warfare as practiced by this youth, as practiced by the Huns. Nevertheless, now after the event, as he contemplated the magnificent artifact, he found himself riveted in fascination, not for its massive size or for the cunning detail of its craftsmanship but for the bright polish of its iron.

How many years had it been—seven, eight perhaps?— since he had last looked at himself in a mirror? The implements were rare in Hunnia, and even on the few occasions when he had encountered one, during visits to the women's quarters or when inspecting the merchandise offered by traveling traders, he had had little interest in such frivolities. Yet now, though fancifully distorted by the convex bowl of the outer surface of the shield and by the numerous scars and scratches hacked into the metal in battle, the reflection staring back at him made him catch his breath.

The large, grayish eyes were familiar—one never forgets one's own eyes or is surprised by them—yet he wondered at the age and coldness he seemed to see in them. The eyes were no longer those of a boy but rather those of a warrior: eyes of iron, eyes of ice. Nor was the hair strange to him—after all, he saw it every day, dressed it every day. Yet the very fact that this was so—that he could actually *see* his hair as he held it—would have caused him to smile in disbelief only a few years ago. Hair long enough to see? He took pride in the chestnut mane that flowed over his shoulders, which he braided and tied back in a warrior's plait when preparing for battle or engaging in competitions. It was a sign of his role, of his status in the close-knit but hierarchical Hunnish world, an indication as telling of accomplishments and acceptance as the small, intricate *tamga* of the royal clan that he bore branded into the skin over his right shoulder blade.

He set the shield on the ground leaning against a post and gathered his clothes, which he had stripped off for the wrestling match. Donning the worn leather leggings, the soft doeskin boots, and the bright crimson woolen shirt he wore only for special occasions, such as this gathering of the clans, he allowed his mind to wander. The roping was concluded, and now he would be returning to duty. It was good, this break from the routine, if only for three days—yet he was ready now to return to his patrols, to his roaming of the steppe with the *zuun* he led, his squadron of a hundred.

He fastened the final straps of his leather corselet over the tunic and then placed the fur-trimmed cap carefully on his head, centering his braid between his shoulders. He began to walk out of the dressing area toward his horse and then stopped and returned to pick up the shield. What would the king have thought had he forgotten it? Picking it up, he stole one last glance at the cloudy reflection, at the tanned and hardened warrior in the furs and leather of the Hunnish cavalryman, and unthinkingly, without vanity or hesitancy, but with pure joy, he smiled.

And in the reflection of the war shield the cavalry officer Flavius Aetius smiled back.

III

Turgrid and Flavius stared into the spitting fire as other young soldiers sprawled about nearby, resting, gnawing on the remains of their dinner, or idly discussing the events of the day. The men's horses wandered aimlessly, snorting and snuffling, occasionally approaching their owners and nosing them affectionately in the back of the head. A few of the troops lounged discreetly at the side of the fire near Flavius, listening silently to the legend Turgrid had been chanting, rhythmic and dreamlike, in the ancient tongue.

Flavius savored the lilting, melodic sound of the words as much as he did their actual meaning. After eight years in the Hunnish court, his command of the spoken language was as fluent as that of a native-born prince. The literary language, however, the obscure and all-but-forgotten form in which the epics were recited and handed down from generation to generation, was altogether different, a mystery and a puzzle that was only now being opened up to him. Time and again he had listened to the Hunnish legends, the stories of the ancient gods and the origins of the Hunnish dynasty, recited in the formidable verses known now only by the oldest of the clan elders and by the members of the Hunnish royal family to whom it was systematically taught. Each time, the power and the beauty of the words became clearer to him. He relished every opportunity to hear the recitations that Hunnish princes were taught to chant strictly from memory. None of the words had ever been written, and none ever would be. The men around the fire were enraptured at the recitation of the remarkable epic, despite the fact that most, like him, could understand only a bare smattering of the actual words.

Turgrid sat cross-legged, hands resting gently on his knees in the traditional position of bards, eyes gazing straight and unblinkingly into the fire as he intoned the dead dialect that Flavius struggled, with every ounce of his concentration, to understand.

". . . One day the ancient sword will be found, the sword forged and beaten by the Father of the Dynasty himself, a blade tested by fire, strengthened by ice, kissed by the wind. It will be secreted in stone, to be recovered only by the Berik Cur, *the Great Leader, for whom the highest destiny is reserved, a king whom every nation will fear above all men. When he possesses that sword, the Sword of the Dynasty, he will be nigh unto the gods, and indeed will become like unto a god himself."*

Turgrid's voice trailed off into silence. The only sounds remaining were the popping of the fire and the muted shuffling of the horses in the darkness. The soldiers who had been listening to the tale yawned and stretched, then gathered over a flat rock to cast lots for the guard shifts that night and prepare for sleep. Flavius stared into the fire a moment longer, a faintly bemused expression on his face. Finally, with a shake of his head as if breaking a spell, he waved his hand in dismissal.

"A sword? I always wondered, Turgrid—why do you place the destiny of your people on the hope of finding an ancient sword? Not on the favor of God, or on the might of your armies, or on the weakness of your enemies—but on finding a magic sword?"

"You misunderstood the legend," Turgrid replied coldly. "Possibly due to your defective knowledge of the language."

"Do you dispute my interpretation of it? I hope one day

to be a Roman commander, like my father—but it will be by the skill of my tactics and the force of my will. I would never place my hopes on the fulfillment of some myth."

"If that was an 'interpretation,' your Roman education is astonishing in its shallowness. We do not place the destiny of our people on the hope of finding a sword, instead of on the favor of the gods. Rather, finding the sword *is the outward sign* of the favor of the gods—the confirmation that all the other conditions are right for our destiny to be fulfilled. That may indeed mean our armies are sufficiently mighty and our enemies sufficiently weak. Or it may mean that the Spirit of Heaven has descended and taken the form of our ruler, or that all the tribes of the earth have recognized the one true way of life, the way of the Hun, or any number of things. It is not for humans to know the specific circumstances."

"You don't question what the circumstances might be? Not even to yourself? You don't wonder at the logic of the story?"

"It is not necessary. The sword will be found. Perhaps tomorrow, perhaps a thousand years from now. When that occurs, we will know—the entire Hunnish nation will know—that the circumstances are right, the stars are in alignment, and our destiny will be achieved. It is a puzzle. But one that I am glad to leave unexamined, and to trust in its potential."

Aetius stared at the fire, shaking his head. "A puzzle, a riddle. Riddles have their place in Roman culture, too, Master Turgrid, but not one that decides the destiny of nations. Ha! I have a riddle for you."

Turgrid looked at him with annoyance. The mood of mystery and melancholy he had sought to create was shattered like a fragile goblet.

"A riddle?" he said. "You wish me to guess a riddle?"

"Yes. An old Roman one my father taught me. You must guess who I am. Listen:

"Hung with my mates in summer's heat,
no drop from rain or well.
Then strong men roughly pulled me down
and threw me in a cell.

"They kicked me, beat me, bled me,
out of pleasure, not of rage,
Then put me in a darken'd tomb
to wait and seethe and age.

"But in the end I'm laughing,
for I bring the strong man down.
I make the whore look like a queen,
and make the king a clown.

"I cheer the soul, turn cowards brave,
cause long-dead hope to wake.
And Hell's own fire cannot inspire
the chaos I can make."

"So—," Flavius continued. "Who am I?"

"Who are you?" Turgrid stared at him for a moment in bewilderment; then his face hardened. "Bah. I pass the night with your *zuun* and I recount for you the greatest legend ever told, of the great sword of the Huns—and you respond with a child's riddle. Ask your riddles of children in the palace, when you return."

"The greatest legend ever told—of an ancient sword? Found by a famous king? It's a great myth, Turgrid, as good as the ones told by the ancient Greeks, which I used to love. But you don't really believe it, do you? It's entertainment, like my riddle, no more and no less. And you still haven't given me the answer."

Turgrid drew his eyes wearily away from the fire into which he had been staring and looked hard at Flavius.

"It is the epic of the Huns. It is the story of our past and our future. As much as the *Iliad* is yours. Oh yes, I know your *Iliad*. Do you think it is believable? And the *Odyssey*! Now *there's* a myth!"

Flavius shrugged. "The Sword of the Dynasty, the *Iliad*—they're all myths. You don't insult me by calling Homer what he really is—a teller of stories. I prefer to hear about real deeds. I prefer to *do* real deeds."

Turgrid grunted. Flavius glanced at him in puzzlement. "What? What did I say?"

"That you prefer to do real deeds. And you shall have the chance."

"What do you mean?" Flavius asked.

"That was an extraordinary performance you gave for the king at the roping. He is considering making you a *cur,* a senior officer, assigning you a true command in his army, not merely leading a *zuun* like this one."

"A *Roman,* commanding in the Hunnish army?"

"A Hun commanding in the Hunnish army. You are no longer Roman to me, nor to King Rugila."

Flavius smiled and looked back into the fire.

"I would be very proud."

Their conversation was interrupted by the panicky whinnying of a horse in the distance, then the animal's scream of pain and shouts of men. Turgrid and Flavius seized their bows with a start and leaped up.

"What was that?" Turgrid asked, peering into the darkness. He picked up a burning stick from the fire, tossed it to Flavius, and they sprinted into the darkness, toward a copse of trees looming like a black shadow into the star-studded night sky.

As they approached, tripping and scrambling over the rock-strewn ground, a riderless horse burst suddenly from the undergrowth, rushing frantically toward them. Flavius leaped out of the way, while Turgrid threw himself at the animal, seized its halter, and dug in his heels, jerking so hard on the strap that the horse twisted its head back and fell screaming to the ground.

Terrified, the animal kicked out and flayed with its sharp hooves, as both men leaped back. In an instant, it had regained its feet and raced into the darkness, whinnying its outrage and fright. Turgrid glanced at Flavius.

"Did you see him in the torchlight? His haunches were covered with blood!"

"I saw," Flavius replied grimly. "Who was assigned to guard the horses tonight?"

Ahead, the frantic animal sounds became even louder.

"It doesn't matter. Something is still up there with the other horses. Hurry!"

Crashing through the underbrush, they charged into the grove of trees, oblivious to the spines and nettles tearing at their clothes. As they were still a week's journey from home by foot the horses must be protected at all costs. Around them, they could hear the shouts of others in their party also scrambling through the vines to the animals' assistance. Flavius cursed. Was there no trail through this damnable brush? The animals must have wandered through from another direction, following grazing paths. Bursting into a clearing with several others of their party, Flavius and Turgrid spotted in the moonlight six horses backed up against a rock outcropping, eyes rolling in terror. A snarling wolf, bloody foam dripping from his jaws, crouched before them, preparing to spring.

"It's one of our own," Turgrid observed, dismayed. "He's gone rabid."

Flavius stood, raising his bow and drawing an arrow from the quiver on his back. Turgrid, too, raised his bow, but Flavius stopped him.

"Don't worry. I'll put him down."

Just as he said this, however, the wolf's ears pricked, and he turned toward the two men. Seeing Flavius taking aim, he slumped his shoulders and slinked into the trees. There was no time to shoot.

Turgrid followed with his eyes as long as he could before the animal disappeared into the darkness. "He can't think straight," he said. "Madness is driving him, so he won't run away. He'll be back for the horses."

Both men nocked arrows and gazed warily into the trees. A dozen other troopers had also arrived, bearing torches and drawn bows, and were carefully scanning the edges of the tree line. Seeing that the undergrowth where the wolf had disappeared was sufficiently guarded by his comrades, Flavius turned toward the group of horses, clustered trembling and terrified against the rough outcropping where the wolf had cornered them.

"I'll calm the horses so we can lead them out. We've already lost one—we don't need six more to bolt from us in the middle of the night."

Just as he lowered his bow and began approaching the frightened animals, a snarl broke from the air above him and the horses again began whinnying their shrill screams. Confused at the source of the sound, Flavius raised his bow again and whirled, looking about wildly. Nothing but blackness and the snarling. It was only when one of the soldiers raised his torch high that the light reflected red off the glowering eyes of the wolf—standing on *top* of the rock outcropping to which he had circled, just above Flavius' head.

"Flavius!" Turgrid shouted. "Eyes to the East!"

"What . . . ?"

Flavius whirled again, but it was too late. The wolf leaped from the rock with a mighty spring, hurtling silently through the air. The beast slammed into him from behind, bowling him to the ground. They rolled through the pine needles and dirt in a shouting, snarling, frantic ball of fur and leather.

Gasping in surprise and rage, Flavius broke free and

scrambled to his feet. With no way to escape, he drew his dagger, but the wolf did not hesitate. Quickly recovering from his roll, he leaped again, massive jaws snapping in fury—this time directly onto Turgrid.

The Hun's knees buckled under the weight of the leaping creature, and Turgrid dropped to the ground, bow and dagger scattering into the darkness. The animal tore into him with a rage, claws digging into the ground for purchase as his teeth sank deep into Turgrid's thick breastplate. The wolf snarled and thrashed as Turgrid clubbed desperately at his sensitive nose with raw and bleeding knuckles, fighting to ward off the razor-sharp teeth, fighting for his life.

Hun and wolf rolled over and around each other, now one, then the other on top, but without weapons a man is scarcely a match for a rabid animal lacking any fear or even sense of self-preservation—it seeks only to kill; it desires only blood; it feels no pain. There was no time to think, only to act. Flavius leaped forward and threw himself onto the beast's back, straddling him with his legs, one arm locked around the animal's throat, the other stabbing again and again with the dagger.

Slowly the wolf weakened, his head turning and his tongue lolling out of the foaming mouth as he gasped for breath, bucking and scrambling like a young colt to rid himself of the deadly burden on his back. Suddenly, almost without warning, the animal coughed once and collapsed dead. Flavius lay panting and breathless on top of him, and beneath them both, dazed from pain, lay Turgrid, his face a mass of blood.

Shouts erupted from all sides, punctuated by the still-terrified whinnying of the horses and their frantic hoofbeats as they stomped in fear while being led safely away. A dozen hands reached down and seized Flavius, lifting him off the blood-matted body of the wolf and setting him shakily on his feet. He looked around for a moment, disoriented, while the soldiers tossed the carcass of the beast outside the circle of torchlight. Instantly Flavius dropped to one knee and gazed at Turgrid, who lay still in the light of the pine brands hovering near his bloodied face. Oddly, none of the soldiers bent to touch or to help him, and Flavius himself, with mounting horror, suddenly realized why.

"Turgrid! My God, he bit you—a rabid wolf bit you in the face! Turgrid . . . ?"

The older man did not move, and Flavius felt fear descend like a cloud. He seized Turgrid's head in his hands and turned it to face him. The eyes fluttered slightly, and he let out a deep sigh. Flavius called for water and then slapped the face lightly between his hands until the eyes opened.

"Turgrid—look at me, Turgrid. Can you see me?"

Turgrid blinked, and his eyes rolled back in his head, closed in pain, and then opened again. Gradually the pupils came into focus, and Turgrid lifted his head and struggled to sit up.

"Flavius . . . the wolf . . . Did we kill the wolf?"

Flavius breathed a sigh of relief and sat back while Turgrid woozily wiped his face with his sleeve and winced. Carefully he ran his hands over his cheeks and forehead, examining his blood-covered fingers with wonder but only wincing in pain when he touched his nose.

"No, he did not bite me. . . . This blood—it's from where I hit the ground."

Flavius peered at his face. "Your nose is broken," he said matter-of factly. "Better than a bite from a mad wolf." Then with a sudden thought, he stood up, eyes flashing.

"Who was on horse duty for this watch?" Flavius asked in a menacing tone, advancing on the knot of soldiers that had gathered around the dead wolf. "Who allowed them to be attacked in the wood?"

The soldiers looked up at him and silently backed away, but for one man who stood where he was, head bowed, showing no fear but in the slight trembling of his hands as they hung at his sides.

"This man?" Flavius growled. "Is it this man? General Turgrid nearly paid for this man's dereliction with his life!"

The others slowly stepped out of the torchlight, and busied themselves rounding up the remaining animals. A man's shame is not something to be willingly witnessed, for guilt, or pleasure at another's guilt, is infectious as a disease. The horseman dropped to his knees before Flavius, his head still bent forward.

Flavius's breath came heavily in his fury.

"Not only did this man risk the life of his commander, but he endangered all our lives," he pronounced. "There is no worse crime than abandoning one's duty."

There was a rustle behind him, and a hand grasped his forearm. Flavius froze, and the hand's grip on his arm turned to iron. He whirled in fury, then stopped at the figure of Turgrid standing before him, blood caking his rapidly swelling face.

"And how would you punish this man?" Turgrid asked quietly.

"In accordance with the law of the Huns," Flavius replied coldly.

"And do you know what that is? The customary punishment for dereliction is death."

Flavius paused, and then spoke up quietly. "If that is truly the Hunnish way . . ."

Turgrid cut him off. "It is indeed the Hunnish way. But it is not my way."

Flavius stared in questioning silence, his face shadowed and inscrutable in the torchlight.

"You are the commander of your *zuun*," Turgrid continued, "and you may discipline your men as you wish—

to a point. But as *your* commander, I order you to keep your sword sheathed."

With relief, Flavius dropped his hands to his side and stood at attention before the older officer. "As you wish, General," he said in a low tone.

Turgrid nodded. "I would not add the execution of an unarmed man to the misfortunes of this night. I have died and been revived, and I do not know whether the gods favor me or wish me evil. Releasing this man will anger no gods. Killing him may. He will be released."

The prisoner looked up, his face stricken with grief. "Kill me," he said simply. "I cannot return."

"Nor will you," said Turgrid. He drew a dagger from his belt and stepped forward. Seizing the man's long soldier braid, he rapidly sawed it off with his blade, close to the skull, and then tossed the hair aside into the darkness. "You have betrayed your comrades by your negligence and are no longer worthy of living among Huns. Go where you will, but you will not return with us."

The man stood up slowly, raised his shorn head, and without a further glance at Flavius or Turgrid walked away, through the copse of trees and east into the plain.

Flavius stared after him until Turgrid interrupted his thoughts. "That, too, is a Hunnish way," he said. "Banishment of the disgraced. Among us, it is a punishment worse than death. But unlike killing an unarmed man, this punishment does not rest so heavily on the judge's shoulders. It is better to regret being too lenient than too harsh."

Flavius began to turn away, but once again Turgrid grasped his arm.

"You saved my life. I am truly in your debt."

"You owe me nothing. You would have done the same. Any of these men would have."

Ripping a strip of linen from the hem of his tunic, he handed it to Turgrid to clean his face. For a moment both men were silent as they pondered what had just happened. Beside them, the Hunnish soldiers animatedly discussed the wolf battle and nudged with their toes the body of the huge beast where it lay on the ground. Finally Flavius broke the silence between them.

"Why do Huns always say, 'Eyes to the East'? I've never understood that."

Turgrid grunted and inspected the bloody rag he was holding to his nose. "It's just an—"

"—old Hunnish saying," Flavius finished for him. "I know. But what does it mean? It sounds like something the Romans would say—'Eyes to the East'—since so many of our enemies come from the East. But why would the Huns say it? You *are* the East. *Your* enemies are in the West!"

Turgrid scoffed and hawked a great gob of blood-streaked phlegm to the ground.

"Spoken like a Roman. You sit on your little peninsula, surrounded by water, look as far east as the Huns, and think we are the end of the world."

"There are few who have been farther east."

"Ah. But we have. You have never even considered what lies behind us. Persia—a civilization older than Rome, which you know only on its western periphery. Indians, mountains, deserts. The *Seres*—silk people of the Far East, defended by a tremendous wall and armies of millions. Millions! Eventually, they say, a vast sea, beyond which who knows what horrors lie. Our entire past, our very ancestors, lie behind us in the east, pushing us forward, for we cannot turn back. The Seres and the spirits of our dead would not let us turn back, though we might try. We face the West, because that is where our future lies, and our closest enemies. But what we truly fear is the East."

"So you keep your 'eyes to the East,'" Flavius muttered. He nodded at Turgrid respectfully but skeptically and then took a burning brand one of the soldiers held out to him, to help light their way back to camp. As he glanced down, however, a flash of something light on his shoulder caught his eye.

"Look at this."

With the tip of his knife, Flavius dug out a large, bloody fang embedded in his leather shoulder piece.

"This one was meant for me. No wonder the wolf was so furious—it must have hurt like Hell's own fire when he broke it off. Here—"

Flavius scratched a crude *tamga* into the canine with his knife.

"A Latin letter 'A,' for 'Aetius.' A memento of this night."

He tossed the fang to Turgrid, who caught it in the air and closed it in his fist without looking at it. His eyes were fixed on Flavius, as if he were about to say something, and then he raised a corner of his mouth painfully with the hint of a wry smile.

"A grape," he said.

"What?" replied Flavius, puzzled.

"Your riddle. It was a grape. Do you think I do not know about grapes? I served many years in the Roman legions. I have drunk my share of grapes."

Flavius returned the smile and then trotted over to assist with one of the balky horses. The clearing within the copse of trees was returning to its former calm. The only sound was the gentle clucking of the men up ahead as they led the reluctant animals down the path they had come and the soft, rhythmic slicing sound made by one of the soldiers, the last one left, who busied himself removing the dead wolf's head and hide.

Turgrid swiped at the drying stream of blood on his face and watched Flavius for a moment, until his torch disappeared into the undergrowth. He then glanced down at the fang he held clasped tightly in his fist. Shaking his head and wincing at the pain of his destroyed nose, he stuffed the artifact inside his shirt and then hastened to make his own way back to camp.

IV

It was a cold November day, before the winter snows had begun in force, and the dry dust of the plains still swirled through the narrow streets, borne on the back of the frozen Hyperborean wind. Gray clouds hung low in the sky, and the vast herds of horses had been brought in from their summer pasturage and safely gathered for the winter around the felted snow shelters brought out from storage, which now dotted the desolate steppe. Field mice and marmots had retired early into hibernation, and the Scythian geese had already, many weeks earlier than usual, passed over the land in their wavy south-pointed arrowheads. Even the ants and crickets had built nests deeper and higher than usual, or at least so said the children, who are careful to observe such things.

A young horseman in exquisite armor and a crimson cape passed through the outer encampment of guards, paused for a moment to gain his bearings through the haze of dung smoke, and then began trotting slowly through the squalid city. He was accompanied by a band of Hunnish warriors, their hoods and cloaks ornamented with the fine ermine trim that only those of the royal household were permitted to wear. He nodded at the people, but they stood wary and silent, staring at him. He, in turn, was puzzled at their reticence, until with a sudden flash of understanding he removed the bronze Roman helmet with the ornamented nasal and the broad cheek plates that obscured most of his face. They gazed in astonishment at the young officer, at the scarred, leathery cheeks, the narrow eyes—could this be a Hun, one of them?—and in sudden recognition they burst into cheers, surging from their tents and precarious wooden houses and mobbing the soldier and his escort.

It was only with great difficulty that he was able to force his way, smiling, through the growing and raucous crowds, to arrive at the palace, where King Rugila, his enormous family, and an honor guard of Huns awaited him. The horseman dismounted, bounded up the steps, and embraced the old king, who seemed to actually grow in stature and strength as the young man enfolded him in his arms.

"Welcome, nephew!" Rugila exclaimed over and over. "Truly, you bring comfort to an old man's heart."

At the sound of the king's voice, which he had never forgotten, tears sprang to Attila's eyes.

"The gods praise you, Uncle—may you reign another fifty years!"

He then turned to Flavius, lingering nearby and watching the reunion. The two young men clasped each other's forearms in greeting.

"Flavius Aetius," Attila said, slowly inspecting the tall young man who stood before him in full Hunnish garb. His solemn expression broke in a smile. "Your mother feared you lost among the 'barbarians.' But I told her you must be fat and happy and have four wives. You may introduce them to me now. . . ."

Flavius chuckled. "King Rugila made me save the best for you. You'll have to change your clothes, though. They're terrified of Romans."

The two young men took leave of the king, who was already deep in conversation with the Hunnish guard captain about the journey from Ravenna, turned, and walked into the palace. Attila fingered at his legionary cloak thoughtfully.

"This wool is very fine, but the armor is much too heavy. I must find some Hunnish gear."

"Not to worry," Flavius replied. "When we received the letter from my father telling us you would be returning, the king ordered some new armor made for you. Finest I've ever seen. You'll be the envy of every officer."

Attila looked at him closely. "Your Hunnish is excellent. Congratulations. No one on earth speaks Hunnish. Except Huns."

"I'm told your Latin is fluent as well."

Attila shrugged. "Bah. I could have learned Latin faster by loitering in the forum with the whores. Wasted years, those schools, all those boys grinding away at their grammars, pale and dried up. They've lost touch with their true nature. What more does a boy need to know, besides how to draw a bow and care for a horse, and a bit of geography?"

Flavius looked at him in surprise, taken aback by his vehemence. "My father enrolled you in the first section. You did go, didn't you?"

"Of course I did. Sitting in a class with eight-year-old boys, bent over like a hunchback because of my size. That damned eunuch Didymus would lay stripes across my knuckles with a stick if I shirked. Until the day I told him I'd shove it up his ass if he ever touched me again."

Flavius smiled approvingly. "It's long past time somebody put Didymus in his place."

Attila shrugged. "You'd have done the same thing."

"Maybe."

Passing into the great hall, empty now but for a lone servant dozing in a corner, Attila suddenly turned serious. "You're free to return home now. I've brought new Roman hostages. They arrive tomorrow, with the wagons."

Flavius fell silent and looked away.

"You don't wish to go?" Attila asked.

Flavius paused. "Of course. But in due time. When I can be sure of my place in Ravenna. Or when I can make my own place. I can only go home once, and I don't want to squander the opportunity."

"You're not so eager to return to your homeland as was I. Have you become a Hun, then?"

"I will always be a Roman. But our circumstances are different. The Huns still seek their Sword of Destiny, and I, too, seek mine. If I return to Ravenna—my father writes me that the situation is in flux. It is uncertain what my position might be if I were to return now. He is even uncertain of his own standing in the court. . . ."

Attila snorted in disgust. "Your father's standing? The court is run by eunuchs and drunkards. Gaudentius should be proud to lack standing."

"Was Ravenna truly so bad?"

Attila thought for a moment. "Let me give you an example. Do you remember the emperor's chickens?"

Flavius winced. "How could I forget? Noisy, foul-tempered, evil-smelling birds. Less meat than pheasants, uglier than crows. What makes him so fond of those creatures is beyond me."

"You know, of course, that a few months after you left, Rome was sacked by Theodoric's father, Alaric, and his Visigoths. When Honorius was informed that Rome had perished, he was so upset he took to bed in a swoon. Before the emperor could recover from his shock, your father had to explain to him that 'Rome' was the city, not the pet chicken Honorius had named after it."

"You must be joking. Father's letters never mentioned that."

"Do you think your father would put such an incident in writing and commit it to the imperial couriers? Your father is a great and honorable man—perhaps the only one left in the court. After Theodoric was imprisoned—"

"Theodoric? In prison?"

Attila nodded grimly. "What did you expect, when Alaric invaded Rome? Theodoric was a hostage for his father's good behavior. Alaric misbehaved, so Theodoric paid the price."

"But he was only a boy!"

Attila shrugged. "After Alaric died and things returned to normal, Theodoric was forgotten about and left to rot in his cell. Your father released him in secret, brought him to his own house to fatten him up with us for a few weeks, and then smuggled him out, to Alaric's relatives in Gaul. To this day, the court in Ravenna is so confused I don't believe they even realize a hostage is missing."

Flavius pondered this for a moment. "My father is indeed a great man. But something like that could have gotten him arrested for treason."

"It is a miracle he has lasted so long," Attila replied. "It is a miracle *I* lasted. If you are an honorable man, Flavius, then you are needed in Ravenna. Though how an honorable man would survive there is another question."

"Rome must change. And perhaps I am the man to effect its change. But as long as that buffoon Honorius is emperor, this is my home. I see no future for myself in his court."

Attila smiled faintly. "So—you have taken a liking to my 'forum' then?"

Flavius gazed thoughtfully out over the empty steppe as he recalled Attila's old jest.

"I am a Roman. Yet in Ravenna I could not be what I am here. You, Attila, returned here to your homeland as complete as ever you expected to be as a prince: with honors and dignity, no doubt a seat on the king's council, a military command. Those things the king has given to me as well. But only as long as I remain among the Huns. What would await me in Ravenna, under Honorius? If even my father's situation is precarious, what would be mine? The time is not right for me to return."

"Perhaps you are not a Roman. But can you ever be a Hun?" asked Attila quietly. "You don't look like one. Can you think like one? Can you plot and connive like one?"

Flavius paused. "These are also my people now, as much as they are yours. I've eaten with them, trained with them. . . . Attila?"

He looked around for a moment in surprise, seeing no one—Attila had disappeared. Suddenly his eyes narrowed in understanding.

". . . I've trained with them. . . ." he murmured, and then, whirling suddenly, he ducked behind a nearby pillar, hearing the soft tap of Attila's sword as it slapped the wood just where he had been standing a moment before. In a lightning movement, he leaped around the back of the pillar and simultaneously drew his own blade, bringing the tip to rest lightly between Attila's shoulders. Attila, standing on the other side of the pillar facing the spot where Flavius had been, froze and then slowly turned, his face flushing red.

"Turgrid has taught you well," he said quietly.

"Plot and connive like a Hun?" Flavius asked. "Perhaps not. But I can watch my back like one. Eyes to the East."

"We have much to discuss," Attila replied, changing the subject and regaining his composure. "But that can wait. Come—they are celebrating!" Both men sheathed their swords, and Attila slapped Flavius' back as he led him out to the courtyard. "Let us see those virgins you saved for me."

Flavius smiled slyly.

"I didn't say they were virgins. . . ."

V

"It is a hard thing to attack a tribe who were once our brothers."

"They were never our brothers, Uncle," Attila replied. "We have no 'brothers'—we are a people unto ourselves, a race like no other. We have allies, and this nation, these Alani, have been our allies in the past. They may be again in the future. For now, however, they have betrayed your confidence in them and they must be punished."

"They stole our horses. . . ."

"*Herds* of horses, and sheep as well, thousands of them. And massacred entire villages of the shepherds who tended these animals. And encroached upon lands that for two generations have been Hunnish domain. These Alani must be punished, Uncle, or we will lose face before their people and before the other tribes around us. We will lose face before *our* people, whose protection is a king's duty. We will lose face before Rome."

King Rugila sighed and turned to Flavius. "Warfare is a young man's task. But because young men may be too eager to take it up, it is the old man's duty to choose the battles. Nevertheless, you both have proven yourselves not only skillful in arms but wise in your restraint. You are the youngest commanders in all of Hunnia, perhaps in the entire history of our people. Young Attila has told me his opinion of these Alani, and of a war against them. I would hear your thoughts as well, Flavius Aetius."

Flavius set down the cup of *airag* from which he had been sipping. *Curious,* he reflected, *how over time one develops a tolerance for the repugnant, even a liking for it.* In fact, he had grown to truly enjoy this nourishing concoction of fermented mare's milk, which the princes of the court seemed to guzzle in endless quantities. He looked into the old king's questioning eyes. For some months now, ever since Attila's return from Ravenna, the old man had allowed him and the prince to attend the meetings of his general staff. Indeed, the honor of being included among the king's chief advisors had been one of Flavius' reasons for postponing his own return to his homeland. This matter, however, was more serious. For the first time, Rugila was asking the young men's advice—and seeming to listen carefully, though this was a private audience, rather than one of the entire council of generals and tribal elders. Flavius would weigh his words with all the care the occasion merited.

"I agree with Attila," he answered slowly. "The Alani raids must be stopped immediately, and punished severely. However, I differ with him in his comment on losing face."

Attila stiffened but remained silent, staring intently at his comrade.

"By suffering the Alani raids, we may 'lose face' before the outlying tribes," Flavius continued, "but not before Rome. Rome has no concept of losing face, which implies some notion of pride or morality. Rome distinguishes only between strength and weakness."

"This is true?" the king asked, puzzled. "No concept of saving face?"

Flavius shrugged. "From my father's letters, the Huns are hardly on the emperor's mind at all, as they pose little threat to the Western Empire's borders. Saving face may be important to some peoples, but a direct threat or a demonstration of strength is all that matters to Rome. It is a subtle difference but I think extremely important. Take action as you see fit, Great King, to save face before the Hunnish people. But unless it directly affects Rome's borders, do not expect Rome to care one way or the other."

Rugila grunted and looked at Attila, who after a long look at Flavius nodded his agreement.

Within a week they departed, and an additional fortnight found them on the southern steppe, near the outer boundary of the ancient domains of Persia, now the territory of the southern clans of the Huns. The two younger men galloped by the light of a full moon, trailed by the two thousand mounted archers they had brought from the king's *keshig,* his personal guard in the capital. An additional five thousand horses cantered in their wake as spares and relays, moving at a slower, less exhausting cadence and led by the old king and Turgrid.

As they ran through the gently undulating grasslands, Attila guided his mount to Flavius' side. He flashed a thin smile, and his teeth gleamed white in the moonlight.

"You ride like a Hun," he said.

"That is a great compliment," Flavius replied.

"It is not idle flattery, nor is it grudging. You have learned many skills under Turgrid. You will need them. The Alani are fierce warriors, and their cavalry and bowmen are nearly as accomplished as our own."

"I hope to do the king honor," Flavius replied simply.

"As do I. He is a warrior, that one. Nearly seventy years old, and still insists on accompanying his troops into battle, even if he must lag behind with the spare animals. His old bones can no longer take the pounding of galloping all night."

"Did you see the distant column of smoke to the south, just before the sun set?"

Attila grunted. "Another Alani raid. It was past the horizon, but near enough that the smoke trail was clear. The flames reflected off the clouds above them, like a sunset. I estimate a distance of fifty miles. We can cover that before sunrise. The enemy will be caught in the darkest part of the night, sleeping off their *airag* and sated with the Hunnish women they have stolen."

"Our men and horses will be tired. We've been riding two weeks already. It would be best to find some sheltered spot, rest a bit, and wait for the king's arrival. We can attack the following night."

Attila shot him a scornful look. "Did Turgrid never ask you what good it is to sprint all day if you do not have the strength to wield your sword when you arrive?"

"He did. The solution is to pull up short of battle, and wait for strength to return before commencing the attack."

"No. You must continue to ride until you arrive, and be strong enough to destroy the enemy immediately, when they *think* you'll have to pull up short. The solution is to have strength to spare before you even start out. Otherwise—don't start out." With that, Attila emitted a high, piercing whistle and sprinted ahead, and two thousand Hunnish horsemen thundered after him in the moon-lit darkness.

The two young men lay on their bellies in the grass at the top of a small rise, peering down at the rolling plains below them, which glowed silver in the moonlight like the vast fields of ice they had heard talk of to the north. The tiny dots of the Alani cooking fires twinkled dimly some two miles to the south. Behind them, the Hunnish riders sat motionless on their mounts, some slumped in a rest-less doze, others chatting quietly to one another as the horses caught their wind and cropped the grass.

"There they are," murmured Attila. "But we've caught no trail of them, encountered no rear guard. These men are not retreating after a raid—they're advancing, into our territory."

"And they're not a band of horse thieves," Flavius con-curred. "They're an army. Look at the number of fires. This is not what King Rugila expected."

Attila squinted up at the sky. "Two hours before dawn. The quietest part of the night. The best time to attack."

"They outnumber us two to one, at least. And the king hasn't arrived yet. He and the spare horses are probably still another three hours behind. We should send a rider back to warn him. . . ."

Attila snorted. "By the time the king arrives, it will be daylight, and too late to hide. We will have lost the element of surprise, and we do not have the force to take on this army in pitched battle. We must attack now."

"Without the king? He'll flay you alive."

Attila turned his head and coolly appraised his comrade. "You were trained as a Hun, but you think like a Roman."

Flavius bristled. "You say that as if it were an insult."

"Romans never move at night. They attack in rank and file in full view of the enemy, or they hunker behind their log walls. They have strength, but no cunning. Courage, but no imagination. . . ."

"And they do not engage battle without the orders of their commanders," Flavius rejoined angrily. "The enemy knows this country well. King Rugila knows this country. But do we? You call it lack of imagination. I call it prudence. We must wait for Rugila's counsel."

"If we do not attack now, there will be no battle," Attila insisted. "We cannot fight this force in daylight, and they will discover our presence before we have another opportunity to surprise them in darkness tomorrow. There is no other way."

"We, too, are an army, not merely raiders," Flavius replied. "We must have the discipline of an army."

Attila ignored him and stood up. "I will take a quarter of the force, swing out in a wide arc, and hit them hard from the rear. They won't have any guards posted on that side. Watch for my signal. When you see a flaming arrow, wait a few moments until they wake up and shift all their forces to the rear of their camp. Then you hit them from the front with the rest of our troops."

Flavius leaped to his feet. "Are you mad? A full attack without even the king's knowledge?"

Attila shrugged and smiled, hoisting himself lightly onto his horse. "Think like a Hun, Flavius! By this evening, Rugila will be toasting us both with *airag* drunk out of an Alani skull."

Wheeling, he trotted softly on a line through the midst of the bowmen, ordering those on his left to ride out with him and those on the right to stay behind. Furious, Flavius mounted his own horse and sat silently watching. Within moments, Attila and his riders had thundered away, and on the vast, rolling plain the sound of their hooves was absorbed into the soft ground and the still air and disappeared like the traces of vapor rising from the horses' nostrils.

Flavius glanced south, toward the lights of the enemy camp. The die had been cast—there was nothing for it but to make sure Attila's plan was successful. He would have to pay close attention to the signal to arrive in fighting order within a few moments of the attack from the rear. But how to approach the camp closely without being detected? Even at night, fifteen hundred massed riders would cast a dark shadow against the light background of the grassy plain, a shadow that would be seen easily by the Alani outposts. So there could be no massed body of riders.

"Dismount," he hissed softly to the men nearby, who passed the word to the other troops and then dropped quickly to their feet, landing like cats in their soft leather riding shoes. The riders out of his earshot quickly followed suit. They then gathered silently around him in the lee of the small hillock separating them from the enemy camp.

"Now walk your horses," he ordered in a harsh whisper. "You'll keep a lower profile against the sky. And spread out—ten paces apart, ranks of fifty. Those in the front, watch my hand signal. Those farther back, and on the flanks, watch the horses around you. All silent! Move slowly."

The men nodded. This was not the customary Hunnish mode of attack, but all could see the intent. Immediately Flavius set out, striding slowly and purposefully beside his horse, his hand gently caressing the beast's neck to calm it and prevent it from whinnying in the tension. On both sides and behind him, fifteen hundred men did the same, gliding carefully through the thigh-high grass. The only sound was the occasional snort from a horse impatient at the slow pace. Flavius prayed that the noise would be absorbed by the light breeze or confused with the snuffling of the Alani animals in their camp.

After a quarter of an hour of silent progress on foot, with an occasional pause to listen for sounds of activity in the enemy camp, Flavius raised his fist above his head for a halt. They were at the base of another small rise, one of the innumerable little hills that rolled like waves on a beach across the endless plain, obscuring his view of the campfires below. Handing off his horse to the man on his left, Flavius dropped to his belly and crawled the final few yards to the summit, from which he could again gauge his distance.

There before him lay the extent of the Alani encampment, scarcely a mile away. They could approach no closer without being seen, for within a quarter mile of his own position he could view a small dark spot in the grass—a guard outpost, no doubt. As his eyes scanned the camp he sucked in his breath. They were right—this was no party of horse thieves. But it was no minor military raid bent on plunder, either. He made a quick estimate of the number of fires and tents. No, it couldn't be. He counted again. Even by his most conservative reckoning it was true. There were at least ten thousand men camped on the plain before him, fresh soldiers, unencumbered by distance, plunder, or captives. His heart sank as he realized what they had stumbled upon. It was a full invading army, outnumbering his and Attila's men five to one.

Flavius thought hard. With such a numerous enemy, when Attila attacked, his force would simply be swallowed up in the maw of the great camp and lost before Flavius would have time to race in with his own troops to relieve the pressure. And once Flavius did charge in with his relief force—what then? Even if Attila was extremely lucky, even if he succeeded in distracting half the camp, which seemed unlikely, an additional five thousand of the enemy would remain to face him down. The odds seemed impossible even under the best of circumstances, but if Flavius arrived as planned, after Attila's attack had commenced, the best of circumstances would be lost. The camp would be aroused, the men armed, and battle already joined.

His mind raced. What were his options? Cut his losses now, retreat back to the safety of the grasslands and the orders of the king, and leave Attila alone to his suicidal foray? The prince and his five hundred bowmen would be lost, certainly, but Flavius and the king could then retreat back to the capital to raise an army large enough to exact vengeance and drive the Alani out permanently. What would Attila do in his place? What would the king do? Flavius shook his head. He could not think along those lines, put himself into another man's mind. He did not have options. He had only a course of action. There must be no delay between the two attacks, for that would allow the more numerous Alani to defeat one strike after the other, like a bison fending off individual wolves with its horns. With simultaneous coordinated attacks, however, a pair of predators could bring down a much larger animal—if they were lucky.

He slid back down the hill to the small knot of riders who stood quietly waiting for him in the center of the front rank. "Pass the word," he said softly. "Spread out farther in formation. I want a half-mile front, one that completely envelops the Alani camp from side to side. Stay on foot until the signal. Then mount and charge. But keep your arrows in quivers, blades in sheathes. Ignore their horses; ignore their men—those will come later."

Flavius paused, and the men looked at him, silent and wide-eyed. No arrows? No blades? This was not the Hunnish way of warfare.

"Go for the fires. Every man seize a brand or torch. Set fire to every tent, every awning, every stack of shields. Everything. There will be no plunder. I want chaos, an inferno. When you are surrounded by flames and confusion, then you will know you have done well."

After a pause, one of the horsemen spoke up. "And what then, *Cur* Flavius? What then, when all is burning?"

The query was obvious, but the soldier's questioning of an officer, a breaking of the custom of silent obedience, was a thing so rare that every man turned to stare at him for a moment and then back at Flavius with hard, glittering eyes. Flavius realized that this was a dangerous moment—perhaps the most dangerous he might face that entire day, if he did not respond with the reasoning and confidence his men demanded. He stared back, masking his own expression in dark shadows as he pulled his battle helmet over his head.

"Then—when all is burning—draw your bows and finish your work."

Word of the unorthodox tactic spread quickly down the lines, and just as quickly the men clambered up the hill on foot, spaced themselves across a wide arc, and began walking steadily forward. Within moments, the dark shape Flavius had seen in front of them earlier materialized into two, and he realized they were a pair of guards, dozing against their spears butted into the ground. A quick motion with his hand brought the bows of a dozen warriors on either side of him into firing position, and at the signal of a quick hiss they loosed their arrows. One of the guards emitted a sharp yelp, and then both dropped to the ground like sacks of grain, dead before they hit. At the sound, a chorus of baying erupted from a pack of dogs in the camp, followed by the angry shouts of wakened soldiers calling for the animals to be silent.

Still, the Huns stalked silently forward. Here and there along the front line, other volleys of silent arrows were loosed, other grunts of dying men were heard, as the archers picked off Alani guards, stray mongrels, and enemy soldiers unfortunate enough to have picked that moment to stumble to the latrines in the darkness. The tension now was palpable, the baying of the hounds was growing louder, and even the horses, on both sides, began whinnying nervously at the silent approach. Yet the alarm had still not been given, and the camp remained restlessly sleeping.

On Flavius' left, to the east, a faint glow was beginning to appear, and the stars in that half of the sky had begun to fade. There was no more time. The sun would be over the horizon in an hour, and by that time the invading army would be awake and preparing for the march. The enemy's buglers would sound at any moment. If there was to be a surprise, it would have to be now.

Flavius was close enough that if he squinted, he could make out individual embers in the half-dead fires. The outlines of skulking dogs could be clearly seen, and here and there a drowsy soldier crawled out of the tent he shared with his comrades, and knelt to blow on the flames and warm his hands. None of the Alani troops had yet thought to look toward the darkness of the plain. Those few who were awake focused only on the coldness of their fingers and on the glowing heat of the fires. . . .

Flavius raised his fist in the air and silently leaped onto the back of his trembling horse. Around him he could hear the quiet rustling of his men doing the same. For the first time he realized the advantage of the Huns' thick leather armor, which caused no clanking or rubbing of metal as the men moved. He paused for a moment, waiting, all his senses on the alert, allowing just a few more seconds for the men at the farthest ends of his line to receive the signal and mount their horses. Just a few seconds more. . . .

And then, high above his head, from the corner of his eye, he saw what he at first took to be a shooting star.

Attila's fire arrow.

There was no need for further orders. Fifteen hundred men surged forward and stormed into the slumbering enemy camp from one end to the other. The horses raced straight through tents and field kitchens, uprooting stakes and trampling sleeping enemy soldiers in their gallop. As the Huns guided their mounts to the fires, each man leaned far down off the side of his animal's back, gripping the shaggy mane with one hand and maintaining only a precarious grip by the heel of one foot. Half-burnt sticks of firewood were seized, glowing embers scooped up in the hollows of battle helmets, and without pausing even to gain their bearings, the riders raced to the nearest tents and sleeping blankets and set them afire.

Screams rose into the air as the coals licked into the dry, half-rotted canvas of the tents and the woolen bedrolls. Half-naked men rolled and stumbled from leaping flames, unable to retrieve the armor and weapons they had stashed inside, and ran panicked through the camp, seeking shelter and escape. The glow of the approaching dawn was smothered by a pall of thick smoke as tents and stacks of provisions burst into flame. Bellowing riders, their faces smudged black, stormed through the roiling clouds on their panicked horses, seizing more firebrands and hurling them in all directions. The terrible flames rose and spread, and soon all was a curtain of fire on the entire north side of the camp. Terrified Alani warriors, some on foot, a few clinging desperately to the manes of runaway horses they had seized, flew blindly from the heat of the flames.

Racing into the center of the camp, the Alani were met by a cloud of arrows, humming like a swarm of evil hornets, as Attila's party surged through from the opposite side. In their panic to escape the lethal missiles, the Alani turned and began staggering back into the wall of smoke and flame, seeking in the choking cloud invisibility and shelter from the onslaught they had stumbled upon. It was as if their very gods had unleashed a flaming hell upon them.

Flavius emerged red-eyed and spitting from the thick haze of smoke his troops had created, cavalry sword brandished in his right hand as he surveyed the destruction of the camp. Through his streaming eyes, he saw Attila's force sitting their horses in close alignment in front of him, raining volley after volley into the masses of bedraggled enemy soldiers who staggered out of the flames and smoke. Flavius' own forces raced from the turmoil on their mounts, hacking at the terrified Alani troops with the swords that now took the place of the firebrands. Flavius grunted in satisfaction. The plan had worked perfectly. The Alani force was destroyed.

Suddenly, from the periphery of his vision, a flash of metal caught his eye. Whirling, he was caught up in a mob of mounted warriors thundering past him. Emerging from the far end of camp, the only sector not yet reached by either his or Attila's archers, the Alani general and a cadre of his personal guard and senior officers had been able to seize weapons and mount nearby horses. Clad in half-fastened remnants of scale armor, some two hundred men rushed past within an arm's length of Flavius' own horse. Ignoring their own burnt and dying troops, they raced laterally through the cloud of Attila's arrow fire, emerging on the other side with scattered losses. At a shouted command, the group consolidated, gathering together all others of their surviving troops who could capture and mount horses in the chaos. With a further shout, they stormed off through the smoldering remains of the camp and into the grasslands, toward the rising sun.

Furious that he had allowed the enemy commander to rush past him so closely and escape, Flavius slapped his horse hard on the haunches and drove back into the smoke and flames, circling around behind Attila's forces to avoid being killed by his bowmen. As he came upon them from the back, he watched them fire arrow after arrow into the terrified Alani stumbling out of the smoke with their hands raised in surrender. Their bodies created a wall of dead and dying where they fell. Flavius galloped up to Attila's side and reined in.

"The fire attack—brilliant!" Attila shouted over the cheers and shouts surrounding him. "The enemy were more numerous than we thought."

"You can take captives now—the survivors are surrendering!"

"Captives? We will take no captives. These men are as good as dead."

Flavius stared at the helpless enemy writhing and dying in the withering hail of arrow fire. "The Alani are unarmed! Call off your men—take these soldiers as slaves!"

"You have done your part," Attila shouted back. "Now I will do mine. Did you kill their general?"

"No!" Flavius replied. "Their general escaped, with a troop of armed guards!"

"They can't run far, without food or supplies. You saw where they went?"

"To the southeast—back toward his own land. . . ."

"Take him!" Attila roared. "We'll present his head as a gift to the king!"

Flavius peered into the gray smoke. Staggering figures that a moment before had been only vague shadows were beginning to take on definition and clarity in the hazy morning light.

"My men are scattered," he shouted back. "It'll take me too long to collect them. Your troops are all here together in formation. Give them to me and I'll track him down!"

Attila was silent for a moment, loosing arrow after arrow in deep concentration.

"Attila!" Flavius exploded. "Stop your accursed target practice and give me your men, or we'll lose the enemy commander!"

"Take them!" Attila bellowed. "I'll collect the rest of the Huns after the camp is destroyed, and ride back to meet my uncle!"

Charging his horse out in front of the Hunnish bowmen, Flavius raised his fist to stop their shooting. "Follow me!"

As of one accord, Attila's five hundred horsemen wheeled their mounts and thundered off behind their new leader. As they departed, the camp fell silent but for the crackling of flames and the moans of the dead and dying. Attila sat his horse in the midst of the destruction and glared about him with satisfaction. The work was almost done. There were few left who would bring back the tale of the Alani defeat to their homeland. It was not often, Attila allowed himself to think, that one gained so handily the gift of an entire enemy army.

One by one, then in groups of six or eight, and then entire companies, the Huns who had attacked along the north side of the camp emerged from the smoke and flames, covered in greasy black soot and spattered with the red spray of battle. Seeing Attila sitting on his horse in the middle of the camp, they trotted up on their exhausted mounts and stood silently awaiting his orders.

None carried plunder or war chests; none carried enemy shields or other trophies of war. This had not been a contest for glory. It had been an exercise in utter destruction.

After most of the troops had gathered in the center of the camp, two more figures came limping out of the thinning smoke to present themselves before Attila. The first was a grimy, blood-spattered Hun whose horse had been hamstrung by an Alani ax and who had fought his way through the melee on foot. He nodded to his mounted comrades as he approached.

The second was an enemy soldier the Hun was prodding forward at the point of a sword. At first, in the dim light of dawn, the others took no notice of him, but as he approached they began staring, for even under the crust of battle he was seen to be different. Unlike the swarthy Alani, this one had pale skin and reddish hair.

"Did Flavius Aetius not tell you to take no plunder?" Attila growled at the Hunnish soldier as the pair joined the crowd of waiting horsemen.

"This is no plunder but a captive," the Hun grunted. "He claims to be Roman. He was escaping the camp with the Alani commander and I pulled him off his horse. He may know of the commander's destination, but I will kill him if you wish."

Attila peered at him for a moment and then shrugged. "There are Romans under every rock on earth," he spat, "even among Alani in the middle of the steppe. We will take him to Rugila. The king will decide his fate."

The troops made one last foray through the smoking camp, poking through smoldering rubble with lances and sticks, putting wounded horses out of their misery, seizing food that remained unburnt by the flames. And then, at Attila's whistle, they gathered at the edge of camp and raced in the direction from which they had just arrived. Nearly ten thousand men had been killed in the space of an hour, and the remainder were being tracked like runaway slaves. Enough food and supplies had been seized to allow the Huns a leisurely trip home without the effort of hunting. And the Alani had been taught a permanent lesson about the borders and possessions of their rivals.

As the sun rose red and malignant in the smoky haze, it witnessed only a silent and smoldering stain on the vast grasslands, without a single living creature to be seen.

Rugila was livid.

"You, Attila, and your absent comrade Flavius Aetius," he intoned hoarsely, his face flustered. "I gave you rein to track down bandits and then await my approach. And yet you ignored me as if I were a dotty old fool. You outran your commander and your supplies and you joined battle, without my orders."

"And against overwhelming numbers," Turgrid added sternly.

"You two are the captains I favor most, yet you defied me," Rugila continued. "The penalty for treason is death or banishment."

Attila stood calmly before him, absentmindedly patting his exhausted horse. He remained silent for a moment, thinking, and then suddenly ripped off his battle helmet and tossed it at the king's feet. Reaching behind him, he seized the handful of arrows still left in his quiver and threw them in a jumble on the ground and then tossed aside the wicker shield still strapped to his forearm.

"Kill me if you like. My neck is yours."

The king's eyes opened wide.

"Do you have no fear?" he asked. "Of the Alani blades, or of my wrath?"

Attila raised an eyebrow. "Fear? Do you think me a coward?"

The king shook his head. "That I do not. Yet there are different kinds of courage, and I seek to know you by your kind. Some have no fear because they are ignorant of the danger. Those men are not brave—merely stupid. Some are, perhaps, brave, but only to a point. Beyond that point, fear grips them, overwhelms their courage, and they run. And you . . ."

"Whether or not I feel fear is of no concern. If I do feel it, I complete my work despite it, which in truth is the same as not feeling it. Call me stupid or call me courageous. What matters is, we were victorious."

"Is that truly all that matters?"

"We defeated ten thousand heavily armed Alani cavalry, with only our two thousand light bowmen. And Flavius is even now tracking down their general."

"Does winning excuse insubordination?" Turgrid queried, peeved at the younger man's flippant tone. "Does it offset the shame you have brought on your uncle by overstepping his authority?"

"Victory softens the sting. No one need know the king did not order our attack."

"That may be," Rugila conceded. "But rich plunder would salve the sting even more effectively. Show me the Alani war chest."

For the first time, Attila dropped his defiant gaze.

"We took no plunder. We were too badly outnumbered. There was no chance to seek it, and everything in the camp was destroyed by fire. Perhaps the Alani general took the war chest with him and Flavius will capture it."

"And prisoners?"

"None also, except—"

"No prisoners?" The king looked up at Attila, surprised. "No slaves? You killed every man in the camp?"

"Many burned in the fires . . . others were killed by arrows. There was but one who survived, a foreigner, who claims Roman citizenship. He was fleeing at the side of the Alani commander, but he has told us nothing of the Alani's whereabouts."

"A foreigner? Bring him to me."

"He is very ugly."

The king scoffed. "And I am to be frightened by this? Bring me this captive. I have seen Romans before."

Attila turned and stalked over to the nearest guard, to whom he gave a message. In a moment, two stout Hunnish soldiers returned, carrying the captive between them, his feet dragging on the ground. His nose and cheekbones had been smashed; his eyes were swollen nearly shut. When he was dropped in front of Rugila he looked up, rose to his knees, and smiled painfully through broken teeth.

"What happened to this man?" the king asked.

"Fell off his horse," Attila replied. "Onto my soldiers' fists."

"He gives no information," one of the soldiers volunteered.

"Fools!" exclaimed the king. "Nephew, at the very least, this man is good for a household slave. He is not to be broken like a common criminal."

"Yes, *Berik Cur,*" Attila responded stiffly.

"Now— Nephew, you speak Latin. Ask him why he works for the Alani. Where is he based? Are there more Romans in the Alani camp? Are they training the enemy? Ask him!"

Attila began a rapid-fire series of questions to which the captive merely laughed or responded with a repeated phrase, over and over. After a moment, Attila gave up in exasperation and then turned to Rugila with an expression of worry.

"He will give no information. He is stubborn, perhaps mad, but I believe he's alone among the Alani, for he mentions no countrymen of his. His Latin is halting, as if he hasn't spoken it in years."

"And what does he keep repeating?"

"He keeps saying, 'Cannae, Cannae—the Huns will meet their Cannae.'"

"Bah—what is this . . . this 'Cannae'? Is he indeed mad?"

Attila hearkened back to his schooling in Ravenna, when he had spent months listening with half a mind as his *magister historiae* dissected the Punic Wars.

"Cannae—it was a great battle fought centuries ago. When Hannibal the Carthaginian invaded Italy, he feigned retreat and led the pursuing Roman legions into a confined area, where they were ambushed. Fifty thousand Roman soldiers died that day."

The old man paused, deep in thought. "The Alani are in alliance with many of the scattered tribes in this area," he said slowly. "When I fought in these parts decades ago, it was not enough simply to subdue the Alani; a dozen allied clans had to be brought into submission as well. They had strongholds in the canyons, and it cost us many lives. How many men did you say were in the enemy camp you destroyed?"

"Ten thousand," Attila said cautiously, his eyes widening with understanding.

"A large party, to be sure—but not large enough for an invasion of the Hunnish lands. Could they have been gathering forces? Waiting for the outlying tribes in the canyons to collect and join them?"

"If what you say is true," Turgrid said, "the Alani commander who escaped may be fleeing to seek refuge at just such a stronghold in the canyons—"

"So this Cannae," the old king interrupted, speaking in a subdued tone, "when the Roman says the Huns will meet their Cannae, he is referring to—to what?"

Attila strode over to the prisoner, whose mocking laugh had now subsided to a nervous chuckle as his gaze shot back and forth between his captors. Without a word, Attila drew a serrated-edged dagger from his belt and seized the wretched man by the hair, jerking his head back and exposing his throat. The blade tore raggedly through the Roman's skin like the slashing jaws of a wolf, and blood spurted in a crimson stream into the grass at the king's feet. As Attila released his grip, the man's head flopped forward and he rolled softly to the side, dead eyes still open in surprise.

"He is referring to the tribesmen of which you spoke," said Attila as he squatted to wipe his blade on the dead man's tunic.

"And to Flavius Aetius."

"You have made the king doubly angry," Turgrid pronounced as he and Attila galloped hard to the southeast, leaving Rugila and the still-smoldering ruins of the Alani camp behind them. The path they followed could not have been clearer—two hundred fleeing Alani guardsmen and five hundred pursuing Huns do not leave faint traces in the grasslands. "First by attacking the enemy, then by riding off without his orders to seek Flavius."

"He refused to give me any men."

"Insolent pup! What would you have him do? Assign you more troops to lose in this ambush you suspect? Leave the king to stumble back to the capital alone, herding the spare horses? You stole two *zuun*—two hundred troops—in the middle of the night, convincing them you were following Rugila's orders. Is this how you gain favor with the king?"

Attila was silent for a moment. "And what would you have me do? Abandon Flavius to a trap that we know about, but that he does not, through no fault of his own? It was through Flavius' quick thinking that we won the victory over the Alani camp in the first place. Is this how the king rewards him?"

Turgrid shook his head vigorously. "This is a lost cause in any event. They have a half day's lead on us. Either Flavius has captured the Alani general and is now returning victorious or he has himself been trapped and is now dead."

"A half day's start? That is nothing. Both the Alani and Flavius are riding exhausted horses; we have fresh ones. They are dodging and feinting; we are running the trail straight. And if this is a lost cause, why are you riding with us? Does that not make you complicit in my 'betrayal'?"

Turgrid glared. "I have trained Flavius for many years, and I trained you before then. If you gain victory in this, I will claim my share of the glory. If the king removes your heads for insubordination, he will undoubtedly remove mine as well, for incompetence, so I may as well not sit silently by waiting for it to happen. Besides . . ."

Attila waited. "Besides what?"

"I owe my own debt to Flavius."

Attila smiled grimly. "Welcome to the 'Band of Two Hundred.'"

Dawn found them in broken country, a land fractured by labyrinths of broken canyons, timeworn escarpments, and steep, crumbling hillsides. The riders' pace had slowed from a gallop to a slow, steady walk and finally to a stop to reconnoiter the terrain. The Hunnish riders dozed upright sitting on their horses. Two days and nights of riding and fighting were beginning to tell on the men, and only Attila seemed unaffected by fatigue. He pushed his mount hard, pausing here and there to examine the depth of tracks in the gravel and the consistency of droppings, then staring off into the shadows cast by the low-hanging cliffs.

"They headed toward that ridge in the distance," he said. "Couldn't have been more than an hour ago, and from the looks of that slope they cannot have climbed it yet."

Turgrid looked and nodded his head. "Flavius plans to corner them there. I'd have done the same. We'll help him finish."

They had traveled scarcely a quarter mile toward their target, however, when Attila again paused, this time looking at the gravel slopes on either side of the dry riverbed through which they were riding.

"Do you see that?" he pointed to Turgrid. "The gravel's been freshly turned. On both sides. Too steep for horses. Some men have come down those slopes. Many men."

Turgrid's eyes narrowed. "Allies of the Alani," he muttered. "Tribesmen."

Attila nodded. "It is as the king said."

Without further word, they urged their horses forward over the boulder-strewn ground as the men behind them, now fully awake, carefully picked their own paths between the cliffs.

After an hour, distant shouts could be heard ahead, and as they rounded a corner the situation became clear. The dry riverbed they had been following ended in a box canyon some forty yards high, over the top of which the river, during the rainy season, flowed in a high waterfall. Now, however, it was simply a dry bowl, an amphitheater of sorts, bounded by cliffs on all sides and occupied only by grayish, sun-faded boulders—and hundreds of furious men.

Everywhere were dead Hunnish horses. None had survived the attack when the Alani troops fled into the dry basin and then wheeled around and trained their arrows on their pursuers, with the mountain clansmen providing supporting fire from the rear. Flavius and his men had leaped off their mounts to take shelter behind rocks and outcroppings, but their panicked animals, unable to hide, had been the first targets of the enemy missiles. In truth, Attila thought, it was for the best, for if the Hunnish ponies were in the same condition as the lame and exhausted Alani mounts he spied trembling against the cliff face, they were best put out of their misery.

The Alani and their canyon-dwelling allies were not aware of the arrival of Attila's band behind them. Pausing for a moment, he assessed the situation. The fighting had initially been furious, for dead and wounded lay everywhere, their bodies forming low barricades across the two sides' firing positions on each side of the dry basin. Nevertheless, as the exhaustion and injuries of both sides began to bear full weight, the men's actions had slowed and become more lethargic. Only the canyon dwellers were still energetic and unhampered by injury. Hundreds of them clambered about the walls of the canyon, naked or wearing only rough skins for protection. As they scurried for cover from boulder to boulder, leaping onto outcroppings to fire arrows and sling stones, it was clear that even with their primitive weapons and poor aim, their freshness and numbers would be the deciding force in the battle. Flavius had indeed met his Cannae.

Attila drew back out of sight. The riverbed was too narrow for his entire force to rush through quickly, too rocky for them to remain safely mounted. Storming into the basin as a single unit would only throw them into the same predicament as Flavius. He looked up. Narrow goat paths crossed the steep slopes above him that ended at the lip of the cliff above the dry waterfall. There was only one way. Indeed, the stone dwellers had had the same idea—the rocks above the basin were already dotted with them.

He pointed to his men. "Turgrid, lead half the men, up to the heights!" he hissed. "And destroy those goat men!"

Though exhausted themselves, the Huns lost no time. Leaping off their horses, they began scrambling up the rocky walls of the slopes, grasping at roots and tufts of grass. As they climbed, every solid perch was used for a pause to draw an arrow and fire at the cave dwellers. Bodies began tumbling to the dry riverbed, bouncing and rolling on the cliff face as they fell.

Within moments, Turgrid and the Hunnish troops had reached the cliff edge at the top and from this vantage point begun firing down onto the helpless Alani and their allies below. "Like shooting fish in a pool!" Turgrid exulted. Roars of pain and anger rose from the basin. Taking the remainder of the Hunnish forces, Attila rushed through the narrow gap in the riverbed. Drawing their swords, they hacked and slashed as they moved forward, fighting their way through the panicked stone dwellers, who rushed to flee back through the same narrow gap. Lacking fighting blades themselves, the barbarians were helpless against the determined thrusts of the Huns, and soon their numbers thinned and dwindled, and their shouts finally died altogether.

The clamor raging through the basin subsided to a few individual moans of the wounded, and Attila cautiously stepped into the open, eyes flitting in every direction to sense threat. It was a scene of terrible carnage.

All about them, behind every boulder, sprawled dead men and horses, pierced from above by arrows or crushed by hurled stones. On the cliff top, a hundred Hunnish warriors stood immobile, outlined against the gray sky of early morning, bows still drawn as they peered into the shadows for any sign of movement among the enemy. All was silent but for the soft trickle of water from the rocks, the only remnant of what would be a raging torrent in the spring.

Attila looked about in amazement. Not a living creature was to be seen in the basin. It would have taken a brave man to endure such a battle in this place, he reflected.

"Flavius?" he called. His voice echoed like a bell in an amphitheater. "Flavius!" he shouted again.

On the left, out of the corner of his eye, he saw movement. No, not mere movement, but a man. Stepping from behind a boulder, a Hunnish trooper lurched forward, a tribesman's arrow emerging from his shoulder, his armor in tatters, face covered with grime. Forcing a grim smile, he staggered to the center of the basin where Attila and his force stood, and sat, exhausted, in the gravel. Slowly, the rocks came alive. Other Huns emerged from the boulders behind which they had taken shelter from the clifftop snipers. Though it had been only a day since Attila had last seen these men, they looked like ghosts—worn beyond words, many injured, with arrow wounds or with limbs swollen and contorted grotesquely from falls among the sharp rocks. They stumbled into the open space in the middle of the basin and sat with their comrades. Among the last was a gaunt figure who staggered from behind a rock up against the cliff face, carrying an injured Hunnish comrade draped over his shoulders like a deer. He picked his way precariously over the rocky path to the rest of the Huns and laid his burden carefully on the ground before walking slowly to Attila and placing his hand on his shoulder.

"It is good that you came," Flavius said simply.

The long ride back to the Hunnish camp was difficult, and the troops, most of them doubled on the Hunnish ponies, traveled slowly to conserve the animals' waning strength. The men leaned against one another for rest, and they kept to their own thoughts, dozing fitfully. Finally Flavius, barely able to stay mounted on his own horse due to his deep fatigue, broke the silence to Attila, who rode beside him, watching him carefully.

"When I killed a wolf that attacked Turgrid, he told me his life was forever in my hands."

"That is true, by custom," Attila replied. "A Hun does not forget a debt. Turgrid owes you his life, and he will not rest until he has repaid that obligation to you somehow. You may be stuck with him for years."

"Then by the same token, since you saved my life, I owe just such an obligation to you."

"Nonsense." Attila shook his head. "You supported my attack at the Alani camp; I did the same for you at the dry river. We are even. Besides, Turgrid is a Hun. This custom is very ancient among the Huns, one that must be followed at all costs. Because of its very seriousness, we would never think to impose it upon others. It applies to Hunnish debts alone."

Flavius bristled. "And a Roman's debts are worthless? Roman honor has no value?"

Attila shrugged. "Even the Romans appear to think so. An entire profession in Rome has been created to force people to honor their debts. They're called lawyers."

"I have been given the rewards of a Hun, and in return I must accept my obligations as a Hun. I owe you my life."

Attila smiled. "Have it your way. But don't worry; I won't hold you to it. I've seen Roman promises and Roman honor."

Flavius considered this for a long moment. "No," he said finally. "You haven't."

VI

Several months after their return, King Rugila sat dozing quietly in his carved wooden chair as a handful of wives and aides moved quietly about. It was the end to a long day for the old man, and Flavius was reluctant to disturb him—but he had been summoned a few moments before. He approached softly, watching for a sign that the king might be examining him through hooded lids, and seeing none, he stealthily observed the sleeping king. How much the old man had aged since he had first met him; how much he had aged just since their return from battle against the Alani. That expedition had exhausted the king so much he had still not recovered—physically or mentally. His head slumped forward, his bald skull shining in the dim light like yellowed alabaster. Flavius bent slowly on one knee and cleared his throat. Rugila started and looked up, slightly bewildered. Then, as he recognized Flavius, his face cracked in a wide grin, exposing his black gums.

"Flavius Aetius, my son, my own *oylan*," he croaked hoarsely. "You are well?"

"Very well, Great King. My father writes me of important news, which I'm sure you have already heard through your own couriers, or you would not have summoned me during your . . . private hours."

"Flavius—I fear what is good for you may not be so for me. I am a very old man now—"

"Not true," Flavius interrupted. "You still ride with the wolves, as I have seen you do many times."

"I cannot even climb onto my horse without assistance."

"You have fifty wives, none of whom appear deprived, even the youngest among them."

"They are trained to look patient with their lot." The king's expression drooped mournfully.

Flavius sighed. "You feast often, and you eat like a wrestler. Last night I saw the servants bringing you a second bowl—"

"—of *airag* and boiled crane eggs. My son, I have only three teeth left in my head."

Flavius was at a loss for further words. Suddenly, however, the king brightened of his own accord.

"But two of them meet!" he cackled happily.

"Great *Cur*," Flavius interrupted, "hear me out."

The king adopted a sober expression and fell suddenly silent. "Speak."

"The Emperor Honorius has been overthrown."

Rugila peered at him closely. "So I have heard. But why is turmoil in Rome good news to you?"

"Because Honorius was a thief and an idiot. He nearly destroyed the empire with his carelessness and neglect.

Even now, hostile tribes are poised to attack the borders from every side. My father has written me often of the situation. He has always had to be very subtle in his letters, but his meanings are always clear to me. Honorius' villainy mocked all that Rome stood for."

"Nevertheless," the king said quietly, "Honorius sent you to live among us, did he not?"

Flavius bowed his head. "That is the one thing for which I am grateful to him."

The king regarded him thoughtfully. "The high fall low, as the low rise above them, and the Fates respect no man. So men's fortunes change, just as do the seasons. I was once told that a countryman of yours—a writer of plays—was killed in a most bizarre fashion, at the very peak of his greatness. It seems that a passing eagle, bearing a turtle in its claws, sought to break it on a hard surface, and dropped the creature directly onto the man's bald head. The result was fatal for the man. For the turtle, too, I presume."

Flavius stifled a smile. "Yes, Great *Cur*. The man's name was Aeschylus, though he was Greek, not Roman."

Rugila nodded with satisfaction. "And what is it you wish to ask of me, young Flavius?"

Flavius took a deep breath. "As you know, King, I often interrogate merchants and diplomats who arrive from the western regions. I read my father's letters closely, and read between their lines. I have long made it my business to keep as closely informed on Roman affairs as possible. It is partly out of my own interest in my homeland, partly because I know it is of assistance to you."

"Indeed, my son, you have many times given me extremely valuable interpretations of the actions of the Roman leaders. For this I am grateful."

Flavius nodded and continued. "The news from my father has been confirmed by a party of Greek traders that arrived from Constantinopolis several days ago, and by diplomatic courier from the eastern Roman court. Honorius was overthrown by a certain Ioannes, known as the Usurper—a commander of legions and an old comrade of my father's. I remember him from years ago when he visited our household in Ravenna. He is an honorable man, uninterested in wealth and glory seeking, and he desires only the empire's best interests. He is also well disposed toward the Huns."

Rugila nodded. "Yes, I, too, know this man. So it is he who has taken control of Rome?"

"Not quite, Great King. He has overthrown the emperor, but he has not consolidated his power, and he is threatened on all sides, both externally and from within. Honorius had heirs, and the eastern Roman emperor, Theodosius, has allied with them and is even now mobilizing a large army to attack from Constantinopolis. Several powerful Roman generals have their own ambitions as well. . . ."

"I shall never understand these republics," Rugila grumbled. "I need a hundred diplomats merely to tell me who is in power in Rome."

"It has been many centuries since Rome was a republic, my lord," Flavius said.

"That may be so, but if Rome is not a republic, then it is something else, and it is therefore lacking a crucial element."

"And what is that, Great *Cur*?"

Rugila paused for a moment before glaring up at Flavius fiercely through his rheumy eyes. "Rome needs a good king!"

Flavius smiled. "Perhaps so. Perhaps you are right. Nevertheless, the situation now is fragile, and with the challenge for leadership, the empire is falling into chaos—"

"So," the king interrupted, "you wish to assist this . . . this Ioannes the Usurper."

"I do. I have delayed many years returning to my homeland. Because of my responsibilities here, and my loyalty to you—but also because I saw no future for myself in Ravenna. I saw that, under Honorius, there would be no place for a man of honorable ambition. Now, Honorius has been deposed. The future of Rome is in balance. It could swing either way. This is the opportunity for which I have hoped for a long time. It is an opportunity for a man to truly make a mark, to gain the trust of a new emperor, to restore an honor to his homeland that has been lost. It is time for me to return and carve out my own future."

"And do you have a plan for this great carving of yours? Young men everywhere hope to change the world. What makes you different from the others?"

"The fact that you have made me a Hun. Never before has a Roman of noble family been able to step outside the empire, view his own homeland so objectively. My views of Rome have not been filtered through a decadent court; my gifts and skills are not beholden to corrupt officials. My motives are pure. You have made me a Hun, but more important, you have made me a Roman the likes of which Rome has never seen."

Rugila regarded him thoughtfully. "An interesting perspective. But one does not conquer a vast civilization with the power of being novel. You are not an entertainer. You are a soldier. What is it you require of me, young Flavius?"

The young man took a deep breath and then looked straight into the old king's eye.

"A body of Hunnish troops. You have already treated me as your own son, made me a *cur*, put me in charge of a cavalry brigade . . ."

"Yes, you and Attila both—for you have both proven your ability and courage, though at times I still question your judgment."

Flavius bowed his head, in acknowledgment of his past rashness and then raised his eyes back to the king.

"And now I wish to command warriors to fight on the side of Ioannes. Not mere mercenaries, but a true Hunnish force. Perhaps, with such troops under my command, I could contribute to consolidating the new emperor's victory."

Rugila gazed dreamily at a point in space behind Flavius' back.

"You were once a Roman; then you became a Hun. Do you remember the day you first arrived here in my court? A lost, confused Roman boy. But still you had a spark of defiance, of curiosity and ambition in your eye. Now you once again become a Roman, and a patriot at that." He shook his head.

"Great King," Flavius broke the king's reverie. "Ioannes could change Rome. This is an opportunity for the Huns, to put Theodosius in his place, and at the same time bring about sanity in the Western Empire. We should not fail to take it. I would attack Rome's attackers to save it, and then cure Rome's wound by cauterizing it. I would bring Hunnish blades and fire to cleanse Rome, to seal off the open sore left by Honorius. But I need men."

King Rugila snapped his attention back to the present. "And if I do not give them to you?"

Flavius held the king's sharp gaze. "Then I shall ride home alone. The carving will be more difficult, but it will be done. And if I have no horse, I shall walk. I shall have no more possessions than when I first arrived in your land, and I will feel no poorer for it."

The king nodded and smiled faintly. "You need men, and you shall have men. Turgrid has already spoken to me of this matter, and the men have been assigned to you. The Army of the North."

Flavius took a step backward, as if hit physically by a blow.

"The Army of the North! But *Great Cur*! That is sixty thousand horsemen!"

Rugila looked at him sternly. "Indeed."

Flavius stepped forward again, his face solemn. "Rome will reward your foresight."

The king winced and his face suddenly became somber. "Do you think I covet Rome's rewards, my son? Does Ioannes truly mean anything to me?"

The young man stared at him, puzzled.

"Do you think I even *respond* to the potential for reward from Rome, or from any party, when I make decisions?" the king pressed.

"No, but . . ."

The king's expression became fierce.

"Look at me! I have not been able to chew food for years, and what food I *can* eat I can barely taste. Music I can scarcely hear, people across the next room I can hardly see, and it has been far too long since I have been able to satisfy my wives. But I survive because I am no puppet, Flavius; I am no tool. I am no mere instrument for collecting stimuli from outside, like a lyre that lies dead and silent unless a man plucks its strings to bring it to life. My body may be gone, Flavius, and my subjects may laugh at that . . ."

"Never, Great King," Flavius said somberly.

". . . but my will survives, and this is what distinguishes me from an instrument. My *will* survives, and my *honor* survives, my honor as a Hun! And I am bestowing this gift upon you, Flavius, this gift of an army, as a force of my will and as a consequence of my honor. Do you understand?"

"Yes, my lord."

King Rugila nodded and began laboriously rising from his chair. A young woman who had been hovering inconspicuously behind him suddenly flitted from the shadows and seized his arm to steady him as he began

tottering unsteadily toward the door to his apartments.
Flavius, too, straightened up. Stepping forward, he hastened to the old man and seized his other arm, but the
king shook him off fiercely, stopped his torturous gait,
and peered up into Flavius' face. Suddenly his eyes became as cold and unblinking as an adder's, and Flavius
knew that this man still had many years left in him and
many wits left about him.

"Young Flavius, whether you are Roman or Hun, I
trust your heart. You are like a son to me. But if you vio-
late my will, then you betray me, as a father. You mock
the only thing I have left—my honor. The success of your
venture depends on your wisdom, and yours alone. Do
justice to this gift."

"I will not disappoint you."

The fierce old man gazed fixedly at Flavius for a long
moment. "You will rise high, young Flavius Aetius."

The interview was at an end. The king turned and hob-
bled away to his bedchamber, leaving Flavius alone in the
darkening atrium, pondering the price that comes attached to all great boons.

A week later Flavius, garbed in the Hunnish battle gear
that was so light and flexible when riding yet so impenetra-
ble to missiles in battle, raced across the steppe, surrounded by a squadron of Hunnish standard-bearers and
aides. Two tiny wolf pups, a parting gift from Turgrid,
peered warily out of the leather saddlebag in which a nest
had been arranged for them, and the polished Gepid war
shield he had won was strapped securely to the horse's
haunch behind his thigh. Following close behind him was
the thunder of the Army of the North, galloping in loose
formation—sixty thousand warriors of the steppe, clad and
armed like their leader but decorated with remnants and
scraps they had taken from fallen enemies in their most recent campaigns: shreds of iron Scythian chain mail, the oc-

casional Germanic battle helmet, even bloody tufts of Alani scalps tied to loops along a trophy strap attached to the back of the saddle, a habit Flavius had always detested.

As he cantered across the grasslands with his troops, the memory of his final conversation with Attila came back to him, a conversation he would long have cause to remember. As Flavius had been about to mount his horse to depart with his new army, Attila had stopped him and grasped his hand in a strong grip. The Hun was not one to express emotion, nor did he this time, but Flavius was surprised at the warmth of his hand and the sincere sorrow in his eyes. Truly theirs had been a friendship forged deep, in both battle and rivalry, but in mutual respect and admiration as well.

"What will you do?" Flavius had asked him, and Attila appeared visibly relieved that the silence of their handclasp had been broken.

"I?" his comrade had answered. "I will not be idle, surely, and much of my work in the months and years to come will be due to you."

"To me? Then you are in luck, because I will be many weeks' march away."

"Yes," Attila replied, with a wry smile. "The king has given you a great gift in this Army of the North. But he did not do it solely out of love for you, though there is much element of that as well."

"Of course."

"It is in the Huns' own interest that Rome be strong," Attila continued. "Not *too* strong, but strong nonetheless. We have seen in the past the results of the collapse of your borders. The Visigoths, who were once our allies, poured across the Rhine to establish their own kingdom in Hispania. The Vandals are now doing much the same."

"But they did not become allies of the Romans," Flavius countered.

"True, but no longer are they our allies, either. Rome's

weakness actually weakened the Huns, drawing away great tribes that might have been useful to us someday."

"And so your duty . . ."

"My duty will be to see to our own borders. When Rome is strengthened by your new army, our allies, especially the Ostrogoths, will be stopped in their movements west, perhaps even pushed back from the territories they have acquired along the Rhine. If they cannot advance west into the empire, they have only two choices: stand where they are and breed like rabbits, or . . ."

"Return east—back toward the Huns."

Attila nodded. "Correct. Therefore the Goths and other tribes had best be our allies, rather than our enemies. I will make them our allies. Persuading them if possible, forcing them if they resist . . ."

"*Forcing* them to be allies?" Flavius asked skeptically.

". . . eliminating them outright if necessary," Attila went on. "Our own borders are as pressured as Rome's. We must expand or die—remaining static is not an option. We must not solve Rome's problems simply by transferring them to ourselves."

"Attila—this we can do together. Our nations each face the same threats, from many of the same tribes. A common solution can be found to this, once the situation in Rome has stabilized. . . ."

"Perhaps." Attila shrugged. "Though when has the situation in Rome last been stable? I wish you great luck and great success, my friend. But friendship, I fear, is not something that can be relied upon in cases such as this."

Flavius had had little time to ponder Attila's words, for the king and his family arrived at that moment, as did Turgrid, to take their leave of the young Roman. This Hunnish strategy was a bold one and, Flavius knew, necessary in light of his own plans. Still, he would have much to discuss with his father when he finally arrived in Ravenna.

Now, however, as he and his horsemen galloped across the steppe, the king's words hammered at his brain in rhythm to the pounding hoofbeats.

You will rise high, Flavius Aetius. . . . Do justice to this gift. . . . Do not disappoint me.

Flavius shook his head to clear it of the echo of the king's final words. He felt hollow. His body was strong, but his spirit was divided, split between two lives, rent down the middle like the notch in a double-bladed battle-ax. Was he a Hun, or was he a Roman? A man of the steppe or of the forum? A comrade of Attila or of Vortigern? Such doubts he had never felt while living in Ravenna as a boy, nor when roaming the plains of Hunnia as a young man, for in both places he had felt complete, undivided by competing loyalties and customs, wholly present where he was. Now, however, he felt doubt gnawing at his belly, like the fox under the tunic of the Spartan boy in the ancient tale. Unlike the Spartan, however, he knew not whether to silently endure the pain or to rip open the fabric hiding his uncertainties and expose himself for what he was: a Roman in Hunnish armor, a Hun with a Roman face.

As if the old king were actually present, Flavius muttered back to him a reply, in a voice inaudible to all but himself and his magnificent Hunnish war pony, itself a farewell gift from Rugila.

"I will not disappoint you, Great *Cur*," he said.

Yet even as he spoke, the face of Rugila that he retained in his mind's eye faded and blurred and nearly disappeared—and then finally returned and became clear again, though in another form.

It was the face of his father.

FOUR

Ravenna, A.D. 425

I

The late-summer air was heavy with the fragrance of wild mint and overripe blackberry, and the sun pulsed hot in the blue sky, lazily eyeing the testing mobs of clouds that gathered unruly on the horizon. Flavius trotted his horse through the carefully cultivated hills of northern Italy, where, though still miles from any city of size, the roads were cobbled more smoothly than any he had seen in fifteen years outside the empire. Carved granite stiles placed at regular intervals announced the distance he had traveled from the last town of consequence and the distance yet to be traveled to Ravenna. Stone estate houses were visible at the ends of long, manicured driveways, and the hillsides were dotted with smaller peasant cottages, rude perhaps by local standards, with their stick or thatched roofs, but still capable of standing a hundred years or more, in sharp contrast to the portable felt structures to which he had become accustomed in the East.

Fruit trees sagged under their heavy burden——figs and late apples, peaches ripe for the tasting; and everywhere, climbing up the sides of houses, trellised in neat rows in fields, even growing wild at the sides of the road, were grapevines——how long had it been since he had seen fresh fruit in such abundance? Though the walls of Ravenna still lay far out of sight beyond the distant horizon, he drank in every detail, every veiny green leaf, every clod of dirt, every breath of fragrant air.

The sixty thousand Hunnish troops trotting behind him remained stolid, impassive, and silent, but he could sense that even they, even these iron men of the steppe, fresh from bloody victory over the legions of the Eastern Roman Empire, were breathing deep the flower-laden air and glancing sidelong in amazement at the lushness of the land through which they passed.

As the terrain began to flatten and to show signs of his home region's familiar salt marshes, Flavius spied a familiar figure sitting motionless on his horse in the middle of the road. Wearing full Roman dress armor, immaculate cloak draped carefully behind him over the white haunches of his magnificent war charger, cavalry lance drawn up at his side, his father, Gaudentius, was an army of one, visibly older but lacking none of the Roman dignity and straight-backed discipline that Flavius remembered. Behind him stood his supporting forces—an accompanying squadron of thirty cavalry guards, equally polished, identically armed, as motionless and impassive as their commander.

Flavius heeled his horse forward, sprinting away from his troops. As he approached the tiny Roman squadron, Gaudentius alone dismounted and walked slowly out toward him. Flavius leaped down in the Hunnish fashion, scissoring his legs behind him and vaulting over the right side of the still-galloping animal, hitting the ground gracefully at full run as the horse veered gently off to the left, slowed, and stopped of its own accord. Flavius trotted up to his father and enveloped him in a joyful embrace, while the lead troops of his army halted in the road a respectful distance behind.

Grasping Flavius' shoulders, the older man pushed away and stared at the son he had not seen in many years. His rapid glance over this strange young officer, with the long braid flowing down his back, the sweat-stained armor decorated with swirling engravings, the rawhide leggings, and the high, fringed boots, raised far more questions than answers—he could scarcely believe that such a barbarian, leading such a troop, had ventured as far as civilized Italy, much less that he was his own son.

"Before I ask you the question I must ask," Gaudentius said, his face impassive, "I want you to know how proud I am of you."

Flavius was moved. "Father, your letters meant a great deal to me."

Gaudentius offered a thin smile with his lips, though his eyes remained stern. He nodded his head toward the huge army standing silent behind Flavius.

"Some things I wrote to you, but others I did not, for fear they would be read by the wrong eyes. But first: Do you come in peace or in war?"

Flavius was taken aback. "Peace or war? You didn't receive news of my victories? I left Hunnia weeks ago, as soon as I heard Honorius had been overthrown. I defeated Theodosius' forces moving in from the Eastern Empire to subdue Ioannes. Since then, I have faced no military challenges on the road to Ravenna—not here, nor in the outer territories. The Roman garrisons let us pass unimpeded. Surely that was your doing, giving us safe conduct. You know how I come!"

Gaudentius shook his head. "The empire is not as you remember it, son. Command is in flux; you don't know who Rome's enemies are. Indeed, sometimes *I* don't know who Rome's enemies are. If the garrisons let you pass without challenge, it was because they were afraid to challenge, not knowing whether the legions would support them. Your army"—and he gestured again toward the massive force—"passed through a door that was left ajar. You defeated the empire's enemies, but that does not necessarily make you its friend. And so I must ask you again, because it is not obvious to the court, nor is it to me: Do you come in peace or in war?"

Flavius glanced behind his father, behind the small squadron of Roman troops, down the road. The cobbled track wound endlessly through the marshlands, eventually disappearing into the distant sea haze that smudged the horizon. Beyond that, he knew, a traveler would soon be able to make sight of the great raised causeway that led across the morasses of the River Padus and then see the tops of Ravenna's walls rising in the shimmering, heated mist. Yet now, for the first time, he spotted a glint of polished steel in the near distance, flashing at the front of a long shadow darkening the road as it threaded over the horizon. The city's powerful garrison. Of course Gaudentius would not simply ride out alone, with only a bodyguard, to meet a potentially hostile force.

Flavius looked into his father's eyes. "Peace or war? I come to defend Ioannes' right. I come to defend Rome."

Gaudentius stared back at him, unblinking. "Then you've come too late."

"How is that? I came as soon as I heard Ioannes had assumed power."

"Ioannes is dead."

Flavius' jaw tightened.

"Two weeks ago," Gaudentius continued. "Killed by assassins sent by Theodosius."

"The city is impregnable. How could they have passed over the causeway undetected?"

"They didn't," Gaudentius replied. "They were led along a secret path through the marshes by a shepherd. Some say he was an angel in disguise; others say the devil. In any event, Ioannes was captured. They cut off his right hand, paraded him through the streets mounted on an ass, and then took him to Aquileia and beheaded him in the Circus. Ravenna yielded and all the leading men pledged loyalty to the eastern emperor—including myself. I rode all this way to tell you personally."

"Loyalty to Theodosius? But he tried to invade the West during its time of weakness. My forces defeated him, weeks ago! He holds no sway. . . ."

"New alliances have been made. Don't ask me to explain—I am a soldier, not a magician. Theodosius is the highest-ranking leader between the two empires. He has appointed a new ruler for the West."

Flavius' face darkened—was his entire journey, and his hard-won battle of a few weeks before, all for naught? He racked his brain for memories of the men he had known in Ravenna as a boy, who might have curried favor with the eastern emperor to gain appointment to this position. "A new ruler?" he asked, the anger in his voice barely controlled.

"Yes," Gaudentius replied evenly. "Theodosius' cousin, Valentinian. You don't know him. Before he left Constantinopolis, Theodosius granted him the title of *Nobilissimus*; on his journey through Thessalonica he was promoted to the rank of Caesar; and upon his arrival in Ravenna after Ioannes' overthrow he was proclaimed Augustus, saluted by the senate, and invested with the imperial purple."

"And this Valentinian—is he a man worthy of his sudden new position?"

"Hardly." Gaudentius set his jaw and gazed into the distance.

"Hardly worthy?"

"Hardly a man. He's six years old."

"Six years old!" Flavius spat. "Has Theodosius taken leave of his senses?"

"Possibly. The Empress Mother Galla Placidia will be regent until he comes of age."

"Galla Placidia—Honorius' sister? That means the court of Ravenna is merely continuing as it always has! It's like a Hydra. You cut off one head, but—"

"I've nothing to say of the Empress Mother," Gaudentius interrupted coldly. "You must understand my position."

Flavius stared at him in silence as Gaudentius turned back to his horse and began slowly mounting in his stiff cavalry armor.

"I'll accompany you on the road to Ravenna," Gaudentius continued. "We have three days of travel, two if we ride quickly. Time enough to catch up on many things, on fifteen years of life in the court. The Empress Mother wishes to see you immediately upon your arrival."

Flavius straightened his shoulders and glanced back at his troops.

"And in that, at least, I'll be happy to oblige," he replied.

Flavius and Gaudentius, each accompanied by a squadron of thirty guards, clattered through Ravenna's gates, into the cobbled streets of the city, and straight to the entrance of the massive, fortresslike palace. Both armies had been left outside the city walls, each a prudent distance from the other but not so far apart that the sharpest-eyed among them could not observe the other side with wary suspicion.

At the main portal, all dismounted and Gaudentius began striding through on foot, though Flavius hesitated. The older man glanced back.

"We leave our guards outside. No legionaries are allowed in the palace grounds—and certainly not Huns."

Flavius shrugged, and gesturing silently to his questioning troops, he bade them stay in the courtyard, while he followed his father inside.

"Will you be showing me to my quarters first?" Flavius asked as he realized his father was leading him in a direction away from the apartments and directly to the central core of the palace, the vestibule and the atrium. "I don't want to show disrespect to the empress by appearing before her straight from the road." He slapped his leather-clad thigh and raised a faint cloud of dust.

Gaudentius glanced at him and merely increased his pace. "The Empress Regent demands you attend her immediately."

Passing directly to the atrium, the two men strode past a line of courtiers and ladies-in-waiting. Informed by scouts hours before of the imminent approach of the Hunnish force, they had turned out in all their finery and curiosity to witness the return of Gaudentius' long-absent son.

As Flavius made his way past the gaping spectators, he thrust out his jaw and tossed back the long mane of chestnut hair, which he had loosed from its braid and hastily combed out with his fingers on his walk through the palace. The room fell silent but for the dry creaking of Gaudentius' stiff cavalry boots on the polished marble floor and the patter of Flavius' soft deerskin riding shoes. His stained armor and the moth-eaten fur trim of his plain woolen cloak were in stark contrast to the courtiers' fine silks and perfumed hairpieces, and a bevy of eunuch functionaries standing at the foot of the dais to the throne smirked with disdain.

Flavius kept his eyes fixed forward, ignoring the stares and whispers all around, and strode confidently toward the seated Empress Placidia. Just as he approached the first step to the dais, however, a young nobleman of Flavius' age, muscular as a gladiator but with eyelids lined with kohl in the Egyptian fashion and with oiled, perfumed hair, suddenly stepped forward and blocked his path.

Flavius stopped, silently observing the man. Gaudentius stepped to his side.

"Son: I present to you the Empress' High Chamberlain, Eugenius of Alexandria."

The chamberlain did not deign even to acknowledge the introduction. Instead he coldly inclined his head toward the cavalry sword Flavius wore slapping at his side.

"Weapons are not permitted in the lady's presence," he growled, in a tone that was low but could nevertheless be clearly heard throughout the room. "And you will pause and kneel for introduction."

Flavius did not move a muscle. "I yield my sword to no man," he said in a voice equally low but equally threatening. "Least of all to a eunuch."

Eugenius stiffened, and the onlookers emitted a collective gasp. Gaudentius leaned forward to whisper in his son's ear.

"Eugenius isn't a eunuch."

Flavius was unfazed. His hand moved to the hilt of his sword, and his eyes flickered to the steward's groin and then back up to his face.

"I will remedy that if he doesn't stand aside."

He then shouldered roughly past the shocked functionary, briefly bent one knee to the Empress Regent and the young Valentinian standing next to her, and then stood up, looking openly into their faces.

The boy emperor, garbed in a miniature version of a Roman general's field uniform, accurate even down to the tin, muscled breastplate painted to resemble a bronze carapace, glanced up at the newcomer, his gaze lingering on the matted hair and the dusty armor. After a moment, as if devoid of curiosity or amazement, his eyes glazed and he looked away, bored and dreamy, at an indefinable point in the crowd of courtiers in the back of the room.

Placidia, resplendent in a court gown of shimmering yellow silk trimmed with strings of tiny ivory-colored pearls, sat with shoulders hunched forward in tension. She glared at Flavius defiantly, her face pinched and narrow, clearly unhappy at the newcomer's demeanor and his treatment of her steward.

"Greetings, young Flavius Aetius," she said, in a voice that was soft and cultured yet seemed strained with the effort of remaining neutral and unexpressive. "I have heard much about you from your father. We are delighted to hear of your safe arrival, and of your desire to serve the emperor." She placed her hand lightly on the shoulder of her distracted son, who jumped as if awakened from a daydream and then gazed again without interest at the dusty, sweaty newcomer standing before him.

"Thank you, Empress Mother," Flavius replied respectfully, without averting his gaze in deference, as was the custom of the court. "And I look forward to serving . . . Rome." The pause in his speech had gone unnoticed by no one, least of all the Empress Regent, who stiffened visibly.

"Serving Rome. Yes, indeed, that you shall do. You have been away a long time, and though I fear you have much to relearn of our ways, I have assigned you to a most enviable post: Procurator for Italy. You will relinquish command of your troop of mercenaries, of course, and assume responsibility for all administrative, financial, and revenue-collection duties on the peninsula, as well as advising this court in—"

Flavius calmly interrupted her speech. "Thank you, my lady, but I respectfully decline."

The empress ceased speaking with a sharp intake of breath, and again gasps were heard throughout the room. His words resounded off the marble walls and fluted columns as if he had shouted them. The courtiers fell silent and edged forward slightly, staring at him. No man had ever had such temerity as to contradict the Empress Regent outright—particularly when offered such a valuable position. Gaudentius gazed straight ahead, expressionless, a bead of perspiration rolling down his temple despite the room's cool draftiness.

Placidia affected a slight smile, as if addressing a child or a dense slave.

"Perhaps you did not quite understand, Flavius Aetius. I have offered you a quite attractive position of civil authority, one very well suited to a man of your age and experience. Many men of higher birth and rank than yours have competed fiercely to obtain such a position—"

Again Flavius interrupted her.

"Empress Regent: My troops await me outside the gates. They are healthy and ambitious, and I must keep them occupied and fed or . . . they become restless. . . ."

The empress and Flavius stared at each other for a long moment as his words trailed off, the unspoken implication hanging in the air like the curling trails of candle smoke from the sconces on the wall.

"In that case," the empress said finally, her eyes narrowing in anger, "we shall have to consider an appointment that is, perhaps, more commensurate with your resources."

"Indeed, Empress," Flavius rejoined, his face expressionless. "It is that very matter that I am most eager to discuss with you."

II

Long moments later, a contented Flavius and a haggard Gaudentius strode back through corridors and galleries.

All around them were signs of the enormous wealth and power of the ruler of the Western Roman Empire: intricate mosaics, fountains splashing in tiny courtyards, potted palms, and the soft rustling of silks as ladies and courtiers glided silently past.

"Flavius," Gaudentius remarked thoughtfully, "though you're my son, I no longer know you. You are the most foreign creature ever to set foot in these palace halls, yet in many ways you're more Roman than . . . than any Roman here."

Flavius glanced at him, puzzled. "How so, Father?"

"You have the largest single force in all of Europe. Oh, certainly, Rome's standing army is larger, but the legions are scattered across a thousand miles, and are disorganized and unreliable, poorly melded of a hundred barbarian nations. Your troops are all here. They're trained and cohesive. You could have seized the palace. You could have seized the empire."

"I still can."

Gaudentius was silent for a moment, looking even more haggard than before. "You give me gray hairs when you say this. I'll be pure white by the end of the day."

Flavius showed no sympathy. "But if I took the empire, could I keep it?"

"Are you asking rhetorically, or sincerely?"

"I always speak sincerely," Flavius replied. "You yourself are a commander of legions, Father, so of all men, you would know. If I took it, could I keep it?"

Gaudentius glanced at his son sharply. "Then I will speak sincerely as well. If you took it, you would be the youngest Roman commander in a century. Possibly the most powerful since Constantine. You departed a boy, and returned at the head of an army."

Flavius stopped and faced his father. "So. That is the sort of story of which heroes are made. But you haven't answered my question. If I took Rome, could I *keep* it?"

Gaudentius looked away. "It's the sort of story of which *tragic* heroes are made. No, I don't believe you could keep it."

"Nor do I. Not with an army of foreign auxiliaries. Not with a troop of Huns."

"But many would disagree," Gaudentius replied. "The empress fears you—or she wouldn't have agreed to rescind your appointment as procurator and offer you military command of all Gaul."

Flavius smiled faintly. "She didn't offer it to me. I suggested it, and she agreed. Could she have expected me to settle for less?"

Gaudentius' face did not betray his feelings. "Beware you don't overstep your capabilities. Many men have been brought down harshly for reaching too far, too fast."

Flavius brushed off his father's concerns. "Seizing power by the sword—that's not for me, Father. If I achieve power I wish it to be legitimate. I wish to deserve it. Taking it as a personal bauble would make me no better than a dictator. A Sulla or a Nero. It would make me no better than Honorius."

"Yet all of Gaul—this is not something to be taken on lightly."

"Nor do I. I've been given command over the world's finest horsemen. That is a boon not to be squandered. I've been stymied in my plan to assist Ioannes—yet there are other needs. Even when living among the Huns I knew of Rome's faltering borders. The Ostrogoths and Alamanni I met in the camps boasted of their raids across the Rhine, how Rome was impotent to prevent them from crossing at will, how it was only a matter of time before they would have the mass to seize Gaul. You yourself often wrote me of the problem—how your armies had been reduced to skeletal levels, the best troops siphoned off for the eastern or African campaigns, the auxiliaries demoralized and deserting."

"These problems have been generations in forming," said Gaudentius, surprised at the impact his letters over the years had had on his son. "And you would solve them like that? The border on the River Rhine is not a leak in the plumbing—it is a dam about to burst!"

"I arrived with the finest cavalry in Europe, and now I have the armies of Gaul as well. I'm not beholden to the court and the eunuchs, and I have free rein to act as I wish, to stem the decay. I have waited for this for a long time—such an opportunity will never rise again. I trust I have your blessing."

Their conversation was interrupted by a burst of tambourines and flutes. Rounding a corner, Flavius and Gaudentius came upon a gaily decorated courtyard, crowded with people. At first it was difficult to see past the lines of servants spilling into the outside gallery through which they were passing. But as the two men pushed their way along the path, they eventually found themselves at the edge of the courtyard itself, where they had a clear view of the festivities.

Tiny lanterns had been hung on cords strung between the walls, each with a single flame dancing merrily inside a brightly dyed box of stiffened Pergamum parchment, the light shining through like a luminous painting, casting colored spots on the walls and floor. Songbirds fluttered inside ornate cages constructed of the finest spun wire. But what attracted Flavius' attention immediately was the people, who looked as if they had stepped out of another time and world—just as he, still in his Hunnish togs, no doubt did to them.

The girls were barefoot, and the flagstones of the open courtyard had been not merely washed but *scrubbed* to a dull gleam, to allow the girls to frolic unshod without dirt or soil marring the soft pinkness of their soles. They wore tunics so short as to barely cover the buttocks, carefully fringed at the bottom to allow an occasional glimpse of white hip if swished just so. The linen garments, of a texture so fine as to hang transparently on every curve, light as air, were cut almost scandalously low at the neckline, to facilitate casual draping off of one smooth, bare shoulder. They wore delicate circlets of flowers on their heads, and their cheeks had been dusted with a light rouge and a shimmering golden dust. The effect was to make them appear as if they were breathless and perspiring, or perhaps that was the natural effect of the wine they sipped from gilded chalices. When Flavius peered into the ornate crystal bowl from which it was being served, he observed that the honey-colored liquid frothed and churned of its own accord—no doubt cut with water from a spring he recalled in the nearby hills, which contained bubbles that made one's nose tickle.

The men were even more astonishing. They were completely bare-chested, though they were clearly young noblemen from the best of families, rather than garden slaves toiling on the emperor's estates. Indeed, they wore practically no clothing at all, but for skin-colored loincloths decorated with strategically placed grape leaves. Unlike the tresses of the carefully coiffed girls, the men's hair was purposely mussed and curled. Their faces were unshaven and painted satyrlike, with stylized eyebrows that turned upward at the corners and mouths painted broadly in an unnatural and bestial shade of red. Many swigged wine sloppily from rustic goatskins slung casually around their necks, like those worn by peasants working the fields, and all swayed happily to the music provided by a trio of Greek musicians in a corner.

Flavius stared in amazement. It was a display that would have been inconceivable, possibly even illegal, and most certainly distasteful in a land such as Hunnia. As he watched, a girl of perhaps eighteen spied him and skipped up, laughing and flushed. Gaudentius immediately fixed her with a disapproving eye.

"Lady—in your position and at your age! A sauce like that"— he nodded at her goblet—"is not meant for girls of noble family."

"General Gaudentius!" she giggled. "It's a masquerade! Have you come with your grim expression to impersonate my late uncle Honorius for the evening? Or perhaps with that long face you wish to look like his horse! You can go straight back to your plans and maps. Or . . . perhaps you wish to join us? Slave!" She beckoned to a bewildered-looking servant girl standing at a nearby column awaiting orders. "Bring General Gaudentius a grape leaf to wear!"

Gaudentius visibly recoiled and a loud laugh could be heard behind the girl.

"What, Old Gaudentius here?" a raucous voice called. "Someone must have pulled the stick out of his blasted—"

The girl turned and interrupted the catcall with a laugh.

"Now, Narcissus, be nice!" She then sidled up to Gaudentius with a loud stage whisper. "He's supposed to be Narcissus. We've all dressed up as our favorite mythological characters."

Flavius' amusement was growing by the moment. "And who are you supposed to be?" he asked.

The girl turned, seeming to notice him for the first time, and flushed with pleasure at the opportunity to act her role. "Can't you see? I'm Echo! Can't you see? I'm Echo! Can't you see—"

Flavius interrupted with a smile. "I thought Echo was supposed to repeat the words of others, not her own."

The girl stopped her chant, slightly confused, then smiled at the laughter she saw in Flavius' eyes. Gaudentius stepped forward, stiff and disapproving.

"Son, allow me to present Princess Justa Grata Honoria, daughter of the Empress Regent and older sister to the young emperor."

Honoria affected a fetching pout. "Oh, Gaudentius, you gave me away! But this is the famous Flavius Aetius? He's handsomer than I expected." She grasped Flavius' hand and began pulling him over to the party in the center of the courtyard.

"Come join us!" she cried, laughing. "You can be . . ."

And she paused for a moment, provocatively stroking the leather shoulder pad and then inspecting with surprise the layer of dust and soot that came off on her fingers.

". . . Let me see . . . Mars, the fierce—and dirty—God of War!"

Flavius smiled and politely withdrew his hand.

"Thank you, Princess, but I really must go . . ."

Again the drunken laughter burst out from somewhere behind the girl.

"Same as his father—they both have sticks up their arses!"

Honoria glanced backward at her friends in irritation and then turned back to Flavius.

"Don't mind them," she said.

Flavius shrugged. "I don't."

She giggled. "Come see us again soon, Flavius Aetius—we'll have more time to talk another day."

Flavius and Gaudentius turned and made their laborious way through the servants and onlookers to the other side of the courtyard, where the gallery once again was clear, and then walked on in silence.

"She's trouble, that one," Gaudentius said, frowning. "Keep your distance."

Flavius sighed and gestured about him, at the carefully potted palm trees in every corner, the mosaics beneath their feet, and the frescoes painted on every wall, their colors so cunningly vibrant they seemed almost to glow in the flickering torchlight.

"This whole court is trouble, Father. Politics and favor trading, all of it. I see it in your eyes—you're afraid to speak, afraid to move, you, one of the most powerful officers in the empire."

"The eunuchs wield the true authority in this court, not the generals," Gaudentius said quietly.

"This may be Rome, but it is not worthy of Rome," Flavius replied.

"Son, Rome is honor and nobility. Emperors come and go like the seasons, but Rome is eternal, because it is built on honorable foundations, and because honor is eternal. Remember that, and live up to it. Fulfill your duty."

"Rome's honor—it's only an ideal, Father," Flavius replied. "It was founded by Aeneas, a refugee from a deceived and defeated army who in turn deceived and abandoned the woman who loved him. Is this honor? Rome's honor will never be achieved. Look around you here. You can't delude yourself."

Gaudentius was silent for a moment, then shook his head. "It is not a delusion, any more than Plato was deluded when he attempted to describe the ideal world, or the ideal republic, though he knew it could never truly exist. You must always strive to overcome the *reality* of Rome. Only then will you live up to the *ideal* of Rome."

"Live up to the ideal," Flavius mused. "Even if that means abandoning the reality."

They fell silent as the singing and shouts of the party faded in the distance behind them. It was only as they neared the palace's main portal, where their guard escorts awaited them, that Gaudentius cleared his throat to speak once again.

"There is something else."

Flavius smiled. "I've been away a long time. There must be much else."

"Something important. Have you thought of taking a wife?"

"I have had many other things to think about."

"Senator Carpilio and I have been discussing an arrangement," Gaudentius went on. "He has a daughter, Priscilla. . . ."

"Carpilio—?"

"The chief magistrate," Gaudentius replied. "His family has been of the senatorial rank for generations. His daughter is young—she won't be ready to marry yet for several years—but because of her father's position, she already has many suitors. The senator has agreed to hear your petition before accepting any others."

Flavius considered the proposal in silence for a moment, then looked up.

"Father, I'm grateful. This is a true honor. But the time is not right. You told me to live up to my duty. My duty is first of all to Rome."

Gaudentius sighed. "You'll be departing for Gaul immediately then?"

"First thing in the morning," Flavius replied swiftly. "No need to stay another day."

So recently had he returned home, but he knew beyond a doubt he must leave. A man could not remain long in this lotus field without losing all desire to achieve, without losing all honor and discipline—or without being forced, like his father, to wage continual battle to maintain them, to use every ounce of energy every moment of the day merely to keep his internal balance. Why live surrounded by sloth and temptation and struggle simply to live up to your own standards when you could work in an honest land, among men who already subscribe to such standards, and then rise even further upon *those* foundations instead? It was all so clear to him that there was no need to agonize, no need even to consider.

His father interrupted his thoughts. "I will send a man with you when you go," he said, "to assist you, as an aide on your staff."

"Is he strong, and can he ride? I intend to move fast and travel hard. I don't wish to maintain a staff."

"Florentius has served me for years now, in war and at the palace. He was my chief cavalry centurion, until he lost a leg in battle against the Slavs. He healed, and now rides again as well as any man, but in the meantime I have kept him on my own staff because he is clever, and has a knack for administration. He also knows me better than any man alive. I cannot go with you myself, but Florentius will serve you in good stead."

Flavius nodded, and the two men fell silent as they rounded the corner and entered the tunnel, the gateway through the sixteen-foot walls that were the outer barrier of the fortress-palace. Just then, a hard object slammed into his shoulder, as if someone had struck him with a club. The impact spun him around and toppled him to the cobbled pavement, where a large man fell onto him with a grunt of pain, and then hurriedly shifted off.

Flavius groaned and rolled to the side before rising unsteadily to his feet. As his eyes gained their focus in the tunnel's semi-darkness, his sense of being stunned gave way to one of anger. "Who is this?" he snapped.

Before him, situated on the shaded cobbles in the middle of the tunnel, was a richly upholstered dining couch, on which sat an enormous man. His clothes were ragged as a beggar's, exposing a heavily muscled chest heaving hairily through the tatters. A bushy black beard climbed across his face to the middle of his cheeks, like ivy on a wall, and his eyebrows met in a single thick line over his broad nose. Were it not for the tears welling up in the giant's eyes as he cowered on the precariously creaking couch, Flavius would have thought he had encountered a troll from a Germanic forest.

"Who is this?" Flavius repeated as his hand rubbed his aching shoulder. The giant heaved a loud sob.

Gaudentius sighed. "Magnus," he replied.

" '*Magnus*'—big. I know he's big. But what's his name?"

"We call him Magnus. Just Magnus."

By this time Flavius' own Hunnish guard had run up from their position at the main gates, swords drawn. Flavius waved them away and eyed the blubbering giant. "Look at the size of those arms—they're as big as my waist. Why isn't he in a traveling circus? And why is he sitting on a silk couch in the middle of the tunnel?"

Flavius' father sighed. "Simple," he said, and looked at Flavius significantly.

Flavius did not understand. "So tell me," he said after a moment. "If it's so simple."

Gaudentius shook his head. "No," he said in a low voice. "Magnus is simple. He can barely speak. He's the son of an old palace retainer who died years ago. Honorius kept him around as a pet. It's useful to have him—to move furniture and whatnot."

Magnus nodded and dropped to his knees before Flavius, grasping his hand and placing it on his unkempt, greasy head.

"He's clumsy," Gaudentius continued. "If you ever hear a pot breaking or a chair collapsing in the palace, you'll know Magnus is about. Eugenius beats him like a stray dog. That's why he cowers. I try to show him a bit of kindness when I can. Stand up, Magnus."

The giant blinked and rose slowly to his feet. To Flavius, it was as if a mountain had risen in front of him. The short Hunnish guards, who barely came to the man's chest, recoiled and gripped their swords more tightly. Magnus wiped the tears from his eyes, thumped his chest with an enormous fist, and laboriously announced, "*M-m-mi-les.*"

" '*Miles*'?" inquired Flavius, still warily. " 'Soldier'? You want to be a soldier?"

"More's the pity," said Gaudentius. "Even with those biceps, what skill could he perform? And what armor would fit him? He'd need a helmet as big as an anchovy barrel. Here, Magnus," he said hurriedly as the titan's eyes began welling again. Gaudentius dipped his fingers into the leather purse at his belt and handed him a pair of small copper coins. "Take the couch inside and go buy a honey cake to cheer yourself up."

Magnus' face brightened immediately into a grin that showed white and gap-toothed through the bird's nest of a beard. As he fingered the coins, though, his brow knit in dismay and a cloud again passed over his face. Looking down into his enormous palm, he gingerly picked up one of the tiny coins with his sausage-like fingers and handed it back to Gaudentius. "*Unus*," he grunted.

Gaudentius smiled. "Magnus may be clumsy, but he's the most honest man in the empire," he said. "He knows a honey cake only costs one *denarius*, so he's returning the other. We play this game every time." He turned back to Magnus. "Keep it, lad," he said. "Buy another for your girlfriend."

The giant nodded happily and clutched the tiny coins tightly in his ham-sized fist. He then stooped, picked up the long couch with one hand as easily as if it were a scroll of parchment, and continued his shuffling path through the gate, accidentally knocking the furniture twice against the walls and leaving chips of gilding on the stonework.

Flavius stared after him for a moment and then turned to his guard, who, until the surprise collision with the palace giant, seemed not to have budged from their positions of readiness at the base of the portal the entire day. They looked at him silently.

"We sleep in Ravenna tonight," he announced.

Still the Huns did not shift their glances. They stood unmoved by the event they had just witnessed, and unmoving, until one of them finally broke the silence.

"And in the morning?" the trooper grunted in the guttural Hunnish tongue.

"In the morning," Flavius replied, "we ride to Gaul."

PART II

FIVE

Gaul and Hunnia, A.D. 425–444

I

Seasons pass, fortunes and loyalties wax and wane like the phases of the moon, but Rome endures eternal—and so, too, do the threats of those who would have it otherwise.

For decades, Rome's border garrisons in Gaul had been thinning and weakening, even periodically collapsing like a burst dam, as new floods of barbarians surged through. Always Rome succeeded in regaining tenuous control, reestablishing a wavering barrier against the encroaching tide. In recent years, a kind of hostile stability between defender and attacker had prevailed, yet now the enemies beyond the Rhine were once again growing in their ambitions. The Alamanni, Vandals, and Franks seethed in resentment at being stymied on the banks of the great river. They wallowed in the poverty and disease of growing populations on poor and untilled land, and their young warriors brooded relentlessly in their desire for the fertile plains of Gaul. Each winter, as the rivers and streams froze solid, the imperial roads filled with snow, and the legions hunkered in their barracks, the fur-clad tribesmen emerged from their smoky huts, summoned by the calls of their warlords. Each winter they took up their roughly wrought blades, hoisted their oaken shields, and mounted their high-flanked horses, inured to the deadly cold. And each winter they surged in furious

masses along ancient paths and hidden mountain cross-
ings, to try their strength and seek access to the temperate
plains of Gaul—against the ever-harried defenses of the
Roman legions.

And so it was this winter, as the pressures of rage and
ambition rose to the boiling point. Now, in this remote
valley, the frozen, fir-studded hills rang with the clash of
battle, the screams of frantic horses, and the roars of angry men. The driving snow lashed relentlessly with the
force of the wind, and the skin of the men's faces was red
and chapped from the biting air. All was chaos, and the
stench and the sounds of fear rose up even above the fury
of the wind-driven snow.

Never had the Franks met such a formidable foe. The
thick forests of eastern Gaul were *their* territory—if not
in fact, then certainly by right of intent and possession,
for their tribesmen had been filtering across the Rhine
and into the mountainous valley for months, waiting for
the right moment, the right circumstances, when they
would have the mass to overwhelm the Roman defenses,
to break through the legions' lines, to swarm unimpeded
into the warmer lands of the south. The Franks had
counted on the Romans' long reluctance to protect these
difficult regions in winter; their ponderous marches and
tenuous supply lines; and their low morale and numbers.

But they had not counted on General Flavius Aetius
and his auxiliaries.

Before the Franks could consummate their plans for
mass assault on Gaul, they had been driven back before
the onslaught of this new weapon of the Romans, these
Huns, mounted killers who knew no fear, felt no cold,
complained of no hardship. These strange horsemen from
the East even required no meat, for it was said they could
survive for weeks in the snowy mountains on nothing but
milk from their mares and blood tapped from veins in the
animals' forelegs. Rumor spread among the Franks that

the Roman commander—a tall, lean man with flowing hair—bled his own horse and drank the steaming liquid along with his men, eschewing the comforts to which his rank entitled him, sleeping in the snow and shouting commands in their own barbarian tongue. This was a man the Franks had not anticipated, and in their ignorance of his skills and of the strength of his dark-faced warriors they had allowed themselves to be cornered, at a place no normal Roman army would ever have ventured and a time no normal Roman commander would ever have dared attack—at dusk, in a driving snowstorm, three days' march from the nearest Roman settlement.

The battle was bitter, but foreordained, for a body of freezing Frankish irregulars, even if fighting on their own territory, even if they outnumbered their adversary two to one, cannot stand up to horse troops such as these, on animals that seem to actually *gain* strength from the harsh conditions. But when one has nowhere to go, when one's back is pressed against a frozen mountainside, and when light is fast fading and the Huns and their damnable wolves still press forward, there is nothing to do but to fight on and try to drag as many down into Hell with you as you can.

Flavius Aetius himself led the final charge of the Hunnish troops across the blood-sprayed snow and into the surviving mass of Franks, who in desperation had stacked the frozen corpses of their horses and comrades as a grisly barricade in front of them. Yet as he surged through the drifts, cavalry sword raised high in the signal to charge, a Frankish soldier lying on the ground in a frozen pool of red suddenly sprang up. With a howl of rage, the Frank lunged at Aetius' horse, wrapping his arms around the animal's neck to drag him down. The horse staggered under the weight of the attacker and rolled his eyes in terror while Aetius lurched and gripped the beast's flanks tightly with his thighs to remain upright.

Without warning, a flash of gray flew through the air and slammed into the Frank's back. Aetius' huge she-wolf tore with her fangs at the neck and shoulder pieces of the attacker's armor, digging her claws into his back and thighs for purchase. The man was caught utterly unawares and dropped off the horse with a scream, whirling and reaching desperately behind him to dislodge the beast clinging to his back with the tenacity of a lion. Leaning over his terrified horse, Aetius thrust his cavalry blade into the unprotected gap in the man's armor just where neck meets shoulder, feeling the crack as the steel bit cleanly through the tendons and collarbone and deep into the soft tissue of the chest. As he jerked the sword out, the wolf leaped off and circled back to the side of his master's mount, snarling angrily, ears flattened to her head in fury.

The Frank, relieved of the burden of wolf and of life, stood swaying on his feet for a moment, the supports of his neck cut through and his head fallen and resting on his shoulder. He stared at Aetius sideways for a moment, eyes blinking in surprise and then clouding in death, and dropped slowly to the ground, under the flashing hooves of a group of passing horsemen.

Aetius wheeled and paused to calm his horse as the Hunnish auxiliaries stormed past him, their animals leaping through the snow, over the makeshift barricade, and into the mob of Franks beyond. For the enemy, it was the end—of their wrongly held assumptions about Rome, of their ambitions to conquer Gaul, of their very lives. In a moment, the forest would again be silent but for the wind whistling through the quivering trees. The bloodied snow beneath ten thousand cadavers would soon soften in its crimson, turning pink with the new layers that fell upon it and finally white, as the drifts obliterated all signs of the destruction that had taken place this day.

Aetius turned toward the final charge, leaning forward

to peer through the flurries, his face unshaven, his eyes red-rimmed from fatigue, his long hair streaked with frozen white. He raised his sword in salute, the hilt still trailing the Frank's blood onto his fist.

"For Rome!" he bellowed, and his voice rang out sharply over the diminishing sounds of battle and the cries of the dying.

As one, the Hunnish troops rampaging through the Frankish lines stood in their stirrups and raised their own swords.

"For Aetius!" they roared in reply before returning back to the slaughter.

Among the northern clans of the vast Slavic tribe, in the farthest reaches of the territory of the Huns, passions ran fierce and loyalty deep, with alliances forged on courage in battle and on tales told during the long and haunted darkness of the winter nights. Outsiders rarely ventured to this harsh land, and it was beyond the memory of even the eldest of the elders that a stranger of royal lineage had penetrated this far. So taken unawares had the tribes been at the arrival of the fur-clad prince from the East that the clan leaders had not even had time to collect their forces for presentation. It was only now, a week after his appearance, that warriors were beginning to congregate from the myriad hamlets dotting the steppe, arriving by river craft, or by thick-shouldered warhorse, or by foot. For days they had been pouring in, and now the frozen fields far around were crowded with haphazardly arranged tents and wooden huts, and the night air rang with the drunken carousing and fighting of the thousands of men who had arrived for this night, this traditional night of the Gathering, on the first full moon after the winter solstice.

But on this night, the council of elders that gathered at the great, roaring fire was not presided over by the hereditary Slav king. The man who stepped forward was the visitor from the East, a man whom few of the warriors had seen before. He was short but powerful, with a broad face scarred in a strange pattern, and the hair streamed from beneath his fox-trimmed cap like a black river springing from a rock. He had come a very great distance to talk to these men, these fierce northern warriors, and his words were compelling—all the more so, for he had come with an army.

Upon arriving at the place of the Gathering, every Slavic warrior had passed through the vast camp of troops who had accompanied this commander from the East. They, too, were short men and silent, men who never removed their thick leather armor or laid down their lances, men who seemed never to dismount their strange, shaggy horses, even to eat or sleep. They were men who moved little, as if conserving their strength. Yet it was said that when called upon to do so, any man of these thousands could strike at astonishing speed: to counter a sudden attack, to capture an unbroken horse with the toss of a cloth rope, or to ride fifty miles in a day without complaint or question.

And as the arriving Slavic tribesmen passed through the camp of these watching, armored men, they realized that decisions had already been made and that their world would be changed forever.

The night was propitious. The air was so cold it seemed almost tangible and solid, as if one could seize the darkness and grasp it in the hand like a piece of iron. Yet the air's bite could scarcely be felt, as excitement ran high and kept the blood running hot under the skin. Above, in the night sky, the aurora blazed with more brilliance and grandeur than had been seen in these lands for generations. Great incandescent swathes of light cascaded and tumbled down invisible heights, swirling in maelstroms and hanging in vast festooned arches of shifting color. The gods themselves had assembled to witness the night's event, announcing their presence with the radiant display. A hundred thousand men stood in silent awe, their frozen breath mingling and hovering over their heads like a phosphorescent mist.

Before the blazing council fire, the leader of these scar-faced men, these Huns from the East, stepped forward to address the tribal elders. But the ring of his voice meant that he was not directing his words merely to them, to the old men. Rather, he was speaking to all the Slavs, to every hard-eyed, yellow-haired warrior gathered about the fire. His voice carried even to those standing so far away in the cold darkness they could scarcely see the flames, much less feel the radiating heat. In the dim light behind the fire stood the darkened silhouettes of his Hunnish warriors, mounted as always, drawn up in battle order in ranks that extended in the other direction far into the cold darkness.

"Honorable Slavs!" the Hun shouted, and by this time every northerner had learned that this commander's name was Attila and that he flaunted not the name of his father and his grandfather, as was the way of the Slavs, but rather stood on his own name alone, like a man on an island without a connecting peninsula to his past and to his forebears.

"Fearsome Slavs!" he roared again. "I stand here tonight to honor your people's warriors. I stand here in respect for your courage, your strength, and your warlike hearts. I come in sorrow for the losses you have endured in the past, at the hands of those who would seek to deprive you of better lives and warmer lands. And I come in anticipation of the victories you will win in the future, and of the lives of plenty you will bequeath to your children's children.

"Great Slavs, I come now to unite us, to bring our peoples together. Your council has heard my words, and accepted them. By binding our nations, we strengthen our swords; by allying our forces, we ensure our freedom! For the way of the Hun is the way of freedom—freedom from oppression and freedom from tyranny. Freedom to roam the earth at will. Freedom to expand and grow. With this alliance between our two great peoples, your strength, which is already formidable, becomes ours, and our strength becomes yours, a strength greater than either kingdom could have alone—a strength greater than has ever been seen!

"Join with me, Slavs, in cementing this friendship, this pact—salute with me, that our peoples, together, may gain ever greater glory and be blessed by the gods, becoming the nations our peoples deserve! For our distant enemies have never seen the Fires of the Gods that we now witness in the night sky above—and they have never seen the likes of the fires of the Huns!"

A hundred thousand warriors raised their arms and roared, clanging their shields with their spears in a deafening clatter that rose into the frosty air and disappeared into the turmoil of the colors above and beyond to the sharp, glittering stars. It would be many hours yet before the eastern horizon would begin to lighten with the feeble glow of day, and only a few hours after that, that the exhausted sun would again sink back beneath the edge of the plain. Yet, as the mob of shaggy giants roared out their support for his cause, Attila turned toward the darkened east to honor the sacred deities of the sun, as was the sacred custom of the Huns. It was necessary for the gods to approve his venture, to be appeased in his efforts. For though now he had secured the Huns' northern and eastern borders by the might of the Slavic tribes, there still remained many more peoples, many more tribes, to consolidate into the vast alliance.

By persuasion or by the sword.

* * *

The Burgundian capital of Borbetomagus, strategically situated on a rocky outcrop high above the left bank of the Rhine, was once one of the most beautiful cities of the lands bordering the Roman Empire. It was also one of the most impregnable, a fact that had encouraged the Burgundian king Gundahar to step up his raiding and plundering of a wide swath of Roman territory. Indeed, the king had even gone so far as to join with the Alani king Goar in declaring allegiance to a new Roman "emperor"—a certain Jovinus, an upstart Gallic senator whose position was supported by a cohort of fierce Burgundian guards. It was an act of war even more blatant than the lightning raids Gundahar had been conducting against the Roman garrisons—for raids are a fact of life in the empire's border regions, almost expected, but an actual challenge to the emperor's supreme authority is not to be tolerated.

Jovinus himself came to a painful end after a short reign—captured by Roman forces in Narbo, his head was given a long and distinguished tour of the empire and finally awarded a permanent home grinning down at travelers from the battlements of the walls of Cartago. Yet his sponsor, Gundahar the Burgundian, remained unpunished. And much to the dismay of the court in Ravenna, Gundahar's plundering even increased, his wealth steadily growing at the expense of the region's suffering Roman landowners and his threat to Roman authority seemingly undeterred.

Until this day.

Aetius stalked a well-trod line before the invincible Burgundian walls, ignoring the clouds of arrows and missiles raining down before his legions massed below. A line of Roman artillery troops stood at nervous attention before him, each man keeping a wary eye at the top of the walls, lest the Burgundians find their range more accurately. Behind the Romans stood dozens of massive onagers, the huge stone-hurling machines whose ferocious recoil was said to be as dangerous as the kick of a wild ass; and behind them in turn, five legions of Hunnish auxiliary cavalry. In the past, Rome's horse troops had rarely totaled more than a tenth the number of foot troops in a battle. Yet when Aetius led a campaign, the proportion was increased to as high as one-half or three-quarters. And when the horse troops in question were his formidable Huns . . . then it was one of the most powerful fighting forces Rome had ever fielded.

Aetius raised his sword above his head, as his enormous, shaggy wolf paced restlessly at his side.

"Ready the incendiary!" he bellowed.

"Ready the incendiary!" the artillery officer echoed back. Lit torches touched down onto the onager payloads—barrels of pitch wrapped tightly with oil-impregnated straw, which burst into flame at contact.

"Release!" Aetius shouted.

"Release!" came the reply.

The cheers of the watching troops were drowned by the crash of oaken arms against stop beams as twenty onagers fired at once, sending flaming missiles soaring into the air and over the walls. At the same signal, the waiting Huns released their own formidable war bows, filling the air with a hellish storm of fire arrows that slammed into the defenders atop the walls, penetrating their armor and sometimes their very shields and setting all within the walls ablaze—thatched roofs, horses' manes, Burgundian flesh. In moments, a devastating firestorm had been unleashed within the crowded confines of the city, an inferno producing a rank cloud of black smoke that blinded troops and trapped civilians within their own homes and shelters before they even realized the danger.

But the assault had only begun. As the chaos atop the walls reached its peak, the Roman artillery troops changed their ammunition. Now large rocks flew from the formidable machines, battering the walls, toppling crenellations, opening gaping holes in the battlements. And suddenly, over the frenzied roar of the attack floated the sound of incessant pounding. On the Roman flanks, far distant from the point where the bulk of the assault was taking place, a huge battering ram, a bronze-sheathed log swinging on chains beneath a shelter protected by a heavy pointed wooden roof, began beating against the city's wooden gates. At the sound, the Burgundian commander on the wall top, himself barely able to remain on his feet with two Hunnish arrows protruding from his shoulder, blanched in desperation. He shouted to his troops to reinforce the garrison at the main gates. But it was too late. There were few still living on the wall top who could even hear him.

With a terrifying crack the gate splintered, and with one more lunge of the powerful ram it collapsed completely. The Roman troops leaped away as flames burst from the opening, consuming the battering log's shelter in a blast of fire. Inside the walls it was a hellish scene, but in a moment the pressure of the flames diminished, and with a bellow of triumph a thousand Roman soldiers sprinted through the flaming gate, leaping over the burning timbers and onto the walls from the inside. They raced along the catwalk, dispatching the surviving defenders and securing the other city strongholds. There would be little plunder or slaves to be taken this day. Borbetomagus was destroyed, the barbarian incursions into Roman territory cut off at the root.

Aetius looked up at his men on the wall. He would have been glad to have accepted Gundahar's sword in surrender, and indeed, the previous day he had demanded it of the king, but to no avail. Aetius knew that surrender was not the Burgundian way—and he deeply regretted that, unlike so many other peoples he had defeated over the years, the warlike Burgundians could not have been converted to allies or auxiliaries. Yet that was the way of war, and the course the Burgundians had chosen was honorable—if suicidal. Dismissing his regrets, he leaped onto his own horse and raised his sword.

"For Rome!" he shouted, with a voice that carried far above the din of battle to the roaring flames within the city. Yet the response from his troops was not an echo but an affirmation.

"For Aetius!" came the bellowing reply.

High on the observation tower on the eastern wall overlooking the river, he could see the dark shadow of a Roman herald laboriously climbing the final ladder to the signal fire platform on the top, perhaps the only spot in the entire city where there was, in fact, no fire. A moment later, cheers erupted from within the city and without, as the troops peered up through the billowing smoke to spy the silhouette of the *aquilifer,* the eagle bearer, holding high the triumphant Roman standard, etched against the clear blue sky.

The distant Maeotian marshes along the barbarian coast of the Black Sea had for centuries been a refuge for those fleeing authority and a quagmire for those seeking to impose it. Half a millennium earlier, fierce King Mithridates of Pontus had confounded Pompey the Great by trekking here through the frigid Caucasus Mountains in the dead of winter, leading a ragtag band of mercenaries. Now the Alani sought to do the same, establishing a formidable stronghold in the swampy wastes of this inhospitable land, where they could consolidate their forces once again to stand against the encroaching tide of Huns pushing their nation west, ever west.

But Attila would have none of it. Those who would not accept the sovereignty of the Huns must become their enemies. Those who would not become allies must be destroyed. In a world of powerful warrior tribes, of empires that must expand or die, of unrelenting outside pressure on ancient territories and borders, there was no other option. Control or conquer—in the end, it was a matter not so much of glory but of survival.

Storming over the low horizon in mid-afternoon, his enormous army arrived at the wood plank city well before nightfall. The Alani watchmen on the log towers had long seen the horsemen's approach, but the actual assault took them completely unawares. Never had an attacking army simply rounded the world's edge and then continued galloping into a full-scale assault without even pausing to catch breath or take a meal. The Huns' supply wagons trailed miles behind, but their cavalry showed no signs of slowing to allow them to catch up. The Alani defenders were astounded. Impossible as it seemed, they had just witnessed a thirty-mile charge. And at the very front of the vast horde of silent wild-haired horsemen was the Hunnish commander himself.

Reaching the city's steep earthen ramparts at the base of the walls, the Huns, rather than slowing, scrambled their horses straight up the slope, into the very teeth of the ferocious Alani arrow fire. Slashing furiously with swords and battle-axes from behind their light wicker shields, the steppe warriors surged forward. They plowed through the palisade of sharpened stakes as if it were made of swamp reeds, their horses trampling the collapsing enemy lines with sharpened hooves. At the very peak of the assault, a sharp whistle could be heard from behind the Hunnish lines, and then, to the terror of the defenders, hundreds of snarling battle wolves leaped into the fray. The ferocious animals threw themselves at the fleeing Alani, shredding their light armor with their claws and slashing at their throats with bloody fangs.

With the first defenses breached, the Alani turned and fled behind the stout log walls of the city, hurriedly barring the thick gates behind them, praying that this barrier

would allow them space to tend their wounded and signal
for reinforcements from the outlying tribes. Still, the
Hunnish horsemen did not hesitate. Casting aside their
shields, the riders seized the coils of rope that each carried slung from his wooden saddle horn. While still at full
gallop, they rose to a crouching position on their horses'
backs, guiding the animals into a sprint parallel to the log
walls. As they approached, the riders used the horses' momentum to leap, seize the tops of the walls with their
hands, and scramble deftly over, while the horses veered
away. The defenders on the catwalk, stunned at the sudden appearance of a thousand Huns at the top of their
twelve-foot barricade, froze in astonishment. The Hunnish ropes whirled, and within moments the outer wall
was thick with the writhing bodies of Alani warriors, dangling by their necks from the upper course of the logs.

Attila cantered to the top of the now-undefended earthen
rampart, pausing momentarily to survey the scene. Nodding grimly, he trotted over to a line of Ostrogoth troopers
who, in the meantime, had hastily built a row of charcoal
fires in the beaten grass. Seizing a torch that one of the men
handed to him, he raised it high above his head, waving it in
a signal, and then hurled it at the walls, where it landed at
the feet of the swaying Alani corpses. A hundred Goths
rushed forward to do the same, and the Huns still standing
on the wall top leaped down inside the fortress. Within moments the entire length of the wall was ablaze.

As the city's defenses collapsed, mobs of people
poured out, some scrambling over still-intact portions of
the burning walls, others struggling to make their way
through the main gates, desperate to escape the flames. At
sight of the screaming townspeople, all discipline by the
attackers was lost. Ostrogoth soldiers leaped off their
mounts and waded into the crowds, seizing plunder and
women and dragging them back to the main lines.

At this, Attila's leathery face grew black with fury. He

galloped toward a Goth he spied nearby who was dragging a terrified Alani woman by her wrist, and as he rode by he slammed the back of the man's head with the flat of his sword, sending his bronze helmet spinning into the air and knocking him facedown and senseless into the dirt. A tall Ostrogoth officer, witnessing the blow, cantered up to Attila, his face grim.

"General Attila," the man shouted over the din of battle, "my men helped you win this victory, and now they are taking their reward. That is the purpose of war! And yet you punish them!"

Wheeling his horse around viciously, Attila pressed his animal directly against the Goth's, reached over, and seized the top of the officer's breastplate, pulling his face down close to his own. He practically spat in his rage.

"No, Captain," he hissed. "That is *not* the purpose of war."

The officer stared in astonishment. In fury Attila nearly pulled him off his horse, then checked himself before continuing in a lower, menacing tone.

"The purpose of war is to *appall*."

The Goth swallowed, and Attila released his iron grip on the man's breastplate and backed his horse away.

"Leave these citizens to disperse at will," Attila growled, gesturing to the terrified mob now milling about the destroyed city. "Their news will spread, and this entire country will be conquered, by fear, if not by the sword. They will become valuable allies of the great Hunnish coalition, securing our borders—and yours, Goth—or they will be eliminated."

He wheeled his horse again and raced off, leaving the officer rubbing his bruised neck and staring after him, with a fear in his heart almost as great as that of the weeping Alani themselves.

II

The hot summer sun of southern Gaul smothered the
earth like a woolen blanket, wringing fragrant oils from
the wild thyme and rosemary dotting the dusty brown
hillsides. The air was so heavy with scent and heat that
people and animals moved as if drugged. Snakes and
toads, if too slow to crawl into the shade after warming
themselves from the nighttime cool, would be found
cooked on the cobbles at mid-day, their bodies mere dried
husks. Men shuffled somberly in a heat haze from shade
tree to shade tree, lying somnolent in the shadows of
stone buildings, drowsing in vine-sheltered courtyards
and alleyways.

Only the lizards remained alert. The tiny splayed-toed
creatures lurked in niches and crevices on every wall, immobile, only their protuberant eyes moving, rolling about
in their heads, inspecting the progress of the droning
flies, waiting for one to approach within tongue shot. Earlier in the season there had been an epidemic of them.
Some people even called it a plague. Lizards by the thousands had filled the streets, methodically crawling from
their unknown point of departure to their equally mysterious destination, searching for mates, for food, for water,
for death underfoot—for whatever reason it was that
lizards congregated on cobbled streets. For a week, the
provincial capital of Arelate had been tormented by these
creatures. They dropped from the ceiling onto plates of
food, from walls onto the hairpieces of noble ladies, from
trees onto the bellies of terrified babes. Slaves were
brought in from the fields to spend entire days stomping
the creatures flat with their feet. They swept and shoveled
the tiny carcasses from the houses into the streets and
from the streets into mortuary wagons to be carted to the
community rubbish ditches outside of town. Scullions

and cooks were commandeered by the prefect to scour the city baths, administrative buildings, and other government facilities. Even young boys were converted to bounty hunters, paid one *denarius* for every hundred of the pests they brought in. For a time, some laborers' children earned more than their fathers.

And then seven days later, as suddenly as they had arrived, the lizards departed. They disappeared to no one knew where, leaving behind only the usual number of one or two per room, calmly performing their time-honored and respected duties of eliminating the quantities of flies that normally plagued the residents. People shook their heads in puzzlement, returned to their former tasks, and awaited, with some foreboding, the next plague to be inflicted upon them. Sores on their bodies? The River Rhodanus running red with blood?

But none came, and the lizard infestation was soon forgotten, and the people once again dozed fitfully in doorways and courtyards in the heavy, fragrant heat of the day.

Outside the basilica of Arelate—a magnificent stone fortresslike structure, the largest church in southern Gaul—the wedding party stood patiently wilting in the heat of the day, crowded together in the small square of shade afforded by the overhanging archway of the main entrance. The procession was to begin at any moment, and the officers of the escort were rebuckling the hot ceremonial armor they had loosened earlier when the metal had begun to scorch their skin. Just as they were arranging themselves in formation to enter the church, the pounding of hoofbeats was heard in the empty street from the direction of the military garrison just outside the city walls. All paused and looked up. In a garrison city such as Arelate, half the traffic on any given day, at least during the heat of the day when shops closed and market traffic dwindled to nothing, consisted of military couriers and transport.

This was no mere courier, however. The garrison commander himself, resplendent in the crimson cloak and polished armor worn only on important occasions, pounded up to the wedding party and leaped off his horse with a hurried salute. General Flavius Aetius, Count of Gaul and Italy and Commander of the Legions of the Western Empire, stepped forward out of the shade to greet him.

"You will be attending the ceremony, then, Tribune?" Aetius asked, with a note of irritation in his voice. "I thought we had agreed the garrison was to remain staffed throughout the day."

The officer dropped his salute and hurriedly wiped his dripping face with the hem of his cloak. "Begging your pardon, sir, but an important dispatch just arrived. I thought it best to bring it to you myself."

"Could it not wait . . . ?"

"It is from the Emperor Valentinian, sir."

The aide Florentius, whom Gaudentius had assigned years previously to serve on Flavius' staff, limped forward out of the shadows where he, too, had been waiting, the brass ball on the end of his wooden leg resounding loudly on the hot flagstones. He was a short man, with the overdeveloped shoulder and arm musculature of one who had spent many years hobbling on crutches before finding a craftsman capable of fitting him with an artificial limb. He was indifferently shaven, but his gray hair was cropped even and short, in the typical legionary style. Though it had been two decades since he had commanded men directly in battle, in his bearing and in his expression he remained every bit the centurion he once had been. He adjusted the collar of his stiff ceremonial armor and glanced impatiently into the darkness of the church. The signal for the procession had not yet been given.

"I'll handle this, sir," he said crisply, and held out his

hand for the dispatch, which the garrison commander gave him. Florentius scanned it.

"The emperor is sending three representatives of the Eastern Empire to discuss state matters with you, sir, and requests that you arrange a full military escort for them and accompany them through the Alps. . . ."

Aetius cut him off, turning to the garrison commander. "Tribune, do you realize what day this is?"

"Yes, sir . . ."

"Do you know the guests in attendance?"

"Sir, I realize they include King Theodoric of the Visigoths. . . ,"

"Theodoric—my oldest friend, Rome's most powerful ally, and potentially its most powerful enemy. And do you imagine the emperor realizes what day this is?"

The tribune paused. "He may have forgotten, sir."

"How long ago did he send that letter?"

Florentius glanced again at the dispatch. "This was dated twenty days ago in Ravenna. It appears to have been delayed— the ambassadors will have long passed through the Alps by now."

Aetius nodded. "So one more day will not matter. I expect the emperor would agree that the wrath of a few eastern diplomats is nothing compared to that of a new bride whose ceremony has been interrupted."

"Sir, is it wise to ignore the emperor's dispatch . . . ?"

"Return to your duties at the garrison, Tribune. Theodoric and his court are in attendance, the bishop is standing by, and this is my wedding day. The emperor can wait one more revolution of the sun."

As Aetius stepped back into the shade he could not help but let his mind wander. Two decades had passed since that day when, as a young man, he had ridden into Ravenna at the head of the largest cavalry force in Europe. If any of the palace residents who had witnessed his

arrival at that time were here in the basilica today, they
would scarcely recognize him. Since taking command in
Gaul he had cut his hair short in the practical, ascetic
manner of the Roman legionaries, although he still retained the habit of occasionally running his fingers over
his scalp, as he had when he had worn his hair in the flam-
boyant Hunnish fashion, hanging over his shoulders. The
Hunnish armor had long been consigned to a cedar storage chest, which Aetius opened only rarely, when seeking
old estate documents or other necessities. The only constant vestige of his Hunnish days was the wolf that was
his inseparable companion. She was not one of the same
animals as had been given to him by Turgrid upon his departure for Ravenna, of course. Those had died years before, the male in a hunting accident, the female of old
age. But since that time, Aetius had carefully bred their
descendents, and every few years he would keep and train
the fittest female of a litter, to replace her mother when
she died.

   The other reminder of his Hunnish life had arrived
only yesterday and was one that stopped bystanders cold
as he rode through the streets. She was a true Hunnish
warhorse, a magnificent beast sent to him from Attila as a
wedding gift. Aetius recalled the presentation of the animal by the Hunnish couriers who had accompanied her—
the knee-length mane braided into a hundred tiny tresses,
each adorned with a dangling pearl; the polished wooden
saddle inlaid with a design of Bactrian lapis lazuli in the
pattern of the royal *tamga*; and the tail, which had been
allowed to grow out to an absurdly impractical length and
which now, washed and brushed to a fluffy sheen, hung so
far as to nearly trail the ground. The garrison tribune,
upon seeing the extravagant animal for the first time, said
she was the most elegant female he had met in years and
wondered aloud if she was married. But Aetius, to prove
she was a true warhorse, displayed the final detail Attila

had discreetly tucked into the embossed leather saddlebag—an ancient, desiccated Scythian scalp. Aetius smiled as he recalled how the tribune had recoiled at the discovery.

His thoughts were interrupted suddenly with the sound of the wedding hymn, and a priest at the door beckoned to him to enter.

An hour later, the ceremony completed, the couple walked slowly down the cool dampness of the basilica's center aisle, past the splendidly dressed and applauding guests, to the steps outside, where they were hit by a blast of heat as intense as if they had just stepped into a blacksmith's furnace. As Aetius and his new wife descended the steps, they stopped to greet the various dignitaries already awaiting them in the receiving line. One man, however, bulled his way out the main doorway of the church behind the couple and directly through the crowds gathering in front. He was exceedingly short but thick-torsoed, bluff and hearty, with a full brown beard that rose up his cheeks nearly as far as his eyes, and he was dressed in finely made but informal attire, like a nobleman on a hunt. He strode directly up behind Aetius and, without pause, engulfed the general in a powerful embrace that pinned his arms to his sides, lifting him briefly into the air before setting him back down again. The man-bear erupted in a booming laugh, his white teeth shining through the fulsome thickness of his beard like a string of pearls displayed on a fur cape.

"You, Flavius, I've seen enough of," he bellowed. "Why in God's name am I embracing *you*, and from behind, no less! Allow me to kiss your lovely bride!"

And before either Aetius or the lady could protest, the man seized her by both shoulders in his huge paws, pulling her forward and down to his height, and gave her a forceful, smacking kiss on each cheek. He then pushed her back to admire her, still grasping her shoulders. The woman, surprised and with her veil knocked askew, smiled demurely and blushed, before glancing toward her husband with pleading eyes.

"A wonderful match, Flavius, wonderful!" the hearty guest exclaimed. "You must visit the queen and me in Tolosa at first opportunity! My dear Priscilla, has Aetius ever told you how I rescued him in a fight with a maddened Hun when we were boys at the palace in Ravenna?"

Aetius stepped forward apologetically.

"Priscilla—King Theodoric of the Visigoths. My oldest friend, and most forward one at that."

" 'Forward'!" the king protested with a loud guffaw. "What kind of lies will he be feeding you next? Me, *forward*! My dear," he said, seizing her arm, "allow me to tell you . . ."

"Time enough later to become acquainted." Aetius smiled, taking his wife's arm to rescue her.

King Theodoric roared with laughter, slapping Aetius on the shoulder, and moved on. Behind him, a dignified older man, wearing a formal toga, waited patiently, a smile on his face. He stepped forward and embraced Priscilla, who hugged him happily.

"My daughter," the old man intoned. "You look lovelier than I've ever seen you. I've waited many, many years for this moment."

"Senator Carpilio, thank you for traveling such a long way for this occasion," Aetius said, with sincere gratitude. "It is indeed a privilege to finally join your family."

"The honor is all mine, General," the old man replied graciously. "I knew your father for many years, and we often spoke of our desire to unite our children. A pity you took so long! Though I must admit, when you first returned from the land of the Huns with that horrendous hair I feared I had made a grave mistake, promising Priscilla to you."

Aetius smiled. "I have had many duties, Senator. And

now your daughter is chief among them." He glanced proudly at the woman at his side.

A smartly coiffed woman in traveling clothes climbed the steps from the street and stepped forward, accompanied by her party: several female attendants, a trio of dignified foreign gentlemen, and a squadron of accompanying Roman cavalry guards. The other noble guests, still filing slowly out of the church, shrank back in surprise and deference, and even Carpilio bowed deeply and stepped away a respectful distance. The woman in traveling clothes, face flushed and damp from the heat, gracefully accepted the hand Aetius extended to her to assist her up the final step.

"General Flavius Aetius—forgive me for arriving late for your wedding," she said languidly. "We were delayed by weather in the Alps."

Aetius bowed his head politely.

"Lady Honoria—what an unexpected pleasure. Had I known sooner to expect the emperor's sister I would have prepared an escort to meet you in the mountains . . ."

Honoria laughed as she climbed the last step.

"Nonsense! You spend so little time in Ravenna I'm amazed you even recognize me. And this must be . . ."

Aetius introduced his wife. "My wife, Priscilla Aemilia. I'm sure you know her father, Senator Carpilio."

"A lovely bride," Honoria continued. "And lucky, too! You know, many a high-born Roman lady's heart is breaking this day, my dear. Our brave General Aetius is the catch of the empire—!"

She looked slyly at Aetius, whose gaze shifted impatiently to the next guests in line.

"Princess," he said in annoyance, "you travel alone, with only your maids?"

"Of course not!" Honoria laughed. "My brother scarcely lets me out of the palace alone, much less travel to Gaul!"

A well-built, muscular man stepped to her side and stared boldly at the general without deigning even to bow in greeting. Puzzled, Aetius studied his face, knowing he should be able to recognize the man but not quite able to make the connection.

"General," Honoria continued, "you've met my chancellor? He used to serve my mother."

"Of course—Eugenius, is it not?" Aetius recalled as he leaned forward to grasp the man's hand. "I remember you well from my presentation to the Empress Mother years ago. And now you serve the princess?"

Eugenius paused at the recollection of the insult he had suffered at the hands of the young general newly arrived from the land of the Huns, then allowed a slight smile to pass over his face. "I serve the princess in ways most satisfactory to us both," the steward replied in a low tone.

Aetius stared at him coldly. "Have you still not been promoted to eunuch?" he asked in a similar low voice before turning away dismissively.

Eugenius stiffened and glared angrily.

Ignorant of the men's brief exchange, Honoria prattled on. "The Augustus was sending an advisory mission to you from the eastern emperor." She glanced back to the three foreigners behind her, who nodded politely. "And since they were traveling to your city, I begged to accompany them—after all, the wedding of Rome's most illustrious general deserves official representation from the palace, does it not?"

Forgetting Eugenius, Aetius looked back at the princess, as if just then realizing she was still present.

"An advisory mission?"

"Oh, don't look so concerned, dear Flavius!" Honoria laughed, laying her hand gently on his forearm. "They're here to *ask* you for advice, not give it! Some question or other about your friend, that Hunnish king."

"Bleda?"

"Yes, of course," she replied. "You know him, do you not?"

"Slightly. His uncle, the late king Rugila, was like a father to me. But Bleda was unwell and stayed isolated in the palace the entire time I lived there, so I knew him but a little."

Honoria wrinkled her nose. "How charming. Still, perhaps you are the man they need to talk to about a little difficulty they are having. But enough of politics. We shall talk later."

Bowing to the princess and nodding to the ambassadors standing behind her, Aetius led his bride quickly through the honor guard of sweating swordsmen and to the entrance of a large villa adjacent to the basilica—his home while not on campaign, the governor's mansion. Just before sweeping through the doors and while receiving the greetings of the servants clustered outside to observe the proceedings, he paused to glance briefly behind him. Princess Honoria still stood exactly where he had left her, staring after him, a smile frozen on her face.

III

In the conference hall of the governor's palace the next morning, Aetius sat at the end of a long wooden table. He rarely scheduled meetings or events in the morning, preferring instead to spend the early hours of the day alone, drafting correspondence or reading the decoded dispatches that had arrived during the night from the various garrisons under his command. The room was plainly decorated, of simple stone and wood, more befitting an army officer's austere tastes than the bright colors and polished marble usually preferred by the empire's provincial governors, in imitation of the court in Ravenna. The raucous sounds of vendors and street life could be faintly heard through the thick stone walls and window holes, which were draped with heavy tapestries to keep the rooms cool during the heat of the day.

Florentius knocked on the door. Without even waiting for Aetius' response, he stumped into the room, the brass knob on the bottom of his wooden leg ringing sharply on the stone floor.

"General—the foreign visitors who arrived yesterday. I told them it was the day after your wedding, but they insisted you would agree to meet with them. . . ."

Aetius put down his papers. "Yes, I expected they might be early risers. Show them in."

Florentius nodded and disappeared. Moments later he returned, throwing the door open wide to let pass the three diplomats, now changed out of their dusty travel clothes and arrayed in brightly colored eastern silk robes, artfully arranged in the latest fashion from Constantinopolis.

"General Aetius," Florentius announced after thumping in behind them. "Ambassadors Plinthas and Epigenes of Constantinopolis, and the scribe Priscus."

Aetius gazed curiously at the three men as they stepped forward. The two envoys both looked to be in their mid-fifties, with neatly trimmed beards and hair cut in the severe straight-banged fashion of the eastern court. The scribe was young and eager-looking and clean-shaven of both head and jaw. He carried under one arm a small portable desk—a folding board, with a compartment for a stoppered bottle of ink and spare writing quills—and under his other arm a roll of several sheets of parchment.

As they entered the room, Aetius pushed back his chair and stood. "Good morning, gentlemen. I trust your lodgings last night were suitable?"

Plinthas nodded. "Quite adequate, General, for our simple tastes. Pardon us for interrupting you on the day after your wedding—but the matter is of some urgency, coming as it does from both your emperor and from ours."

Aetius shrugged and opened his hands in a welcoming gesture. Florentius loudly dragged three straight-backed wooden chairs up to the table across from Aetius.

"The day after my wedding," Aetius repeated. "It is of no concern—my wife knows she is married to a soldier, and absences are part of the bargain. Perhaps that is what attracted her to me in the first place." The diplomats chuckled politely. "Please be seated. Wine?"

Plinthas waved off the offer with a grimace. "Thank you, my lord, but now that we are no longer accompanied by the princess, I believe we would rather . . . um . . . eat our breakfast than drink it."

Aetius clapped his hands. A Gallic servant backed into the room through a side door with a tray of fruit and cheeses, and carefully arranged plates of the food in the center of the table. Plinthas and Epigenes each picked up a slice of cheese and morsel of bread and began nibbling elegantly, while Priscus gazed up at the ceiling and tried to ignore the rumbling in his belly until after his superiors had breakfasted. Aetius waited until the servant had finished setting the meal and had slipped out of the room. Then, as the door clicked shut, he leaned forward, impatience written in the expression on his face and the tilt of his shoulders.

"How may I be of service to you, gentlemen?"

Epigenes popped a piece of cheese into his mouth and dabbed appreciatively at his beard with a linen napkin. "General Aetius, as I'm sure you are aware, for some time now—many years, in fact—the eastern emperor Theodosius has been conducting . . . er . . . diplomacy among the tribes of the Danuvius."

Aetius looked at him sharply. "The tribes of the Danuvius? Along the Black Sea? In fact, I did *not* know that, though it explains some of their behavior. Nevertheless, those tribes are subjects of the Huns, and I know the Hunnish general Attila watches his foreign alliances closely. What manner of 'diplomacy' is the emperor conducting among them?"

The ambassadors glanced at each other warily but said nothing, each apparently waiting for the other to speak. Finally Priscus paused in his scribbling and broke the silence.

"Diplomacy of a financial nature, my lord," he muttered quietly, without looking up.

Aetius sat back in his chair. "I understand," he replied. "Bribes. Standard policy, of course, among both the Eastern and Western Empires. It keeps the trade flowing. And King Bleda of the Huns is aware of this?"

Epigenes shook his head uncertainly, but his colleague stopped his denial with a glance and then looked at Aetius with an exasperated expression.

"Oh, he has long suspected," Plinthas answered, "but he has had no proof. Until now."

Epigenes broke in. "We denied everything, of course, but a company of Hunnish scouts captured a bag of Roman gold and some . . . documents."

Aetius glanced at him suspiciously. "What kind of documents?"

"Certain . . . plans, my lord." Plinthas groped for words. "The bribes were not actually to facilitate trade relations with the barbarians. They were to, ah, install Hunnish leaders more, ah, sympathetic to Roman interests. . . ."

Aetius angrily slapped the palm of his hand down onto the tabletop. "You made plans to overthrow Bleda?"

"Merely plans and conjectures, my lord . . . ," Epigenes reassured him. "We felt that strategically it would be in the empire's interest if the Huns could be made more pliable, more . . . amenable to Constantinopolis' policy regarding trade routes and borders in the East. . . ."

"More *pliable*?" Aetius scoffed. "The Huns are already under pressure from their allies, particularly the Alamanni and the Ostrogoths. Those tribes are growing quickly, clamoring for more land and territory. Now that we have strengthened our own borders along the Rhine and Danuvius, they have nowhere to go. If you turn them against their Hunnish masters, how can you imagine that will be good for Rome? Either Bleda must react against his allies by overrunning them, which would bring the Huns themselves to our borders, with no Ostrogoth and Alamanni buffer between us, or Bleda will be overthrown, to be replaced by an even more powerful Hunnish leader who can stand up to the demands of his allies. The clan and tribal leaders would accept nothing less. Is either of these cases what you truly want?"

The ambassadors averted their gaze in silence.

Aetius softened his tone. "And what was King Bleda's reaction to your interference?"

Plinthas affected a defiant expression. "He is threatening war on the empire."

Aetius stood and began pacing the floor. "So Bleda has backbone after all. Nevertheless, the damage has been done."

"Indeed, my lord, the Huns have become more brazen than ever about their incursions into Roman territory across the Danuvius. Their herders and settlers ignore all boundary markers. . . ."

Aetius shook his head. "Boundary markers? Lines drawn on maps in the offices of Ravenna and Constantinopolis are meaningless to the Huns. No Hun rider would stop at a boundary marker. Few even understand the concept."

Epigenes cleared his throat. "Be that as it may, we thought that perhaps, given your personal experience with the Huns, you might suggest a course of action. . . ."

"A course of action? Of course I can suggest one. Tried

and tested by every Roman emperor for centuries." The diplomats eagerly leaned forward to listen. "It is not a secret. You pay the king off. Like everyone, he has his price. You were caught in the act; now take your penalty. Boys caught stealing orchard fruit are made to pay for it by their fathers. Any well-brought-up emperor should do the same. Apologize, pay the penalty, and retreat with honor."

The ambassadors looked at each other in dismay, and after a momentary pause, Epigenes raised a finger in objection.

"Indeed, the Huns have already made demands for financial reparations. But they are completely unacceptable to Constantinopolis."

Aetius stopped his pacing and turned to look at the Greek. "Unacceptable?" he asked, an amused expression on his face. "Is the eastern treasury not so full anymore as to ensure its safety from attack? You three do not seem to be suffering."

The two ambassadors looked down unhappily at their gold-ringed fingers and awkwardly placed them under the table, while Priscus took advantage of the pause in the conversation to reach for a slice of peach.

"If it were only the Huns," Epigenes continued, "we could certainly afford to pay off Bleda. But once word spreads that we have increased the stipend, every tribe from Pannonia to the Persian border will be demanding the same thing."

Aetius suddenly felt overwhelmingly bored with the discussion, no longer capable of feigning interest or even respect for these men who came feigning poverty and asking him to feign fear. He sat back in his chair and began absentmindedly leafing through a sheaf of papers. Priscus, who had resumed scribbling every word of the discussion in rapid and efficient shorthand, lowered his head to hide the amused smile that kept threatening to creep across his face in response to his superiors' discomfort.

"So don't pay the stipend to Bleda, then," Aetius said distractedly. "Go to war with him. That, too, is a valid and honorable option."

Plinthas stared at him in alarm. "My lord, perhaps we have been too vague in our meaning and in the purpose of our visit. Let me make myself very clear: The Eastern Empire alone is not capable of confronting the Huns, even if they are led by a weak king."

Aetius paused in his paper shuffling and looked at the men with exasperation. "Why do you come to me with this matter? It is your emperor's request to make and my emperor's decision as to whether to commit western troops. I am merely—"

"You are the Supreme General of Italy and Gaul," Plinthas interrupted. "The entire world knows who truly controls the military resources of the Western Empire. The heart of command, General, is here—in this room. You are an honest man. More important, everyone knows you are an honest man. Your counsel in this matter is crucial."

"I see," Aetius responded quietly. He again stood and began pacing, dismayed that his efforts to avoid involvement had been unsuccessful. Finally, he paused in front of the easterners and placed his hands on the table.

"Bleda is weak of body," he continued. "But he is also wily."

The ambassadors nodded in relief and even ventured small sidelong smiles at each other.

"However," he went on, "I am in no position to send troops to assist you. The Armorics are proclaiming independence in the northwest, and the Burgundians remain troublesome, even after the death of their King Gundahar only two years ago. And here, though Theodoric is my friend and the Visigoths are nominally our allies, still they are unruly. Hairy, painted giants who scarcely know a bath from a pig trough. With friends like these—"

"But you have Hunnish troops, do you not?" Plinthas interrupted.

Aetius shook his head impatiently. "A few auxiliaries only. Most were released after the Burgundian campaign, when their twenty-year hitches were up. They have returned to their homeland, or retired."

"But . . ."

"Your ruler was ignorant and offensive in his diplomacy," Aetius continued. "He cannot escape this situation with impunity."

The ambassadors' smiles abruptly disappeared.

"Despite Bleda's threats," Aetius said, "I suspect he wants war even less than you. His body is not strong, so he is unable to lead troops into battle, and would therefore have to assign this task to another man, and potentially lose control of his command. Yet he is still not to be toyed with. He has been ruling by sheer force of will for ten years now, ever since Rugila died, and for all I know he may do so for another ten. He cannot back down, for to a Hun, retreat is tantamount to dying. Nor would his clan leaders and barbarian allies even let him back down."

"What do you suggest?" Epigenes cut in impatiently. "Do we go to war with him, or not?"

Aetius looked at him pityingly. "I thought you easterners had a reputation for being crafty."

Epigenes looked away in annoyance.

"More important even than his will," Aetius continued, "is that Bleda is like his uncle Rugila, and has a true sense of honor. And for that reason alone, it is in your interest to keep him in power for as long as possible, for you do not know who might succeed him. An honorable man can be relied upon to keep his word. He will not surprise you, as you surprised him."

"Are you accusing us of dishonor?" Plinthas scowled.

Aetius shot him a glance that caused him to shrink back in his seat. "This is what you will do," he said, ignoring his guest's anger. "Call his bluff—but in secret. Tell him you will not pay his price. At the same time, you must allow him to save face before his barbarian allies and clan leaders. Otherwise even I cannot predict what might happen. Offer him a token increase in the stipend, so he can tell his warlords the Romans have been duly punished."

"But the other tribes!" Plinthas protested. "When they hear we have increased the payment . . ."

"They will not hear. As I said, the deal must be kept secret. Make the payment contingent upon his silence. Have him formally agree to confidentiality . . ."

Priscus looked up in surprise and spoke again, for the first time since his earlier interruption. "A contract? Make a Hun sign a contract? Of what use is that?"

Aetius looked at him sharply. "You are too accustomed to Roman traditions, scribe. Among the Huns, an oath is worth something. No paper is necessary. Indeed, it would be useless, as few Huns can read or write. All their scribes are Roman or Goth exiles."

Aetius glanced toward the door, indicating that the interview was over. Seeing this, the ambassadors rose to leave.

"Thank you, General, for your advice," Plinthas said curtly. "You are too kind."

Aetius nodded impatiently and began arranging the dispatches on the table. But as the easterners filed out the door, he looked up suddenly.

"One more thing."

The three men stopped in the doorway and looked back at him.

"When you deal with the Huns, leave me out of it. You did not speak to me of this matter. Is that understood?"

The three men nodded solemnly, and without further word Florentius ushered them out into the blinding sunlight, where the escort from the garrison stood patiently waiting to accompany them on their return journey.

SIX

Hunnia and Ravenna, A.D. 445

I

The massive procession wound through the muddy Hunnish streets, under an iron gray sky that threatened downpour at any instant. A wave of thunder rolled from the distant horizon and washed over the vast crowd of mourners, then just as swiftly swept past toward the opposite horizon. Another followed, rhythmic as the tide. Between surges, a drum beat slowly and deeply, the steady, hypnotic cadence smothered at regular intervals by the crash of a mournful gong. The overtones fluttered and rose in pitch, in dissonant counterpoint to the bass of the drum and the thunder.

Ten thousand people, and more—ten times ten thousand—wailed and keened wordlessly, swaying to their own rhythms, unconstrained by the pulsing beat of the drum and the rending cry of the gong. Some bent to pick up mud and offal from the street, which they smeared into their faces and clothing. Others tore at their hair, abrading their scalps until they were raw and bloody, or flailed at their flesh with leather horsewhips. Men and women alike ripped at their own clothing, baring themselves to the waist in their self-inflicted suffering, rendering themselves indistinguishable from one other, their torsos garbed in streaked layers of mud and blood.

At the head of the procession, marching slowly under

the command of the drum, a thousand armed warriors tramped stolidly through the crowd, their stern faces ignoring the pandemonium around them. In their midst, four identical dun-colored Hunnish ponies swayed slowly in a two-by-two deployment, linked to one another by poles and bearing between them a large wooden bier, intricately carved of ancient and precious wood imported at great cost from a distant place of heat and flood, a hundred days' march to the east.

On top of the bier was a sheet so densely and finely embroidered with swirling patterns of fantastic creatures and mythological images as to hide even the underlying linen fabric. With the rocking of the horses and the explorations of the wind, the silk-threaded creatures swayed and rippled on the sheet so vividly they seemed to be of another world—a world more colorful and exotic and terrible than the monochromatic dreariness of the glowering clouds above and the filthy street below, a fantasy world of dragons and wolf people and winged horses with bloodred eyes.

Resting under the embroidered linen sheet, with only the golden crown on his head exposed, lay a dead man.

The deep drum exploded in a frenzy of pounding, punctuated by the crowd's rising wail and the increasingly ominous roll of the thunder. The column of soldiers stopped at the edge of a small square, and an honor guard of eight foot soldiers, waiting for them in the center, marched stiffly to the bier. Seizing the leather grips fastened to each of the four corners, they carefully lifted it from the poles linking the four horses. They then hoisted the heavy platform to their shoulders, taking care not to tip it lest the precious burden be jarred or disturbed in any way. Without further pause, they carried it to the stone altar in the center of the space and solemnly set it down on the flat pedestal.

On all sides of the raised platform, dry brush and kindling had been loosely piled and drenched in naphtha. The heady, medicinal scent of the substance floated into the air around the altar, masking the stench of the streets. Stacked neatly onto the impregnated brush was the treasure of an empire: statuary and idols, chests of valuables, heaps of silver plate and ingot, thick bolts of silk. An elderly *qam*, a tribal shaman, stepped forward and breathed deep from the smoke of the holy herbs smoldering on a brazier beside him. Then, taking a long, sucking breath, he commenced a wailing chant of *sygyt*, the ancient and mysterious throat singing that allows its practitioners to sing in two voices simultaneously. Beginning with a low, guttural moan, he closed his eyes and hunched his shoulders in deep concentration, forcing the air through his throat and increasing the tone in strength and volume. The sound rose gradually to a harsh buzz that vibrated and resonated until it filled the altar, then the entire central square, floating even above the pounding of the drum. In ecstasy, his eyes rolled back into his head and forward again; the crowd hushed in awe and the pounding drum rose to a fever pitch. Suddenly a high flutelike overtone soared from his mouth, clear as the clinking of a glass, piercing the air to the farthest reaches of the square, even as the deep, anguished moan simultaneously remained as a bass counterpoint. The piercing harmonic, womanlike in tone, swelled and quavered, combining with the gravelly bass, weaving around it, yet remaining a separate, distinct note. Upon achieving the miraculous effect, the ancient priest sustained both tones for a long moment, his face darkening in effort and concentration, while the drum exploded to a final whirling crescendo and then fell silent. Only the high-pitched wail and the moan held the air, and then they, too, faded to nothingness. The *qam* slumped for a moment in exhaustion, eyes rolling in and out of focus; then he took a deep breath and reached into the brazier to lift out a lit brand.

A hundred thousand pairs of eyes stared avidly, almost hungrily, at the funeral pyre. The *qam* staggered forward through the strewn furniture and wealth, impeded by age and narcotics, eyes rolling and lips mouthing syllables incomprehensible to all but his own gods or demons. He stepped on the upraised nock-ear of a war bow, one of dozens taken from the armory and cast onto the pyre to assist the dead man in his journey through the Land Beyond. The bow sprang up and slammed against the old man's shin, causing him to stumble and almost fall. The crowd gasped as he paused, wincing in pain; and then once again they fell silent, and he resumed his path through the heaped treasure, to the stone altar in the center. There he stopped, raised his torch above his head, and stared into the crowd.

There are civilizations that preserve the dead bodies of their great men through clever embalming, through layers of linen wrappings, through entombment in vast stone edifices. There are even those who coat their dead with wax or pitch or immerse them in vats of honey, to dry and solidify like flies in amber. These are civilizations that remain fixed in place for generations and millennia and who seek for their dead men to remain fixed in time, so there is scarcely a difference between the dead and the living. These are peoples who stay immobile even with the passing of the seasons, who have lost the custom of traveling with their herds, whose cities are of granite, permanent and eternal.

The Huns are not such a people.

Life is transitory; the seasons change and the herds move on. The Huns' dead are afforded the greatest of honors. They are ushered to the next world with magnificent lamentations and feasting, the *strava* for which the Huns are justly famous. But they are not preserved.

As the *qam* stood with the smoking torch held above his head, a chant started, one syllable, a guttural, almost animal-like grunt from the back of the crowd, gaining in volume and intensity as it swept forward, like the thunder and drumbeats of a moment earlier.

"Fire! Fire! Fire!" the crowd roared, though the *qam* seemed not to notice, for he neither acknowledged the sound nor hurried his movements in any way.

Lips moving in inaudible prayer, he finally bent down, lifted the shriveled hand of the dead man from where it lay under the sheet, and carefully touched it first to his own forehead, then to both cheeks and mouth. Finally, he dropped it, almost carelessly, back to its former place on the motionless belly. Straightening himself once again, the *qam* looked to the sky and opened his mouth in a black, toothless scream, a sudden howl all the more startling for its soundlessness under the cries of the crowd. As he wailed his death song, the torch dropped from his hand into the impregnated brush at his feet. Flames exploded around the altar, leaping up the robes of the shaman, who stood motionless, his arms still raised high, head thrown back, and mouth opened wide in pain and ecstasy.

A sudden breeze arose, fanning the flames into an intense heat that licked at the chests of precious jewels, the rare silks, the priceless weapons and furnishings. In a moment, the *qam* collapsed backward into the fire. Black smoke swirled and drifted into the crowd, raising tears to the eyes and the stench of burning flesh and narcotics to the nostrils. Again the wind picked up, a strong gust this time, momentarily flattening the flames in front of the altar and clearing the acrid smoke from the people's view. Wind rippled and billowed at the heavy linen covering the body, and in a moment the fire recovered, stronger now than before with the steady fanning, and leaped, avid and hungry, at the hem of the embroidered cloth. Just as the roaring flames had completed their possession of the sacrifice, a last gust whistled through, flipping back the hem of the fabric from the head of the body and exposing the pink, gaping flesh wound across the throat, raggedly torn, rather than cut, as if by the teeth of a wolf—or the edge of a serrated blade.

The crowd roared in lamentation and ecstasy, and King Bleda stared one last time at the glowering, storm-laden skies of Hunnia before the braid of his hair burst into flame and his pale, gaunt face disappeared forever behind a curtain of black smoke.

On the desolate plain an hour's march distant, there was no sign of the event taking place in the Hunnish capital, just beyond view over the low, grassy ridge on the horizon. Indeed there was no sign of civilization, or even human habitation, for as far as one could see on every side. All was silent but for the wind whistling mournfully through the grass.

The three Roman diplomats and their small protective escort of *equitates,* cavalry guards, sat dusty and travel-worn on their tall warhorses, shoulders drooping in fatigue. Before them stood a large squadron of armed Hunnish warriors, mounted on hook-nosed ponies and garbed in full battle armor. The Romans towered over their Hunnish counterparts by a full head or more, perhaps two if the greater height of their horses were considered. However, the Hunnish squadron outnumbered the Romans by a factor of ten and carried spears and battle-axes unsheathed. More ominously, their faces bore not a twitch of intimidation, much less fear, at these short-haired trespassers on their oversized horses, who had arrived, as bad news periodically did, without announcement or fanfare, from the lands to the west.

"We have been sent at the behest of the eastern Roman emperor Theodosius Augustus to treat with King Bleda," announced Plinthas in the most commanding voice he could muster. When this elicited no response from the impassive faces before him, he sighed and considered his next words. He never failed to be confounded by these barbarians, who seemed unable to understand even the simplest Latin or Greek, as every educated individual in the world should be required to do. Again Plinthas raised his voice, speaking this time more loudly and slowly, certain that this technique would convey his message.

"We have been sent at the orders of the eastern Roman emperor . . ." he brayed harshly.

A broad-shouldered Alaman in Hunnish battle gear, his reddish hair pulled back in a warrior's braid, trotted forward from the back of the Hunnish squadron and cut short Plinthas' pronouncement with a sudden hiss, punctuated by an angry glare from his penetrating blue eyes.

"Iam audivimus, canis Romane," he intoned. "We heard you the first time, Roman dog."

The Alaman nudged his horse until he stood face-to-face with the Roman ambassadors. They fell silent at the unexpected sight of the pale-skinned barbarian commanding the squadron of Huns, at his display of Latin, at his baleful glare. Not a sound could be heard but for the rushing of the wind, which was beginning to gain speed and even seemed to be pushing them, with increasing urgency, into movement, toward or away, anywhere but here. The plain and the wind are intolerant of those who do not move, do not adapt—do not flee. The Alaman eyed them suspiciously, without a hint of welcome.

"You are too late."

"Too late?" Plinthas objected. "What do you mean, 'too late'? We have prepared an embassy to King Bleda, long may he reign, to convey a message from Emperor Theodosius. You would deny us the honor of expressing the emperor's good wishes?"

The red-haired warrior snorted, and Plinthas flushed with frustration.

"Emperor Theodosius has given us a commission!" he shouted. "Who are you to tell us our business?"

The Alaman stared at him unblinkingly, eyebrows raised in disdain.

"I am General Orestes, hereditary chieftain of the Silesian clan of the Alamanni, commander of the Hunnish royal bodyguard. King Bleda is dead."

There was a long pause. Neither side moved, and the rushing wind seemed to intensify, laden now with heavy drops. The gray thunderheads seemed to bear down on them with an almost physical weight, oppressive and suffocating.

"Dead?" Plinthas stammered. "We did not know! But then who . . . ?"

"Silence!" Orestes said in a low, menacing tone. "You did not know, because you did not ask, because in your damnable Roman arrogance you gave no thought to the changing circumstances around you. May your emperor fear and tremble at the might of the new leader of the united Hunnish peoples and allies. You will now be treating with . . ."

". . . King Attila!" General Turgrid bellowed to the intricately carved beams of the log ceiling as he raised his golden goblet high above his head.

A gong crashed, and the room exploded with laughter and cheering and with the shrill, dissonant keening of flutes. Fires blazed in hearths set in all four walls, and the large, lavishly decorated dining hall was bathed in the roaring heat and dancing light of the flames. Long tables had been arranged around three sides of the room, and a hundred finely dressed guests rose to their feet around them. All raised their exquisitely wrought gilded cups into the air, toasting their host, who stood placidly beside

his throne at the center of the middle table. A crowd of
unruly Hunnish boys, shave-headed and rambunctious,
giggled in the corners and jostled with one another to see
better. Turgrid stood in the midst of it all, bearing an un-
characteristic smile as he gazed at his expressionless
host.

Among all the glittering company and the elegance
of the palace furnishings and settings, Attila was the
most plainly dressed, his clothing more akin to that of a
servant than a king. Unlike his guests, many of whom
displayed their wealth and the trophies they had captured in battle, he wore no adornments whatsoever. No
silver brooches or buckles fastened his garments; no
embroidery or stripes hemmed his robes. His garb was
of the meanest and sturdiest oiled leather and sheep's
wool. And his austerity, whether genuine or feigned,
was not limited merely to his clothing. The cup he
raised to his lips was of crudely turned wood, cracked
and dried along the thick, rounded edge. The chair the
steward pushed in behind him was a hard, straight-
backed wooden affair, with an uncushioned seat, though
all the guests who took their own seats after him were
satisfied with plush leather pads stuffed with horsehair
and fitted at angles that allowed them to relax in positions of greater ease.

After the entire company had been noisily seated and
were tasting their wine at leisure, a gong rang for the second time. The guests looked up expectantly as a line of
servants filed in, each bearing a polished silver platter
of rustic presentation—mounds of sliced fruits and farls
of bread, bowls of steaming mutton soup, and boundless
platters of deep red, succulent meat.

Just as the servants entered, a pair of shave-headed
boys, the swiftest and most audacious of the grinning
mob huddling mischievously in the warm corner, burst
from one of the side doors. Between them, they bore a

large platter they had stolen from the kitchen, loaded high with steaming offal. They were followed a moment later by a cursing servant, and as the two urchins raced up to their comrades with the tray of delicacies they were accompanied by roars of laughter from the onlookers. When they arrived, a dozen thin brown arms shot out, spearing the boiled livers and stomachs with knives and thrusting them into hungry mouths. By the time the red-faced servant had threaded his way through the guests to the scene of the crime, the platter was empty and a dozen grinning faces stared up at him wide-eyed, their expressions ones of utter innocence, but for the bloody gravy dripping from their chins.

The servants fanned about the room and began serving the guests from the elegant platters—all, that is, but the lead servant, who moved straight to King Attila. Unlike his comrades, this man bore only a plain wooden trencher, containing a single large uncut shin of mutton, which Attila seized in his hands and began gnawing with his teeth. The guests feasted on more desirable meat and far choicer bits: the tender cheeks and brains of young kid, the tail nub of lamb, the shoulder blade, breastbone, and ribs of horse. For a time, all was utter gluttony, the only sound that of swallowing and chewing, as the guests tipped their platters to drink in the succulent juices, smearing fat on their collars and beards, rolling up their grease-soaked sleeves, and holding out their plates for more. As they became sated, voices again rose, in mirth and joking, until at length Attila stood, wiping his fingers on the hem of his tunic, and the room fell silent.

"In welcome to my clansmen, my sons"—he glanced fondly at the gap-toothed urchins grinning at him in the corner—"and especially our three Roman guests from the Eastern Empire, we are pleased to offer a sample of our humble Hunnish hospitality and entertainment. Treaties and alliances can be discussed tomorrow. Tonight, friends, we shall be merry!"

With a roll of drums, a troupe of Chinese acrobats burst into the room and launched into a series of outlandish contortions and throws, flying over the tables and the very heads of the astonished and ducking guests. From another corner, a new quartet of flutes suddenly began skirling in a quick tempo, and excited by the lively music and the whirling acrobats, a number of guests seized archery bows from their hooks on the wall and began plucking the strings with a rhythmic, discordant twang. In a burst of flame and acrid smoke, a team of fire swallowers leaped into the room and set the boys scurrying in all directions as flames erupted from the performers' mouths, threatening to turn the wall tapestries into an inferno. The hall rang with drunken shouts, and in the very midst of the chaos, a Moorish dwarf, Zercon, tumbled out from where he had been hiding under the table at Attila's feet. The tiny man had formerly been the buffoon of Bleda, who had given him as a gift to Aetius, who had passed him along to the Eastern Roman general Asper, who in turn had sent him back to the Hunnish court. The dwarf launched into a nonsensical song in a mixture of Hunnish, Gothic, and Latin, replete with broad sight gags and lewd gestures, that soon had the diners in stitches, despite the formidable distractions of the tumblers and flame throwers.

By the end of the evening, the guests were exhausted, bellies replete from swilling barrels of *airag* and decades-old wine, jaws slack from fine meat and fruit, and ribs aching from laughter. Every man, that is, but Attila, who had sat still and unapproachable, quietly pondering and observing the behavior of those around him. Throughout the evening, he had displayed not a trace of a smile, and his eyes—those thin black arrow slits of eyes, seeing all yet giving away nothing, absorbing everything yet yield-

ing only a faint expression of contempt—he had fixed
unwaveringly on the three red-faced, laughing Romans.

The next dawn witnessed the sordid aftermath of the previous night's entertainment. Around the room, covering
the surfaces of every table but for one that had been overturned, sat half-eaten platters of food and empty goblets.
Pitchers of wine lay tipped and broken, the dregs dripping slowly from the shards and onto the floor, and fat-
soaked linens lay crumpled and discarded under the
chairs. In the corner a Gothic nobleman, too drunk to
make his way through the narrow streets to his own
dwelling the night before, slumped groaning over the
table, a greasy chop bone protruding from his lips like the
tusk of a wild boar. A Chinese tapestry on the wall
smoked slightly and emitted a foul stench of burnt wool,
and in one corner a dozen small boys lay curled in a heap,
sated and snoring like so many piglets.

The three Romans, woozy and squinting from the
bright morning light outside, were led back into the
shadowy room they had left only a few hours before.
They picked their way carefully across the floor, skirt-
ing the disarranged tables. The steward announced their
presence in a grating voice that set the room's groggy
inhabitants to groaning in their plates, and the ill-used
ambassadors winced at the sound. Yet the dais where Attila had sat the previous night and where the steward had
obviously expected to find him now was empty. The
man shrugged and led them through a small side door
partially hidden by another tapestry hanging crookedly
on the wall.

As they entered the small anteroom, the ambassadors paused in surprise. From floor to ceiling, all four
walls of the room contained shelves groaning with
scholarship. Books, scrolls, papyri, codices of all
kinds, of every binding, in every size and condition.

Reclining easily on a couch in the corner was Attila, calmly picking at a leg of roasted fowl in one hand as he read a small traveler's volume of Strabo in the other. He still wore the simple garb of the night before, although in deference to the morning chill he had now donned a snug-fitting cap of marmot hide, and a woolen military cape. He made no acknowledgment of the ambassadors' presence, and indeed his eyes continued to scan the lines on the page for several moments until finally, with a grunt of satisfaction, he completed the passage he had been reading, closed the volume, and set it carefully on a nearby table.

"Wonderful geographer, Strabo," he remarked casually.

The Romans stared in wonder. Attila alone, of all the men they had seen that morning, seemed alert and even amused, and his expression appeared more contented than it had the night before—indeed, at seeing their surprise, the corners of his mouth even appeared to turn up in a wry smile.

"You enjoy geography, Great King?" Plinthas asked.

"Almost as much as seeing your look of incredulity that an ignorant barbarian can read. Yes, Strabo is clearly a master, as are Pomponius Mela and Arrian. Though I prefer Arrian in translation, as my Greek has become rather clumsy over the years."

The Romans gazed about at the book-laden shelves, at a loss for words.

"I trust you enjoyed the feast last night?" Attila queried politely, observing their puffy faces and unshaven chins. "A *strava* is the traditional Hunnish farewell to a king who has . . . died."

"Indeed, Great King." Epigenes nodded. "The wine was exquisite . . ."

"And the meat?" Attila persisted.

Plinthas looked up with a half smile. "The meat, Great

King, was delectable. Never have I tasted such delicate, tender veal—"

"Horse," Attila corrected him. The ambassadors stared at him blankly. "Unborn horse, to be precise. Stillborn foals. The flesh is of a quality most highly valued by my people."

The Romans blanched. At a nod from the chamberlain, however, they saw that it was time to come to the point.

"Great King," Plinthas continued, "we have been sent on behalf of Emperor Theodosius, who in his wisdom and magnanimity has empowered us to negotiate the terms of a treaty of cooperation between the Huns and the Eastern Roman Empire. We are to seek the conditions for a trade alliance between our two great nations—"

A flicker of amusement passed across Attila's face before he interrupted Plinthas.

"Trade?" he asked. "What might you have to trade, besides insults, and bribes to the enemies on my borders?"

Plinthas took a deep breath. "We have many things from which your people could benefit, Great King. Technology, for example. Weapons. Textiles. Works of art. Books! In exchange, you could provide us with iron. Horses. Luxuries from the East . . ."

Attila stared at him, unimpressed.

". . . gold," Plinthas continued. "Monkeys."

Attila raised one eyebrow. "Monkeys?"

Plinthas glanced down, disconcerted. "Perhaps not monkeys. In any event, we are empowered to negotiate the terms of cooperation between our respective nations. . . ."

"No you are not," the king stated simply.

Both diplomats stood silently waiting for a more complete answer. After a moment they concluded that the king had perhaps not understood Plinthas' words.

The diplomat opened his mouth to explain, glancing at his comrade. "My lord, we shall negotiate—"

Again Attila interrupted. "It takes two willing parties to negotiate. In this court, there is only one—you. There will be no negotiations between us."

Plinthas snorted in anger. "And what am I to tell the emperor?"

"What do I care what you tell your emperor?" Attila replied.

At this Epigenes broke his silence and stepped forward. "Have you no respect for our position? Have you no respect for the power of Rome?"

Attila stared at him coldly. Over the years he had become proficient in that art in which few men are truly accomplished, that of disguising all emotion. His face betrayed no more expression than that of a stone monument. "No. However, since you are so eager to discuss the setting of conditions and fulfillment of demands, I have several of my own. One: that your emperor swear never again to aid my enemies. Two: that he return to me all Huns currently serving in the Roman armies, both East and West. And three: that your empire's tribute be doubled, from three hundred fifty pounds of gold per year to seven hundred."

"But King Attila!" Plinthas protested. "Seven hundred pounds of gold—that is outrageous! Impossible! The empire—"

"Discussion is useless," Attila retorted dryly. "I have spoken."

"But King Attila! Be reasonable. . . ."

At this, Turgrid silently stepped from the shadows of the door behind them and saluted his king. He then turned to the three dismayed Romans.

"I will accompany you to the road south to Nyssa," he said simply.

Attila watched impassively as Turgrid and the Romans

filed out of the room, and then, as the door closed behind them, he turned to a side entrance.

"Orestes!" he called.

Immediately the tall Alaman, clad in a rough Hunnish tunic of felted wool, stepped into the room. Attila sat motionless for a moment, deep in thought, and then stood and walked slowly to an unadorned cedar chest in the corner.

"It is time," he said, "to carry out what we discussed many months ago. Do you still remember the site, my friend?"

"I do, Great King. I have ridden there several times since, on the hunt. It is still occupied by none but the old Goth farmer, a second-generation slave. He rotates his land, plowing only a third at a time and allowing the remainder to lie fallow the other years."

Attila opened the chest, peered in, and then tipped it to its side. With a clatter, a small collection of ancient hardware spilled onto the wooden floor: a pair of broken battle helmets, a rusty dagger, the head of an unusual battle-ax of Goth manufacture. Attila picked up each piece, examining them carefully.

"Rugila's battle trophies. He refused to keep plunder for himself—distributed it all to his warriors. His habit was merely to keep a personal memento of each man he killed."

Orestes remained silent, watching the king.

"This is what I was looking for," Attila continued. Unwrapping a length of greased cloth, he revealed an ancient, bent sword, its handle once inlaid with precious stones, most of them now missing. Holding the hilt tightly in his grasp, he placed the tip onto the floor at an angle and then stepped onto the middle of the blade, snapping it in half. Wrapping the two broken pieces neatly inside the cloth once again, he handed the small bundle to the Alaman.

"As we planned," he told Orestes. "Your tribe has long been one of my closest allies, and you have commanded many warriors as chief of the royal bodyguard in my service. When the time comes, you will command many more. I hold you to silence."

The Alaman nodded and departed as swiftly as he had appeared.

Turgrid and a Hunnish *zuun* accompanied the Romans out of the city. As they veered off the main road onto a sparsely traveled trail, scarcely more than a goat path, Turgrid explained that it was a shortcut to the more heavily traveled trade road to the south.

The Hunnish ponies trotted sure-footedly along the trail, which was only faintly visible, but the Romans struggled to keep up on their long-legged war chargers. Passing a stone outcropping, they noted a dozen pairs of timbers that had been erected in the form of crosses. They had clearly last been used many months before, for the bodies hanging on them were mostly skeletons. Nevertheless, they still bore traces of rusty armor and scarlet cloaks.

As the Romans passed by and realized what they were seeing, they pulled up in outrage.

"General Turgrid!" Epigenes roared out. "What is this?"

"What does it look like?" Turgrid replied coldly. "The place of execution, of course. Every city has one, does it not?"

"But . . . the scarlet cloaks!" Epigenes protested. "These are Romans!"

Turgrid stopped as well, reaching out and fingering the rotted hem of one crucified soldier's cape. He examined the fabric clinically.

"They used to be Romans," he said, "but they enlisted with us. A Hunnish soldier is a Hunnish soldier, regardless of his origin. If you desert from the Hunnish army, you are treated as a Hunnish deserter."

"But they're *Romans,* damn you!" Plinthas roared.

Turgrid seemed to consider this for a moment, as he gazed up into the vacant eyeholes of the skull of the crucified soldier. Turgrid dropped his hard gaze back down to Plinthas.

"They used to be Romans," he said, his voice soft yet menacing. "Now they are just dead."

Wheeling his horse, he again began trotting down the ancient path with his men. The Romans, dismayed and discouraged, had no choice but to follow.

II

In Ravenna, Plinthas and Epigenes stood nervously before the Emperor Valentinian, awaiting his response to their news. Only the scribe Priscus seemed untroubled by the emperor's potential reaction, and rather than shifting nervously on the balls of his feet as did his two superiors, he stood calmly behind them. He wore a bored expression as he contemplated the bald spot on the back of Plinthas' head, which had been spreading at an alarming rate in recent weeks. They had arrived in Ravenna from their long journey to Hunnia only the night before and had not yet even had time to steam the wrinkles from their silks before being summoned to the court. The diplomats' feelings of rumpledness and squalor merely added to their unease.

The young emperor had attained the age of majority only five years before and was still consistently bewildered at the position to which he had risen. Ostensibly he had been groomed for leadership of the Western Empire since the age of six. In fact, however, his mother and regent, Galla Placidia, had sheltered him not only from all responsibility but also from all opportunities even to *learn* responsibility. Upon her recent death, Valentinian had ordered her body carefully embalmed in imperial robes and seated in a position of command on a cypress-wood throne in the Chapel of Saints Nazarius and Celsus; yet though he visited and consulted her in the crypt daily, he found her to be of little assistance or comfort. In his strategic and day-to-day governance of the empire he now relied unconditionally upon the advice and guidance of two men: Flavius Aetius, Commander of the Legions, who divided his duties between the armies in Gaul and the palace in Ravenna; and Eugenius of Alexandria, Master of the Household.

But even they were not enough to give him full confidence in his current role. The absence of his mother had left a hole he had found difficult to fill, a deep desire for the closeness and comfort of family. Of his immediate relations, only his elder sister, Honoria, remained. And though she had never willingly demonstrated even the slightest interest in affairs of state, nevertheless he craved her company like that of an inseparable pet dog. This day, as she was accustomed to doing every day since the death of their mother, the princess remained in the atrium with Valentinian as he conducted the empire's business. Bored and vacant, she wandered listlessly among the courtiers and guests, listening absently. Yet even this half presence of his sister was a comfort to the nervous young emperor.

As the two diplomats finished the summary of their recent journey beyond the Danuvius, Valentinian stared at them, attempting an expression of nonchalance, feigning a confidence and knowledge of foreign diplomacy that he did not in the least feel.

"You say Rugila's nephew Attila is now in power?" he asked Plinthas. "Aetius, tell me: You knew this man Attila, did you not?"

Aetius, who was sitting at a table on the emperor's right, put down the diplomats' travel report he had been reading. "I did, Augustus, and there are many old ones here in the palace who can say the same. Attila lived here in Ravenna, in your uncle's court. He is honorable, but hard. We do not want war with him."

Eugenius, standing coolly at the emperor's left shoulder, smirked. "You almost sound as if you are afraid of him, General. I would have thought that to be unlikely for a man of your skills and resources."

Princess Honoria looked up with interest at the chamberlain's barbed comment. "Eugenius, that was unkind," she mockingly scolded. "Our general is not afraid of anyone—except me, perhaps."

"General Aetius," Plinthas cut in, "you call him an honorable man. And yet he threatens war against the empire! How do you reconcile—"

"Is this true, Lord Plinthas?" Valentinian interrupted timidly. "You have told us he is threatening war against the *Eastern Empire*. But here in the West, I have no quarrel with the Huns. Surely this Attila can be made a friend. . . ." The emperor's expression was fearful, almost pleading, making him appear even younger than he was.

Aetius sighed, wondering, as he had every day for the past twenty years, how a mere stripling could ever have been put in the position of emperor.

"With all due respect, Augustus," he explained, "the Huns make little distinction between the Eastern and Western Empires. The two empires have supported each other in ventures in the past, particularly against the barbarians. Therefore Attila has good reason to view both as one. In that sense, he perhaps anticipates your own ambitious dreams, does he not?"

Valentinian smiled slightly. "Yes . . . perhaps. A very clever man, Attila."

Aetius continued. "What is important, however, is that

Attila has lived many years in Ravenna. He is familiar with the empire; he speaks fluent Latin; he knows Roman custom. . . ."

Eugenius turned impatiently to the king, causing the young ruler to start slightly at his chamberlain's vehemence.

"Attila 'knows' Rome? Utter nonsense! Look at the treaty Lord Plinthas has brought us. How can that rogue expect any nation, even Rome, to pay seven hundred pounds of gold each year to a band of barbarians!"

Aetius snatched the sheet of parchment away from Eugenius and slammed it on the table. All in the room fell silent.

"You are correct, chamberlain—this treaty is outrageous. And what is even more outrageous is that the eastern emperor signed it."

"What choice did he have?" Plinthas shot back. "Now, concerning the seven hundred pounds of gold the lord chamberlain so perceptively mentioned: Since both Eastern and Western Empires are at risk in this case . . ."

"Hang the seven hundred pounds!" Aetius retorted, shocking the others again into silence. "Can you not see beyond the gold?"

"Seven hundred pounds is a considerable sum, General," Epigenes responded gently.

"The gold doesn't matter," Aetius continued. "Not in the slightest."

Eugenius laughed disdainfully. "Then you pay it. I wager you've gathered a bit of a stash during your years in Gaul."

Aetius ignored him. "More important, Attila doesn't care about the gold."

"What do you mean?" asked Valentinian, his face bobbing back and forth between Aetius and Eugenius and his cheeks flushed with the excitement of the argument.

Aetius held out the treaty for the emperor to view.

"This is the key clause: 'Return all Hunnish expatriates serving Rome.' That is what Attila wants. That is his trump."

Valentinian was confused. "But why would he demand such a thing? Surely he is not short of men. I understand that with his allied coalition he commands almost a million already."

"That is not the point," Aetius explained gently. "There are thousands, perhaps tens of thousands, of Hunnish expatriates in Roman auxiliary units scattered all about Europe and Asia, familiar with Roman weaponry, language, motives, tactics. And now all of them will be brought back into the Hunnish fold."

"But would he dare to attack the West?" the emperor persisted.

"Not without a pretext, he would not," replied Aetius.

Eugenius looked at him skeptically. "A 'pretext'?"

"Of course," Aetius replied. "He needs justification—a reason for calling together his allies, an impetus to attack. Attila does not view war as an end—it is a means—and he would have to give his clan leaders and allies a true motive to risk their men with him in such a venture."

The emperor pondered this for a moment in silence before finally leaning forward and locking his gaze on Plinthas.

"Then," the emperor said slowly, "we must avoid at all costs giving him such a pretext."

III

That night, Aetius stepped out of the private apartments he used at the palace during his visits to Ravenna and crossed through a short gallery to a large courtyard, open to the night sky. All was silent but for the soft splashing of the fountain in the center, and a cool breeze floated the heavy scent of climbing wisteria to his nostrils. As he looked about, he realized that this was the very courtyard in which he had witnessed the "mythology" party years ago. It was amazing to him to consider that that young soldier from Hunnia would within a few years become the most powerful man in the Western Empire. *How the wheels of fortune change,* he thought. *And how one must be careful, lest they roll back whence they started.*

He breathed deeply, relieved to be out of the stuffy rooms and in the fresh air, but was startled out of his reverie by the sudden crash of ceramic breaking behind him. Glancing back, he saw a large shadow flit behind a column, and he sighed.

"Magnus, come out," he called quietly into the darkness, and after a moment of silence the servant stepped sheepishly out, head hung, right foot bleeding from the flowerpot he had stumbled into and booted across the courtyard like a ball.

"What are you doing lurking about at night?" Aetius said calmly, and not expecting an answer, he turned along a gallery that led toward the far side of the palace compound. The giant fell into shuffling step behind him.

"Flavius—*m-m-mi-les,*" Magnus said softly after a moment, and Aetius stopped and turned to look at him. He thumped his chest with his fist. *"Mi-les,"* he repeated.

Aetius shook his head. "The emperor needs you here at the palace." Magnus looked down in disappointment. "My friend, it's time you were off to bed. I'm taking a bit of air and then I will turn in, too. Good night."

Magnus stared dumbly for a moment and then nodded, turned, and began shuffling back the way he had come.

Aetius continued his stroll and looked up. It was rare that he could afford himself the luxury of a few moments of leisure to contemplate the stars. But after squinting into the darkness for a moment he looked back down in annoyance. Half his life he had spent in the open plains of Hunnia and the stony hills of Gaul, with views unimpeded by so much as a scrub tree. While visiting Ravenna or the other cities of the empire, he could never accustom himself to the difficulty of seeing the stars and planets. On the sides of the buildings all around were torches to light up the galleries and courtyards, lending a bright cast to everything he saw. Impossible to view the stars under these conditions. Even Venus, which he still thought of by its Hunnish name, the shepherd star *zolbon*, was obscured by a rooftop. Looking around, Aetius spied a tower at the corner of the palace compound, with a flat terrace on the top surrounded by a low iron rail. He began walking toward it and then stopped. The door at the base of the tower was closed and most certainly locked. How to get to the top?

His thoughts were interrupted again by the sound of a torch being knocked off the wall behind him, and a grunt.

"Magnus," he said, this time without even turning around to look. "How does one climb to the top of that tower?"

He heard the giant shuffle slowly up behind him. *"S-s-stellae?"* the deep voice queried.

Aetius nodded. "Yes, *stellae*, the stars. I wish to see the stars."

He turned and saw Magnus' expression of concern, the stern shaking of his head. Magnus pointed to another tower at the opposite corner of the palace compound.

"Too far," Aetius objected. "I'll climb this one. Surely there is an exterior stair." Magnus glanced at the side of the tower, and when Aetius followed the line of his gaze, he could make out a narrow passageway, almost hidden in the shadows.

The big man looked back at Aetius, his expression still nervous, and shook his head, this time adding what he thought was a nonchalant shrug.

"Is there a staircase in that passageway, Magnus?" Aetius asked.

Magnus paused a long moment and then, barely perceptibly, nodded his head.

Aetius smiled. "The most honest man in the empire," he said, reaching into the purse at his belt. "Here, Magnus—buy yourself a cup of wine, and go to bed."

Leaving the giant standing helplessly in the courtyard, he strode into the passageway and up the staircase.

Moments later Aetius passed through the door at the top and onto the rooftop terrace, which was furnished with comfortable lounge chairs and small tables. A single oil lamp guttered in a corner. He stepped to the edge of the terrace, grasped the cool iron railing, and gazed down at the silent city before him in the moonlight—streets and plazas, the luxurious manors of the wealthy clustered close to the palace walls, beyond them the customhouse and other government offices, the central baths, and still beyond them the hundreds of *insulae,* the apartment blocks and tenements housing the city's workers and poorer inhabitants. Over it all, the low moon hovered like a brilliant golden shield, unimpeded by the surrounding buildings. Just then he heard a woman's voice behind him.

"I was hoping you'd come. I saw you standing in the courtyard below."

Annoyed at the interruption, Aetius turned and peered into the shadows. Seeing nothing, he seized the small oil lamp and walked toward the voice.

Honoria sat half-reclining on a lounge chair, wearing a thin silk dressing gown tied at the waist, which had fallen open to the navel.

"Princess—pardon me for disturbing you," Aetius said. He averted his eyes to allow her to arrange her clothing, but Honoria made no move to do so. Rather, stretching catlike and emitting a slight yawn, she smiled up at him in the lamplight.

"I couldn't sleep, and came up here for a cup of wine. I must have dozed off."

Aetius bowed slightly and began walking back to the stairway, but Honoria sat up and called him back.

"General, please—sit here beside me."

Aetius stopped and turned. Walking back, he sat down at the end of the couch. Honoria watched him, her eyes glittering in the lamplight.

"Why do you always avoid me?" she asked. She bore a slight amused smile.

"Far be it from me to avoid you, my lady," he said distantly. "I am a busy man."

"Busy, busy. The priest always advises me to keep myself busy to avoid temptation. 'Idle hands are the tools of the devil,' he tells me."

"Wise words. I merely do my duty, my lady."

"And you must be very proud for doing it so well— such determination, such steadfastness. . . ."

He peered at her closely. Despite her mocking tone, she had raised a notion he always found strange. *Proud* to do his duty? How could that make him proud, unless he only did it sometimes? He would just as soon be proud of eating his breakfast as of doing his duty. To be proud would be a sign of how infrequently he actually did his duty and how little shame he saw in not doing it. Could anyone but a fool be proud merely of not being shameful?

"Is that why you keep yourself so busy?" she pressed. "Are you fleeing temptation?"

Aetius allowed himself a wry smile. "Fleeing temptation? No, Princess, I am burdened with business of state, with your brother's affairs. I have no—"

"Have no what?" Honoria interrupted. "Temptations? We all have them, General; we all have our appetites."

"Perhaps, my lady."

"Me, for instance. You and I have known each other for

many years, and yet you avoid me. Do you not think it propitious—as if fate had a hand—that we now find ourselves in almost exactly the same place as when we first met?"

Aetius looked at her coldly. "I am a married man, Princess."

Honoria laughed, with a scoffing flip of her hand. "What, plump little Carpilia?"

"Priscilla."

"But General, everyone knows it's a marriage of convenience. She happened to be of good family, the right rank, a prefect's widow—virgins are so hard to come by these days—and at the same time, you needed a wife with a suitable dowry. A fine arrangement, I would say. I would also say this: So what?"

Aetius smiled warily. "So one woman is enough. How any man could handle more I'll never know. . . ."

Honoria sighed loudly in exasperation. "Are you willfully misunderstanding me, my dear general, or are you simply beyond all tempting?"

"With all due respect, Princess . . . I do not betray my wife."

"Then don't! Divorce her. Pay her off. They all do it. Every girl has her price, no?"

Aetius stared at her in silence.

"And then," Honoria concluded with a triumphant flourish, "marry me."

Aetius scoffed. "Marry you!"

"Oh, it's quite simple"—Honoria smiled—"and logical as well, which your steel-trap mind should appreciate. You are the most powerful man in the empire, apart from the emperor. I am the emperor's sister—which makes me the most powerful woman in the empire. A perfect match, don't you think? And—"

She snuggled close to him on the couch, and he smelled the strong scent of wine on her breath.

"—I can make life much easier for you than little Carpilia."

Aetius sat immobile, staring into the moonlight. Despite his repugnance for this woman, he felt a flutter of intrigue.

"Easier," he repeated. "How so?"

"Don't play dense with me, Aetius," she snapped. "Marry me. Valentinian will not be siring any children— trust me on that, unless eunuchs learn to give birth. *You* will be next in line for the throne . . ."

She took his fingers in her hands.

". . . and first in line for this."

With a swift movement, Honoria slipped his hand inside her open gown, then leaned back against him, eyes closed, purring like a cat at the warmth of his fingers.

Aetius sat motionless. Never, perhaps, in the history of Rome had any man held so much potential, so much power, in his five fingers. With one slight squeeze of assent, one soft stroke across the smooth curve of her breast, all of Rome, the entire Western Empire, the title of Augustus, could be his. The emperor was merely a puppet, easily maneuvered, capable of being cleanly disposed of if need be. The legions were loyal to Aetius, and though their support alone might not be sufficient, a marriage to Honoria would more than tip the balance in his favor. The slightest twitch of his finger, the gentlest rub against her warm flesh, would make all the difference, in his career and his life and possibly the very fate of Rome.

Still, he remained frozen. Staring at the moon, he realized that Priscilla might at that very moment be gazing at the same orb, thinking of him as she strolled about their villa in Gaul at the end of the day, kissing the children good night before the maids bustled them off to bed. Her face, pink and plump, filled his vision, and he recalled the first time he had thought of her, of the possibility of marriage to her, of the entirely different kind of potential from the one he faced here. His father—dead these so many years—had made the initial arrangements, had proudly broached the subject with his son, advising him of the advantages of the match, and all Aetius could think of at the time was his Hunnish troops, his next great adventure. His father's voice whispered softly in his head, growing louder and more distinct, and his weathered face soon replaced his vision of Priscilla. What was it he had said? What was it Aetius had neglected, had lost sight of, in the confusion and challenges of court politics and command of the legions all these years?

Rome is honor and nobility. . . . You must always strive to overcome the reality *of Rome. . . .*

Impatient with Aetius' hesitation, Honoria leaned closer against him, arching her back slightly, adjusting herself under the warm weight of his hand as she turned her head toward him, smiling and lusty.

"I'm the prize and the empire is the bonus," she murmured dreamily. "Or is it the other way around?"

Aetius suddenly jerked his hand away and stood up, while Honoria's eyes fluttered open in astonishment.

"Rome is not a piece of fruit to be haggled over in the marketplace," he said simply, his voice controlled and icy.

Honoria leaped to her feet and furiously yanked shut her robe.

"Who do you think is doing the haggling?" she snapped. "Piece of fruit! You may know how to seize every moment in battle, General, but you will regret missing this opportunity."

Aetius nodded and bowed his head in sarcastic reverence. "It will have been my pleasure to miss such a chance, my lady."

"No, *my* pleasure, you thickheaded fool. And I take my pleasure where I will."

Seizing a tiny bell she had placed on the table beside

her, she rang it impatiently. Footsteps sounded in the outer corridor and the door opened behind her. Aetius tensed. With no backlight, the door was simply a black opening, and the person entering the terrace was unidentifiable. Without even looking back, the princess spoke.

"Eugenius, show General Aetius out. Out of the building, out of Ravenna, and out of the empire." She shot a malevolent glance at Aetius before puckering up her face in a forced expression of distress. "He has tried to . . . take liberties with me."

At the princess' words, Eugenius smiled and stepped into the light. Aetius' eyes narrowed in contempt. Honoria gave her steward a long, lingering glance and then a sly smile crossed her face. She glided in front of Aetius, to Eugenius' side, and placed her hand lightly on his shoulder.

"I've changed my mind," she said, her voice quavering as she wiped a tear from her eye with the sleeve of her dressing gown. "Eugenius, you stay. The general can find his own way out. We shall make his travel arrangements tomorrow."

"As you wish, my lady," the steward smirked.

Aetius strode out angrily. As he returned down the dark stairs, out the passageway, and into the courtyard, he nearly collided with Magnus, who stood in the shadows, a hangdog expression on his face.

"You knew they were upstairs all along, didn't you?" Aetius demanded. "That's why you refused to show me the way." But he was in no mood for conversation, nor did Magnus have any words to contribute. "Hell, we've both been in Ravenna too long," Aetius growled, and brushed roughly past the giant, who remained where he stood, watching in the shadows.

Aetius strode through the marbled galleries, his expression set in silent fury. Everything seemed magnified, out of all proportion to their true essence—stars glared at him like stage lights; the tinkle of a tiny corner fountain grated on him like the sound of breaking glass. At the edge of a darkened courtyard, the night trail of a snail glowed with mysterious phosphorescence, forming glistening, accusatory script at the base of the wall. Thoughts raced through his mind—of his career, of the safety of his family, of the future of Rome. He briefly considered reporting the conversation with Honoria immediately to the emperor—then discarded that idea, for though the emperor was dependent upon him for advice, if it came to his word against the princess', there was no doubt whose side Valentinian would take. He would lose the battle for the emperor's allegiance, be made to look a fool, and be deemed a traitor besides, for accusing the emperor's sister of . . . what? Tempting him? In his anger he almost laughed out loud, that she had struck so deeply with her weapon, yet he, the Commander of the Legions of the Western Empire, had not a single defense with which to counter her. Is a man's fate so fragile that he can be brought down by such a small thing—while remaining innocent no less? The stars glared at him all the more brightly.

He hardly had time to work through the ramifications of the ill-fated encounter when, rounding a final corner on his way to his apartments, he came face to face with the emperor himself, who was passing beneath an archway, conferring in low tones with several courtiers. A pair of armed praetorian guards stood at attention close by. There was no opportunity for Aetius to reverse his path, to delay the meeting until a later time. The young emperor had already seen him.

"Ah, General Aetius," Valentinian said, reaching out to place his hand on Aetius's shoulder and to feign a camaraderie and superiority of position he always felt lacking when in his officers' presence. "I was just going out for some fresh air before bed. Why are you wandering the corridors at this hour?"

Aetius' expression was stony. "Just clearing my mind, Augustus. If you will excuse me, I am very tired. I'm sure you would prefer a moment of solitude, rather than my poor company."

The emperor stared at him in surprise, then smiled. "Not so!" he rejoined with false enthusiasm. "But I understand. I'm feeling a bit tired myself. Good night." He turned back to his courtiers. "Come. Allow the general his rest."

Aetius bowed, walked past, and turned the corner out of their sight. Suddenly he heard a loud crash of ceramic and a grunt. He stopped dead in his tracks and listened.

"Ah, Magnus!" the emperor called out jovially.

There was the sound of heavy feet shuffling along the flagstones and then stopping.

"What are you doing out here so late at night? I thought you turned in early?"

There was a pause and then a single, stuttered word. "S-s-stellae."

Aetius turned. Was that simpleton Magnus now talking to the emperor?

"Stars?" the emperor replied. "Ah, the stars! Wonderful idea, Magnus! I enjoy stargazing myself. I remember that very tower—I often climbed it with Mother, though I haven't been up since she passed away. It has a splendid view from the rooftop. Well, good night, Magnus. Oh, here—buy yourself a honey cake in the morning. . . ."

Aetius stood dumbfounded as he listened to the footsteps grow fainter and then disappear.

A moment later, Valentinian and his party began climbing the external staircase to the tower. Reaching the top, slightly breathless, he opened the door and strode onto the rooftop. At the sound of a woman's surprised yelp, the timorous emperor leaped back, startled. The two praetorians rushed forward, swords drawn, and peered about in consternation, their eyes still adjusting to the dim rooftop, lit only by the moonlight and the guttering lamp. Valentinian himself was the first to make out the source of the noise. With a triumphant smile, he spied a nude couple beside a couch near the railing, scrambling on the floor to disentangle themselves and find their clothes. Their skin glowed pale in the soft moonlight.

"What are you . . . ? Get away from here!" the woman shrieked.

The young emperor was highly amused at finding such entertainment when he had been expecting pensive solitude. "Oh ho," he chortled, "and who is this?"

Seizing a torch brought in from the hallway by one of the courtiers, he approached the struggling couple like a hunter circling his quarry trapped in a net. "Better than a masquerade," he laughed. "The lovers only have two hands. If they use them to hide their bodies, I'll spy their faces. If they hide their faces, all the better!"

But his own face turned ashen when the light of the torch fell full upon them.

"Honoria?" he said, frozen in astonishment, and his high voice cracked and rose in pitch as the impact of what he was seeing sank in. "And . . . Eugenius? . . . My chamberlain? The palace *chamberlain*?! Sister, I'll have you flogged! What would Mother have thought . . . !"

Below, Aetius stood in the shadows, listening to the sound of scuffling and confused voices. Suddenly three figures appeared on the staircase outside the wall and began descending. When they reached the bottom and stepped into the torchlight, he recognized the emperor's two praetorians, dragging Eugenius, naked and furious. The guards struggled up to Aetius, who stood motionless while they paused to adjust their grip on their writhing captive.

"Aetius—you jackal!" Eugenius hissed at him furiously. One of the praetorians struck him a blow across the face with the butt of his spear.

Aetius nodded and stared impassively. "Congratulations, Eugenius," he said quietly. "I believe you will finally be getting your promotion to eunuch."

The praetorians grinned, firmed up their grip, and dragged the chamberlain down the corridor and out of sight.

The cell had plain stone walls, a table, a chair, and a small cot. A thin shaft of sunlight filtering through a high window illuminated the table brightly, though the rest of the room remained obscured in shadows. It was not damp or cold; the floor was paved with rough-cut flagstones rather than left as packed dirt; and there were no leaks, spider holes, or other inconveniences. But it was a prison nonetheless, with bars on the window and a heavy iron brace on the thick oaken door.

Honoria sat hunched over the table, feverishly scratching out a long letter with a quill. Her hair was unkempt, and it had been weeks since she had bothered to wear makeup. Her jailers were little impressed with beauty, and it was impossible to keep up appearances under these conditions in any case. She poured a bit of wine into a plain wooden cup from an earthenware flagon on the table and gulped it quickly, silently saying a prayer of thanks that her brother had at least allowed her that meager luxury. Finally completing her letter, she signed the parchment with a flourish, folded it, and then refolded it into another, larger piece of parchment. Removing the signet ring from her right hand, she had just seized the candle and was preparing to drip wax onto the envelope to seal it when she paused.

Carefully holding the ring to her eyes, she gazed at it for a moment in thought. Then coming back to her senses, she kissed it and, rather than pressing it into the hot wax, hastily stuffed it inside the envelope. Closing the fold, she dribbled a bit of wax onto the edge but then hesitated, at a loss because now that she had inserted the ring into the envelope, she lacked a signet to press into the seal. With a quick smile, she jabbed her thumb into the wet wax, blew the seal dry, and scribbled quickly on the outside of the envelope. Giving the final product one last, hasty inspection, she nodded in satisfaction, then rang her tiny bell.

After a moment, the jailer's footsteps could be heard approaching, and he stopped, slid open the viewing window, and peered in with suspicious eyes.

Honoria looked up and sighed. "Not you, idiot!" she snapped. "Bring my girl."

The window slammed shut, and a moment later fearful female eyes appeared through the hatch. Honoria stood and passed the envelope through.

"Give this to Marcus the courier. Hurry now! He can use the post relay stations. Tell him it will earn him fifty gold pieces if he delivers it quickly."

The maid nodded and disappeared.

Moments later, after a breathless trot to the stables, the girl handed the missive to a young, fit-looking rider, who was currying a sweating horse.

"What's this?" he asked in dismay. "I've just arrived, from Neapolis. Does your mistress not even allow me half a day to wet my gullet and go to the baths?"

"Half a day?" the servant girl retorted. "I haven't had half a day free since I began working here. And to wet your gullet no less! Who's to say you would only be gone half a day?"

"Ah, well, if you don't trust me—you can come with me then, Lavinia, to keep an eye on things." He reached around and gave her a full-handed pinch on the haunches. "Easy to get distracted in the baths, if you don't have a bodyguard." He winked.

Lavinia yelped and slapped his hand away, though smiling in spite of herself.

"For shame! A pity, too. I suppose I'll have to find another courier. Mistress was in such a hurry to have this letter delivered, she promised fifty gold pieces when the rider returned. . . ."

Marcus stepped forward and snatched at the letter, but Lavinia backed away.

"Fifty gold pieces!" he exclaimed, grabbing her around the waist and struggling to reach the letter in her outstretched hand. "I'd ride to Hell and back for that!"

Lavinia giggled and planted a kiss on his cheek. "For this one you may have to."

The boy stopped and smiled, touching his cheek. "You haven't done that before! What's the occasion?"

She thrust the letter into his hand and skipped away. "This. Good-bye! See you next fall!"

As she slipped through the stable doors, he looked down at the scribbling on the outside of the envelope and his face darkened.

"God save me. Attila, king of the Huns?" He stood lost in thought for a moment, his lips moving silently as he calculated the distances he would be required to travel. He gave his horse one last swipe of the curry brush.

"See her next fall," he muttered, "if I'm lucky to be back that soon!"

He climbed up onto the saddle and trotted through the stable doors.

IV

Attila sat in the dark, smoke-filled great hall, with Turgrid standing just behind his right shoulder. They were surrounded by a cadre of hard-looking military men, the chiefs of his Gothic and Hunnish forces. The room had changed dramatically since the night of the feast—the walls hung bare, without a tapestry to soften the rough-planed fir planks; the tables had all been pushed to the edge of the room and tipped to their sides, but for a small one drawn up in front of the throne and stacked with a variety of parchments and maps; and even the fireplace remained dark and cold, despite the late-summer chill and the approaching dusk. The officers were dressed just as austerely, and some even wore sweat-stained riding togs and bore streaks of mud on their boots. Only the presence of a half-dozen shave-headed little boys, Attila's ubiquitous sons, softened the harshness of the room as they scampered about the bare floor and bickered over some scraps of food. The smallest one lost out in the tussle and ran tearfully to Attila, crying to be lifted onto his lap. The king did so absentmindedly, without glancing down, as he carefully read the dispatches being handed to him.

"This one just arrived, my lord," said Turgrid, handing him a worn, folded sheet of parchment. "From the Roman court in Ravenna."

Attila looked at the envelope curiously. "A strange seal, is it not? This looks almost like a thumbprint."

As he slit open the seal with his finger, a ring fell out and clattered onto the table in front of him. He picked it up and examined it.

"The letter 'H'," he said, surprised. "Emperor Honorius? That brute has been dead for years now. I know the mail is slow, but . . ."

"No, my lord," said Turgrid, peering over his shoulder at the strange letter. "It's from the Princess Honoria, Emperor Valentinian's sister."

"His sister? Why would his sister . . . ?" His voice trailed off into silence as he rapidly scanned the document.

"This is very strange," he said after a moment, setting the letter on the table and absently squeezing the shoulder of the young urchin he dandled on one leg. "She says she's been unjustly imprisoned and denied a trial . . . and that as a fellow sovereign I am duty-bound to assist her. She sends this personal signet ring as proof of her identity."

He looked up, half-smiling, while the men chuckled.

"She's always been a bit 'off,' my lord," Turgrid cautiously explained. "Loose with the wine, and with the men. Her brother, the emperor, has never been successful in matching her to a husband—she's too much the hellcat, I imagine. He probably locked her up for safekeeping."

"Ha!" Attila exclaimed. "So now *I'm* her Hercules, who will rescue her from her wicked brother. What a tale for housewives! With the ring, it sounds almost like a marriage proposal!"

The men laughed again, even more loudly, but this time Attila did not join in. Rather, he stared vacantly into space, idly sliding the ring up and down his little finger.

"Like a marriage proposal . . . ," he repeated.

In the court of Ravenna, the young emperor sat in the map room surrounded by courtiers, quickly scanning dispatches as they were handed to him. Aetius, wearing riding gear spattered by the morning's autumn rains, sat at the ornate marble table directly across from him, pointing out important passages in the documents and explaining them to the young emperor. Suddenly the small group of advisors parted and the room fell silent as Marcus the courier rushed into the room, breathless and dirty, trailed by an exasperated eunuch.

"Begging your pardon, Augustus," Marcus interrupted, extending a letter. "Just arrived. An urgent dispatch for you."

Valentinian raised an eyebrow and grinned mockingly. "Oh? Where from this time, Marcus? Thought you might have left us. The servant girls have been moping about all summer."

Marcus blushed. "From the Hunnish capital, Augustus."

Valentinian reached out and took the letter, though with some trepidation. Before breaking the seal, however, he paused.

"The more I learn about your Huns, General Aetius, the more I dislike receiving communications from them," he said, turning the folded parchment over in his hand. "It reminds me of when I once snuck into the palace cellars as a boy and put my hand into an apple barrel and felt something furry inside. I wasn't sure what it was, but I knew it wasn't good."

Aetius looked up for a moment absentmindedly, then returned to the dispatch he was examining. The emperor tore open the outer parchment, and as he did so, a gold signet ring dropped into his lap, which he picked up with puzzlement. After a moment, he let his hands drop onto the table.

"And I'm positive this is not good," he said.

Aetius glanced at the ring. "That looks like Honoria's signet. How did it come to be in the Huns' possession?"

Valentinian slowly unfolded the letter and read it to himself. "Oh God."

Aetius flashed a sharp glance at the curious courtiers to ward them away, then stood and reached over to take the letter from the trembling hands of the emperor. The general scanned the parchment quickly, then looked up, staring into the distance.

"Attila agrees to the princess' offer of marriage and will gladly accept half the Western Empire as his rightful dowry," Aetius intoned. His voice was calm, but his jaw tightened in anger.

The court fell speechless as every man stared at the emperor, whose lips were working soundlessly. Finally, Valentinian started chuckling, several of the courtiers joined in, and in a moment everyone was roaring with laughter. Only Aetius remained somber.

"Marriage to a Hun?" Valentinian gasped, wiping his eyes with the edge of his sleeve. "Who would have thought Attila had such a sense of humor? And a dowry to that yellow-faced ape!" As his shoulders shook and the room rang with the men's laughter, Aetius beckoned one of the assistant stewards to approach, behind the emperor. Placing his hand on the man's shoulder, he leaned quietly toward his ear.

"Remove the princess' pen, and change the guards and ladies attending her cell," he whispered. The steward nodded and slipped out.

The emperor pushed back his chair and stood up, slapping his hands together cheerfully. His joking expression, however, was belied by the fear in his eyes.

"Enough dispatches for today!" he exclaimed. "General Aetius—would you walk me to my apartments? I believe I'm ready for lunch!" The two men opened a path through the courtiers, descended the steps to the gallery outside, and began walking, as each man's pair of praetorian bodyguards fell into step behind them. Valentinian placed his hand on the older man's shoulder, a sign of respect, as a son would give to his father. Yet the weight of his hand was uncommonly heavy, as if the emperor were leaning, like an old man or a cripple. Aetius tensed at the pressure, and Valentinian, sensing his anger, dropped his hand and stopped, forcing Aetius, too, to stop and turn.

"General," Valentinian said quietly after a moment, "though I wear the purple, you and I both know the truth. I have never had the experience of command. The legions, possibly the whole empire, look upon me as an untested youth. It is you who bear the weight, like a . . . like a—"

"Like a crutch," Aetius interrupted, looking at him pointedly. "A crutch or a cane."

The young emperor's face fell. "Yes, like a crutch. Yet it is I, the cripple, who get the credit for walking. I know that is what you are thinking, and I cannot fault you for that. But how could I have done differently?" He looked up at Aetius' face, and his tone was almost pleading. "Little things—it was little things that escaped my control, that grew into momentous events. Not even Julius Caesar was able to control the effects of a woman's appetite. Cleopatra herself was ravenous, and after Caesar's death—"

Aetius interrupted impatiently. "What did you wish to speak with me about, Augustus?"

Valentinian sighed. "This matter of the dowry—is this the pretext we had cause to fear?"

Aetius paused. "This is not sufficient pretext for Attila to attack the empire. He is ambitious, but he is not mad."

"Then it is merely his idea of a joke?"

Aetius reflected for a moment. "It is not that, either. Attila has no sense of humor."

"Then . . . we should . . . perhaps . . ."

Aetius nodded grimly. "Prepare for the worst. Mobilize the legions at the points of entry to the empire—the Danuvius, the Rhine. As a precaution."

The emperor's eyes opened wide. "But the borders! If our garrison reports are accurate, Attila has countless tribes at his command, desperate for the land and wealth of the Roman Empire. If he resolves to march, he has a . . . a . . ."

"A million men." Aetius finished the sentence for him. "I am aware of his resources."

The emperor swallowed. "And with a million men, surely our border garrisons cannot hold, even if reinforced by the regular army units! Rather than mobilize at the borders, should we not pull them back to Italy, strengthen Rome, strengthen Ravenna? At all costs?"

Aetius turned away and began walking toward his apartments on the opposite side of the palace compound, as Valentinian followed behind.

"Attila is not the only commander who maintains allies," he said, without glancing back at the emperor. "An invasion from the East would affect not only Rome but countless tribes within our own empire—the Visigoths, the Burgundians, various friendly clans of the Alamanni, the Franks. I have my own resources. You needn't be concerned."

"General?"

Aetius ignored him and continued walking, forcing the emperor again to pick up his pace until he caught up with him.

"One more thing, General."

"I have a great deal of work, Augustus. I leave in the morning to tend to this matter of the allies."

"General, you forget your place. I said I have one more thing."

Aetius stopped and then slowly turned, casting a stony gaze on the emperor. The younger man's voice quavered, yet he held the general's formidable stare.

"I am a cripple," he said, "and you are my crutch of seasoned wood."

Aetius looked at him evenly but said nothing.

"And if a man's crutch fails him," the emperor continued, "if it slips on the ground and causes the man to fall, the man may be injured. But he will not be killed. Rather, he will pick himself up, curse the crutch for its betrayal, and break it over his knee."

Aetius narrowed his eyes. Seeing his expression, the two praetorian guards shadowing Valentinian edged carefully nearer.

"Perhaps your history with the Huns has given you blinders," Valentinian went on, with slightly more confidence in his voice. "Perhaps preparations for this event should have been made years ago, when Attila first began assembling his coalition. Perhaps you should have anticipated Attila's aggression, and the land hunger of his allied tribes."

"Perhaps," Aetius said coldly.

"Or, perhaps your past knowledge of Attila and his ways is still the empire's greatest bulwark, rather than a hindrance, as some people might think."

"I claim neither excuse nor credit for my past actions," Aetius replied. "I command as I have always commanded—for the good and the honor of Rome."

The emperor nodded. "And you shall continue to do so. And you shall be rewarded well if you avert this threat of invasion, whether by diplomacy or by arms. Attila's aggression must not be allowed to stand. Nevertheless, General, if you fail . . ."

"I look upon talk of failure as a personal affront, Augustus."

The emperor hesitated but held his ground. "If you fail, General, remember the fate of that crutch. If you are determined to meet Attila in battle in the field, rather than pull back to defend Ravenna, then your action must be decisive. Attila must be destroyed."

Dropping his gaze once again, the emperor stared at the floor for a moment and then with a sharp intake of breath, as if recovering from a vast physical effort, he resumed his walk and swept past Aetius, followed by his two guards.

Aetius stood motionless, staring at the emperor. So it had come to this. Leading the legions into war with the Huns. Reporting to a boy emperor. Orders to destroy Attila. Yet did he have a choice? Of course this was the path he had taken long ago, when he chose this life. But had he really chosen it? Had he truly *chosen* to lead legions, rather than, say, ferment grapes or build stone walls? Or lead Huns? Does a man not have to know that he has a choice before he can truly value what he does? It was too late. Speculation was useless, regret worse.

For a soldier, a Roman soldier, there is only one direction to look: forward. Nodding to his praetorians, he squared his shoulders and resumed his stride.

Just as he turned a corner he heard a crash of breaking ceramic. Instinctively he flinched, and then stepped around a column to investigate. There in front of him stood a dismayed Magnus, shards of pottery at his feet, legs purple to the thighs with the splashings from the amphora of red wine he had just dropped. At sight of Aetius, the bearded face immediately brightened, and he thumped his chest loudly. *"Mi-les!"* he announced. The soldiers behind Aetius snickered.

This time, however, Aetius did not scoff or dismiss the giant. Rather, he paused, and then slowly walked around Magnus, stepping over the puddle of wine, inspecting the man's enormous, rippling muscles through his tattered tunic.

"You know," Aetius mused, "I believe you are due for a promotion out of the palace, Magnus. It is time we made you a soldier."

Magnus' eyes grew wide, his beard split in an enormous grin, and he threw his arms open to Aetius for a crushing embrace. Aetius' guard immediately stepped forward, swords extended, barring the giant's path, but it did not stop him from emitting a deafening, wordless bellow of joy.

"Sir," one of the guards whispered to Aetius. "This man is too big for armor, and he eats too much. Besides, he's dumb as a post."

Aetius affected wide-eyed surprise at this revelation. "As a post, eh? That would make him smarter than half my officers." The guards grinned and relaxed their blades.

"Magnus," Aetius continued as he strode past, "with arms like those, I have just the job for you."

In the courtyard just outside the palace entrance, the courier Marcus checked the cinch of the saddle and adjusted the strap of the leather pouch slung over his back.

Though it was already dark and he had scarcely arrived, there would be no rest for him tonight. He had not even had time for the bath he had been dreaming of for so many weeks, and his hopes of enjoying the favors of Lavinia had long since flown his mind. Marcus cursed angrily as he swung up into the saddle and slapped his horse into a gallop, once again back toward the eastern road.

" 'Fifty gold pieces,' she told me. *'Fifty gold pieces'!"*

V

In a field below a rocky bluff, a day's march plainsward from the current location of the Hunnish capital, an old Ostrogoth farmer trudged barefoot through the gravelly soil of his plot. Every four steps he lazily slapped the ropes on the back of the bony mule heaving the plow in front of him. The man had been farming this wretched land for sixty years and had cursed every miserable day of it, for the only things that grew more prolifically than the weeds were the stones. Grain always came in a distant third. Here and there he stooped to pick up and toss aside a rock that had been churned up by the chipped blade of the plow. Six decades, he muttered, he had been tilling this soil. Six children and a wife he had buried in this dirt, in propitiation to the gods, whichever gods they might be who would require such losses to be deterred from their mischief making. And still stones rose to the surface like bubbles on a pond. Would he ever find the last one, before he died? Would he ever toss aside the last stone? Would he ever see his plow blade course smoothly through a furrow of fine dirt, rather than scrape and jump behind the foul-tempered mule and become lodged in rocks that required prying with his digging stick?

He sighed and silently asked the gods' forgiveness for

his blasphemy and ungratefulness. Yet his black mood remained. As it had for six decades.

Would gold coins ever sprout on trees and strong sons on onion shoots?

The farmer's reverie was broken suddenly when he felt a sharp pain in his foot. He winced, called his mule to a stop, and sat in the dirt to examine the scaly, calloused sole. It was bleeding, but it would heal. If the stones had been unable to cripple him when his feet were those of a young and tender boy, they certainly would not be able to harm him now, with his old hide thicker than the mule's and twice as ugly. He glanced around in irritation to find the object on which he had stepped.

Seeing a sharp, pointed rock emerging from the ground a few paces away, he muttered a curse, pulled himself on his digging stick to a standing position, and with much effort and grunting limped to the spot to pull the stone. Oddly, it didn't budge. Sixty years of plowing this field, and suddenly a boulder appears where there had been none before and refuses to move? He shook his head in annoyance, but not wonder, for in his dirt stones grew like a crop, and if any were missed in one year, they would simply be bigger the next. Again he pulled, and again the object resisted but this time cut his hand as he grasped it. He stared at his leathery, bleeding palm—this time with genuine surprise—and with sudden interest he knelt and began digging around the object with his fingers, earnestly but carefully.

Suddenly it emerged from its tomb—an ancient, rusting sword, the blade broken off short, the honed edges crumbling with corrosion, but with the remains of an agate-encrusted gold pommel still visible beneath the dirt.

The farmer examined it in amazement for a long moment, then carefully laid it on the ground, kissed it, and looked up to the sky in adoration. His old, cloudy eyes filled with tears.

After sixty years, the gods were finally pleased.

* * *

In the palace's rough-planked atrium, Attila smilingly received the latest letter handed him by an exhausted Marcus, who had just staggered off his horse and been brought to the king's presence, supported under the arms by two stolid Hunnish guards.

"Thank you, Roman," the king replied jovially. "Continue your practice and you'll become almost as fast as a Hun. Orestes! Get this man a new horse—and make it a Hunnish one, to replace his worthless Roman nag."

"Great King . . ." Marcus looked up at him with pleading eyes.

Attila peered down at the courier distractedly. "Hmm? What is it, Roman? By the gods, you're filthier than a Goth swineherd. Is this how Ravenna sends out its couriers these days? Guards—get this man a bath and some supper, and *then* send him on his way. I'll not have him report to his masters that the Huns were lacking in hospitality, even to a Roman."

Marcus gave a slight nod of satisfaction and then staggered back out, arms again draped over the sturdy shoulders of the two Hunnish guards.

Attila leisurely opened the letter and read it to himself, snorting in disgust as he finished it. " 'A jest,' they call it. A jest! Turgrid!"

Attila wadded the parchment in his hand and threw it to the floor as Turgrid stepped through a side door.

"Yes, King."

"It is time to make claim on our 'dowry.' "

Turgrid frowned in disapproval. "Great King, with all due respect, it will be difficult to convince your allies to march on the West simply because you seek a Roman wife. There are three hundred wives in the harem already, from every nation under your rule. The average soldier under your command can barely afford even one wife to pluck the lice from his head at night, let alone three hundred."

"It appears even you are unconvinced," Attila said with a mocking smile.

Turgrid gazed at him evenly. "I? *Cur,* I am an old man. Three hundred women would be far too many for me."

"Age is inconsequential," Attila said. "It matters not whether you have one wife or three hundred . . . or whether you rule over one nation or twenty. All possessions are imperfect. If they are of this world, they are imperfect, and therefore insufficient. The only thing a man can do, a true man, a king, is constantly seek perfection."

"But if nothing by itself is perfect, then it is impossible to attain perfection, no matter how hard one may seek it."

"Not quite," the king explained. "Perfection itself may be unattainable—but it may be approximated. Two slightly imperfect objects are closer to the ideal than one."

"In that case," said Turgrid, "the only way to improve one's station in life is not to seek perfection but to seek . . . *more.* But where can that end, I ask you?"

"Where does the conclusion lead you?"

Turgrid paused for a moment in thought.

"The closest one can get to attaining perfection in an imperfect world is to . . . attain everything," he finally concluded.

Attila nodded. "Precisely."

Turgrid looked at him with a puzzled expression. "So for this we are going to war? To attain . . ."

". . . perfection," Attila responded. "That is correct."

"There is nothing perfect about war on this scale."

Attila's mocking smile disappeared abruptly. "Do you truly believe I would march even to the next room, much less to Europe, merely to gain another wife? There are enough good reasons to destroy Rome without resorting to a justification as weak as that. Rome is a menace not only to the Huns but to the entire world. Their greatest man, Julius Caesar, whom his countrymen have deified— *deified!*—killed a million innocent people in Gaul. He was a mass murderer, and yet every Roman emperor since has taken his very name as their title."

Turgrid frowned. "This may be true, but—"

"I am not finished. I have lived with the Romans, and know them well. Their gestures of friendship are false; their alliances serve only their own interests. If they are strong, they conquer. If they are weak, they bluff and retrench, hoping the enemy will not notice, until they become strong again. Outsiders—*barbarians*, they call us—have never been sufficiently strong or unified to take advantage of the precise times when Rome is weak. Until *now*!"

Turgrid stared at him. "And for this . . . this vague claim of Roman evil, you would attack even Flavius Aetius? If anything, he has reined back Rome's excesses. He is the one man of sense in Valentinian's court. . . ."

"That may be. I have thought much of this, but I attack Rome, not Flavius. It is up to him to decide whether he is to make war on us."

"Flavius is one of us. He is a Hun."

"If he is a Hun then let him join us. I will welcome him, and generously reward him. Yet I know in my heart he will not. Roman born, Roman forever. The Romans themselves have a saying: *'Naturam expellas furca, tamen usque recurret.'* You may throw nature out with a pitchfork, but she always returns."

"You are certain of this?"

"Mere friendship must never be allowed to stand in the way of destiny. This is an opportunity for rule, for a Hunnish kingdom that will endure for all time. It must not be squandered."

"Great King," Turgrid said, his face a hard mask. "These are matters for the sophists and the scholars. You do not have a just cause for war on all of Europe. The allies see only the three hundred wives. They will not follow you. . . ."

Attila scoffed. "The allies will not follow me? For decades the Ostrogoths and Alamanni have been massing on the Roman borders, starving, seething, and overbreeding. They are bursting with anger and ambition. The allies can be held back no longer, Turgrid—our own lands are at risk. No, it is not a case of the allies following me. I will follow them! My cavalry will merely be the battering ram of the gates. Once the Roman defenses are broken, we need only unleash the horde and step aside."

Just then, a guard ran in, followed by the limping peasant from the hinterland. Orestes stared intently, fixing his icy Germanic eyes on the old man's face.

"Great King!" the guard shouted. "A miracle! Behold what this old Goth has discovered in his field!"

Unwrapping a filthy piece of sacking cloth, he revealed an ancient dirt-encrusted sword, stunning all into silence.

Muttering softly but distinctly, Turgrid repeated the ancient legend that had been passed down for generations.

" 'One day the ancient sword will be found, the sword forged and beaten by the Father of the Dynasty . . . It will be recovered only by the Berik Cur, the Great Leader, for whom the highest destiny is reserved. . . . When he possesses the Sword of the Dynasty, he will be nigh unto the gods, and indeed will become like unto a god himself. . . .' "

Attila glanced quickly up at Orestes. The Alaman's expression remained stony, but he gave an almost imperceptible nod. The king then took the sword in his hands and stared at it avidly. " *'Like unto a god himself,'* " he repeated with reverence, turning the relic carefully over in his hands. "Behold: my justification."

Turgrid closed his eyes for a moment in dismay, but Attila was so enraptured at the vision in his mind he did not even notice.

"It is time, Turgrid," Attila said, looking up with a gleam in his eye. "Assemble the horde."

SEVEN

The Road to Campi Catalaunici, A.D. 451

I

Above all, it was the Hunnish drums.

Throbbing, all-encompassing, they beat from sunrise to sunset, keeping the time for the incessant tramping of marching feet. Even at night the men were not free of the drums, for the hours of beating had hammered deep grooves into their brains, and they retained the pounding long after the marching had stopped. Indeed, the more silent the night, the more relentless the internal beat pulsing in their heads that made their sleep fitful, that woke them at dawn, and that finally, almost as a relief, melded once again with the genuine, physical pounding of the ox-hide drums as the men again fell into march. For their feet were carried not in the high-sewn doeskin boots of the cavalry, nor in the sturdy, hobnailed sandals of those thousands who had served their years in the Roman auxiliary legions. Their feet were contained and protected in these fittings, of course, but nothing more. It was not these poor layers of leather and iron that carried the soldiers' feet along, that lifted them from step to step, that caused the miles to pass relentlessly beneath their soles.

It was the drums.

And spersed among the solid, leaden beats were other sounds as well. The rapid tattoo of horses' hooves rose and fell like rolling thunder as the massed cavalry swept

through the grassy plain. A dust cloud churned in their
wake, climbing to the heavens and trailing behind in the
wind, leaving a yellow, feathery path, a staircase on
which the gods themselves might descend to inspect the
mighty force below. Metal sang on metal as Gothic war
shields, slung from hard, knotted shoulders, clanked
bronzed rims against the iron shafts of the javelins
strapped loosely in back harnesses. Thick, grinding
wagon wheels creaked along the ruts worn deep in the
road by the rims of a hundred thousand carts before them.

The troops were inured to these sounds, the clamor
and roil of an army on the march, and scarcely any single
man was completely aware of the full, terrifying grandeur of the vast force, for scarcely any man could see beyond the small circle of *arvani* and *zuuni,* the squadrons
of ten men and a hundred, surrounding him. There, to the
right, the profile of an iron-helmeted head—yellow hair
flowing from beneath the rim, straight Gothic nose, the
gigantic frame of a tribesman whose forefathers dwelt far
to the north, where the pale sun fights a losing battle with
the frozen moon and where other gods rule the day.
There, up ahead, a thousand-man wing of swarthy black-
bearded Persian cavalrymen, with high-pointed helmets
and fish-scale armor, stiffly mounted on skittish, thin-
legged stallions; and everywhere, in every unit, leading
every brigade and division and forming the great mass of
cavalry, the leather-clad Huns with their compact, high-
boned faces and wispy beards. Their eyes were nearly
closed against the suffocating dust, their close-fitting helmets masked their brows, and they rocked in rhythm to
the beat of the drums and the pounding hooves of their
hook-headed ponies, swaying with the animals as if they
and the horses were one, sharing the same blood, the
same heartbeat, the same will to live, and to fight, and
to die.

Watching his troops pass, Attila was suddenly distracted by a shout, and he whirled his horse. In front of him stood one of his younger sons, a sturdy lad of twelve, in makeshift Hunnish military garb, cobbled together from cast-off pieces of armor and weaponry he had found in camp or pilfered from the armory when the black-smiths' backs were turned. Behind him stood a mob of other boys, forty or fifty in total, all of them sons of Attila or other Hunnish noblemen, ranging in age from eight to twelve years. Their heads were shaved, and they were garbed with fox-head capes and mismatched armor simi-lar to that of their young leader. Most were armed with hatchets and daggers, though a few were lucky enough to have training bows and arrows, while an equal number had nothing but wooden clubs. They stood facing Attila and their leader, in stiff military formation.

Attila stared at them sternly.

"What is this? Son, is this your doing?"

"Wolf Cub *zuun*, Father," the boy replied. "Reporting for duty."

Attila permitted himself a slight smile. "Reporting for duty? And what *is* your duty?"

The boy screwed up his face, at a momentary loss for words. "Killing Romans, sir!" he said, after a pause.

"Killing Romans!" Attila exclaimed. "Brave wolf cubs! But you're too young. How did you get here?"

The boy pointed to some horses milling about behind them. "We rode."

"You rode? There aren't enough horses there for all of you."

The boy puffed out his chest in pride. "We doubled up. Sometimes tripled. We'll make it, Father. We've been training for this war our whole lives."

"Your whole lives, eh? Well, you'll need to train a bit longer. Back home with you now."

The boy's face flushed red in protest.

"But Father! We've come this far! Besides, we're five

days out from the city now—you wouldn't send us back alone? The sons of King Attila and his nobles? Alone on the steppe? Fighting off wolves and bandits?"

He looked up at Attila pleadingly.

The king stared down at him sternly. "You hid among the wagons for five days before approaching me, and now it's too far to return alone? Ride with the army if you will. But there will be no fighting for you."

The boys whooped and hollered, breaking up their formation. Joyfully they ran to the horses and leaped onto their backs, the smaller boys riding in front and the older ones sitting behind. Attila watched them race down the hill toward the marching army and shook his head in admiration.

"Clever little savages," he muttered, then resumed his viewing of the massive force as it marched past. The rumbling of the heavy wagons and the gallop of the horses could be felt in his gut as much as heard with his ears, and the farther he stood from the army, the more he sensed the vast scope of the arena, the distant, delicate sounds twining around with those more proximate and harsh, like ivy round the bark of an oak. The skirling of the Gothic pipes and the moaning of the Hunnish marching chants embellished and carried the thudding depth of the drums, a rising assault on the senses.

He sat his horse alone as a massive gray wolf paced restlessly nearby, torn between his ancient instinct to howl and rail at the upheaval before him and the fear he felt of his master. Attila surveyed his army, his creation, his offspring, with satisfaction. It was his greatest accomplishment, in a lifetime of accomplishments. It was the most lethal body his enemies had ever faced, and the largest armed force ever assembled in the history of the world.

It was Attila's horde. And it was moving west.

* * *

Through a haze of nausea, Aetius forced himself to ignore the incessant rolling of the deck beneath his feet. He had to concentrate, to think about his overall goal, one that for weeks now had occupied every one of his waking moments: the coalition. A coalition had to be formed, alliances revived among Rome's subject tribes—and quickly. Reports from traveling merchants and diplomats of the eastern court were bringing increasingly worrisome news of the gathering of the tribes in the East. Still, as the gray waves surged before him, he was hard-pressed to think of anything more than surviving this crossing and stepping ashore again as quickly as possible.

He riveted his eyes on the approaching beach as his tiny fleet drew near. Gulls rocked and wheeled above the churning surf, mischievous thieves that had followed the vessel all the way from Gaul, now swooping down toward the deck to peck at a shiny nail, now skimming out a hand's breadth above the water, matching every swell and trough in their effortless glide. Behind the strand, the white cliffs of Britannia rose up like the walls of a fortress. The dull beat of a mallet on a wooden block kept the slave rowers' rhythm, and as the hull finally scraped bottom the captain shouted orders to ship oars.

Before the crew could ready landing craft, Aetius nodded to his men, and he and the dozen Gallic guards accompanying him leaped over the side into the thigh-deep water. As the two other ships in his squadron approached on either side, he saw his men there, too, vault the wales of the ship and begin wading. He smiled in grim satisfaction. Though he might hate water with every fiber of his being, his men would be the last to know it. Leaping into the icy surf, wading nonchalantly toward shore, disregarding the treacherous footing and the breakers that slammed into his back, stoically enduring the drenching that soaked him through from shoulders to feet, showed a certain Roman determination, a fearlessness and disdain for the elements, that was critical for a general to retain the trust of his men.

But he still despised the sea.

On the beach stood a small honor guard of Briton officials, led by a tall, thin red-haired officer in a brightly striped cape hemmed with soft fur. As Aetius and his men surged out of the surf like Neptune's own legions, this man stepped forward and his deeply lined face broke into a wide smile. Aetius stood on the sand for a moment to let the water run off and waited for his men, and then, seeing the chieftain approach, he, too, smiled broadly and stepped forward to receive his embrace. The chieftain did not flinch from the cold soaking he received from Aetius' sodden woolen cloak. Britons seemed scarcely ever to notice the cold or the damp.

"Vortigern!" Aetius exclaimed, pulling him back from the bear hug and pounding him on the shoulders. "So many years, yet I'd recognize you in a moment!"

Vortigern laughed and gestured to a large weathered plank house set back from the beach, on a stone ledge halfway up the cliffs. A narrow path, set with wooden stairs attached precariously to the rocks, wound up from the beach to the dwelling.

"Come, Flavius," the Briton said. "My beach retreat. It is rustic, but private. I use it only for the most special occasions, and indeed you are the first Roman to see it. You and your men must dry your clothes and rest yourselves. We have much to catch up on!" He clapped Aetius on the back, signaled to one of his men to throw a dry woolen rug over the general's shoulders, and led the way up the steep path.

They arrived moments later, panting from the climb in their sodden clothes and armor. They clattered in through the door and noisily threw down their gear and gathered by the hot driftwood fire that had already been built in a large beach-stone chimney in the corner. Aetius shouldered his way through to the front, chatting easily with his men and rubbing his hands in pleasure at the heat. Already the air was filling with the moist, goaty odor of woolens drying. A trio of serving maids, plump and pink-cheeked from the heat of the kitchen, emerged from a side door, bearing trays of steaming tin goblets of a hot beverage to distribute to the men. Vortigern took a hot cup by the rim, wincing and hastily handing it to Aetius to seize by the handle, then raised his own cup in salute to his guest.

"A local specialty." He smiled. "Hot British ale, sweetened with honey and herbs. We call it mead. It'll warm you twice as fast as that lazy grape juice you Romans insist on trying to produce everywhere from Africa to the Baltic."

Aetius tasted the concoction, grimaced, and set the cup down on the carved wooden mantelpiece. "I'm afraid, King, that I cannot stay. I've given instructions to the fleet captains to stand by on the beach. I have only the duration of the tide."

Vortigern looked at him with puzzlement before nodding to his officers nearby. With some reluctance, the Britons and Romans crowding around the roaring fireplace collected their damp woolen cloaks and filed through the door to the windy veranda outside, overlooking the beach, taking their mead with them.

"Why the haste?" Vortigern inquired. "For forty years I've waited to show you my hospitality, and . . ."

"God willing, we will have more opportunities in the future," Aetius replied.

"This invasion you mentioned in your letter—you are worried, then?"

Aetius took another sip of the steaming brown liquid. "Attila has massed many tribes."

Vortigern scoffed. "Then what have I to fear? Attila wouldn't dare set foot on a ship. He wouldn't be able to acquire a fleet in any case. There are few land armies to threaten us here in Britannia . . . except you Romans!"

Aetius smiled thinly. "It is not the Britons I'm concerned about. The Franks and the Gauls are undermanned and disorganized. They will be no match for an attack by the Huns. We require assistance—men."

"Flavius, Flavius," Vortigern sighed. "For this you finally pay me a visit—to demand heads and hands? Of all the things you might have asked for, men are what I can least afford to give. Skilled soldiers are worth their weight in gold, and I dole them out like a miser even to my own chieftains."

"You have the deepest moat in the world—the Channel. Why the need for such large armies?"

"The Channel serves its purpose well. The threats I face are not from that quarter. My northern borders are attacked daily by blue-painted Picts, and the Roman wall built by Hadrian to keep them out crumbles to dust. The Saxons, whom I invited in to fight for me as mercenaries, turn on me like alley dogs at the slightest provocation, and are even now rebelling in the south. Even the Hibernians, across the western sea, occasionally rise out of their drunken stupors long enough to drift over to Britannia in their leather bathtubs and burn a village or two before I can stop them. I cannot spare men to assist some distant Gauls—who would just as soon have my head as my help!"

Aetius stared gloomily into the fire. "I asked you for troops as a friend. Must I resort to demanding them? Though Britain is no longer officially subject to Rome, the Augustus might seek to reverse that situation, if hard-pressed."

Vortigern sucked in his breath sharply at the obvious threat, then after a moment sighed again. "Demand all you like, Flavius—in your name or the emperor's. The Britons will not go unless I lead them. And that I will not and cannot do. Rome would have to mount an expedition against Britannia to force me to. You would eventually win, of course—but at what cost? And with enough time to levy my warriors against the Huns? I tell you this as a friend, Flavius—and as a potential enemy. Do not make such a demand."

Aetius looked away grimly. "Your decision is final, then?"

"It is not a decision—these are the circumstances. You might as well ask me to change the weather. But why be concerned? Your efforts at building a coalition are wasted, and unnecessary. The Alamanni east of the Rhine will never let a Hunnish army pass through their land, eating its way through their crops and livestock. And then crossing the Rhine itself? Impossible. Make the river your line of defense. With a bit of luck, you can set the Alamanni and Huns against each other like two cats. Rome's worst enemies doing Rome's own work, fighting each other. You can destroy them both, without lifting a finger. Now drink."

Aetius stared moodily out the window, where the surf crashing on the beach below indicated a rising wind and a lifting tide. He contemplated the long voyage back to Gaul. He had not even returned yet to the deck of the flagship, yet his stomach was already rising up in protest at the thought of the rolling swells. To hell with the Britons. There would be allies in plenty elsewhere.

He downed the mead in a single gulp and held out his cup for a refill.

For months the Thuringian tribesmen of the upper Danuvius had been anticipating invasion from the Huns. The entire world was aware that a great army of warriors was gathering and closing in from the East. Sketchy reports had filtered through from survivors: Oddly, the invaders did not occupy the lands through which they passed, yet their legacy was death and devastation nonetheless. The countryside for miles on either side of their path was stripped bare of food and valuables. Resisters were killed outright, wives and children taken as plunder. Those who yielded were pressed into service, and the land was left abandoned. Houses, churches, and bridges were destroyed. The path of destruction was a message; the invaders' heralds called out: Surrender to Attila, or face annihilation.

For generations the Thuringians had survived such messages and threats. The proud tribesmen had withstood Rome's halfhearted attempts to conquer them over the years and indeed had even resisted the temptation to join forces with the neighboring tribes in their invasions of Gaul. To quietly live the life of their ancestors on their ancient territory between the grasslands and the Great Forest was a goal to aspire to—a life worth fighting for. Invaders had come and gone over the centuries—and this horde of yellow men from the East, like other enemies, would soon see what it was like to meet true Thuringian warriors.

The leader of the council of elders, Yoric the Squinter, had had ample time to prepare for the invaders' arrival. Indeed, his most formidable stronghold—the stone fortress guarding the critical passage over the River Albis, protecting the eastern approach into the forest—was well organized to resist. Women and children had weeks before been shuttled to outlying villages. Herds had been driven inside the city walls to provide sustenance to the defenders for the long siege to come. Winter wheat was harvested early and green, the thick walls of the garrison reinforced, the keep in the center of the town subjected to a long-overdue restoration to prepare it as a last bastion. Indeed, Yoric had even reinforced the fortress' regular garrison with five thousand additional troops. Their sole task would be to delay the Huns on their sweep through

Thuringia, to fragment the enemy forces as they passed through the forest, gaining Yoric time to build additional defenses to throw against them, perhaps to destroy them once and for all.

Time was of the essence. By blocking the horde's progress here, at the gates to the forest, the Thuringians could weaken the enemy for want of food and supplies. Yoric needed time to assemble his confederation of clans. Delaying the invaders at the stronghold for six weeks—perhaps eight if he was fortunate and the Huns were incompetent—would prevent them from entering the forest until mid-summer. Then, crushing attacks on the enemy *within* the forest would be sufficient to deal the fatal blow—delaying and disorienting the enemy in those fearsome woods, picking off their units one by one until the horde simply evaporated, by death and attrition.

That was the plan. It was the best he had.

Yoric's troops were led by a hard-bitten Saxon commander, Theolaif, who had learned his trade through long years in the Roman legions. He quickly took control of the fortress from its regular garrison and threw himself into a frenzy of activity. He supervised the restoration of the castle walls, the installation of the defensive works, the "wolves" and the "scorpions," on the wall turrets, and the testing and tuning of the artillery. In the best Roman tradition, he ordered the erection of a series of high signal towers of fir-tree scaffolding on a ridge of hills running east fifty miles, to spy out and provide early news of the horde's approach over the plains by smoke signal; and he himself took charge of the field defenses, a task he enjoyed as worthy of his strategic mind. Commandeering a thousand men from the surrounding countryside, he spent much blood and sweat digging an ingenious series of defensive ditches around the stronghold, lining the bottoms of some with sharpened stakes, diverting a stream into others to fill them with water, backing them by easily defended mounds of soft earth, devising palisades and log barricades—every trick his experience told him would allow his outnumbered troops to stall the enemy.

Indeed, his quest for preparedness was so wide-ranging that he even called the garrison's scribe one day to translate and summarize for him a passage from a Latin copy of Herodotus, which he vaguely remembered from his service in the legions. The puzzled secretary searched through the well-thumbed volume and commenced a rapid translation into Saxon. It appeared that, centuries earlier, when the Great King Darius had besieged the city of Babylon for upward of two years without success, one of his Persian officers, Zopyrus, had stepped forward to claim that since the city was so all-important, he himself would give Babylon as a gift to his king.

Calling in a butcher, Zopyrus ordered him to amputate his lips, nose, and ears. He then pretended to defect to the Babylonians, pointing to his ruined features as proof that the Great King had convicted him of some crime and banished him. In his bloody, mutilated condition, how could he not be believed?

And indeed, Zopyrus was believed and even taken into the confidence of the governors of the city, whom he advised to kill all the women so as to spare enough food for the besieged soldiers on the walls. Five thousand women were killed, and the morale of the surviving defenders plummeted, so much so that the gates were only laxly guarded. One night, as the Babylonians were performing religious rites, Zopyrus slipped away and opened a gate to the conquering Persians, who entered and vanquished the recalcitrant city that very night.

As Theolaif reflected on the tale later, however, he could not help but feel dissatisfied. He was certain there must be many lessons to be learned from it, though he could not fathom what they might be. He finally resolved on the most obvious—to beware the arrival of lipless men—and after spreading word among the guards, he returned to his work, focusing all his efforts henceforth on the stronghold and its last bastion of defense—the tower keep.

Theolaif had no ambitions of heroism or martyrdom, for this was no suicide mission he had volunteered to lead. His most important defensive asset was one he had found quite by accident, when restoring the keep. It was the hole—the deep and secret hole, discovered and enlarged by a handful of diggers in the keep's cellar. It burrowed into one of the fortress' ancient and semi-forgotten escape tunnels leading directly under the massive back walls and emerged several hundred feet into the forest's thick undergrowth. Of the tunnel's existence he had told no one, and he had paid the diggers a king's ransom to ensure silence. The troops, he knew, would fight better, or at least more fiercely, if they thought they were fighting for their lives and did not have the option of escape when the struggle became hot. There would be plenty of time to inform them of the hole's presence later, if it ever came to that.

For weeks after Theolaif's arrival, all was uneventful. Days were filled with endless carting of stones and mixing of mortar, nights with the boredom and gambling of soldiers serving garrison duty in the outposts. Scouts sent east on the trade roads reported back that though all was tense, no signs of Attila were to be seen. Rumors arose and flew. Perhaps the Huns had taken a southerly route west? Perhaps they would avoid Yoric and the Great Forest altogether, march through Lower Pannonia and take ship at the Mediterranean? Indeed, the troops even allowed themselves to relax for a space of a few days. How not to laugh in relief when one's worst fear was about to be proven groundless, as when a man wakes from a terrible nightmare to find only the comfort of his own bed and woman.

But it was the animals—the lions and deer of the vast grasslands to the east—that gave the first indication of the Huns' arrival.

Never had the Thuringians seen anything like it. When the first dust cloud rose on the horizon, every man ran to his battle station and tensely waited, though the cloud was perhaps a dozen miles away. When the cloud finally approached, so late the following day that the men had tired and already fallen into their routine of shifts, they were astonished to find that it was produced not by the marching feet of men and Hunnish warhorses but rather by a large herd of steppe antelope—thousands of them, with various other beasts and birds mingled in with them, including wild plains horses, stray sheep, and goats from tribes based so far east the garrison troops could not even identify the brand marks on their sides. Even the occasional lion slunk along the edges of the vast herd of refugee beasts, as both predator and refugee himself. Ignoring the harvested fields and city walls, the animals thundered down the road at the side of the fortress town and straight into the forest, leaving behind them a silence, a dearth of the usual bird and animal noises, which added to the bewilderment and trepidation suddenly felt by the previously fearless members of the Squinter's handpicked division.

For the Thuringians were well aware that God is not random and that such things as the evacuation of an entire plain of all its wildlife is not a random event. The land was emptying itself before their eyes, as a child empties a jar he has filled with grasshoppers picked from a wheat field, and it was doing so for a reason, a reason told in the sparse eloquence of the line of signal towers that disappeared over the eastern horizon. Thin purple columns of smoke rose in straight plumes from the distance, in the prearranged signal. And then, just as suddenly as the smoke had appeared, it was extinguished, and there was nothing. An hour later, as the men strained their eyes toward the east, a plume rose again, then a hundred, a thousand other plumes all across the eastern horizon, melding into a dense black curtain of roiling smoke. Theolaif, standing on the last watchtower in the line, which had been set up on the flat roof of the stronghold keep itself, suddenly lost the jaunty confidence he had felt over the past few weeks. The entire east was on fire, and from the watchtower one could even see the faint glow on the nighttime horizon as towns and fields in the horde's path went up in flames. And for the first time in Theolaif's long career as a soldier, he felt a hopeless knot of despair in his gut.

By the next afternoon, if he lay on the ground, he could sense the tramping of distant feet, through his very belly and bowels, as the ground shook and reverberated to a low, pounding beat. Within an hour the ground's ominous trembling could even be felt by the guards on watch duty on the top of the walls, and the pair of soldiers assigned to the watchtower nervously reported that the structure was swaying as if in a wind, though no breeze could be felt. The watchmen's services were not needed, in any case. By that time the distant cloud of dust could be seen not only from the wall tops but from the ground as well. Indeed, at first some could not even agree as to what it was, for the cloud was so widely dispersed as to resemble a storm sweeping out of the eastern horizon in a vast, swirling arc.

Within another hour, the cloud's dark shadow had begun to be visible on the distant green and brown earth and now began to compress, to collapse into itself like a tunnel dug in sand, for within moments of marking the appearance of the shadow the watchers understood that the vast dark smudge on the horizon was not a shadow of the dark cloud above it but rather a thing itself, and within moments after that they realized that the thing was living and sweeping toward them with the fury of a biblical plague of locusts.

And soon after that, they began envying Pharaoh, that the plague he had faced was of mere locusts.

The horde swarmed through the grasslands and over the low rise of hills below the forest, thundering by the thousands on their warhorses, leading a veritable moving city of wagons and chariots. They disdained even to follow the road but cut their own swath through fields, across meandering streams, over and through hedgerows. It was an implacable, rolling tide on land, hesitating for nothing, stopping for no one, the wide, uneven leading line of horses and men advancing steadily at the head of a moving black mass.

Upon arriving at the fortress, the Huns stopped neither to parley with the inhabitants nor to camp. No visible or audible orders were given—indeed, no officers were even apparent, so closely did the Hunnish commanders dress and ride like the men they led. The army simply split and routed itself around both sides of the garrison's defenses. Five hundred wagons were driven into the ditches to provide makeshift bridges for crossing, and five thousand men were detailed to dig drainage to empty the moats before sunset. Boards were placed over the spikes, and defensive palisades were simply toppled and marched over as the defenders fled in terror without firing. Solemnly, with great discipline and skill, the enormous force gathered in a circle around the walls, like a vast column of ants surrounding the body of a dead rodent.

The attack on the city began without hesitation, without demand for surrender. It began even without drawing up lines of battle, preparing a camp for the besiegers, or taking time to don armor. It began even without an attempt to besiege. When the lead pincers in the formation of the marching horde closed the circle around the fortress, the attack simply began. The darkening sky of dusk suddenly lit as bright as a midsummer's day as thousands of fire arrows poured over the battlements. Theolaif had anticipated such a maneuver and had ordered the roofs of the town inside the walls to be cleared of their customary thatch and dried straw. Nevertheless, the sheer number of flaming missiles caught his troops by surprise and wreaked havoc. Men and animals inside the town fled away from the walls, racing through the streets with wool, hair, and clothing aflame. As the defenses were abandoned, the Huns hurled grappling hooks up to the crenellations, and faster even than the remaining defenders could heave them back down or cut the ropes and keep the hooks for themselves, even more were thrown up, and the walls soon crawled with men scaling the slender lines hand over hand. Within moments, the air rang with the clanging of swords, the whinnying of horses, and the shouts of angry and dying men.

Theolaif stood at a guard post on the wall, watching the attack with horror. Delay the Huns' advance for two months? He had been unable to delay them for two hours! He immediately ordered the final retreat, the order he had hoped not to give for many more weeks, into the impregnable stone of the massive keep. Theolaif and a hundred of his troops, those close enough to hear his command, abandoned their artillery and leaped down from the walls, taking the stairs by twos and threes. Racing across the garrison's main square, they climbed the ladder to the keep entrance, which was built into the smooth wall twenty feet above the ground, pulled the ladder up behind them, and barred the stout iron door tight.

Moments later, by the light of torches seized from the defenders themselves, blood-spattered Huns stormed through the opened gates and into the single street on lunging horses, as the remaining Thuringian troops and garrison soldiers fled in terror. One man only walked his horse slowly through the gates; one man did not whip his animal in a frantic fury. Attila rode calmly through the blood-soaked mud, his horse deftly stepping over the bodies lying in the filth at his feet. He paused for a moment to inspect the pattern of sprayed blood defacing a dingy white wall and then continued his slow advance. A crudely fashioned, stick-and-rag doll lay abandoned in the mud at his feet, with other belongings from a house that had been ransacked, and a squadron of Hunnish horse galloped triumphantly over it, trampling it into the sludge.

At daybreak, columns of black smoke poured from the city, obscuring it and hovering in a low, writhing pall over the surrounding fields. Through the toppled walls, the thick smoke was pierced by glimpses of raging flames. The stronghold that was to have stopped the horde for the season had fallen in a single night. As Theolaif emerged with his surviving troops from the spider hole a hundred feet into the forest, he was quickly struck down by foraging Hunnish horsemen seeking fodder for their animals among the scrub at woods edge. Before his eyes clouded in death, the last sight he witnessed was the toppling of the fortress' formidable west wall—the wall he had thought to be always immune from attack, because it backed up upon the forbidding forest itself.

The Huns would not even deign to occupy the stronghold. Their intent was nothing less than complete destruction.

Once again, all was silent. The killing was accomplished quickly, the looting more so. Like so many other towns on the horde's path across the Germanic plains, this one now was a pile of rubble, its houses reduced to burnt-out hulks, its streets abandoned. The only sound was the wailing of the few mad survivors, left scarred and wandering, like the ghosts of their dead townsmen, flitting into the shadows and hiding at the sound of every footfall. The horde continued its path west, streaming around both sides of the ruined town and then combining again, like a stream whose flow has been temporarily split by a boulder. It had flowed over and around the obstacle and obliterated it from its path.

And then the horde—every last man, horse, and wagon—was swallowed into the Great Forest.

The woods of Rome's territory in eastern Gaul are dense and damp, the leafy precursors of the impassable and endless Germanic forests that begin just the other side of the Rhine and extend to God only knows where. Indeed, only God truly *does* know where, for so far as human knowledge extends, no man has ever passed through that fearsome wilderness from end to end and returned to describe the experience. Many others have made their way back, after days or weeks, to the point of civilization where they started—raving mad from fear or sheer boredom, or delirious from the bites of wild forest animals, or starving, or sick from ingesting unfamiliar plants and mushrooms to ward off starvation. Such are the forests of Germania.

But even the woods of eastern Gaul are terminated and eclipsed by the mighty peaks of the Alps, a barrier at least as formidable to travelers and armies as ever the forest was. Through these mountain wastelands, fierce tribes once warred and hunted, and indeed, during the spring thaws on the high mountain passes the shriveled remains of some of their members are occasionally found still, frozen whole in the very spot they were killed or buried a thousand years before. On an earlier journey through the mountains, Aetius had once discovered an elephant tusk, a relic from Hannibal the Carthaginian's invasion half a millennium before; and scouts seeking new routes had once brought him back stone seashells they had found nestled into the very sides of these mighty peaks. This was a strange land, a haunted land, a land of dizzying heights, but where elephants and mollusks had once ventured. And it was a land almost uninhabited by people, but for a few wild tribes of goat herders who moved across the snow on wooden boards strapped to their feet.

Yet this time, the purpose of his venture into the Alps was not exploration or mere passage. For two weeks Aetius and his escort of cavalry guards had wended their way through the passes, which even now, in mid-spring, were so clogged with snow as to slow progress to a paltry few miles a day. It had been years—generations perhaps—since the few Roman roads through these parts had been maintained or way stations stocked with fresh horses and food. Aetius reflected that soon the routes themselves would become overgrown and forgotten and the precarious passes that had cost Roman legions so much blood to discover and defend in centuries past would once again revert to nature or to the strange peoples who stubbornly eked a living from these remote valleys and hillsides.

As he rounded a corner at the top of a long gravel ascent, Aetius caught his breath at the view of the endless mountain ranges before him. The air was frigid, but he paused for a moment to take in the splendor, glancing at one-legged Florentius, who rode silently at his side.

"There it is, just beyond that long valley," he said. "Sapaudia, capital of the Burgundians, where we exiled their King Gundahar and the survivors when we defeated them ten years ago. They're led by Gundioc now. I know him, but I don't imagine he will welcome us with open arms."

Florentius chewed thoughtfully at a piece of dried meat. "Looks like a hunting camp. This is truly the capital of the Burgundians? I remember the fight they gave us. They were once a mighty people."

Aetius nodded. "They still are, though now they've dispersed, since their old city on the Rhine was destroyed."

"I remember," Florentius replied. "After the siege, the

auxiliaries razed Borbetomagus before we could stop them. A pity. The walls were good and the palace keep was magnificent. We could have used it ourselves."

Aetius shrugged. "But the land was left untouched, and it is good land. It is land to which Gundioc and his people might wish to return. And we might allow them to do so, for their assistance."

Florentius stared straight ahead. "I don't see why the Burgundians would do us any favors," he grunted. "We defeated them. In fact, we massacred them."

"Not *we*," Aetius corrected him. "It was Huns who destroyed their city and killed their king . . ."

"They may have been Huns, but they were *our* Huns, *our* auxiliary troops. You are as much an enemy to the Burgundians as Attila."

". . . but it is also the Huns who would be marching through the Burgundians' old lands on the Rhine, unless they are stopped," Aetius continued. "When Gundioc hears the Huns are again approaching, he will bring his people into line with us. The Burgundians may be surly, but they are warriors."

"Why would we even want allies such as these? They'd stab us in the back as happily as a Hun in the chest."

Aetius frowned. "The legions cannot hold the river alone. We exiled the Burgundians, but they still know the lands along the Rhine. We have no choice but to come to terms with them."

He set heel to his horse and galloped off as the squadron followed close behind.

At the entrance to the city, they were met by a force of Burgundian cavalry guards drawn up in formation before the main gate. From the appearance of their gilded dress armor, which was now tarnished and ill-kept, Aetius surmised they were the king's palace guards—crack troops all, though fallen on hard times. They stared at him with hostility plainly written on their faces. Rome exercised at least nominal sovereignty over these people, Aetius reflected, but he was still many days' march from the nearest Roman garrison and badly outnumbered. It would not do to needlessly anger them—not now.

He drew his own escort up before the Burgundian line, cavalry pikes at the ready, and then advanced forward alone, his hands conspicuously empty.

"State your name and purpose, Roman!" their captain called out in heavily accented Latin, himself advancing his horse forward a few paces.

Aetius blinked in surprise that they did not recognize him, yet with a moment of reflection he realized why. He had been traveling now almost two weeks and was muddy and unshaven. Despite the herald behind him who bore the eagle standard of a commander of legions, there was no reason to believe the isolated Burgundians would be familiar with the insignia of rank. He paused in front of the captain, sizing him up.

"General Flavius Aetius, Commander in Chief of the Roman Legions. I come in peace, to confer with King Gundioc of the noble Burgundian tribe."

The Burgundian captain now registered his own surprise and, deftly wheeling his horse, retreated to confer in low tones with one of his aides. After a moment, he dismounted and walked toward Aetius, gesturing for him, too, to step down.

"We received no advance word of your arrival, General," the officer said with grudging respect. "Only reports from our lookouts that a Roman force was advancing through the passes, and we feared the worst."

"As I said, I come in peace."

"I understand. You defeated us in battle, General Aetius, and Rome is sovereign over our people. We acknowledge that. Yet we do not pretend to offer you a glad welcome."

"I expect nothing from you but to show me the way to your king."

The officer paused a long moment. "The king is occupied."

"Then I will enter your city and wait."

"He is entertaining visitors. He will be occupied for some time."

"In that case, you will inform the king that I will see him immediately. If you attempt to block my progress I will force my way through. If I am harmed in any way, you will see three Roman legions camped within your walls before the month is out."

Again the captain stepped back to confer with his officers, while Aetius patiently waited. Finally, he returned with his answer.

"You, General Aetius, may enter, but your men must remain outside the walls. They will be given food and supplies and may remain as long as necessary. I will escort you in all safety to the king."

At these words, Florentius, who had been listening carefully, sidled his horse up to Aetius' side.

"Do not do this, General," he whispered in a tone loud enough for the Burgundian captain to hear. "Your personal safety is not to be entrusted to the barbarians."

The captain glared but said nothing, and Aetius stared straight ahead without looking up at Florentius.

"King Gundioc is an old friend of mine. I would trust my life to his hands."

And without further word, Aetius strode forward. The ranks of mounted horsemen divided to let him pass, and he and the captain walked through the gates, preceded by a Burgundian rider who galloped ahead to announce Aetius's arrival to the king.

The ramshackle city was of a poverty that Aetius had not seen since his arrival in the Hunnish capital forty years before, yet in atmosphere it was infinitely worse.

For here, the women and children squatted in the streets out of desperation and hunger, rather than of preference for the outdoors, as in Hunnia. Here the animals and fowl stood in the doorways out of lack of other shelter, rather than for human companionship as in Hunnia. Here the buildings were precarious and rudimentary out of sheer squalor, rather than in order to be easily transported. Aetius looked straight ahead, willing himself not to add to the Burgundians' shame of defeat by observing their destitution as well—and the escort captain, perhaps sensing Aetius' reticence, himself remained silent, offering neither explanation nor apology. From all sides, Aetius could sense the anger of a defeated but still-proud people, glaring at their conqueror.

Within a few moments they had arrived at the palace, a low stone structure that had been hastily erected upon the tribe's arrival at this place several years before. The main entrance was guarded by a pair of slouching soldiers, while the courier's horse tied at the front indicated that the Roman's presence was even at that moment being announced inside. Aetius and the captain strode up to the guards and then stood awkward and silent. If Gundioc was entertaining guests, Aetius reflected, the somberness of the city and the lack of guards at the palace was a strange and unassuming way to welcome them.

Suddenly the doors jerked open, and the two palace guards stepped back and stood at attention. First to stride through was a finely dressed older man, with an erect, stately bearing that suggested a high position in the king's circle. The luxuriant fur collar of his linen robe stood out in stark contrast to the threadbare and faded clothing of the guards and passersby, and the polished golden hilt of the sword at his waist indicated he was a man of wealth. Ignoring Aetius, he strode imperiously past.

"The royal chamberlain," the Burgundian captain muttered to Aetius.

"Ah," Aetius replied. "A steward. The whole race of them should be exterminated."

Behind the chamberlain walked a nobleman: a tall gray-haired Goth garbed in immaculate ceremonial robes and wearing over his shoulders a golden fillet of high office. His unusual clothing, however, Aetius ignored completely. What drew his eyes immediately was the Goth's incongruous headgear: as protection against the sharp mountain chill that penetrated even to the drafty palace, the man wore a close-fitting fox-trimmed leather cap of . . . Hunnia.

As the nobleman swept slowly past, he paused for a moment, coolly appraising Aetius and noting his surprise. Then he continued on without a word.

Aetius had waited long enough. Striding impatiently to the doorway, he entered alone, as his escort protested behind him.

"Gundioc!" Aetius bellowed, walking into the dim room.

"I know that voice!" said a man from deep inside the room. "It couldn't be—is it really . . . ?"

Before Aetius could respond, the captain had hastened to his side.

"General Flavius Aetius," the officer announced to the king inside. "Supreme Commander of the Roman Legions."

"Flavius, is that you?" the voice bellowed from inside. "Bring that Pannonian in here, Captain. Good God, Flavius, step into the light—what are you waiting for? Forty years since you've seen me last and you loll about on the doorstep like some peasant. . . ."

Aetius strode across the room and into the strong clasp of the king of the Burgundians. A bluff, hearty man, he seemed to bear none of the poorly disguised resentment that the other residents of the squalid city had been displaying toward Aetius since he had entered the gates. Indeed, his blue eyes, set deeply into the heavily lined face, seemed even to twinkle with pleasure at seeing his old schoolmate. Aetius could not help wondering at such cheerfulness, expressed by a man whose kingdom and capital city Aetius had destroyed only a few years before. Yet there was no time to analyze his character. Aetius immediately launched into his assessment of the situation.

An hour later, Gundioc, despite his practiced joviality, was losing his patience. Noticing this, Aetius pointed with the tip of his sword to the large parchment map the king had produced and spread out on a table.

"The Huns have already conquered all the territories east of the Great Forest," Aetius explained. "Attila boasts that when he is finished with a city, his horse can ride straight over the place where it stood without stumbling. Your kingdom, located adjacent to the Rhine and at the gateway to Gaul, is ideally situated to send men and arms to stop their progress."

"My *former* kingdom, you mean," Gundioc replied with a tense smile. "We have not held that land since your own Huns slaughtered Gundahar and destroyed Borbetomagus. I think my people would find it hard to defend that land from . . . here." He gestured laconically out the window.

Aetius leveled his gaze at him. "Should you wish to defend that land from the barbarians, I am sure we could come to an arrangement for your return to it."

Gundioc snorted. "The Huns—barbarians? Flavius, did not you yourself spend a decade living with them? Surely your familiarity with them did not breed such contempt. For the past two days I have been entertaining the Huns' own ambassador, the Greek Onegesius. Perhaps you know him? He presented me with several interesting proposals."

"These Huns," Aetius replied, "are not the Huns I knew and lived with. . . ."

"Not even Attila? I understand he is leading this defensive force."

"*Defensive* force! Gundioc, they are pillaging and destroying everything on their path as they advance west! I fear Attila has lost control of this mob to his warlords."

"Are you not overreacting?" Gundioc replied calmly. "The Hunnish ambassador has assured me they desire no trouble—they simply wish to pass through Burgundy's former lands, without tarrying. In view of their peaceful intentions, it would not be prudent for me to impede them. Particularly if it means going to the trouble and expense of transporting all my forces back to Borbetomagus."

Aetius stared hard at his old friend. "Pass through? So they admit they seek to pass through! On their way to—"

"Yes, yes, Rome, of course," the king interrupted impatiently. "But surely you are not concerned? An army such as Attila's will never get that far. The Alamanni east of the Rhine are even now massing their forces. They will counter the threat. The Huns will never pass the river. The point is moot. But in the meantime, I am happy to receive their ambassadors."

"So you will not mobilize forces against them?" Aetius pressed.

Gundioc's face hardened, finally losing its forced smile. "Mobilize all my forces to counter a threat that may not be real? Spill my people's blood to protect a Roman general who killed my king and half my army? Your 'coalition,' as you call it, will only bring the Huns' wrath down upon my nation, just as we are beginning to recover from the slaughter you dealt us earlier. Are we rag toys, to be so easily used and trashed by Rome? I want no part of it."

"You realize," Aetius continued, his voice assuming a menacing tone, "that the Huns have no intention of stopping with minor conquests in the East. . . ."

"Certainly. But you, Flavius, of all people, can distinguish between true threats and false ones. Leave the Alamanni and the Huns to wear themselves out against each other."

"I would remind you, Gundioc, that you are a conquered nation, and that you still owe allegiance, and indeed your very position on this throne, to the will of the emperor—and to my own. Do not mistake my tolerance in allowing you free hand to govern for release from your duties."

The king froze for a moment and then leaned forward, face flushed red and eyes bulging.

"Do you threaten me, Flavius?" he asked, seething with quiet fury. "Do you *threaten* me? For if your demands are truly in the emperor's name, I will not neglect my duty to the empire. Yes, the emperor will have his men. But I will not be responsible for the quality or motivations of the men I send to your antiquated legions. You can demand all the men you wish, but if they are not freely given they will be worse than useless to you. You might as well demand coins of gold *solidi* but receive bronze *nummi* for all the good they will do you."

"Do you dare say you would send me inferior troops?" Aetius asked, the fury in his own voice barely contained. "For that, King, I could have you . . ."

"I have said nothing of the sort. I merely point out that if you are not killed in battle because of incompetent conscripts from your 'allies,' the emperor himself will have you executed when he sees the sorry quality of the army you have recruited."

Aetius stared at him in silence for a moment, then slowly stood up and, without further word, strode out. He set an even, unhurried pace through the town's muddy streets, accompanied by the Burgundian captain who had been waiting for him outside in the cold sunshine. Upon arriving at the gates, he and his men remounted and thundered off along the mountain trails upon which they had just arrived.

* * *

The Hunnish force continued its advance through the heavily forested hills, its horses and wooden wagons progressing implacably over all obstacles. Not since the foray of the Roman emperor Julian, nearly a century earlier, had an army passed successfully through the depths of the Great Forest, and never in all of history had one so large made its way through these byways. The cavalrymen maintained close formation, faces stony and eyes chary but inscrutable. The forest was strange—never had they seen trees growing so large, as wide across as a four-horse wagon, or so thickly, like giant stalks of grain, so that at times one could scarcely walk between them. Yet trees are but trees. There are few forests in Hunnia and therefore few forest gods to worship or forest demons to fear. The forest is simply another obstacle to cautiously overcome, like a mountain range, a snowy pass, or a river.

For the wagon drivers and camp followers, unarmed and vulnerable, however, the forest held myriad terrors. Stories had been passed on to them from Germanic captives, tales of fearsome beasts, elephantlike and with bloody tusks, or of werewolves and phantoms, kin to those who stalked the Hunnish steppe as well, the foul hauntings of dead men left unburied or of souls tormented for vengeance. More realistic fears assailed them, too—fears borne perhaps more soundly on the basis of fact. Local tribes were said to waylay innocent travelers in these dark and lonely regions. Roads were cleverly blocked and detoured into traps; trees were felled onto other trees and yet other trees, to crush entire armies under their trunks from a distance; life-giving streams could be diverted or poisoned, game chased away so that the army might starve.

It was a fertile land but not a bounteous one, where plants seemed to grow overnight to tremendous size but yielded nothing edible or useful to man. Indeed, the forest was so green and alive that it was permeated with death, and decay everywhere stalked like a slow, patient assassin. Once, when camped by a river in a thicket so dense that a sunbeam was as rare as a precious gem, a foraging party came across the body of a drowned goat that had floated down from a hidden settlement far upstream. By next morning a mushroom had pushed up from its carcass, and by mid-day it had swelled to the size of a battle helmet. The land was saturated, overflowing with moist, green death, and men joked joylessly of being unwilling even to sleep, for fear they might themselves awaken to find lichens encrusting their skin and a toadstool sprouting from their flesh.

All of these thoughts assailed them, swirling and magnifying in their minds, under the dark canopy of the swaying, sighing, centuries-old spruces and firs. Here and there, bird and animal calls sounded, but not the calls of any animals the men knew. Shadows of *ayac-eri*, forest men, flitted between the trees, and eyes were everywhere. Once a sharp-eyed Hunnish sniper even tagged one with an arrow—blood was found on the leaves where the intruder had been shot; tatters of cloth hung on the brambles where he had escaped into the thick undergrowth—but the Hunnish scout, even with a squadron of heavily armed comrades, dared not venture any deeper into the forest to seek out their quarry or his lair. The forest contained objects of fear, but worse yet, it created fears, by its very darkness, by its silence when one sought the comfort of noise, and by its noise when one sought the solace of silence.

After three weeks of marching along a muddy track beaten into even deeper mud by the nail-studded wheels of the wagons and the pawing of countless hooves, the air lightened, at first imperceptibly to all senses but scent, which detected a minuscule lessening of the odor of damp rot that pervaded all. Soon this lightening became noticeable to even the eyes. The edge of the forest was approaching. Trees were thinning, becoming more widely spaced, and here and there one could even see true ax-cut stumps and relics of isolated homesteads and hunting lodges, now abandoned in the face of the army's march. The massive column of men and horses visibly increased its pace in the excitement and anticipation of finally emerging from the dark prison in which they had struggled for the past weeks. Above, patches of iron gray sky now became visible, and ahead, to the west, the afternoon light for the first time showed brightly through the trees.

Suddenly the column stopped. This was not unusual—an army on the march stops many times during the course of the day, for meals, reconnoitering of terrain, water breaks for the animals, or simply no good reason at all but for the fact that thousands of men following behind one another string and bunch in an endless cycle of contraction and extension. In such a case, the air normally fills with the shouts of officers racing up and down the line, orders to engineers to remove an obstacle, cheers from the lead troops when they encounter a long sought-after goal or an unanticipated gift of a watercourse or a plunderable town. A marching army, or a stopped one for that matter, is rarely silent.

This, however, was not such a stop. Indeed, no sound came from the front ranks of the miles-long line of men and animals at all. The army simply ground to a silent halt.

Attila, who had been riding in the middle of the column, cursed and abruptly began cantering along the muddy road to the front of the line. He was preceded by a squadron of Hunnish guards, whose shouts of, "Way! Way for the king!" cleared a path through the puzzled troops and the wagons.

After nearly an hour of struggling and pushing through

the massed men, Attila broke through to the head of the line, which had stopped just at the forest edge. Before it stretched a series of broad plains, low undulating foothills broken here and there by small peasant cottages and placid herds of grazing sheep. The pastures and small farms stretched as far as a range of hills on the far horizon, a march of perhaps a day or two in distance. Beyond those hills, Attila knew, lay a formidable obstacle, the Rhine, one that would take every bit of his ingenuity to pass. Yet an even more formidable obstacle lay right here, directly in front of his massive army.

At the far end of the long slope, scarcely visible beneath the glaring light of the low-setting western sun, stood another army—as vast as, perhaps even vaster than, the one stalled behind him in the forest. Even from this distance they could be seen spread over a huge arc, and not spread thinly, either, for the rise behind the lead ranks was filled to the summit with a thickly massed body of men.

Turgrid cantered up to Attila's side where he stood observing the maneuver. He pressed his horse up against Attila's and spoke quietly.

"The Alamanni forces, Great *Cur*, led by Yoric himself, it seems. Our scouts say the tribes have overcome their internal squabbles and have now formed a united front."

Attila nodded. "Orestes has been sent ahead, to his tribesmen?"

"He has, Great King. A week ago, as planned. However, we have not heard from him since."

Attila peered straight ahead, trotting his horse silently for a moment across the front of his column, as the officers and guards following him murmured quietly among themselves. Then suddenly halting, he looked straight at the advancing Alamanni force and raised his closed fist. The troops behind him fell silent, and all movement stopped. Not a muscle moved, not a sound was heard but for the soft rustling of the wind and the groan of the trees in the forest behind them. Every Hunnish face stared impassively ahead, at the advancing army of the united Alamanni tribes.

The enormous force drew up in full battle array, the sun glinting on polished cuirasses and helmets. This was no mere tribal militia but rather a trained force, a huge confederation of clans and tribes. And like the other Alamanni Attila had encountered in the past, these men were of terrific size—even from this distance, their stature and musculature were impressive— and they carried a fearsome array of weaponry: broadswords nearly as long as a normal man was tall, battle-axes slung over shoulders for close-range hacking, long pikes with curved, scythelike blades on the ends, designed to reach over and behind shields, to tear weapons straight out of the hands of their opponents, to cut a man's neck from the side or the back even when facing him head-on.

On both flanks of the long infantry front, wings of Germanic horsemen moved forward in close alignment, long cavalry lances dropped to the charging position, heavy shields held high in the erect Germanic cavalry stance. The horses were enormous, a full head and shoulders higher than the short Hunnish ponies, and even from this distance, several hundred yards away, the weight of their heavy hooves made the ground tremble.

The horsemen advanced at a trot, faster than their footbound counterparts in the middle of the line, squeezing the broad front to form a long semi-circular barrier facing the Hunnish column. As they moved, the infantry compressed and the two horns of the crescent of advancing horsemen turned inward, narrowing the open space in the front of the Huns, shaping it to the form of a long cavity, a hollow or a tunnel. If Attila moved his troops forward, he would be surrounded on three sides. If he withdrew—

no, withdrawal was not possible. Turning a massive army such as his completely around on the narrow track and retreating back into the dark woods, where who-knows-what other forces might have circled around behind him, was not an option.

Attila watched the maneuvers calmly, moving scarcely a muscle, and Turgrid and the officers did the same. The troops behind them, however, those who had pushed forward to emerge from the darkness of the trees to spy out the cause of the delay, shifted restlessly in their saddles as they witnessed the steady approach of the Alamanni. They murmured their opinions to the ranks behind them, who did the same to their own comrades rearward, until every man in the Hunnish army was aware that here, in this vulnerable, lengthened column, without hope of emerging from the forest into feasible battle formation, the army was facing the greatest European force ever gathered in one place.

Silently Attila observed the Alamanni approach, until even his own officers began glancing at him wonderingly, restlessly—nervously. The Alamanni horse troops were now within arrow range on either side of the leading ranks of the Hunnish column, and the Alamanni foot troops were within distance of a running charge. Suddenly, with a shrill whistle from a source behind the Alamanni lines, all troops halted in their advance. Every man froze in his position, cavalry lances aimed forward, horses restlessly pawing the turf beneath them, foot soldiers peering through the locks of yellow hair blowing past their eyes. All stood still, silently watching the Hunnish king, his officers, and the vanguard of the horde observing them where they stood on the narrow dirt road that emerged from the forest.

And the Huns stood stone-still, staring back at them, with an intensity that betrayed no fear or hesitation.

For a long moment the two forces faced each other,

gazing at each other, silently calculating the strength behind each other's lines, the determination of each other's leaders, the range of their weapons, and the speed of their horses. For a long moment, a million men stood across from each other, on a deserted pasture at the edge of the forest, and assessed each other's strengths. For a long moment, the fate of both armies hung in the balance.

And then, without herald or warning, a tall Alamanni warrior heeled his horse and galloped out ahead of the column of his countrymen. The long red hair flying behind him, in the Hunnish fashion, was unmistakable. As he raced alone toward the Hunnish lines, he threw off his battle helmet and raised his fist in a triumphant salute.

Attila smiled with satisfaction. "Orestes," he murmured.

With a nod of the king's head, the Hunnish column lurched and creaked forward, like a single living organism, advancing steadily and serpentlike, cavalry following king, wagons following cavalry, more cavalry, foot soldiers, cavalry and spare animals, and always more cavalry, advancing steadily, slowly, in perfect order . . .

Straight into the middle of the Germanic tunnel.

The Hunnish column advanced into the massed force of armed men, and the Alamanni ranks parted, like wheat before a reaper, making way, making way for the eastern king and his army. Into the very middle of the Germanic ranks Attila rode, slowly and without hesitation, looking to neither right nor left, nor even acknowledging the presence of the vast collection of painted and armed barbarian troops on either side of him, huge and muscular, mounted on their enormous warhorses. And as the Hunnish army passed through the lines of horsemen and into the front ranks of the foot troops, the Alamanni silently stepped forward and fell into formation beside the Hunnish column—doubling its width, tripling it, lending the serpentine column a strength and a thickness, a size and a length, never before seen, perhaps in the entire world.

They stepped into the Huns' rhythm, fell into the Huns' speed of advance, and began marching alongside them.

Overhead, flocks of gulls from a distant sea circled and called daringly, waiting for the men and animals to pass, that they might dive down and pick from the scraps of the camp followers and cooks. For many hours the birds circled, however, and still the army continued slowly to emerge from the forest. The allied force covered the land black, carpeted it with a roiling layer of men and animals and wagons on a slow, steady progression, a vast horde more numerous than any ever seen on the face of the earth, marching now under one leader and with one objective: toward the West, toward the Rhine—toward Rome.

Early that spring, on a hillside near Tolosa, in southwest Gaul, Aetius cantered along in company with a man of his own age and several younger riders. All were dressed informally, in leather and rough woolen hunting garb, and were followed at some distance by a crowd of retainers.

"A hunt!" Theodoric shouted heartily. "Never let a day go by, Flavius, without killing something. It's just what the doctor ordered, to take your mind off your woes!"

"There is only one cure for my woes, King. . . ."

"Thorismund!" Theodoric bellowed. "Frideric! Bring your brothers! Hurry now!"

Five young men rode up to Theodoric and Aetius and reined in their pawing, stamping horses. Men and animals were restless, eager for action. The oldest of the five, a sturdy rider perhaps twenty-five years of age, resembled his father so closely that it startled Aetius the first time he laid eyes on him, thinking that somehow Theodoric had discovered the fountain of youth. Thorismund slipped his horse in between Aetius' and Theodoric's animals, clearly maneuvering for close position in whatever was to come next.

"Lads, you see that rise over there?" Theodoric roared. *Was there ever a time Theodoric spoke in a normal tone of voice?* Aetius wondered with a slight smile. It was no wonder he had been given the nickname Earache by his boyhood comrades in the palace. Unfortunately, he seemed somehow to have failed to take this unsubtle hint to heart—if anything, his voice had become even more strident with the passing of the years.

"I say, do you see that rise yonder? That's where I spied the big stag yesterday—a six-pointer, by God! Pity I didn't have my bow with me, or we'd be having cold venison for lunch today. The man who brings me his antlers wins that prize stallion I've been training. Go!"

The young men raced off, yipping and whooping, and Theodoric grinned fondly.

Aetius watched wistfully. "Five strapping sons! You're a lucky man, Theodoric!"

"Thorismund—he's my eldest—he's the best shot of them all," the king replied. "But he's too impatient. Can't ever seem to wait for the right moment. Now my youngest, Himmerit, he's a different story altogether—"

"King Theodoric," Aetius interrupted, reining in his horse and taking a more serious tone. "We must talk. The Huns have allied with the Alamanni. Countless cities and towns have been destroyed. The remaining Gallic tribes are weak and unable to defend their lands. There is nothing between Rome and complete disaster but a river of eight hundred yards' width, our border garrisons, and . . . you."

Theodoric squinted ahead. "Surely you must know why Attila is doing this? Why is he attacking Rome? Why is he attacking you?"

Aetius shook his head. "He has long despised Rome—though I did not realize the extent. Yet he has never been strong enough to challenge us, until now. The planets are aligned in his favor—his allies are powerful and hungry for

Roman land; his own domestic control is secure; Rome's emperor is young and inexperienced, its borders weak."

Theodoric scoffed. "All those are reasons, but not enough. The word I hear is that as the Huns passed through eastern Europe, they razed entire cities to the ground, pillaged churches and monasteries, even slew monks and virgins. Such destruction goes far beyond military targets. Why such savagery?"

Aetius paused. "I fear Attila may have a form of madness. . . ."

"Madness my ass!" growled Theodoric. "Unless it's that peculiar form of madness that comes from craving power. You are merely making excuses for him as a friend. It is time to take his actions at face value."

"That is why I am here."

Theodoric's face took on a somber cast. "It is a tough battle, Flavius—and I don't mean against the Huns. My own rule is not absolute, for I still require the approval of the council of elders and the clan leaders to undertake war."

"But surely the elders can agree on this course of action. . . ."

"Agree?" Theodoric snorted in disdain. "They can't agree on the color of shit. The old Visigoths—those of my father's generation—do not have fond memories of Rome. They shed blood to capture Rome once—and yet now they are no better off for it, and indeed see Rome as once again exhibiting arrogance. The younger clan leaders are eager to test their blades but fear Roman advantage if they win. They fear committing our men to do all the dying, while Rome remains unbloodied to seize control afterward. If they fight, they would rather do it alone. They have their own ambitions."

Aetius stared at him. "Do they not see that neither Rome nor Visigoth alone can prevail over the Huns? The sheer numbers are impossible—and the Huns' numbers are growing with every step they take west. We must combine forces."

Theodoric looked out at the horizon thoughtfully.

"Attila's ambassadors have been here," he confided. "They have promised me that if we allow the Huns free passage through our territory, they will leave my people unmolested. However, if we oppose them, and lose . . ."

"You will not lose. You *cannot* lose. Not with Roman support and backing. We will help you. . . ."

"Roman 'backing' is not enough, Flavius. Roman troops must take the lead. Roman blood must be shed before any other. *Your* blood must be shed before any other."

"And if I do promise Roman legions in the front line?" Aetius immediately shot back.

Theodoric scanned the horizon for sight of his sons, wondering if they had encountered the stag. "*If* you promise and deliver Roman legions to the front line—and *if* the Huns actually do cross the Rhine and threaten Gaul—then I will join the coalition. But my men fight for *you*—not for Rome. Otherwise, I must accept the Huns' offer of protection for my kingdom. I must remain neutral."

Aetius considered this. "Only if they pose a threat to Gaul?"

Theodoric glanced at him. "Flavius: The Huns have yet to cross the Rhine. No army that size has ever succeeded in crossing the river. You know that. You have legions guarding the bridges and the major fords. And you know how wide the Rhine is, especially after the spring rains and the snowmelt in the Alps. Watch. The Rhine will do for us what all your diplomacy has failed at. The river will turn back Attila."

Aetius shook his head skeptically. "And you, Theodoric—," he said mockingly. "How do *you* avoid this madness you spoke of earlier? This madness of power?"

"Me? I don't crave power, except that it allows me the leisure to hunt. By God, Flavius, I'd live as a floor sweeper in a monastery for the rest of my days if the abbot allowed me to hunt every afternoon!"

"That's your goal? That's your only ambition? To hunt?"

"Enough philosophizing, Roman. I'm not a sophist. To the stag!" Theodoric whipped his horse forward, practically lunging in his excitement to join the chase.

Aetius paused a moment before following suit, staring in disappointment at the retreating back of his friend.

"And that, King Theodoric," he murmured, "is why Attila rules half the world."

With a grunt, the Hunnish carpenter finished the splice, pulled tight the double hitch knot, and cleanly sliced off the dangling end with his dagger. To be sure, it was only a foot or so of extraneous rope, which easily could have been tucked into the lashing, out of sight but for a slight visible loop where it was passed through. That kind of job would have been perfectly adequate—good enough for army work. His method was much more difficult, for neatly knotting, splicing, and tying ends of lines was no trivial task.

But this was no trivial job and this man's army no trivial army. All the skills he had learned his entire life, constructing rope-knotted wooden houses, sturdy but portable for transport on the Hunnish steppe, he had brought to bear on this single structure: a makeshift flat-bottomed barge, soundly built of pitch-covered pine planks from disassembled Hunnish shelters and wagons. He stepped back from the final splice to review his work, nodded in satisfaction, then strode to the end of the vessel and clambered up onto the dock to which it had been tightly lashed.

As he climbed the short ladder, a half-dozen hands

reached to help him, grasping his upper arms and shoulders and lifting him off the rungs and onto the thick oaken planks of the quay. As they released him, a roar of many men rose up behind him and he knew that at this moment, on this dock, he had attained a level of renown that few kings ever aspire to, much less mere carpenters. Turning to face the cheer, he raised his arms above his head like a champion wrestler. The throng of men bellowed their approval, slapping his back and lifting him onto their shoulders, affording him a view far beyond the foot of the dock, to the muddy riverbank and the stumps of the newly logged hills beyond. Every bit of space was covered by men and horses.

Other carpenters, too, clambered up and were lifted onto the dock, again to the resounding cheers and laughter of the men. Suddenly, at the base of the dock, a rider appeared on a powerfully built Hunnish war pony, and every voice fell silent. He was clad in sweat-stained armor and wore a fur-trimmed cap pulled down low over his ears and brow, with a black cloak of soft goat wool draped casually behind him, clasped at the neck by an iron brooch. Trotting below him, beside the horse, was an enormous gray wolf, the fur around the neck and shoulders as thick as the mane of a lion, the powerful muscles rolling easily beneath the soft coat as he moved. The beast's eyes glared out from his face, yellow and alert, and the men around the rider stepped back warily, forming a wide path down the middle of the dock to where the cluster of carpenters stood nervously waiting.

Attila rode slowly down the quay, his horse's hooves clopping on the wooden planks, and then, standing before the workmen, he deftly wheeled around. The gigantic throng behind him fell silent.

"If after so many victories," he shouted, "if after conquering so many great peoples, you were to be halted by a river, I would be a fool to think I could goad you with mere speech, as if you did not know what was at stake. Only an untested leader would resort to that."

The men nodded and murmured, and here and there enthusiastic cries floated above the mob.

"Never would I demean you with banal words," he continued, "nor would you honor me falsely by listening to them. War is not something you need be prodded to undertake. For what is war but your very bread and meat? What is there sweeter in this life than for a brave man to seek glory with his own hand, to sate his soul with conquest? What is there more pure than for a man to forgo his personal comforts and ambitions and friendships, to achieve victory for his people?"

A buzz of excitement rose from the men surrounding him, and the mob pressed forward, toward the dock where Attila stood. The wolf, uneasy, gave a low growl and the guards at the front edge of the throng pushed back, resisting the pressure behind. Several men, even a horse and rider, lost their balance and toppled off the edge of the quay, though not a single eye even glanced their way as they struggled out of the water and onto the beach. Every man, every face, was focused on the stern visage of their leader.

"We will rise to the occasion, the Huns and their mighty allies; we will attack the Romans eagerly! For despite their machines and their fire, despite their drills and their training, they cower in terror. They know not whether to seek the heights, seize the hills, or clamor for cover in the open fields. Our greatest ally, Fortune, has joined us, and with her we cannot lose. If we are fated to die, death would overtake us anyway, even in peace, in our own beds. But if we are fated to live, no spear can harm us. And we *are* fated to live—for why else would Fortune have made us victorious over so many nations, unless it were to prepare us for this great victory? I myself will hurl the first spear at the foe. If any can endure rest while Attila fights, he is a dead man!"

The cries grew louder, more pressing, and Attila raised his voice to be heard.

"These men . . . ," he shouted, gesturing at the workers before him, "these carpenters, trained in the simple tasks of their daily lives, have performed a great feat! Skilled in the making of wagons and huts, these men have built us a path to victory. With ropes made of Hunnish grass, wood from the planks of Hunnish wagons and houses, and strength from the muscles of Hunnish riders, these men have constructed a road to destiny. The purity and simplicity and glory of the Hunnish nation have been brought to bear, to defeat the decadence of mighty Rome!"

The men surged, and the guards struggled to hold them back, to prevent them from overwhelming the very dock on which the king stood.

"And this!" Attila bellowed. "*This* will be our path, the Hunnish path that will bring Rome, the scourge of the world, to its knees!"

Whirling on his steed, startling the wolf at his feet, the king pointed his long sword to the simple barge lashed tightly by the bow to the edge of the dock below him. The men roared in triumph as he slowly raised the sword, pointing it to the vessel's stern, which was lashed to the bow of another barge . . . and that barge to another . . . forming a long, flat line of vessels crossing the vast expanse of the smooth river, the crafts in the middle bowing out gently in a graceful arc from the pressure of the current but clinging fast to their brethren craft. The carpenters' careful joining and knotting and planing had held true.

"To our destiny!" Attila shouted, and the cheers rose deafeningly around him. A dozen workmen lifted up a broad wooden ramp at his feet, staggered forward, and dropped the end off the edge of the dock to the bridge of barges floating placidly below, quickly lashing the near ends of the ramp to the wharf posts to prevent it from slipping.

"To Rome!" he bellowed, and driving forward, he urged his warhorse at a trot down the ramp and onto the first barge, which floated as steadily and calmly as if it were a road on solid ground. The horse did not so much as hesitate, and the wolf bounded across the ramp to catch up with his master.

Behind them, Huns, Ostrogoths, Alamanni, Rugi, Sciri, Gepidae, Vandals, and a myriad other tribes who had flocked to the support of this new leader, this new ruler of the world, quickly formed their cavalry and wag-ons into the formation to which they were long accus-tomed, for they had marched five hundred miles to reach this point and they had that distance more still to go to reach Rome.

The million men of the horde began their march across the Rhine.

II

"A story, Father," the young voice begged.

"It's past time you were in bed."

"Flavius," said Priscilla, "you leave tomorrow. Surely the boy can stay up a bit longer."

Aetius considered this with a smile. "So. I'm as out-numbered at home as I am in the field. Which story will it be? About when I was a boy? About your grandfather?"

"A myth! A myth by the Greeks!"

The smile faded. "A myth. It's been a long time—I don't know many . . ."

"Please?"

Aetius paused a long moment, his eyes gazing at the ceiling of the dining room of the house in Arelate. How long would it be before he would again recline on this couch, gaze at this ceiling, hold his child on his lap?

"There was a young man, a brilliant young man," Aetius began, "rich and famous."

"A warrior, like Achilles? Hercules?"

"No. . . ."

"A sailor, like Jason?"

"No, he was a musician."

"Oh." There was a tinge of disappointment in the tone. "He didn't conquer anyone?"

"Indeed he did. He conquered the most terrible of the Greek gods, Pluto himself."

"But he wasn't a warrior?"

"His name was Orpheus, and his weapon was the lyre and his voice."

He glanced to his wife and saw her wave away the servant girl who had begun to clear the plates. Priscilla then turned back and fixed a penetrating stare on him. Aetius immediately regretted his choice of story, but it was too late. There was nothing to it but to continue.

"Orpheus' music was so entrancing that when men listened to him, all the chains that bound their minds to earth fell away and were left behind. When he played, the rooted trees would move toward him on the ground, the shifting rivers would halt their flow, and even the gray rocks in the fields would rise from the earth and begin to sing. His music was the most sublime of all human accomplishments, the greatest of all the gods' creations.

"But Orpheus was not a god. He was a man, and like all men he suffered. To his great sorrow, his beautiful wife, Eurydice, whom he loved more than even his music, died, and her soul passed to the Underworld. Orpheus was crushed. In his deep mourning he sang all the more passionately. But for all he sang, for all he conquered the fierceness of the world with his music, he was unable to subdue the sorrow in his heart. So great was his love for Eurydice, so little did he value his own life without her, that he resolved to go down into Hell itself, to seek her out and to bring her back from the grasp of her dark guardian."

The dining room had fallen silent as Aetius' wife and son listened. Twilight began to descend, the shadows in the room lengthened and grew deep and cold, but no one thought even to light a tallow.

"Finding the secret entrance to the Underworld, he descended into the darkness. All around him, the souls of the dead fluttered about, screeching like bats, warning him away with their unintelligible words. Yet Orpheus was undeterred, and when it became too overwhelming even for him, he lifted his lyre and began to sing. And there, even in the very depths of Hell, his music and his longing began to take effect. The great three-headed hound Cerberus stood in silent amazement and let him pass; the Furies, who avenge men's sins and steal men's happiness, dropped tears of sorrow. Tantalus in his accursed prison forgot the eternally rising waters and his fatal thirst, and even the vulture who day after day tore out and devoured the organs of the living giant Tityus ceased for a time his terrible shredding.

"At last, after singing for a day and a night, Orpheus heard the words he longed for. 'We yield,' came the voice of the Monarch of the Dead, Pluto himself. 'Take thy wife, for by thy music truly thou hast redeemed her.' Orpheus began to dash forward to embrace her but halted at the god's next words: 'Yet only this law obey: Thou must not look upon thy beloved with thine eyes until both have reached the light of the sun. For only then can she truly again be thine.'

"Orpheus was not dismayed and with great joy began leading his wife along the winding, dark path through the Underworld and back to their earthly home. Yet who but a god can give such a law as that, a law forbidding a man to look upon his beloved? And who can obey such a law but another god only? For a man, for Orpheus at least, it was impossible. Just when he reached sight of the cave that would lead them out of the Kingdom of the Dead, he glanced back at his wife in affection, and upon looking, he lost and killed her there."

The room had fallen into darkness, and for a moment all was silent.

"And he wasn't able to get her again?" the small voice asked, subdued.

Aetius paused a long time, thinking. "He was not. But the ancients tell us there was a lesson to be learned from Orpheus' tale. That whoever would seek the upward way, the way of light, and serenity, and truth, must always look forward. And whoever would look backward for these things—into the past, into the darkness, into lost friendships and loves, into the ways of old—himself gives way to darkness."

The child slid off Aetius' lap, kissed him good night, and then slipped out of the room to his waiting nurse, though Aetius scarcely noticed. His wife, too, remained silent on the other side of the room, yet in the darkness, and in the depth of his own thoughts, he scarcely noticed that as well.

For his thoughts were completely taken up with memories of his own past, of his own ways of old, of his own lost friends. And he knew now, of a certainty—as clearly as if he had heard the very voice of Orpheus singing in his ear—that he could no longer look back, that he could no longer seek reconciliation with the shadows of the past.

A man cannot live his life in two worlds. He must look to the future or fall by the wayside. He is alive, or he is dead. He is Roman or a Hun. There comes a time when there is no room for questioning, no occasion for self-doubt or regret. There comes a time when there is no looking back.

Aetius stood up abruptly and strode to the door. There

was still much work to be done to prepare, but his conscience was clear.

He was Roman.

III

Aetius sat his horse before the palisaded walls at Arelate. For months he had been massing his troops here, at the site of the Roman high command for Gaul, and though the huge camp was already bursting with troops newly arrived from garrisons as far distant as Lusitania and Sicily, still more were marching in daily, in disciplined order and high spirits. Even now, shouting could be heard from the road leading north from the city as ox drovers trailing an incoming contingent from Transalpine Gaul now demanded that their Spanish counterparts, who were already departing on the outbound march ahead of the main army, make way for them.

Before Aetius, the Roman army stood in review, armor polished, woolen cloaks newly washed and steaming in the hot morning sun, leather straps of sandals and shoulder pieces deftly repaired and oiled. The body of troops was enormous, larger than perhaps any other ever seen on the soil of Gaul, certainly the largest Roman army that had been gathered in one place since—Aetius idly reviewed figures from Roman history in his head—since when? The Emperor Julian's massing in the previous century? Perhaps as far back as the conquests of Julius Caesar himself. Still, Aetius shook his head in dismay. From the scouting reports he had received of the approaching Hunnish army, even discounting the factor of fearful exaggeration, his troops seemed pitifully few.

Nodding at Florentius to accompany him, Aetius wheeled and cantered toward a young Visigoth nobleman sitting quietly astride his horse a hundred paces away with a small knot of retainers. Their clothing was dusty and sweat-stained, and the horses panted and pawed the earth as they caught their breath in the cool shade of the city walls.

"Prince Thorismund," Aetius called as he approached, smiling at the young commander whose stocky and muscular build so reminded him of the Visigoth king Theodoric. "Welcome. I didn't see you arrive, but your presence gives my men confidence of the Visigoths' support."

The prince turned and grinned broadly. "General Aetius!" he exclaimed. "I rushed from Tolosa as soon as our forces were assembled—Father asked that I attach myself to your staff, and keep him informed of your progress north. I've brought my own couriers to run messages and scout the roads—they know the territory well."

Florentius galloped to Aetius' side, eyeing the small knot of horsemen that hovered behind Thorismund.

"Theodoric promised soldiers," he said, without preliminaries. "Many soldiers."

Thorismund gazed at the older man with resentment, his eyes lingering disdainfully on the wooden leg. "Who is this?"

"Centurion Florentius," Aetius said. "A man of trust. He speaks for me."

The prince nodded skeptically. "My father will deliver the troops you requested. It was not an easy task—the tribal council of elders opposed lending any soldiers to the cause. Father eventually overruled them—"

"Overruled them? I thought the Visigoth council would agree . . . ?"

The young man gave a thin smile. "They did. But only after Father locked them in the palace council room until they did so. They are still locked up—it's safer they remain that way until our army departs."

"And when will that be? Our troops are outnumbered by the Huns four to one. The situation is critical."

The prince nodded. "My father is aware of that, General. He asks me to inform you that he will meet you with his army at Aurelia in exactly three weeks' time. From there the two armies can continue on together."

"How large a force did he gather?"

"Every man but the border garrisons. Two hundred thousand troops."

Florentius snorted and turned away. "Well, that's good news," he replied. "Now we'll only be outnumbered two to one."

Thorismund stared at Florentius with an expression of shock, and Aetius reached out to slap him on the shoulder with a grim smile.

"Only two to one! A big relief, don't you think?"

He cantered off, sending Florentius away to help organize the troop departure, shouting an order to his officers. With a crash of drums and a roar from the throats of three hundred thousand men, the troops quickly shouldered their gear and armor, fell into position by company, and began the long process of marching out. As column after column of infantry filed by at a Roman trot, Aetius observed their progress distractedly. He then resumed his gallop, beyond the encampment's long wooden palisades and around the southeast corner of the city walls, to the shaded and sheltered side. Waiting anxiously for him in front of a large field tent in the midst of the high command's quarters was Priscilla, her two children flanking her as well as several other women and children of the senior officers.

Aetius reined in his horse, dismounted, and stepped to Priscilla's side. His face was still preoccupied and distracted as he addressed her, and his voice had not yet lost the harsh edge of command it always assumed when addressing his troops. His expression showed that he was eager to be away.

"Three weeks' march to Aurelia," he said. "Then let's

hope to God Theodoric keeps his word and meets us there with the Visigoths. He's never let me down, ever since we were boys, but anything can happen in three weeks, while herding that many men."

"Is there no other way?" she asked softly.

Aetius seemed almost startled to hear her voice, and as he looked at her he struggled to focus his thoughts. He shook his head. "One might have been found earlier, before Attila started out. Now it is too late. Three weeks from now and we will know."

A small boy sidled close. "What will we know, Papa?"

Aetius looked down, smiled, and ruffled the child's hair, considering what, and how much, he should tell the youngster. How to tell a young boy, who is scolded whenever he pinches his little sister, that it is his father's job to kill other men? How to explain that his sole task is to deprive other young boys of their own fathers?

"Whether . . . we are to be Romans or Huns."

The small boy peered up excitedly. "Huns! When can we be Huns, Papa?"

Aetius picked the boy up and peered closely into his face. "If we become Huns, we will never be Roman again, Son. We will always be Huns. Forever."

With a eunuch's shrill call of, "Way for the senator!" a sedan chair arrived behind them, borne on the shoulders of four muscular slaves, and was gently lowered to the ground. A small knot of attendants quickly gathered around it. Priscilla peered at the commotion in surprise, then at her husband.

"Could it be?" she exclaimed.

Carpilio, in his customary formal Roman toga, stepped stiffly from the sedan and looked toward Priscilla and Aetius.

"Father!" Priscilla called.

She ran to him and embraced him but pulled back suddenly and stared at him with concern at his formal and distracted greeting. The old senator barely saw his daughter as he continued looking past her, toward Aetius. Aetius stepped forward and seized Carpilio's arm in a hearty greeting.

"Senator!" he said with a broad smile. "Good to see you again!"

Carpilio returned his affectionate clasp. "Flavius— how many times must I remind you to call me Father?"

Priscilla seized her father's arm again. "We've waited for your visit for so long! But now it's late—Flavius is leaving this morning."

"Ah, but the timing is perfect," Aetius corrected her. "The good senator—'Father'—can keep you company while I'm away. Help keep my boys here from turning completely barbarian."

Carpilio smiled but shook his head. "Unfortunately, Rome does not finance trips to Gaul simply for senators to visit their grandchildren. I've arranged an appointment to Flavius' camp as an observer—to report back to the emperor on his disciplining of the Huns!"

Aetius nodded. "And I'm happy to welcome you to my staff. But Senator—my troops are departing now, and I must join them. I will leave a detachment to escort you at a more civilized pace."

Carpilio waved him off. "Fine, fine, be off with you! Give me a moment to acquaint myself with my daughter's family before I march off to do battle with Attila!"

Aetius began edging toward his horse, but Priscilla stepped forward, away from the chattering old man and boys, to embrace her husband. He glanced at her and then, with a smile, stretched out his arms and drew her close to him. They stood together long and silently as the other officers around them looked away and tactfully walked a wide berth around them, for it was a rare occasion that the general displayed emotion in public. Suddenly she pulled away, as if remembering something, and drew from her vestments a gift—a small plain glass bottle topped with a cork, decorated with a loop of bright purple yarn.

Aetius looked at it curiously. "What's this?"

"Olive oil from our estate," Priscilla replied. "The first pressing. It's wonderful. For luck."

"Purple yarn. That's either very lucky or very, very unlucky."

"In this case, it's very lucky. Trust me."

Aetius pulled the cork, took a quick whiff, and smiled. "Luck is always useful. Thank you."

Priscilla took back the open bottle, tipped its mouth against her finger, and dabbed a bit of the oil onto her neck, as if it were perfume. She smiled.

"I'll save it for you," she said.

Aetius nodded, kissing her on the forehead. He then mounted and cantered to his troops, the fastest units of which were already several miles down the road. Priscilla turned from her children and Carpilio, facing her husband as he heeled his horse. Long after he had disappeared from sight, she stared silently into the rising cloud of dust raised by his marching troops.

PART III

PART III

EIGHT

Campi Catalaunici, Gaul, June 20, A.D. 451

I

What for most civilizations in the world would be a capital city is to the Roman legions a mere daily camp. "Mere" is perhaps not the correct word. If there is anything Rome's opponents have learned over the centuries of fighting the legions, it is this: Roman soldiers are not caught by surprise in their beds.

Tonight their camp was constructed as it had been the previous night, twenty miles away, and the night before, twenty miles beyond that. A fortified stronghold, one exceeded in strength by few others in Gaul, but for the occasional citadels perched above strategic road and river junctions. The outer entrenchments were deep, twelve feet, and wide, another twelve feet, extending in a vast square around the camp, with the only openings being the main gate in the front, a smaller one in the rear, and a passage on either side through which a small creek passed and exited. Dirt was still flying from the trenching as the last of the column of troops and supplies filed into the square, but Roman soldiers dig quickly—many had dug just such a ditch every day for the past twenty years, each time after a hard march carrying eighty pounds of tools and weapons. It was an effort that, the first time, makes one's back muscles burn and spasm but which over time diminishes to a dull, aching routine. One learns to adapt, to bear with the pain, for training and drilling and digging ditches is as much of the mind as of the body, and it is good that the brain is a malleable organ, for the digging is always there—as is the pain—and if a man could not adapt, he would go mad.

On the inside of the square, the dirt from the trenching had been thrown into a high embankment, beaten and packed solid with stamping and wooden boards. On top of the fill wall, sharpened stakes were installed for the palisade, as cartloads of freshly trimmed young pines arrived from a stand of trees the scouts had identified a mile up the road. Inside the camp, engineers had already laid out the streets in a neat grid, roping off areas near the walls for livestock and prisoners, tenting areas for the various units farther toward the center, away from missile range, and the heavily guarded general staff area in the center. Hospitals, kitchens, armories, carpentry shops—an entire city was laid out and constructed in a matter of hours, along standardized lines and patterns. If a Roman soldier from Syria could be somehow transported overnight to a legionary camp in Iberia, he would feel perfectly at home, and indeed, looking around himself at the camp city in which he had landed, he might not even realize he had moved. Rome is known as the Eternal City, but it is its legionary camps—built of dirt and logs, rather than of marble and brick—that are truly eternal and constant. Under Nero, Rome burned, under Honorius it was sacked, and both times it was rebuilt in a new fashion. But a legionary camp—a legionary camp remains always the same, torn down in the morning and rising again like a phoenix in the evening, identical and unchanging.

There are few attacking forces in the world capable of storming a camp surrounded by a twelve-foot moat, topped by a palisade of sharpened logs, defended by a quarter million Roman legionaries, and backed by an equal number of auxiliaries.

But Aetius had no illusions. The Huns were one such force.

Couriers dashed about madly, on foot and on horse, bringing dispatches from the rear lines of the column. Scouts thundered in from the far outposts, identifying the route of the next day's march and the site of the next day's encampment. A new delivery of pine logs clattered to the ground from a tip wagon, narrowly missing a flock of bleating sheep being driven past to the livestock yard. Centurions shouted orders and obscenities, claiming sites for their companies in the most desirable parts of the grid. The pounding of thousands of tent stakes was deafening. Aetius rode through the chaos, looking about distractedly as he surveyed the legions' progress. A scout galloped up to his side on a frothing horse, leaped off, and saluted breathlessly.

"Sir, the outposts report that the Hunnish force is only a day's march east."

"They're marching as fast as we are," Aetius replied, his mouth set in a grim line.

"They have horses, sir."

"And we have Romans. What of the land around the Huns?"

The scout blinked. "The towns ravaged, sir, all the land burnt black for miles. The people are so desperate they rejoice for the dead and lament for the living. Refugees are being pushed out in all directions. They are laying the land waste with their thievery, as much as the Huns with their torches. If they spy our supply column, it may be as difficult to hold them off as it will be the enemy."

Aetius nodded. "Burnt black. It's a sorry truth—where the Huns have passed, no grass will grow. Yet the enemy cannot stay and wait for us to attack—they will starve. They must advance upon us here. What is the name of this plain?"

"The locals call it Campi Catalaunici, General."

Aetius nodded and squinted into the distance. "Cata-launici. So be it. And what is that party riding in from the east?"

The officer looked. "Part of one of our cavalry co-horts, sir. Sent out yesterday to try to stop the harassment on our flanks from Hunnish outriders. Looks like they have some prisoners."

Aetius kneed his horse and galloped alone toward the riders trotting in on their foam-flecked mounts. Some fifty Romans in the squadron, their faces drawn and eyes red-rimmed from fatigue, rode two abreast. A dozen or so Hunnish prisoners rode in a group in the middle, sitting erect and solemn on their shaggy ponies, eyes blind-folded, hands tied behind their backs, feet fastened to-gether by lengths of rope passing under the horses' bellies. Despite their situation, the prisoners held their heads high, with the dignity of victors who lack only the final battle to claim their titles. Aetius reined in and stared at the party as it approached.

"What do we have here, centurion?" he called.

The squad leader, a wiry Celt with a three-day growth of beard, saluted with outstretched arm. "Prisoners, sir. Attacked our lead party and then bolted after the skir-mish. We killed most, but this crew here became sepa-rated from the main pack and we trapped them in a blind draw. Looks like we got their leader."

He nodded to one of the Huns, a stocky young man of perhaps twenty-five, who sat motionless on his mount. His dress and demeanor were identical to those of his comrades, the only difference being the bit and bridle fit-tings, which were of gold rather than the customary iron. Aetius approached on his horse, his eyes ranging over the Hunnish rider, who continued to sit stolidly, unaware be-hind his blindfold that he was being scrutinized. Aetius' gaze lingered long on the man's face. That forehead, that jaw—this face was not strange to him.

"Their leader, eh?"

"Can't know for sure. They won't say a word, even to our interpreter."

Aetius faced the Hunnish riders. "You men are prisoners of Rome," he announced firmly, in the Hunnish language. "You will be taken to interrogation, and your level of cooperation will decide your fate. Whether you live or die is up to you."

The Huns did not move, nor even acknowledge Aetius' words. *And why should they?* he thought. Being blindfolded, they had no way of knowing his identity from that of a common camp interpreter.

Drawing the knife at his side, Aetius leaned over and with a single swift motion cut away the gold clasp on the lead Hunnish horse's halter and examined it. It was as he thought—the *tamga* of Attila's clan. He slipped the piece into his own belt. The bit, no longer fastened, fell loose and the horse spat it out, allowing it to dangle at the side of its neck, though the well-trained animal did not turn. Aetius nodded to the centurion, and the riders resumed their walk past him toward the Roman camp.

Just then, Florentius cantered up, extending a scrap of parchment to Aetius.

"Just received from a courier, sir. King Theodoric is arriving. The Visigoths will be deployed by the end of the day."

Aetius stared at him a moment, collecting his thoughts, and then allowed himself a wan smile.

"Good. Send word to Theodoric not to make himself comfortable."

"*Not* to make himself comfortable, sir?"

"Correct. He'll be fighting by morning."

Florentius looked around skeptically. "Do battle here?

On a broad open plain? It favors their cavalry, sir. We have none ourselves to speak of. We should pick a better location."

"We have no choice. The conditions are the same ahead of us, and we cannot retreat or the men will lose morale. We make our stand here."

Florentius glanced around once more, then shrugged laconically. "Could be worse."

Aetius raised an eyebrow. "Possibly. But the stakes couldn't be higher. Our fate will be decided on this plain, the fate of the Western Empire. Perhaps the fate of civilization itself."

Florentius stared into the distance, shifting a piece of grass on which he was chewing.

"You don't seem concerned," Aetius said.

The old veteran looked at him. "About the empire? Sir, every time I fight, I fight as if the empire were at stake. But that's not what I think about. I think about fighting as if *your* life were at stake. And my comrades' lives. Hang the philosophy—a man must fight for something bigger than himself, but not so big that losing his life wouldn't matter. Romans don't fight for their empire. That's too vague. They fight for their comrades, and for their commander."

"This battle is different."

"Sure it's different. More comrades."

"Florentius," Aetius said, "you've been with me for many years, and you accompanied me while I built this coalition. You know there is much more at stake. I told my son that if we lose, we'll all become Huns."

"You told him wrong, sir. If we lose, we'll all be dead," the centurion replied.

"You don't care that all of Gaul will be lost, that Rome may be destroyed, that our very civilization could be wiped out?"

Florentius shrugged. "You tell the men that, sir, and I

don't know what they'll do. It may inspire them, or it may paralyze them."

"And what do you say I should tell them?"

Florentius paused for a moment. "To fight for their families. And for the men at their side."

"Is that all? Is that enough?"

"You want the men to really fight?"

"That's why I'm asking you."

"Then," the old centurion replied, "you tell them to fight for *you*."

Aetius stared away, in silence.

II

The Hunnish scout thundered up to the heavily guarded main entrance to Attila's camp, his horse panting, his woolen cape torn, and his leather gear spattered. A blood-soaked rag covered his face and all but one eye, and he turned his head at a peculiar angle in order to peer through the darkness. "Way for the king's scout!" he shouted. "Way for the king's scout!" Two heavily armored Ostrogoths stepped forward out of the ring of torchlight, away from the crowd of guards blocking the main road into the camp. They motioned for the rider to stop, which he did, in ill temper.

"Password?" one of them barked, in heavily accented Hunnish.

"Fuck you and your passwords," the rider growled. "I've been riding three days and three nights, and I'm wounded. How do I know what tonight's password is?"

"You don't enter the camp without a passw—"

The Goth's words were cut short as the Hun's cavalry sword pierced his throat and emerged, dripping, out the back of his neck above the edge of his armored carapace. With a roar, the other guards leaped forward to the attack, but paused as the rider's horse suddenly reared onto its

hind legs and began kicking dangerously with its sharpened forehooves.

"Put down your weapons!" a commanding voice called
from the gates, which consisted of a blockade of two
overturned wagons set into a barricade of rough-hewn
logs.

The Goths warily lowered their blades and stepped
back.

"Idiots." Turgrid stepped forward from the entrance
and glanced in distaste at the body of the dead guard lying in the darkness at his feet. "The password is meant to
repel Roman spies, not our own scouts reporting intelligence." He looked up at the rider. "Identify yourself."

"Outrider," the man croaked, panting in pain from his
injuries. "Probing Roman supply lines to the south and
west. We were ambushed by an enemy cavalry squadron.
The king must be informed. . . ."

Turgrid's eyes opened wide. "You were with the Raven
Squadron? And the rest of the men?"

"I will report to the king."

"Indeed you will. And then if he allows you to live, you
will face disciplinary action for your stupidity here. Drop
your sword to the ground, dismount, and come with me."

Moments later the two passed through a series of
rickety blockades of wagon planks and into Attila's
compound and then into an unassuming felt tent in the
far corner. The king sat brooding before a wrought-iron
brazier of charcoal, a wolf dozing at his side. He
glanced up at Turgrid and the rider as they ducked into
the tent.

"Intelligence, my lord," Turgrid announced.

"So take it from him and then join me here—we have
work to do."

"He insists on giving it personally to the king. He appears to be the only rider who returned—from the Raven
Squadron."

Attila looked up sharply at Turgrid and then at the rider. "Well, out with it, man."

The rider peered at the king through the shadows of his face wrappings. "I would speak with the king alone," he said in a strong voice.

Attila's eyes narrowed, and he sat up straight in his seat. He stared at the man for a long moment, seeming to peer directly through the filthy wrappings to the man's body beneath and to his soul beyond that. "Leave us, Turgrid."

The old man hesitated, looking from the king to the rider and back again, then turned and walked out. Attila waited carefully until the tent flap had dropped behind his old general. He then turned back to the rider, slowly stood, and placed his hand on the hilt of his sword. His stance was low and threatening, balanced on the balls of his feet, lithe as a cat.

"Now, Flavius Aetius," he said in Latin, "why do you enter the wolf's den? Do you seek to kill the pack leader? Or are you simply mad?"

Aetius slowly unwrapped the rags covering his face "Neither. When the fate of entire peoples lies in our hands, it behooves us to speak with each other before committing ourselves. Some actions cannot be reversed."

"And you do so by sneaking into my camp in the dead of night?"

"You have a strange definition of 'sneaking.' I'd wager your dead guard at the gate would not agree with it. How would you have me meet you?"

"Send a herald," Attila replied. "Like any normal Roman commander."

"For months you have turned away every courier I have sent to you. What would you do with a herald bellowing at your gates?"

"Shoot him," Attila conceded, "before he tried to bribe my officers. I have no further patience with Roman lies and arrogance."

"That is why I came myself."

Attila snorted. "Three decades have passed since we last fought together. Then it was as comrades. Now it is as enemies. Is there any reason why I should not simply kill you now, and thereby win the battle before it even begins?"

"I am not the legions," Aetius replied calmly. "I am merely their general."

"The Romans are no Hydra. If I cut off the head, new ones will not spring up in its place. You have placed the fate of your entire army in my hands this night. History will remember you as Rome's most foolish general."

Aetius stared at him evenly. "Kill me now if you wish. But there are two reasons why you should not."

"I would be very interested to hear them."

"The first is your honor. I come into your presence alone and unarmed, as an ambassador. As a friend. To discuss peace. Ambassadors are not to be harmed, by long-standing tradition and by ties of honor between princes. And friends are not to be harmed—by friendship itself, and by risk of displeasing God."

Attila laughed. "Your friendship, Flavius—that I accept. But honor? That is not yours to give. Honor is empty without power to define it and iron to back it. Honor begins with the quest for power, and ends with the conquest of nations. Power and conquest are tangible; they exist independently and are absolute. Honor is relative. It shifts with the views of the man conceding it, and therefore is not to be trusted. I will not compromise quest and conquest for mere honor. Besides, if your protest of friendship is sincere, why is it that *I* must yield the concession?"

Aetius stared at him a long moment, his face expressionless but his eyes unable to disguise his disappointment. "That is your answer?" he asked.

"That is my answer to your first reason. I hope your second is more convincing."

Aetius nodded. "It is this."

He reached into his belt, brought out the gold harness clasp, and tossed it at Attila's feet. "I believe it belongs to your son."

Attila glanced down at the trinket, then back at Aetius, his face betraying no hint of consternation or alarm.

"Dengizich. You have killed him, then?"

"No. He is well. For now."

"I have a hundred sons. . . ."

"Congratulations. But you have only one first-born. Only one heir to your throne."

"If you believe the life of my son is of sufficient value to dissuade me from taking Gaul, to convince me to reverse the course of my army, then you do not deserve your rank."

"I do not believe that at all," Aetius rejoined. "I do believe, however, that your son's life is of sufficient value to guarantee my own safety while I am in your camp. If I am allowed to return unharmed, your son and his comrades will be released unharmed. If not, they will be crucified at sunrise in view of your army."

"You seek to frighten me, but I know that Romans no longer practice crucifixion. Your threats are empty."

"The carpenters are at work even as we speak."

Attila stared at him for a long moment, appraising him. Finally, he nodded in agreement. "Very well. I guarantee your safety—out of friendship, not your threats. Speak."

Aetius took a deep breath. "I will make you a proposition. Turn your army now. Go back across the Rhine and return to your home. In exchange, I guarantee the safety of you and your men as long as you are within the borders of the empire. There will be no retaliation for the damage you have already wreaked and the plunder you have already taken."

The two men eyed each other. "This is your proposal?"

Attila finally asked. "For this you risked your life to meet with me?"

"I would not have been a man, or a friend, had I not allowed you a way of escape."

Attila let loose a short, sharp burst of laughter. "Even if I accepted your ridiculous offer, you would not let me depart in peace. You *could* not! Your emperor would have your head, for allowing the villain who destroyed eastern Gaul to march away unharmed. No, Flavius, there is no middle ground here. For Rome to survive, I must die. Did you truly need *me* to tell you this hard truth?"

"So you refuse?" Aetius persisted.

Attila shook his head in exasperation. "Since you claim to be a friend, let me make a counter-proposal. Disband *your* army. You will save the lives of thousands of men who would otherwise die by Hunnish blades. Join with me in my conquest. I will give you one-third of the conquered empire to rule—and a place of honor. You will then have achieved all of your goals—peace, honor, and command. Have I left out anything?"

"Only this," Aetius replied. "I already command the *entire* empire, in fact if not in name. Why should I give up two-thirds of what I already control?"

"You may command the legions, but you do not have the title of 'Augustus.' I am the only man in the world who can give you that."

"The history books are full of emperors appointed by edict. None survived for long, and most left the empire worse than they found it. I will not add to the ranks of those traitors."

"Rome is on its deathbed, Flavius. It is weaker now than when we first stole fruit in the streets of Ravenna forty years ago."

"Rome will recover. It always has, and always will, as both a world power and a state of mind. Rome is eternal, and neither you nor your horde can change that."

Attila shook his head. "And they call *me* mad. I have no more time for talk, with friends or enemies. Give me your answer, once and for all."

Aetius paused for a moment before responding. "I cannot accept. Why would you want me to? If I agreed, I would not be a man worthy to rule a third of an empire."

"And is the empire you think you would betray truly worth defending?" Attila persisted.

"If it is not, then nothing is worth defending. I have no choice."

"No choice? That is your greatest defect, and Rome's," Attila replied. "If power is within my grasp, I *choose* to seize it without hesitation, without distraction of mere friendship or principle. I *choose* my own fate, pounce on it like a lion, guzzle it like a bowl of uncut wine, without fear. In doing so, I put even the gods to shame, those gods who seek to control my destiny. You, however, are beholden to your tradition, your definition of honor, your god. Your fate is preordained, and it is to lose everything."

"I must go now," Aetius said simply, arranging the bloody wrappings around his face once again.

Attila stared at him coldly. "How could I have expected otherwise? You have refused the domain of an emperor, and will be left with only your name. Perhaps that is enough for you. But it is not for me. Turgrid!"

As the old general shuffled in, Attila turned away dismissively. "Find this man a fresh horse, and send him on his way. He has his instructions, and is not to be questioned or disturbed."

Turgrid nodded and ducked back out the tent flap. Aetius turned to follow but stopped as Attila suddenly called him back. The king's expression had once again become hard and inscrutable.

"In three hours," he growled, "the sun will rise and illuminate your army's dying day. Look at that sun, Flavius; observe that star closely, and the rays it casts and the length of its shadows. Think about the choice you have made, the men it will affect, the lives it will change. And know this—that before the day is out, I will control every region of the earth lightened by those rays. And Rome will be in darkness."

Aetius stooped and ducked out of the tent without a word. Before him lay the vast encampment of the Huns. He had hardly noticed it on his way to Attila's tent an hour before, in the tension of the moment, but now the enormous scope of the horde was apparent—and overwhelming. A million men—it was the largest city in the Western Empire, a moving metropolis, a population without culture, history, or governance, a huge, rolling machine of death. Across the plain, the twinkling lights of the cook fires and torches spread to the dark horizon, disappearing to tiny pinpricks of light in the distance, melding with the cold, winking stars of the sky to form an uninterrupted, dizzying pattern of lights that began at his feet, spun outward in all directions, and met in the great heavenly dome overhead.

He followed Turgrid through the camp, threading his way between the fires, feeling the heat from each roaring blaze in turn beating on one side of his face, then on the other, like a hot pulse. This was not a city or a camp with which he was familiar. No neat rows of tents here, no carefully plotted streets or drill grounds, no impregnable stockades and ditches surrounding the perimeter. This was a vast barbarian mob, with loutish Ostrogoths swaggering belligerently among hard-looking Hunnish soldiers, women and children of both tribes scampering indiscriminately among them, wooden wagons parked helter-skelter among the tents or toppled to their sides to form lean-tos, and above all the horses—horses everywhere, the shaggy patient Hunnish horses, standing beside the men and staring into the fires, poking their long, hooked noses into the tents, resting lazily on their sides in the middle of the paths. Horses, a million horses, as many horses as there were men, and spares besides. *What chance did Rome have,* Aetius thought grimly, *against such an enemy? They lack discipline, they lack order, yet what force on earth can stand up to horses and horsemen such as these?*

He thought bitterly of the months of struggle he had consumed merely to gather his own unwieldy coalition—the reluctance of the emperor to commit troops and treasure, the scoffing of the allies. Yet here, in the camp of the Huns, he saw that all his work had yielded a force so inferior as to be laughable, so foot-bound and stodgy that his troops' sandals might as well be nailed to the ground, against the speed and mobility of this great force, with its infinite quantity of horses. *I would give up all the stockades and discipline of my own camp,* he reflected, *for only half the horses of the Huns, and my troops would be no worse off for it.*

Turgrid sidled up to him. "The king ordered you a horse, and your release," he said in low tones, "though I personally would have had you flogged and executed for your conduct at the gate."

"Farewell, old man," Aetius replied behind his rags.

Turgrid paused and stared. "I know you," he muttered, more to himself than to Actius. "I know you."

Aetius climbed upon the fresh horse Turgrid had brought him.

"Perhaps it's just an old man's mind playing tricks upon him," Aetius said before cantering away.

Turgrid gazed after him, wondering, and then returned to making his rounds of the camp in preparation for the morning.

III

The day dawned with promise of bright sunshine, though this was difficult to imagine in the cold, thick mist that hung low over the field. Romans and Visigoths formed up on the near end of the plain outside their camp. Half a million men covered the slope, a mass of warriors so huge that its farthest reaches disappeared from sight in the silvery fog. As far as the eye could see, the land was covered with a roiling carpet of gleaming metal armor and crimson cloaks, and a thousand olive-wreathed eagle standards marking the individual units jauntily spiked the air.

In the tension before battle, no man could stand still. Some jogged in place or swung their arms in circles to loosen their stiff limbs and warm their blood in the bracing air. Others squatted on their heels, nervously sharpening a spearhead for the hundredth time or polishing a shield with a pumice. Some collected in small groups, chatting quietly and peering anxiously through the mist, in the direction the enemy was said to be approaching, while others withdrew into themselves, remaining alone though surrounded by throngs of men. Every soldier reacts differently to the notion of impending death, and in the moments before battle is joined, a man's true nature—whether as a loner, a lion, or a believer in God—suddenly rises to the fore.

Behind them stood a long battery of missile-launching onagers, twenty such monsters, heavy wooden timbers and iron fittings laboriously dragged from the Roman garrisons at Lutetia and Aurelia by oxcart and hastily erected in the night. Each weapon was set on a massive wooden carriage, supported on iron wheels that would not buckle or flex with the stress of firing the loads. The front of each carriage was positioned flush against the edge of a twelve-foot protective trench and anchored to the ground with spikes and heavy ropes to prevent it from tipping backward when the firing arm was winched down. The row of artillery was aligned facing the enemy position, each machine twenty paces from its neighbor to allow room to maneuver. The far end of the artillery battery faded and disappeared into the shifting mist.

As Aetius trotted his horse along the row of onagers, his eye was suddenly caught by a familiar face. Standing next to one of the devices, the huge soldier stood out from his comrades because of his lack of armor. He wore only a loincloth and sandals, with an undersized helmet perched precariously on the top of his head like a cap on a wall knob, yet as he stood at attention with his squadron he thrust out his gigantic chest as proudly as if he were wearing the finest electrum-graven breastplate. Unlike the other onager operators, whose jaws were grimly set in anticipation of the effort to come, he flashed a gap-toothed grin through his shrublike beard. Aetius grinned back and reined in his horse.

"Magnus!" he shouted. "How are they treating you in the legions?"

Magnus grinned even more broadly, raised his gigantic fist, and thumped his chest. *"Mi-les!"* he announced triumphantly. *"Mi-les!"*

His fellow legionaries, standing at attention, could barely contain themselves, and their shoulders shook with silent laughter.

"Centurion!" Aetius called to the officer in charge of the artillery. "How is this man serving?"

A weather-beaten, wiry veteran whose head barely came to the middle of Magnus' chest stepped forward. "First-class recruit, General," he pronounced with satisfaction. "I'll admit I was skeptical at first, because he eats as much as two men. But he does the work of four, so I believe the legions got the better end of the bargain."

Aetius nodded in approval, raised his hand to Magnus

in salute, and touched heels to his horse, continuing his review of the troops.

As he approached each unit, the men stood silent, falling into formation, armor donned, helmets pulled over their faces, shields poised. The long wooden onager arms hovered in the air over their heads like so many enormous dragonflies. The standards of each century and cohort stood proudly in the still air. Here and there a man cautiously removed his helmet to adjust the woolen skullcap he wore beneath, to shield his scalp from the burrs and rough seams of the legion-issue bronze headgear. The sun could now be seen as a blurry white disk shimmering through the fog, and though the mist was not yet dissipated, the heat of the day was beginning to rise uncomfortably for men in full armor and battle gear. Already it was so humid that the stray dogs following in the army's wake were panting.

Aetius, Florentius, King Theodoric, Prince Thorismund, and a handful of senior officers paced their horses before the long line of men, restlessly wheeling their mounts and turning their heads to peer off over the plain into the distance. The fog was lifting almost as they watched, and a light haze now swirled low over the expanse of grass, the sun-steamed vestiges of the previous night's dew. It, too, would soon burn off with the day's heat, but the warm, damp air would make the men feel as if they were standing in a bread oven.

Looking out at the troops waiting in the fog and the shimmer, Aetius raised his sword, commanding their attention.

"Romans and allies!" he shouted, in a voice that rang like a bell over the silent, sweltering formation. "We stand here today, the greatest western army ever assembled, to defend our people, our homeland—but most of all, our honor."

He paused and paced his horse slowly along the front ranks of the legions, peering into the eyes of individual soldiers, carefully watching their faces. And just as carefully, the men maintained their stony expressions and avoided his gaze. Their responsibility was to fight, they were hired and paid to do battle, and their allegiance was to Rome. But whether they did so fiercely, wholeheartedly contributing their entire being, or merely lent their arms and their sword was a matter for Rome's general to inspire, and they remained to be convinced. For though it was Aetius himself who was speaking to them, a man known throughout the empire for his bravery and skill, in reality he was merely an advocate pleading a case, the case of the emperor, and the legions were the skeptical jury, listening and preparing to render judgment as to whether or not this man's argument was soundly made. Thus far, they were keeping their opinions to themselves. Aetius continued his harangue.

"The Huns see our traditions and call us weak," he shouted. "They see our culture and call us decadent. They see the freedom and mercy we show our enemies and call us fearful. But the Huns are wrong! A millennium of Roman victories does not derive from weakness. A thousand years of Roman progress and triumph do not stem from decadence. No nation has ever prevailed over Rome. No nation has ever trampled Visigoth honor. And the Huns shall not prevail now!"

With each ringing phrase, the troops loosed a desultory chorus of cheers and acclamations—but they were languid and unconvincing, and Aetius saw that they were not even spontaneous but rather instigated by his own officers, in an attempt to excite the men to join in. Even the centurions remained silent, and this was the most dangerous observation of all. For if any army's centurions are not enthusiastic, the battle is lost before it is even begun. The men were simply not reacting. In a rising voice, Aetius repeated his final phrase.

"I said, the Huns shall not prevail now!"

The cheers were slightly louder but still not satisfactory. The troops were holding back. They were not hostile, merely hesitant. Aetius trotted to King Theodoric and spoke quietly, an expression of concern and puzzlement written on his face.

"Theodoric—are the men drunk? Or tired? Why do they not respond?"

"Aetius, I cannot speak for the Romans. But as for my own men, they are terrified of the horses."

Aetius again glanced across the plain. Far in the distance was the sight his troops had been warily observing since first light. Through the swirling mist, a huge body of Hunnish armored cavalry was forming—hundreds of thousands, vastly outnumbering even the enormous army assembled here before him. The Hunnish forces darkened the ground, and as they slowly approached, details began to emerge—of racing and weaving riders, their helmets gleaming in the low sun; of lumbering wagons with their loads covered under dirty tarpaulins; but most of all, of horses, so many horses as to make it seem that every pony in the world had gathered in this one spot. The vastness of the Hunnish mounted forces was overwhelming, even to a veteran Roman legionary. To the inexperienced auxiliaries, it was terrifying.

"You see?" Theodoric continued. "Attila has positioned his strongest forces—his own cavalry—in the very middle of his lines. That's where our own strength must lie—in the center. Yet you've positioned your weakest troops there. Alani auxiliaries, for God's sake, led by their worthless king, Sangiban! Only the devil knows what hole they crawled out of, but they're untrained and they look half-starved. You said the Romans would be first to shed blood. Shift the positions, Flavius, while we still have time."

Aetius squinted out over the field. "No," he responded, after a moment. "The Huns always place their strongest troops in the center. They'll be expecting us to reciprocate. We'll keep the Alani there—they have a hatred for the Huns like no other people. Let Attila drive a wedge down our middle, straight in toward the camp and the onagers."

"You're pitting our weakest forces against their strongest? The Hunnish cavalry will trample them like straw men, and we'll lose the center."

"The center is backed by the ditch and the camp," Aetius responded. "That's the final line."

"And when they reach that line? Against the Alani, it won't take the Huns long."

"Long enough for what we need to do. You, Theodoric, will advance your Visigoths up the right flank—against Attila's Ostrogoths. Giant against giant. Keep twenty thousand men in reserve, out of sight behind the camp. No telling when they'll be needed. I'll march the Roman regulars up the left. Scouts say he's placed his Germanic auxiliaries on that flank. They'll be commanded by the Gepid king Ardaric. His men are strong, but undisciplined."

Theodoric reflected for a moment. "So you *want* the Huns to punch down through our center?"

"The Alani simply have to hold at the trenches in front of the onagers and the camp. Even Alani can hold—or die—in front of a trench. Our flanks are stronger than theirs—you and I will advance our troops up the left and right and surround the enemy, then close in on the sides."

"That's your plan? You're outnumbered two to one, and you're going to *flank* the Huns?"

"That's my plan."

Theodoric shook his head. "You're mad. I don't wonder the troops are terrified. You assured me the Romans would be the first to shed blood, but here they are on the flank. My men are expecting you to take the brunt of the punishment."

"There will be plenty of blood shed this day, by all of us," Aetius replied.

Theodoric glared at him skeptically. "And the horses?" he asked.

Aetius gazed away. "I know Attila. It is death to attack fresh Hunnish horse directly—his cavalry will be invincible. His frontal assault will collapse our center, and the Alani must simply hold them fast, wear them down, form a wall before the trenches. With their corpses, if need be. Until we can move our flanks forward and then rush in from the sides . . ."

"This is what you are going to tell the Alani? That they have to take a heavy cavalry charge full in the teeth? To die, but to die grinning, because eventually we'll be able to win our own battles and then flank Attila's horse when they are distracted by the slaughter?"

Aetius turned back to his troops. The plan sounded preposterous, even to him, but it was the only one with even the smallest chance of succeeding. Of course he could not tell them the enormous odds they faced, the fact that they were all—Alani, Roman, and Visigoth alike—likely to die, even in victory and most certainly in loss. Yet the evidence could not be denied. It was there behind him, a huge body of approaching Hunnish horse, flanked by auxiliary foot troops, stretching across a front of nearly two miles. His men could scarcely focus their eyes upon him for the fear that was filling their hearts at sight of the terrible force thundering toward them. The onslaught must be faced, the men's fears countered. He recalled reading a harangue Xenophon had given to his own outnumbered forces in a similar situation a thousand years before, and setting heel to his horse, he began trotting sternly before the assembled lines of his men.

"The horses!" he shouted. "You're discouraged because the enemy has cavalry and we do not?"

There was scattered muttering from the men as they shifted uncomfortably on their feet and glanced sideways at one another.

Aetius assumed an incredulous expression. "Cavalry! Is that all? Cavalry are merely men on horseback! I would pit a hundred Alani on solid ground to a thousand Huns on their sow-bellied ponies any day. And I know of what I speak—I myself commanded Hunnish cavalry!"

The men fell silent again, listening to him intently. But their expressions became more open, less skeptical. Aetius was wrenching them from their fears, bringing about a change in their views by the very force of his confidence.

"Does a man die in battle from the kick of a horse?" he shouted.

The men stood silent.

"Answer me, legions! I say, does a man . . ."

"No!" the troops roared back. "No!"

Aetius waited for the clamor to die down.

"Of course not!" he bellowed. "A man dies in battle from a sword or a spear, not from a hoof. And your own blades will spend more time in barbarian bellies than ever a weapon was meant to do. The Huns are forming up on the plain as we watch, screwing up their courage to attack us, knowing and fearing they are facing granite—Roman granite! The hard granite mountain of Rome and its victorious allies!"

The men began clanging their shields on their knees, rising to the reaction Aetius had hoped to create. He forged on, raising his pitch, his voice ringing with excitement.

"They are screwing up their courage to attack us, yet

they fear a fall off their damnable horses as much as they fear the cold steel of our swords in their bowels. I am a trained cavalryman—I am a *Hunnish*-trained cavalryman—and I know this: Horses are no match against our legions and allies—except that Huns can flee more swiftly on horses!"

The men broke into a deafening cheer, slapping one another's shoulders and loudly banging spears against knees. Glancing to the side, Aetius saw the grizzled veteran Florentius watching him intently, and he remembered the earlier discussion with his aide. *"Romans don't fight for their empire,"* he had said. *"That's too vague. They fight for their comrades, and for their commander . . . for their commander!"* Standing now in his stirrups, Aetius' voice rang out over the ranks of assembled troops.

"Romans!" he shouted. "Fight for Rome, for the honor and ideals our great nation stands for, has always stood for these thousand years. Visigoths! Fight for the glory of your great people, the strength of your arms, the courage of your hearts. Alani! Fight for vengeance, fight to the death, against an enemy who has pillaged your lands, stolen your women, sought to erase even the very memory of your proud name. And in this battle—which will be remembered throughout history as the greatest battle ever fought—seek only one goal, the goal of victory, even as your eyes cloud with death and the spear falls from your grasp. Whatever you fight for, men, whether honor, glory, or vengeance, whatever you fight for, *warriors!*, fight for me! Even as I'"—and seizing a javelin from a centurion standing in the front rank, he hurled it flying, far out into the plain, where it pierced the ground and stood swaying and defiant, like a Roman standard, a stark challenge to the approaching enemy—"even as I will fight with every fiber of my body for *you!*"

The men bellowed and surged forward, the blood rising to their faces, the hot lust for combat impelling them and driving them. Aetius raised his sword high above his head, saluting their courage, basking in his men's excitement and adulation.

But only for a moment. The enemy was fast approaching.

Lowering his sword, he nodded to King Theodoric and his officers, who cantered to their positions in the line, shouting orders. Scattered trumpets blared the fanfares signaling orders. With an even louder cheer the men stepped forward.

This was no mere march. Rather, it was a Roman battle march, with a strut and a cadence calculated to strike terror into the heart of the enemy even before the clash of the opposing lines. The ox-hide drums sounded their gut-thumping rhythm, the deep, repetitive, three-beat tattoo that marked the Pyrrhic march step. Developed by the Spartans centuries before, adopted by the Romans who understood its terrorizing effect on opponents, it was dancelike in its movement, hypnotic in its relentless, deadly rhythm. Three steps forward, pause for a beat. The Roman legionaries had been trained in this step since their first day of service, and they knew the drill well. Three steps forward, pause for a beat. Swing the shield in unison with the men on either side, grunt the cadence.

The legionaries' faces bore expressions of utter concentration as they stared ahead, no longer fearing the enemy, nor even thinking of them, as they concentrated on the rhythm. Sweat beaded on their foreheads, as each man worked to keep in perfect step with his comrades. The hypnotic beat occupied their minds completely, as it was designed to do, distracting them from any thought of pain or death, fortifying their backbones with Roman iron. Three steps, pause. Thud, thud, thud, silence.

The legions of the Western Empire advanced across the field in precision, gleaming shields swinging in strict unison.

The forces of the allies marched in ragged rhythm on the Roman right, their armor a motley collection of the gear of the individual tribes. Most were disheveled, some bearded, others painted and shaved. Those who had never seen the Pyrrhic step looked at first with alarm at the synchronized movements of their Roman comrades. Then, clumsily at first, with hesitation but with increasing confidence, they, too, fell into the same mesmerizing rhythm. Three steps, grunt. Every man struggled to keep pace with the thumping beat of the Roman drums, eyes glancing to the side, to the shield of the man at one's shoulder. For a brief, glorious moment, every man felt only the might, the precision, and the strength of the Roman legions. For an instant every man—Visigoth, Alani, or other—was Roman. For a single, blessed moment in time, the men's fears were allayed, their minds distracted from the steady approach of the Huns, who themselves advanced undeterred by the vast wall of men approaching the center of the field. The sense of power, of invincibility, at being part of this enormous force, was intoxicating. Three steps, pause. Thud, thud, thud, silence.

Aetius, closely observing from the left wing, raised his cavalry sword and waved it to watching couriers, who picked up the signal and immediately passed it on to Theodoric, leading the Visigoths on the opposite flank. At a sudden shout from a tribune, which was picked up and carried across the entire force within two cycles of the Pyrrhic step, the Romans all broke in unison into a harsh chant, the ancient hymn to Mars and Mithras, a fearsome prayer a thousand years old, retained as a last vestige of their warlike ancestors, even as the legions had converted from the old pagan gods. It was a rumbling growl felt almost as a vibration in the gut rather than heard as a song and calculated, like the booming drums and the mechanical lockstep, to demoralize and terrify the enemy. The vast, swaying monster of metal and death, a force otherworldly and almost inhuman, advanced slowly and implacably toward the lines of Hunnish horsemen, whose faces had now become visible in the near distance through the swirling mist.

The first volley of arrows, thousands of whistling missiles, struck the front ranks squarely, but from this distance feebly. From two hundred fifty paces the Hunnish arrows could do only slight damage, most sticking harmlessly in shields or skittering off helmets. Nevertheless, a few struck soft flesh, and men fell, dropping to the ground with choking grunts. Still the mesmerizing rhythm of the drums accomplished its intended task: There was no faltering among the main body of troops. The ranks behind simply stepped over the fallen and moved up to fill the gaps. Those auxiliaries who from the beginning had disdained to join in the march step, neophyte warriors unaccustomed to the discipline, or veterans who thought themselves too experienced to require the mind-numbing cadence, paused in wonder at the striking of the arrows. *Two hundred fifty paces!* From *horseback!* Only demons could shoot such a distance, while galloping, no less. If this was a demonstration of the Huns' aim and strength when they were so far distant, what damage, then, could they wreak once the space separating the two forces had narrowed? The auxiliaries began to waver in their ranks.

Yet the Romans on the left remained steadfast, and Theodoric urged on the Visigoths with his raspy bellow. Thump, thump, thump, pause. The effect was powerful, but the Huns were undeterred. They fired another volley of arrows, this time from a more lethal range. More men stumbled and fell, this time among the stronger troops on the Roman flanks. It was becoming difficult to concentrate on the step, and gaps began opening in the lines that could not be filled as quickly as before.

Aetius sensed an object brushing his right forearm, tugging at his sleeve with brief insistence. He reached across absentmindedly with his other hand and looked down in wonder when he felt the hot wetness of blood. His arm had been deeply grazed by an arrow and was now bleeding heavily. Bleeding, he knew, was a good sign— much better than a bloodless puncture. Provided he could stop the flow. He looked around. No one had noticed his injury, not even Florentius, as every man's face was fixed straight ahead or to the shield of the man at his side. Only Lucilla, his wolf, who trotted along gamely at the horse's side, looked up at him quizzically, ears cocked upright and yellow eyes gleaming brightly. No time to gallop to the rear for a surgeon. Without dismounting or even slowing his pace, he tore a strip of cloth from the hem of his scarlet cloak and bound the wound quickly using his other hand and his teeth. There was no pain, which caused him mild surprise and even a bit of perverse pleasure. In his many years of battles, this was the first time he had ever been wounded. Still, a mere arrow graze was hardly something to boast about to his sons.

The Hunnish horsemen facing them galloped and whirled, weaving in and out of formation in maneuvers that allowed them to fire their arrows and then quickly duck out of the way as another rank of horsemen raced in to shoot. Their archery fire was steady, without pause or respite, and now became heavier and more lethal as the two battle lines approached each other. With the steady rain of missiles, the front ranks of even the Roman lines began hesitating, as if the troops were marching through a marsh that sucked at their feet and held them back. Wheeling to the side and driving his heels into his horse's flanks, Aetius began sprinting across the front. Raising his sword high in the air, he opened his mouth to bellow the command to charge, but before he could even utter the words, they were drowned by the shrill howl of the Alani battle cry, a scream of rage at the generations of defeats the Huns had inflicted on their people. In an instant, the entire army had taken up the terrifying cry as its own.

Romans, Alani, and Visigoths burst out of their synchronized rhythm, into a furious dash. Enemy arrows rained down upon them in a thick hail, hissing like a swarm of adders. Heads down behind their shields, they bulled through, still keeping close formation, as the Hunnish horsemen wheeled and reined in, retreating and dancing their ponies, seeming to melt like wraiths just beyond the reach of the charging Romans. But this was no retreat. The Alani lunged forward, the Hunnish cavalry dispersed and skittered back, and along the horsemen's flanks there appeared a towering wall of armored infantry—the leading ranks of Attila's Ostrogoth and Germanic allies.

With a terrifying crash of steel on steel, the stolid forward lines of the Romans collided with the mass of furious Alamanni. The tight, orderly formation of a moment before exploded, collapsing into a chaotic mob of furious men and writhing horses. From the first point of collision, at the leading edge of the Hunnish wedge against the Alani, the impact spread right and left down the lines, like a great shock wave, a surge of water from a broken dam suddenly crashing with unstoppable force against an immovable stone wall. Half a million men from both sides were swallowed in the maw of swirling mist and roiling dust. At the shrill whistles and shouts of the commanders, still thousands more poured into the vast, bloody fray.

His wound forgotten, Aetius raced through the lines, bellowing hoarsely into the deafening chaos, urging his men on, dipping into the fringes of the dusty whirlwind of death and slashing and hacking with his own sword as he forced his way through groups of attackers. After what seemed an eternity of struggling through the surging combat, he paused a moment, squinting through the dust and chaos before him, seeking to get his bearings. Men pressed against him from all sides, and the clamor of battle was deafening, yet he could scarcely see ten paces on either side for the cloud of mist and dust that had descended over the field. In an instant, he realized his place was not here, that his men could not see him or hear him, that he risked losing the battle for attempting to win it with his own hands. Cursing, he whirled his horse and began forcing his way back through the mob of charging legionaries, back out of the blinding cloud, back to the rear of the lines, to contact with his couriers and generals—to a view of Attila.

In Aetius' urgency to commence the next phase of his plan, the path back to the Roman fortifications seemed endless, though it was only as far as it had taken his infantry to charge a few moments earlier. Fighting his way through his own men, he cursed again, furious that visibility was so poor he could not make out the deployment of his troops or his reserves.

Suddenly, before he even realized he had arrived, there loomed above him out of the haze the menacing arms of the onagers he had so carefully placed the night before. And just as suddenly the swirling morning mist finally began to clear. Reining in his horse, he turned and peered back, across the field through which he had just charged. It was precisely as he had planned: Like ghosts in twilight he could make out through the yellowish haze of dust the crimson-cloaked line of Romans on the left flank and the wraithlike figures of the furious Germanic infantry directly before them. On the right, Goth was fighting against Goth, their ancient tribal battle cries soaring up over the clamor of battle. But in the center— in the center, incredibly, the Alani auxiliaries were still holding. Against all odds, but fighting with the rage of a people who had been humiliated by their enemy for decades, the Alani maintained an orderly line, refusing to collapse under the weight of the Hunnish horse. They were only slowly falling back toward him, toward the gates of the encampment, absorbing terrible losses but buying him time, just as he had hoped. The strategy was working. He turned to the onagers. It was time to start the next stage.

"Centurion!" he shouted from his horse across the protective entrenchment separating him from the battery of artillery. The wiry onager commander raced up to face him from the other side. "Plank down!"

The officer shouted behind him, and two men hurriedly seized a pair of wide planks and laid them across the ditch. Aetius carefully urged his skittish mount across the swaying boards and over to the other side, where the operators stood at ready.

"Fire at will!" Aetius shouted. The centurion flashed a yellow-toothed grin and whirled to face his artillery crews. With a bellow that carried over the clash of battle, he shouted the slow, methodical orders that would unleash a rain of death on the advancing enemy.

"Onagers, ready!" the officer roared as he raced along the length of the artillery line, sword in hand, eyes darting in every direction to observe the troops' progress. Eight men per unit, two stationed at each corner, strained and pulled to rock each piece into place and align it in firing position. The ever-nearing sound of battle lent a vital urgency to their task, and Aetius shifted his gaze between the artillery before him and the battle raging at his back, while his horse pranced nervously.

"Draw! . . ." the centurion bellowed, and Aetius glared at him for what seemed the leisurely pace of his orders, though in truth the men could work no faster nor more frantically than they already were. Four soldiers per machine, stripped bare to the waist, with even their helmets thrown aside, struggled to crank the two cogged winches that slowly drew down the arm. The strength required for this operation was breathtaking, and even these men, specially recruited for the task, strained and panted at the effort, muscles bulging and sweat running into their eyes. In the intensity of his stare, Aetius could make out a throbbing purple vein at the temple of the nearest winch operator, through the patchy hair of his closely shorn head. Glancing farther down the row of machines, he caught sight of the undersized helmet still propped on Magnus' dome. Beneath it, the big man's face was twisted in a rictus of effort, the first time Aetius had ever seen him actually strain at a task—as well he might, for with his Herculean strength Magnus operated one of his own machine's winches alone, as a matter of professional pride.

The onager arms locked into position at the bottom of their arc and the winch operators stepped back, winded. Aetius glanced back impatiently at the battle. The situation was critical. Although the center was not collapsing under the Hunnish horse, the Alani were nevertheless retreating, and they would not be able to maintain order much longer in the face of their stupefying losses. The enemy's forward momentum had to be stopped now, or Aetius would be forced to signal a general retreat of all his troops to protect the camp.

"Load . . . ," the tribune bawled in a long, drawn-out command that exasperated Aetius with its sensation of leisure, though the soldiers manning the units were working their machines flawlessly and with a celerity that could not have been matched by any other army on earth. At each weapon, a legionary staggered up from the supply wagons behind them, bearing a heavy barrel of naphtha and sulfur. This they gingerly set in place in the leather slings attached to each winched firing arm.

After what seemed an eternity, the centurion again

sprinted red-faced and breathless along the length of the onager line, at last shouting the order Aetius had so longed to hear.

"*Fire!*"

At each piece, a winch operator seized a lit torch that had been spiked into the ground nearby and touched it to the naphtha barrel, setting the oil-soaked wood aflame. At almost the same instant, the other winchman raised a wooden mallet over his head and slammed it down on the trigger block, tripping the catch off the winch cog. With a crash, the mallet struck home and the arm whipped up, at a speed faster than the eye could follow. There was a whoosh and a roar that startled Aetius' horse and set him to rearing, and twenty missiles were slung simultaneously through the air, trailing sparks in their searing wake and landing in a fiery, oily shower in the midst of the enemy lines. Scarcely had the lethal fire-bombs landed than Aetius urged his horse back over the plank, to the summit of a small rise just ahead, between the artillery battery and the main clash of the troops. There he had spied a knot of senior officers gathering to take stock of the situation. Behind him, he heard the tribune's furious bellow again begin the laborious cycle.

"Onagers, ready!"

Arriving at the top of the hillock, just over the thickest part of the fighting, Aetius was gratified to see that a slight breeze had picked up and was blowing the choking cloud of dust away from his position and back toward the Hunnish lines. *Give Attila a taste of blindness in the middle of battle,* he thought to himself grimly, and he reined in his horse to watch the onagers hurl their lethal loads. Fiery missiles shot through the air above him like comets, landing in the midst of the enemy ranks just behind the battle line. With every impact of the fireballs, tortured screams rose from horses and men as the liquid flames of the barrels exploded and coated them with a sticky, flaming fluid that burned through the skin and could not be extinguished. The missiles hammered gaps in the line and the enemy fell at an astonishing rate. As the Roman artillerymen found their range, they pounded not only the enemy front but the trailing ranks behind them as well. It was impossible to miss.

Yet it was also impossible to arrest the enemy advance. For every horseman that fell, another charged into his place, and those in the front ranks were pressured by the zeal of the men behind. Grass fires broke out, terrifying the animals and blinding the riders with the smoke that blew directly into their faces. Here and there, individual trees on the plain burst into flame, adding to the hellish vision. Black columns of smoke rose everywhere and then melded into a solid curtain, a shifting, writhing wall that refused to rise or disperse, mixing with the dank mist produced by the heat of the sun and creating a greasy, foul-smelling pall that wafted over the field.

Still, the Huns' inexorable advance over the Alani continued, and the enemy auxiliaries on the flanks did not appear to be weakening, either. Every step the Romans and Visigoths advanced into the smoke-blackened carnage brought them into contact with the same fire and darkness as the Alamanni and Ostrogoths were suffering. Movement in either direction had stopped, yet the battle raged invisibly behind the black curtain of smoke, and the roars of a million men rose from the swirling cloud. Aetius cantered down the hillock, back toward the main battlefield, and hailed a Roman officer whose horse had stumbled out of the cloud from the left flank, gasping. Wheeling his mount around, the officer pounded breathlessly up to Aetius, his face streaked with black sweat and his red, swollen eyes streaming tears.

"Damn that artillery to hell!" the officer spat hoarsely, and then recognizing Aetius standing before him, he hurriedly saluted.

"That artillery saved your lives, Tribune," Aetius repri-
manded him. "How goes your cohort?"

The tribune gawked at him. "Cohort? I can't *find* my
cohort! I can *hear* them, or hear *someone's* cohort, all
around me, but I can't even see the ground to piss on in
there, much less my cohort! Sir!"

"The enemy are in flames, Tribune. I can see them
burning from here. Look!"

The tribune peered down the hill, straining to see behind the wave of smoke to the rear of the enemy lines.

"They may be in flames, sir, but they continue to fight!
My men are even killing their own comrades in their
blindness, but the enemy continues to fight. Any other
men would have run by now."

"Yes," Aetius conceded. "But this is not just any other
enemy. Tribune, our onagers have eased the task of the
infantry, but they are themselves undefended. If the Huns
continue to bear down on us from the center, they'll jump
the trenches and take the artillery and the camp. We have
to pull troops from the flanks and reinforce the center."

The tribune simply stared at him dumbly.

"Tribune!" Aetius roared. "Our Alani are about to collapse. Reinforce that center!"

"Reinforce the . . . with *what*, sir? I don't know where
my troops are!"

"Then damn it all to hell, I'll go find them myself!"
Aetius roared. Savagely slapping his horse's haunch with
the flat of his sword, he raced down the hill and again
dove blindly into the black cloud, as the bewildered tribune flew red-faced after him.

IV

Attila wheeled his horse furiously, eyes flashing in rage
as he viewed the battle below him. The morning mist that
had so annoyed him when the Romans had made their ini-

tial charge had all burnt off. Yet visibility was even worse now, as a thick pall of smoke from the Romans' fire missiles blanketed the center of the battlefield. In a rage, he whipped off his bronze helmet and dashed it to the ground, followed by the leather cap he wore beneath it, letting the long graying hair fall loose over the bronze armor his officers had insisted he wear. He peered up at the clear sky, now turning a dingy yellow with the rising smoke. Barely noon yet, and the sun was already bearing down like a hammer on an anvil. All around him horsemen shouted and galloped in confusion as the fiery missiles rained down upon them, and the screams of dying horses, tortured by the pain of the flaming droplets, nearly drove him mad with distraction. The dying of his own troops was hard enough to bear, but what man can endure the death throes of a well-trained horse?

Puddles of flame underfoot provided perspective and frame of reference in the twilight of the billowing smoke, though at the same time turning the landscape into a treacherous wasteland. A man stepping or falling into such a puddle might leave his feet behind as blackened stumps. A horse sprinted past in panic, its tail and its rider's long hair streaming in flames behind, yet the horseman ignored the pain as he emptied his quiver of arrows, quickly and blindly, into the dark cloud where he knew his enemies were striving. Men and animals by the hundreds lay writhing and dying in the flaming mud. The Huns' momentum had been stymied. His plans for an early and decisive rout had been shattered.

Suddenly, peering through a brief clearing in the grayness below, Attila saw an opening. The Roman onagers! If he could hasten the collapse of the Alani in the center, his horsemen could breach the trenches and overrun the artillery, while driving a wedge between the two Roman flanks.

"Mass in the center!" he barked, his hoarse voice

carrying into the depth of the smoke cloud like the clanging of a gong. "Pull in the cavalry and the Goths, and mass in the center! Take out those accursed machines!"

At the command, the cavalry officers nearest him leaped forward. They raced to the left flank, where the battle between the Ostrogoths and Rome's Visigothic allies had been furiously joined. Surging into the midst of the desperate fighting, they split off a large battalion of foot soldiers, five thousand men, and quickly diverted them to the center to lead out the Hunnish cavalry mired in the deadly smoke. A large body of foot troops, closer to the ground and more maneuverable than horses over the rising mounds of corpses, would be able to make the final break through the embattled Alani. Then nothing would separate the surging Hunnish horsemen from the lethal artillery.

Attila continued to bellow orders, lunging toward the cantering troops and then backing off, urging them on, pounding at the hindquarters of the horses and men with the flat of his sword.

Behind the coalition lines, all was as clear to Aetius as if Attila had drawn out the tactic on a scrap of parchment and delivered it to him in the hands of a courier. Emerging into the clear to check on the progress of the Hunnish horsemen, Aetius noted the Ostrogoth foot troops consolidating behind the central battle line, preparing for a massive charge against the exhausted Alani auxiliaries. The Alani needed to be reinforced at all costs, but the very weapons that had saved his center thus far—the thick smoke and the furious volleys of fireballs from the onagers—were preventing him from identifying reinforcements to bolster the middle. Having lost his couriers in the confusion, he himself raced toward the smoke cloud to warn his officers. Charging into the murk, he nearly collided with Theodoric, who was galloping out, black as a demon, sword trailing blood. His beard was so thick with dust and grime it looked as if it were made of baked clay, and his nose flowed mucus. He was followed close behind by Thorismund and a handful of other officers, coughing sharply to clear their throats, eyes glowing white in their smoke-stained faces.

As they galloped into the clear, an enormous Gothic cavalryman who had been following them burst out of the smoke, mouth open as he gasped for air, bloodshot eyes wide and focused on Theodoric. Aetius turned just as the Goth raised his long striking sword for a blow.

"Theodoric!" he shouted.

The Visigoth king jumped as if stung and whirled instinctively, at the same time ducking his head below his horse's neck. The Goth's heavy blade slashed harmlessly through the air inches from the king's head, and he roared in dismay.

"I've got the bastard now!" Theodoric bellowed as his horse reared in alarm, and from its great height the king brought the weight of his own sword down onto the barbarian with as much force as his muscular arm could offer. Landing square on the horseman's neck at the edge of the breastplate, it sliced like butter through the clavicle and into the soft tissue below, piercing the man's body and armor diagonally to the opposite hip, stopping only when it hit the pelvic pan. Theodoric jerked the blade out, and the upper half of the Goth's body, still bearing a dumbfounded expression on its face, fell free to the ground. The legs, tightly gripping the horse's side in the stiff cavalry armor, remained fixed in place as the panicked horse raced off.

"By God!" Theodoric roared in astonishment. "The wretch had no bones!"

Yet there was no time to dwell on the king's feat of strength.

"Theodoric!" Aetius bellowed. "The Alani can hold no longer! They're collapsing in the center!"

"Give me a drink!" Theodoric roared back. "And that Goth—do I have to do everything around here myself?"

Wordlessly Aetius handed him his own leather canteen. Theodoric took it and guzzled the watered wine in great, breathless gulps, finally handing it back nearly empty. He wiped his lips with the back of his hand, though droplets still hung suspended in his beard, like blood.

"So the Alani have fallen back now?" he demanded. "This was the plan—we turn our flanks inward now and pen the Huns in like sheep!"

"It is still the plan, but our troops on the flanks have not advanced far enough," Aetius replied hurriedly. "And we can wait no longer. Attila is pouring men into the center to breach the artillery trenches. Call in your reserve troops now!"

Theodoric nodded, and one of the officers riding with him put a dented brass horn to his lips. With the long, drawn-out wail of the Visigoth call to arms, there was a sudden rumble, which gave momentary pause to the exhausted lines of battling legionaries below them, as they peered back to see the response to the trumpet's blare. Aetius whirled his horse and raced to the artillery lines, where once again he rode gingerly over the trench plank and this time ordered it to be taken up behind him.

From behind the far side of the fortified encampment, twenty thousand Visigoth foot troops raced out from the clearing where they had been waiting impatiently. Their deployment was loose and motley, though what they lacked in precision they made up for in determined courage. Falling into formation just in front of the deep trench protecting the artillery battery, they lined up in ranks eight deep, bracing themselves for the Hunnish horse charge they could see forming in front of them, through the dissipating smoke. At Theodoric's commands, twenty thousand shields were raised, spears snapped down into the horizontal thrusting position and feet dug in, nearly as efficiently as Roman troops themselves could have performed the maneuver. Just as they had fixed themselves in their positions, they themselves sensed a low vibration, a deep thundering that grew louder, building ominously. Breaking through the smoke were the pounding hooves of the horses, then the animals' deep chests, and finally the dark, grim faces of the enormous mass of Hunnish horsemen. They charged in a front five hundred riders wide, directly over the decimated line of Alani, toward the Visigoths and, behind them, their ultimate target—the lethal battery of artillery.

The lead Visigoths in the defensive line hunkered behind their shields, bent forward on flexed knees, and braced themselves. The smoke was still too thick—by the time the Hunnish cavalry had become visible there was no time to loose spears, much less arrows, to soften up the attacking horde. The full strength of the charging horsemen—on their stirrups—would have to be met. No army on foot—barbarian or Roman—had been able to stand up to such a charge before. And no cavalry charge before had been as massive as this.

Behind the lead ranks of the Visigoths, those in the second rank held their breath and also leaned forward, pressing the bosses of their shields into the backs of the men in front of them. In the third rank, the men did the same, again and again, to the rearmost line. No man would be able to waver and step back—none would be able to dodge the charging Hunnish horse. It was a human wall, which would have to stand, would have to persevere against each thousand-pound animal bearing down on them. It would *have* to stand. The alternative was impossible to contemplate.

The Hunnish cavalry slammed into the massed Visigothic lines with a deafening crash. Horses reared and screamed at the impact, the lead animals in the charge impaled on the spear points that the Visigothic defenders had braced butt-end into the ground, angled up toward their bellies. Dying as they stood, with snapped spear shafts protruding from their deep chests, hundreds of horses collapsed frothing and bleeding on top of the very troops who had impaled them, and their riders leaped furiously off their backs, cavalry swords whirling, onto the heads of the Visigoths below. Behind them horse after horse slammed relentlessly into the haunches of the animals before them, whinnying in terror and fury, as their riders, too, leaped off, hacking and slashing with their swords.

The first line of defenders collapsed under the terrible weight of the charging horses, and then the second line and the third. The carnage was appalling, as the Visigoths fell to the fury of the careening horses and riders. Yet, by the weight of the Huns' own horses, the defenders succeeded in depriving them of their greatest weapon—momentum. For as the first rank of horses dissolved on the Visigoths' butted spears, the second rank was impeded by their bodies and was able to advance only a few feet farther into the solid block of the phalanx before themselves being stopped. Dying horses rolled to the ground, crushing riders and attackers alike. The Visigoth reserves swarmed over the writhing animals, dragging Hunnish riders off and grappling in hand-to-hand combat. Still, rank upon rank of horsemen charged into the line and leaped over the carnage before them, advancing again another few paces before they, too, were overwhelmed. The field degenerated into chaos, all lines of formation destroyed.

The Visigoths wavered at the terrible attack, but they had nowhere to retreat from the Huns' fury, apart from the deep ditch behind them. So they remained, repulsing each successive wave of charging cavalry. Above the tumult could be heard the furious shouts of Theodoric as he drove his men to even greater exertions, roaring at them to remain in their positions, or die. With mounting fury, the Huns continued to hurl themselves at the wall of bodies along the line—but the stubborn Visigoth phalanx continued to hold.

Behind the trench, the onager operators frantically fired their burning missiles into the lines of Gothic and Hunnish troops before them. Though half-dead with exhaustion, the artillery commander had ratcheted up the rate of firing and the distance of the pitched fireballs. So preoccupied were the artillerymen with their work that they scarcely looked up to observe the Hunnish cavalry attack and the brutal defense of the Visigoth reserves, only yards away from their machines. Throughout the infernal roaring and screaming and dying that was taking place just before their eyes, the firing crews continued to rain molten death upon the enemy across the plain.

Suddenly a squadron of Hunnish cavalry attackers appeared, seemingly from nowhere, racing down the Roman side of the defensive trench and along the path worn by the centurion shouting his firing orders to the artillerymen. Having seen the murderous reception given their comrades by the Visigoths, these riders had raced far over to the right flank of their cavalry unit and around the far end of the trench, where they had cut down the squadron posted to defend it. They now rampaged unopposed through the Roman side of the artillery lines, running down the firing crews, who had stripped their armor to work faster and carried not so much as a dagger in defense. Leaning over their horses, the Huns slashed with their swords, beheading and killing several of the artillery crew outright. The onager men paused for a moment in surprise, then rushed to the supply carts to seize shields and weapons to defend themselves.

Aetius sprinted along the line, furiously rousing the operators to pick up blades and fight. Even in the midst of the attack, however, he suddenly reined his horse: There, just before him, exactly at the spot he had been posted, stood Magnus, bearded face twisted in bewilderment and pain, the upper muscle of his massive right arm bleeding profusely from a deep cut inflicted by a Hunnish horseman's blade. *My God,* Aetius thought, *how could I have put him in this position? The poor brute is too slow to defend himself, can't even wear proper armor.* Even at that moment, surrounded by terror and chaos, he felt a depth of remorse for this one man before him that rivaled what he had ever felt for the thousands of men who had fallen in battle under his command in the past three decades.

Magnus stared dumbly at him, unable to hold shield or weapon as the lifeblood gushed from the deep wound in his arm. For Aetius, time seemed to slow and freeze, the deafening clamor to fade into a far distance. He was transfixed at the sight of the wounded Magnus, blinded by rage and sorrow, incapable of reacting even as another Hunnish pony raced directly toward him, the rider's yellow grin gleaming from the dark shadows of his cavalry helmet.

As the rider bore down, Magnus turned his head dully, and his half-clouded eyes focused on the glinting sword. Suddenly an expression of realization and horror flashed across his face.

"Ae-ae-aetius!" he roared, pointing with his uninjured arm.

Whirling, Aetius turned to find the charging Hun nearly upon him. There was no time to draw his sword, nor even to leap his horse out of the rider's path. Lunging to the side, he rolled off the horse and onto the ground,

just as the Hun's sword crashed down with the full impetus of his charge. The terrible blow sliced cleanly through
the vertebrae and neck of his mount, killing it instantly.
Before Aetius could even dive out of the way, the animal's
huge body had fallen on top of him, pinning his legs to
the ground.

Stumbling to his friend's side, Magnus bent and seized
the horse's hind hoof, heaving with his one hand. The
huge burden budged, but only slightly.

"Pull, Magnus!" Aetius shouted. "Pull, if you've ever
pulled in your life!"

Adjusting his grip, Magnus again set his feet and
leaned into the pull. Straining, his face purpling at the effort, he slowly slid the carcass off Aetius' legs.

Fifty paces away, the Hunnish attacker, cursing his
missed blow, skidded to a stop and looked behind him.
Seeing the general on the ground, covered with the blood
of his animal, he grinned, heeled his horse, and charged
in for the final blow.

Magnus looked up at the charging horseman, and suddenly the most basic, the most desperate, instincts of his
brain were triggered. A surging desire—for survival? for
revenge?—overwhelmed him. Dropping the hoof he held
in one hand, Magnus stumbled forward and with all his
remaining strength launched himself at the onrushing
horse. Lunging with the erratic step of a drunkard but
with the force of a charging bull, he careened directly into
the ribs of the Hunnish horse.

The horse screamed in pain and fell to the ground,
plowing jaw-first through the dirt, its hind legs still
churning. It happened so quickly the rider continued to
cling to the horse's back by his own unthinking instinct.
The animal's momentum sent it slamming into the onager operated by Magnus, which was already winched
and waiting only to be loaded for the pounding of the
mallet to trip the release. With the impact, the rider lost

his grip on the animal's back and flew over the iron rim of the wheel, slamming his head onto the device's platform, on which a flaming puddle burnt, the remains of the previous shot.

The Hun's body on the trigger tripped the release. With a loud crack and a rush of hot wind, the firing arm leaped and shot skyward, the sling snagging the Hun's head and plucking it off his shoulders as neatly as a turnip being popped from its furrow. It flew, grimacing, through the air back toward the enemy lines, a flaming, wide-eyed missile, Magnus' most effective shot of the day. After Aetius struggled free of the horse's crushing weight, he leaped to Magnus' side, finding him lying dazed, his helmet askew and his face pale from loss of blood.

Quickly tearing a strip from his ripped cloak, Aetius tied it around Magnus' bicep, inserting a broken winch pin into the knot and twisting it to cinch the tourniquet tightly and cut off the blood supply to the arm.

"That'll do for now, old friend," he said, clasping the man's enormous paw for a moment in his own hand. Then looking up, he spied a Hunnish horse whose rider had just been killed. Running up beside the frantic animal, he vaulted onto its back in the Hunnish fashion he had learned so many years before and, scarcely pausing to get his bearings, set heel and raced away to rally the defense of the onagers.

V

Behind the Hunnish lines, Turgrid cantered up to Attila. Seeing the old man, Attila shook his head in wonder. *Eighty years old if he's a day,* Attila thought. *He can still outride any horseman west of the Rhine, and his sword is drenched with Roman blood. It is because of men like these that Rome will never be able to prevail against us.*

But Turgrid himself gave in to no such vanities.

"Rome's auxiliaries are repulsing the cavalry!" he reported hoarsely, his eyes red and watering from peering through the smoke at the Hunnish charge. "The artillery still holds!"

Attila furrowed his brows in anger. "The artillery is their strength. We *must* destroy it!"

He glared about in frustration. Solutions he had in plenty, but all entailed high costs in terms of men, and there was still much territory to conquer before he reached Rome. In a stalemate of strength, he knew, the force with superior numbers would eventually win—for if half a million men died on both sides it would mean the extinction of the Roman coalition but the death of only half his forces. But at such a cost . . . He recalled his studies of Pyrrhus' futile victory over the Romans centuries before. Winning had meant that great general's doom. Could he win the battle while suffering such heavy losses and then still have the strength to continue on to the ultimate goal? It was a subtle calculus that would give pause to even the most seasoned commander, and his mind raced as he considered his options.

Looking behind him, he spied the squadron of small boys with their fox-head capes clustered nearby, eyes wide, doubled and tripled up on their war ponies, waving their hatchets and cheering the troops as if they were watching horse races on the steppe. Seeing Attila's nod, the boys' leader broke away and raced up to him, an eager look on his face. The king paused for a moment, considering the youthfulness of his son, his thin arms and legs, the shaven, knobby head, the miniature bow and arrows slung over his back. Then, seeming to make up his mind, he leaned over his horse and conferred for a moment with the lad, who nodded his head. When Attila sat back up, the boy shouted something to his comrades, who cheered lustily and then rushed away at a gallop, waving their hatchets, warlike, over their heads.

Turgrid maneuvered his horse back to Attila and looked at him sternly.

"Those boys should be back with the supply wagons, out of danger," he said. "What did you tell them?"

Attila set his mouth in a thin, straight line. "I just sent in my secret weapon."

Turgrid stared at him for a moment, then scoffed as he nodded at the boys disappearing into the cloud of smoke and dust. "Secret weapon? I didn't know we had one."

"I was a boy once," Attila responded as he cantered away. "No one burns for victory like a boy."

At the onager entrenchments, the combat continued to rage between the Hunnish horse troops and the Visigoth reserves. All lines separating the two forces had now disintegrated; all formation had collapsed into a mob action. Victory by the Huns here, on this front, would drive an enemy wedge between the main Roman force and the allied Visigoths on the two flanks, as well as stifle the machines. The position was crucial, and both sides began pouring in additional troops. Thousands of fresh horsemen thundered into the fray from the Hunnish lines, while Aetius worked frantically with his senior officers, dipping back and forth into the choking smoke on the flanks, urging their units to rush forces to the secondary conflict behind them, at the artillery lines. The flank battles began to wane, a consequence of both sides' exhaustion and the orders of their officers to withdraw; but the struggle at the artillery battery grew steadily fiercer and more chaotic, and the mounds of dead and wounded fronting the onager trench grew to sickening proportions, rivaling the walls of corpses that had developed on the main battlefield itself.

Through the thick of the chaos, dozens of boys suddenly appeared, crawling on their hands and knees, clutching hatchets and abandoned swords in their fists.

Darting for shelter, here hiding behind the cadaver of a
horse, there behind a mound of grotesquely contorted
bodies of dead Visigoths, they raced in and out of the
shouting and chaos, themselves silent and wary. Like agile monkeys, they threw themselves into the thick of the
battle, squirming between combatants' legs, slipping
through their grasp, dodging fists and blades, until they finally emerged behind the Visigoth lines, on the very
brink of the blood-filled trench. Even when the Visigoth
warriors saw them, they ignored them as being simply
Hunnish camp followers, overeager for plunder but harm-
less. Scamps of boys were nothing compared to the endless swarms of Hunnish horsemen who were gradually
pushing the Visigoths back toward the camp walls.

As the boys slipped behind the Visigoths, they jumped
into the protective trench below the onagers, rolling down
the soft dirt of the sides and landing among the grasping
fingers of the dead and dying men whose bodies covered
the bottom. Leaping up, they stifled their horror and
clambered through the carnage along the length of the
trench, spacing themselves beneath each of the eight onagers in the center. With unutterable relief, they then
leaped free of the grisly path on which they had been
walking and scrambled up the far wall, digging in their
hatchets as grips to allow them to clamber hand over hand
up the steep slope. Just below the upper lip, each boy
paused, jamming his sword point-first into the wall and
standing on the swaying blade, teetering like tree cutters
on step boards preparing to begin chopping above the
flaring of the root.

As the Roman artillery commander shouted, "Ready,"
the row of cubs drew their daggers and began frantically
sawing at the thick ropes that anchored the front of each
device to heavy stakes in the ground. At the "Draw" command, they put away their daggers, though the ropes were
barely half-severed, and drew their hatchets. The boys'

leader, stealthily peering over the upper lip of the trench
to observe the preparations, mimed the centurion's orders
to the hidden lads. Just as the torchbearers touched the
flames to the missiles, and before the centurion was able
to open his mouth, the wolf cub leader shouted, in his
shrill, high-pitched voice.

"Strike!"

A row of hatchets slashed simultaneously through the
half-severed anchor ropes, and the front of each onager
carriage, already groaning with the leverage applied to it
by the winched firing arm, leaped into the air. With a terrifying crash, the eight devices flipped backward like
monstrous insects, crushing the winch operators and
torchbearers behind them. At once, the line of artillery
burst into flame. The centurion standing in the midst of
the devastation stared in astonishment at the destruction
in the center of his battery, silently mouthing the word
Fire! . . .

From a nearby hillock behind the Hunnish lines, Attila
surveyed the ruin of the artillery with satisfaction.

"Cunning little monkeys," he mused, shaking his head
in admiration. "Better than my own cavalry. Turgrid!"

The old general galloped to his side, his eyes glinting
beneath the visor of his war helmet.

"Yes, Great King."

"The Visigoth reserves are massed at the gates to the
Roman encampment, still defending their artillery
trenches, though only their own helpless god knows
why—the onagers are being obliterated. Aetius is pulling
Roman troops in from his left flank and sending them in
as reinforcements. He's worried—if he's shifting men
who are already fighting, then he has no reserves left. You
see how they are all knotted up together before the camp
gates, repelling our cavalry?"

Turgrid nodded, knowing his commander's thoughts
better, perhaps, than his own. "Yes, *Cur*. The ropes?"

"While they are massed in a tight phalanx. The ropes."

At a signal from the general, a Hunnish courier blew a mournful note on a curved brass-tipped sheep horn. The wavering cry carried its message, like the drifting smoke of incense, far above the chaos and carnage of the field below. From behind the Hunnish lines a mass of horsemen surged forward. The animals were painted with phantasmagoric designs, mythical beasts, swirls, and other tribal oddities, an ancient practice Turgrid had revived to distract and strike fear in the hearts of the enemy by the sheer strangeness of the sight. Each rider was ornamented in colors and designs similar to those of his steed—swirling motifs etched deeply into the leather breastplates and on bronze helmets. The warriors on either side of this new force of cavalry, both Alamanni and Goth, shrank back, as if encountering their enemies rather than their allies. But it was with good reason that this body of cavalry provoked revulsion even among the battle-hardened barbarian troops past whom they proudly trotted. For each rider was equipped not with bow and lance but with dagger at the waist, shield in the left hand, and in the right a long coil of cloth rope. And every barbarian nation under Hunnish dominion had felt the bite of those deadly coils.

The force of fresh riders trotted up to Attila, who appraised them critically.

"It is good we kept a reserve," he said to Turgrid.

The old man nodded. "Half a *tümen*," he replied, "five thousand men. There is another half behind them, awaiting their chance, and yet more can be diverted from elsewhere, if necessary."

Attila took a last long look at the field, then pointed with his cavalry sword off to the flank, where a full legion of Roman reinforcements from the battle against the Gepidae was being redeployed toward the overwhelmed Visigoths at the artillery trench.

"Ropers!" Attila shouted at the eager men halted in formation before him, horses snorting and stamping with impatience. "Victory is before you—you hold it in your hands! Toughen your hearts, steel your muscles to lunge into the fray, while the enemy still reels from our attack! Despise their battle line! Attack the Alani; destroy the Visigoths! Seek swift victory over Rome by surging deep into its vitals. When the sinews are cut, the limbs drop; when the bones are broken, the body cannot stand! Show your cunning, Huns; show your strength! Avenge your wounded comrades through death to the foe, and let those who are sound revel in the slaughter of the enemy!"

The men roared, their horses quivering.

"Hear me!" Attila bellowed. "The man who brings me back the head of Theodoric, the Visigoth king, will receive a chest of gold for each member of his household!"

The horsemen lunged and drew back, scarcely able to contain their bloodlust, desperate to begin the rush toward the mass of tight-packed Roman legionaries they could see joining the Visigoths in the distance before them.

". . . And the man who brings me back the head of Aetius, the Roman commander . . ."

The horsemen fell suddenly silent in anticipation.

". . . will be served for dinner to my wolf tonight!"

The wolf, trotting restlessly at the side of Attila's horse, glared at the men with slanted yellow eyes.

"Did you hear me?" Attila roared. "Aetius is to be brought back alive. Now go!"

With another resounding cry of the horn and a bellow from the men, the rope cavalry leaped forward, racing over the pitted, cadaver-littered ground in a wide, straight front, directly toward the Roman lines.

Below, in the thick of the fighting in front of the trench before the raging flames of the upended artillery, the Hunnish regulars who were still engaged with the Visigoth troops perked their ears at the sound of the horn. Without hesitation, they began executing a slow, orderly withdrawal—on horseback for those with surviving mounts, on foot for those many who had lost their animals in the furious fighting at the trench. The Visigoths stood exhausted, watching the enemy retreat with a mixture of relief and bewilderment. Before them, the ground was covered with horses and men, mounds of bodies, some still, others moaning and writhing in agony. They were heaped haphazardly in contorted, makeshift barrier walls where they had fallen during the repeated Hunnish cavalry charges, and they filled the muddy ditch, where they had been thrown by the momentum of the Huns' brutal attacks. All before them was anguish and death, and the survivors were covered with such gore that even men who were lifelong friends could scarcely recognize one another. Trembling with exhaustion, they reeled at the horror they had just witnessed.

Equally battered reinforcements of Roman legionaries began pouring into the gaps in the Visigoth lines, breathless from their forced sprint from their previous deployment on the left flank. With the arrival of the Roman troops, the shattered Visigoths allowed themselves some guarded optimism, and scattered cheers rose from their ragged lines. Their hopes had already been strengthened when the bleating of the Hunnish horns had signaled the enemy to withdraw. Yet there was a determination and order about the Huns' movements that caused Aetius to observe them with tense suspicion. Attila's strategy thus far had been to apply relentless pressure with his overwhelming forces at every point on the allies' front, particularly the center. Why, now, would he allow time for the Romans to regroup and regain their strength?

At the gates to the camp, behind the destroyed artillery, Florentius thundered up on his horse, face blackened by smoke and wooden leg shattered by an enemy sword but otherwise unharmed. He reined in and wheeled his horse this way and that, seeking to gain a clearer view of the scene before him through the dense haze.

A cry broke from a courier nearby. "General Aetius," he shouted hoarsely. "They're retreating! We've beaten them back—the Hunnish cavalry is retreating!"

Aetius trotted forward several paces to gain a clearer view, and Florentius wheeled and raced up to his side. The old centurion peered again into the haze, and shook his head. "They're retreating, sir, I'll grant you that, but I don't like the looks of it. The Huns haven't been defeated—not even close. Why would they withdraw?"

"I agree," Aetius replied. "I know that horn signal. Tell the officers to keep their troops in formation."

Prince Thorismund raced up to the two men on his war charger, the animal's face flecked with bloody foam. "General Aetius," he exclaimed, breathless. "The enemy is retreating! We have beaten them back from the onager trenches, they're falling back! Order a charge now, while they're bloodied and confused—this may be the turning point!"

Ignoring the prince, Florentius squinted again toward the enemy lines. "Sir, the Huns have only withdrawn a short distance. You see there? That other squadron? Fresh reserves."

Aetius nodded his head. "Half a *tümen,* I'd wager. . . ."

Thorismund snorted in annoyance at the unfamiliar Hunnish word. "Reserves? There aren't enough of them to make a difference, now that your legions have reinforced the Visigoth line. General, let us signal our troops to the attack while the enemy is falling back!"

Florentius sidled his horse closer to Aetius' animal. "Sir," he said in a low tone, "whether or not this is the battle to end all civilization, I don't know. But it's the biggest damn fight I've ever seen, and I've seen a lot. We can't make out either of our flanks. Hell, we can barely see what's going on twenty paces in front of our noses. You send twenty thousand men into a charge you're not sure about, you may be sending every one of them to his death."

"General Aetius!" Thorismund shouted with increased urgency. "The enemy is on the retreat—order the attack!"

Aetius trotted his horse forward a few more paces. Florentius' words had put him on the alert. The warning he had spoken to Theodoric before the battle echoed in his head. *It is death to attack fresh Hunnish horse directly. . . .*

As he stared intently, a breeze lifted the swirling smoke for an instant. The moment was brief, but long enough for him to spy the coils of rope each horseman carried at his side. Suddenly he realized Attila's intent, as surely as if he had heard the command himself. Never before had he seen the Huns use this tactic in open battle, and certainly his troops had never trained to defend against it.

He spun his horse around, bellowing to his officers, "Disperse the troops!"

Thorismund and the men nearby stared at him in astonishment, and the cheers they had been raising at the Huns' retreat died in their throats. Still, the bulk of the troops continued to surge forward, for they smelled a change in the wind, sensed that the momentum had shifted in their favor, that victory might now be in their grasp. As the first force of Huns methodically withdrew, the Visigoth reserves and the Roman reinforcements who had just joined them advanced at the same pace, eagerly securing the sector of battlefield they had lost earlier when they had been pushed back against the artillery trench.

"They couldn't break through with their first wave of cavalry," came a contemptuous shout from the Visigoth lines, "and they're not going to break through with the second!" A chorus of cheers rose up from the man's comrades nearby.

From the lead rank, a Roman hefted his dented, bloodied shield and waved it in the air. "Ha! I'll get that big yellow devil in the front, see if I don't. Somebody give me a spear—I'll take him from here."

"None of us got spears!" came the shouted reply several units back. "Just means you have to get intimate with your sword!" A round of laughing and catcalls swept the field as the joke was quickly passed through the ranks.

"Halt and disperse!" Aetius roared from behind the legionaries. Troops in the vicinity froze and looked up to see the general racing past on his horse. "Do not attack the cavalry!" he shouted. "Disperse!"

"Disperse . . . ?" some voices began protesting, but their questioning was drowned by the rising clamor of thousands of men shouting in excitement as the enemy began its charge.

In the confusion, Aetius' calls to disperse were still picked up by only a few of his officers, who themselves realized the danger only tardily. Trumpeters could not be found to spread the orders more quickly—some had been killed in the earlier Hunnish cavalry charge; the rest had tossed aside their horns in desperation, to take up arms themselves. The allied legions remained in the tightly packed formation they had adopted at the defense of the artillery trenches, and the cheers rose even more loudly as they began their own desperate dash forward.

The two lines were fast approaching. Suddenly the Romans in the front ranks, those who could best see the threat before them, began to falter and hesitate.

"They're ropers!" a trooper shouted, too late. "Get back!"

But the allied troops were deployed too densely to move any direction but forward. The Hunnish cavalry raced toward them, knowing there was no need to fear spears or arrows, for the Romans and Visigoths had already thrown or broken all of theirs hours before. Charging to within ten paces of the Roman front line, the lead Huns suddenly skidded to a stop and loosed the coiled ropes they carried, directly into the massed packs of foot soldiers facing them. A thousand loops descended like an enormous net over the heads of the astonished troops, and with unerring skill the Huns quickly jerked the ropes taut.

The Romans onto whose shoulders the ropes had dropped were the fortunate ones—their necks were broken instantly as the Hunnish ponies reared back with their great strength. Those on whom the ropes had dropped farther down, over the shoulders, tightly binding their arms to their sides, were thrown brutally, face-first, into the gore-filled mud and then dragged like great squirming fish into the Hunnish lines and trampled beneath the hooves of the enemy horses. As the first line of ropers pulled in their struggling catches with shouts of triumph, a second line surged forward, and then a third, each time casting their deadly ropes into the bewildered mob of allied forces before them. A centurion turned and opened wide his mouth in another frantic order to retreat, but his shout was cut short by a rope cast from his blind side, which was jerked so sharply it half-severed his throat.

There was no escape. Choked cries filled the air as the leading ranks of the legion turned and attempted to retreat. Those in the rear, who had not yet realized the danger, continued to press forward, compounding the chaos as soldiers tripped and fell over one another, scrambling over their comrades beneath them, clumsy in their exhaustion and in the heavy armor that weighed them down, unable to use their skills or their swords on attackers who stood just beyond their reach. The enemy advanced implacably and in the end was slowed only by the mounds of bodies that had built up at their feet, those who had been dragged out from the Roman lines and those who had been trampled by their own panicked forces. The Hunnish horses frantically stamped their dance of death on their quarry, and the spray coated the dead and the living with a crimson sheen, rendering the ground a slurry of viscera. One horseman, pausing for a moment in his lethal hunt, leaned over the side of his mount and picked up a Roman helmet on which the end of his rope had snagged. Holding the trophy triumphantly aloft by the crimson officer's crest, he gave it a sharp shake, and a severed head rolled out onto the ground, to the jeering laughter of his comrades.

On the viewing hillock near the Romans' right flank, Aetius was furious at his inability to make himself heard. "Disperse the troops!" he roared, racing back and forth behind the lines, charging into the ranks and swatting at the men with the flat of his sword to enforce his meaning. Thorismund followed Aetius' lead, while Florentius, casting about sharply with his keen gaze, cantered over to a single terrified trumpeter who sat frozen on his horse, spellbound at the bloody spectacle before him.

"Are you the only trumpeter left in the entire army?" the old centurion shouted, his gray eyes flashing fire. "Sound the order to spread! Disperse them, by God!"

With a start, the soldier raised the horn to his lips. The instrument sounded a staccato command, over and over, a repeated rhythm. The terrified Visigoths stared in bewilderment as Aetius stormed into their ranks on his horse, forcing their attention by the blows of his swords. The Romans, however, or at least those who had fought under his command in Gaul, squared their shoulders and seemed to gain strength by his presence.

"Where the hell is Theodoric?" he shouted. "Disperse! Romans, Visigoths, disperse! Spread yourselves out! Let the ropes fall between your ranks, and then seize them with your hands! Theodoric, disperse your men! Order your troops, damn you!"

At last the men understood. In rapid order they re-formed ranks, this time in an extended deployment, each man six or eight feet from his neighbor. The ropers had by now also re-formed their lines and had commenced their advance for another rampage against the allied lines.

This time, however, the Romans were prepared. Sheathing their swords and standing bravely in formation as the whirring ropes flew toward them like so many wing-borne serpents, at the very last instant each man leaped to the side, and with the new formation each man had room to do so. Seizing the ropes with their free hands, they gave sharp tugs before the Hunnish mounts had braced them-selves for their own pull. Instantly a number of the Hun-nish ropers were jerked from their horses in surprise, while others let drop the coils from their hands, leaving themselves exposed and defenseless. Cries of rage rang out from the allied lines as the battered Romans and Visi-goths found new strength in the tactic and leaped forward, over the bodies of their fallen comrades and into the lead-ing ranks of the startled Hunnish horsemen.

Surging into the cavalry lines, they bludgeoned the wild-eyed animals with their shields and slashed blindly with their swords, loosing all their frustration at the Huns' surprise tactic. The furious Visigoths, seeking to redeem their near collapse at the artillery trenches, leaped directly onto the horses, throwing themselves into hand-to-hand combat with the wheeling and struggling riders.

Within moments, the cavalry was stopped, its front ranks disabled by the attacks on the horses and riders, each struggling animal smothered with swarming sol-diers. This time, it was the advance lines of the Hunnish cavalry that desperately wheeled about for a retreat, only to be thrown into chaos and confusion as they collided with their still advancing rear forces. Horses and riders fell under the same sharpened forehooves as had deci-

mated the Roman lines moments before, and it was only
with terrible effort that the Huns were able to reverse
their forward momentum and execute a retreat, to a point
just out of range of the allied infantry, where they halted
to regain order.

Romans and Visigoths alike collapsed to their knees in
exhaustion. A throaty, wordless bellow of triumph roared
out over the plain, an animal-like cry of desperation, of
relief and emotion that they had once again thrown back
their attackers, once again repelled the best that Attila
could hurl against them. Yet their cry was tempered, too,
by anguish and frustration, for despite this small moment
of victory, this further confirmation of God's favor, the
losses from the Hunnish ropers' first charge had been almost inconceivable. And the Huns themselves still sat
watching them on their panting, foaming mounts, glaring
at them, scarcely a spear's throw away—though the Romans had no spears to throw.

Aetius reined in his horse in the midst of the carnage
and gazed about, taking advantage of the brief respite to
assess the situation. Thus far he has resisted the enemy's
every advance—but at what cost to his men? On every
side, from the very gates of the Roman encampment behind him out to the middle of the plain, the ground was
covered with a writhing blanket of dead and wounded.
From a distance, it seemed almost alive with the agonized
movements of horses and men in their death throes, and a
rider could in some places scarcely pick his way through
the fallen without stepping on a limb or splashing through
a puddle of crimson.

The Hunnish horsemen had not resumed the attack but
rather waited warily beyond range after their rope men
had been repelled. Yet all was not yet silent. From the
flanks the clamor of the furious battle still being waged
wafted over the sultry heat of the late afternoon. Aetius
sprinted up to an exhausted tribune who was staggering

on foot at the edge of a circled mound of bodies, searching for the remnants of his cohort.

"Tribune—you come from the left flank? How goes the fighting?"

The officer stared back at him dully, and Aetius spied a trickle of blood dripping to the ground at his feet and a broken arrow shaft protruding from beneath the man's breastplate.

"I come from the right flank, sir," the tribune rasped hoarsely, striving to stand at attention as Aetius approached, but wincing in pain at the effort. "My troops were sent there as reinforcements because the Visigoths were being pressed. That was an hour ago. But I've lost them now." He collapsed to one knee, exhausted, and braced himself against a spear he had jammed into the ground.

Aetius squinted at the eastern sky, where thunderheads roiled and tumbled over one another in blackening threat.

"It'll be dark soon," he told the young officer. "A storm is coming, and will stay the battle. Pray Theodoric can hold out until then."

"I fear he may not, sir."

Aetius stared harder at the approaching clouds. "I have no more reserves, and my men here are in no condition to help him. What is your name, Tribune?"

The officer swallowed laboriously and gathered his breath.

"Quintus Valerius, sir," he croaked. "Eleventh Legion, First Cohort." He paused for a moment; then his mouth twisted in a painful grin. "My first battle, sir. My father arranged a year's posting for me, but I thought I might apply for a new commission when my time is up."

Aetius averted his face at the tribune's appalling suffering. A man dying bravely does not wish others to see his pain. And a man who does not know he is dying does not wish to see news of his fate in another's expression.

"Tribune Quintus Valerius," he finally said, "I shall make good report of your valor today. Your sons and grandsons will be proud of you."

The tribune pulled himself laboriously back to his feet, leaning heavily on the spear as if it were a crutch. "Thank you, sir. I will inform King Theodoric to hold out on his own. I'm told he's been calling for more reinforcements."

With a tremendous effort he staggered off toward the distant sound of the still-raging battle, weaving a painstaking path among the bodies of the six hundred men who, only that morning, had proudly marched under the standard of his cohort. Aetius watched him for a moment and then cantered back to the lines of Visigoths and Romans. The troops lay exhausted from their ordeal with the ropers, sprawled on the ground in mindless consort with their dead comrades, the living indistinguishable from the lifeless, the wounded from the hale. On a small rise in the midst of the troops, surrounded by fallen soldiers, stood the indomitable Florentius, leaning on two infantry swords he was using as canes, his wooden leg completely gone. Staring into the smoky haze with bloodshot eyes and blackened face, he looked up as Aetius trotted up to his side and dismounted.

"Florentius!" he said. "I had thought you lost!"

Florentius glanced at him and snorted. "Hard to keep up when your horse is shot out from under you, and your leg is hacked off by a Goth. I traded my peg for his neck, though," he said, lifting one of his swords and inspecting the sheen of blood that coated it for half its length.

"I'd hate to be the enemy who thought he could best you, old man," Aetius said.

Florentius grunted. "Your son may be disappointed," he replied. "We're not Huns yet."

"It isn't over," Aetius said, glancing about at the carnage.

"True. Best rally the troops in case the enemy gets it in his mind to charge us again."

Aetius strode among the shattered men, gently encouraging them to rise to their feet. Eliciting no response, he began toeing them with his cavalry boot, then applying the flat of his sword to their backs and thighs.

"On your feet, men! The Huns might try another ruse before sundown, but if we can hold them off once more, they won't fight after dark."

Weary and groaning, the troops shakily stood. Aetius was astonished at the number who remained lying where they were, unable to rise at any cost. Slowly and deliberately, the men shuffled back into position, shields held on trembling arms, swollen, bloodshot eyes peering through their visors as the Hunnish mounted warriors before them sallied forward in small groups, charging recklessly and then pulling back at the last moment, shouting taunts and shrill yips.

"My God—do they never quit?" groaned a half-dead legionary, swaying on his feet, to an exhausted comrade nursing an arrow wound in the shoulder. "You kill one and three more take his place."

"Still," the other rejoined, "we held the devils off! Didn't we do it? Didn't we just hold the bastards off?"

The first soldier grunted a weary assent but would not admit a triumph, even grudgingly. "Another victory like this," he rejoined, "and we'll all be dead."

Turgrid cantered up to Attila, who sat his horse motionless on a low hillock, peering down at the battlefield.

"The ropers have been stopped, *Cur*. The other troops are still fighting on all fronts, but they are exhausted and are making no further progress. Night will fall within the hour. We should organize a withdrawal."

Attila cursed. "Turgrid—I must assemble the *keshig*, the royal bodyguard. Find Orestes, and five hundred men, with fresh horses. The Roman camp is large, and the road behind it is long."

Turgrid looked at him warily. "The road behind it? Where will you go? The horde is not fit to fight further, either this day or tomorrow, and our supplies are drained. My advice, *Cur*, is to—"

"Let the horde turn back, or go to the devil if they wish! My army may be stopped, but Aetius will not live this night to savor his victory. I must assemble the guard!"

"Is this no longer a battle for Europe? Is this merely a personal struggle, your own feud against a man who was your friend, who has done you no harm?"

Attila stopped short and glared at the old general. "Flavius Aetius has done more harm than can ever be calculated, more than anyone but a king can ever know," he hissed. "He was offered a share in command of the world, which he turned down, to cause this . . . annihilation! Destiny—our *common* destiny—has been thwarted! The will of the gods has been repulsed! Is there any greater evil than this? Aetius must be destroyed! To excuse him is to condone him. Are you a Hun or a Roman?"

Turgrid met his gaze unflinchingly. "A Hun, Great King. I will always be a Hun." There was no hesitation.

With a quick nod, Attila wheeled his horse and raced off, leaving Turgrid staring after him. The weight of his many years descended upon him like a heavy cloud, and he suddenly felt very old. His shoulders slumped, and for a moment his face crumpled in an expression of despair.

But only for a moment.

Suddenly straightening and setting his mouth in its customary line of determination, he dismounted and slapped the haunch of his horse, sending it trotting away back toward the Hunnish camp. He watched it for a moment as it joined the herds of riderless animals moving slowly in the same direction, away from the continuing clamor of the battle. He then quickly removed the heavy helmet and officer's armor he wore, reflecting on the half century of protection they had afforded him, the countless gashes they bore, the stains of enemy blood, both old and recent, that had soaked so thickly into the leather as to color it a motley black. The armor was legendary among the Hunnish troops he had commanded over the years.

Last, he removed the woolen cloak and the insignia of rank he wore as a brooch at the neck. It was a bronze pin, of ancient barbarian manufacture, that had been gifted him by King Rugila many decades before for valor in battle, and which he had worn every day since.

All these things he scattered on the ground before him, mingling them with the torn clothing, broken weapons, and other detritus covering the field for many hundreds of paces in all directions. He was left with only his camp clothing, his riding boots, and a crudely carved wolf tooth, which hung like a gleaming talisman on a thong at his neck.

"I am a Hun," he repeated, holding the yellow fang between his fingers. "And a Hun always pays his debts."

Pausing to pick up a discarded Roman legionary helmet lying on the ground and place it loosely on his head, the old man walked alone toward the center of the battlefield, and though he was surrounded by a thousand thousand fighting men, his departure went unnoticed by all as he disappeared into the dense cloud of smoke and dust from the battle that still raged.

VI

Twilight finally descended, and with it rose the wind, bringing treason and rebellion to the skies. Black-armored clouds assembled in formation, forgetting their late wars and lack of discipline. As the moon advanced silently across the sky, they launched themselves upon its trail, overwhelming it like mute assassins. Down from the blackness came at first a few desultory drops, and then more, until at length the thunderclouds were full overhead and the water fell in a stinging rain, washing the dead and chilling the living.

A herald in full regalia galloped out alone from the ragged Roman lines, bearing a lance with a white pennant flapping.

"A truce!" The herald's voice rang out over the field that had fallen almost silent since the last troops had broken off the battle with the falling of night. "General Aetius calls for a truce during the hours of darkness to collect the dead and wounded. Do you accept?"

There was no response from the restless Hunnish lines, but for a general outburst of catcalls and taunts.

The herald ventured a few steps farther, lifting his white pennant and praying it could be well seen in the darkness and the rain, and that his exposed torso, on the other hand, could not be. He raised his formidable voice even more loudly, struggling to stifle the fear he felt. "Do you accept, I said?"

After a moment, Attila cantered out a few feet in front of his troops on a snorting and pawing war pony. It was his fourth mount that day. Two had been shot out from under him, and the third had slipped on a fallen Roman and snapped its leg. The king bore a torch in his hand.

"A truce, Romans," Attila bellowed out in mocking Latin. "You have until sunrise to remove your trash from the field!"

As the camp savants translated his words into Hunnish and Goth, laughter roared out from the Hunnish lines. Attila glared angrily in the direction of his enemy, hurled his torch into the darkness toward the voice of the invisible herald, then wheeled and trotted back to the waiting horde.

The vast plain of Catalaunici now belonged only to the ambulance crews and the collectors of the dead.

NINE

Campi Catalaunici, Gaul, Night, June 20, A.D. 451

I

Aetius slumped in fatigue on a camp stool near Turgrid's cot, hands drooping between his knees. Despite the throbbing pain in his forearm where the arrow had grazed him, sheer exhaustion had finally overwhelmed him, and his head nodded forward. The oil lamps were sputtering out, and all was quiet but for the incessant rattling of the rain on the canvas roof and the faint nighttime noises of the camp—the guards calling the watch, the restless snuffle of horses.

Suddenly he was startled awake by voices nearby, as the young tribune Antony, wearing a rain-drenched cloak and mud-spattered armor, burst into the tent without even the customary announcement from the guard. Aetius sat up with a start and squinted at him, running a hand through his dirt-encrusted hair. The officer's demeanor was eager, but, Aetius noted grimly, his expression was somber. Clearly he had important news to impart—but bad news. What Aetius wouldn't give to be back in Arelate with Priscilla this night. What he wouldn't give to be in Turgrid's place—sleeping, under a blanket, with no further responsibilities. Hell, even the wound might be worth it.

"General Aetius!" the tribune barked, much too loudly for the closed space of the tent. Aetius glared, and the officer cleared his throat and began again, only slightly more softly. "You ordered me to report at the next watch. The night squad has finished their count. The news is not good, sir!"

"Quiet, Antony," Aetius growled. "Can you not see we have a patient here?"

The tribune did a double take at the sleeping form lying on the cot. "A . . . a Hun? In your quarters, General?"

"So it seems. What is the news, Tribune?"

The officer paused to collect himself and peered at a scrap of parchment he held in his hand, turning it this way and that in the flickering light. "Close to a hundred thousand casualties on our side, sir, dead and wounded. We estimate the Huns lost twice as many, which would normally be good news, but—"

Aetius cut him off dismissively. "But there's twice as many of them to begin with. Right?"

"Yes, sir. I would say more."

Aetius shrugged. "This is nothing new."

Antony threw back his shoulders. "Our strength is badly depleted, sir. Shall I spread word to begin the retreat?"

"Retreat? Are you out of your mind?" Aetius asked evenly. "Spread word to hold fast—this is the greatest victory the Western Empire has ever achieved."

The tribune stared at him incredulously. " 'Victory'? Victory! Beg pardon, sir, but perhaps you didn't hear me: Our forces are depleted!"

"Yes, and the Huns have been stopped—that's all that matters. For two full days now they have been camped on this wretched plain, unable to go through us, around us, or over us. Attila has never faced such an obstacle. We are Romans, and he knows we can hold out another two or three days, if necessary."

"Another three days! We'll all be dead!"

Aetius sighed. "Don't worry, Tribune; it won't come to that. There is a reason why Attila's men are a 'horde' and we are 'legions.' His men live for pillage and plunder. What you see as a loss I see as victory. And the longer we stay in front of him, blocking his path forward, the more secure that victory becomes."

"But sir," the officer protested, "their numbers are their strength!"

Aetius shrugged, stood up, and walked back to his desk. "No, Tribune—their numbers are *our* strength."

"The enemy's million men are *our* strength?"

"Of course," Aetius patiently explained. "They have no supply line, as we do. With a million men they must keep moving to eat. They cannot stop, not even for a day. They suck the countryside dry for miles around within hours, and they burn what they cannot eat on the spot. You don't need to *destroy* the horde to attain victory— you need only stop them. Hunger will do the rest. If they can't pass us, they must turn back—or starve. Even now, in the rush to prepare for battle, I would venture they haven't eaten for three days."

"But sir, with all our casualties—"

Just then the veteran tribune Pellus burst into the tent with additional news. Aetius looked at him in surprise. "Are my guards not on duty tonight? This tent is becoming a circus. . . ."

Pellus interrupted him. "Sir—the Hunnish camp has come alive. They are forming ranks, preparing to march—"

"It's an attack!" Antony burst out.

Pellus looked at him with disdain. "No, sir," he replied. "We believe it is a withdrawal. Word is already spreading among the troops!"

With that, all three men paused to listen. There was a bustling outside, a sound alien to them, unlike the somber quiet and the moans of the wounded they had been hearing for hours. There were even hints of distant cheering and celebrating in the camp. Florentius swung into the tent on crutches, the stump of his leg dangling uselessly without its wooden extension and brass knob, and Senator Carpilio shuffled in wearing oversized army boots.

"General Aetius," Florentius announced, "it is confirmed. The Huns are preparing to break camp!"

Carpilio stepped forward and clasped Aetius' arm. "Well done, son! When I betrothed to you my own daughter, I had no idea I would become father-in-law to the savior of Western civilization."

Aetius nodded. "Your arrival seems to have brought us good fortune, Senator. Perhaps tomorrow you will be able to witness the retreat of the enemy."

Carpilio stepped back and wagged his finger, but the broad grin never left his face. "Ah—let us not be premature. Victory is not assured quite yet. There still remains much to do before the horde is destroyed—"

Suddenly Prince Thorismund burst into the tent, a wild expression on his face. Alongside the Roman officers, the prince looked every inch the barbarian chieftain in defeat. His leather vest hung open, exposing his chest, bound across one side by a grimy strip of rag through which blood from a wound had soaked and stained brown. His long hair was tied up loosely on his head in a topknot, his arms were bare, and his baggy woolen pants hung loose and sodden on his legs, mud-caked from the knees down as if he had been trudging on the road alongside his men. He glared about angrily, and after getting his bearings inside the close quarters of the command tent, he strode up to Aetius, his chin jutting forward belligerently.

"My father is dead!" His voice cracked and he broke off, staring straight into Aetius' eyes.

Aetius gazed back at him calmly and reached out a hand to his shoulder. "Son . . ."

But Thorismund shook off the gesture angrily. "He was cut down in the midst of battle, cut down like a dog by those infernal Hunnish cavalry—and yet your camp celebrates?" He glared at Carpilio. "Even your guards have given up their posts outside the tent—they're swigging hot wine at the quartermaster's yard. Is this the Roman protection you promised? Is this the great Roman discipline? The promise to stand on the front lines in defense of your empire?"

Aetius stared at him for a moment in silence and then gestured for him to sit.

"King Theodoric was a brave man, Prince," he said quietly. "A king like no other, with honor to spare . . ."

Thorismund kicked the camp chair angrily, shattering it against the tent post and bringing a torrent of beaded drops down upon their heads. "He was also a loyal ally," he replied accusingly.

". . . and his death is a great loss to the Visigoths, and to Rome," Aetius calmly continued.

Carpilio stepped forward. "His name shall be honored for all time, young prince, for he has contributed greatly to this Roman victory!"

Thorismund wheeled on the old man in anger. "*Contributed*, you say! Were it not for the Visigoth army, there would be no victory, Senator. This was a Visigoth victory, a complete Visigoth victory, but it is not yet finished!"

Aetius looked at him. "What do you mean, Prince?"

Thorismund turned on him savagely. "I mean that Attila still lives, and so long as he does, my father's death is unavenged. We must destroy the Huns once and for all!"

"We will do no such thing," Aetius replied quietly. "The Huns are on the retreat."

"That is a lie. They have not been conquered . . . only stopped!"

Aetius shook his head slowly. "Stopping them is defeating them. The Huns are still dangerous, like a cornered bear, and our own forces are depleted. By attacking now we could lose the advantage we have gained. We could even lose victory itself."

Thorismund gaped at him. "You refuse to attack? You refuse to avenge my father? If you allow Attila to fight another day, will your emperor allow *you* to live?"

"Listen to the general, boy," Carpilio interrupted angrily. "Rejoice in what you have gained, rather than curse what you have lost."

"But—"

"I refuse to risk further life when there is no need," Aetius said coldly. "The emperor's reaction bears no weight in this decision. I look to the good of my men, and to the good of Rome."

"By God!" Thorismund shouted. "If the Romans are afraid to attack these yellow dogs, I'll do it alone!"

The tent erupted in shouting and insults as every man tried to speak at once. Aetius, however, remained apart, carefully studying the Visigoth's face. Finally, he spoke again, and all fell silent.

"So you will attack the Huns without Rome," Aetius repeated. "By what authority do you do this? Are you now king of the Visigoths?"

Thorismund paused, for the first time showing a hint of uncertainty. "My army has acclaimed me king. . . ."

"Ah," said Aetius. "But you have brothers in Tolosa. I have met at least four. All of them have some claim to the Visigoth throne. And they are all in your capital, living in the palace, so they are in a better position to assert their claims, are they not?"

"Your words are an insult, Roman," Thorismund burst out angrily. "Do you deny my authority to lead my army? Do you doubt my ability—"

"No," interrupted Aetius. "But every moment you remain here, seeking vengeance on the Huns, allows your brothers in Tolosa additional time to seize control."

"Do you think I have not thought of this?" Thorismund

exclaimed heatedly. "If I were to leave at once, I might arrive in Tolosa before they receive word of Father's death. Yet by doing so, I would betray the coalition. Has any man ever faced such a wretched choice, between gaining control of a kingdom and remaining loyal to his duty?"

"Yes," Aetius said quietly.

"All the worse for him," Thorismund snapped.

"I accept full responsibility for your actions," Aetius replied. "Go now to Tolosa. Consolidate your crown, and remain a Roman ally. We will have the opportunity to serve each other in the future."

Thorismund looked at him warily. "You release me of my commitment to you?"

"It is what your father would have wanted."

"My father would have wanted his blood avenged, not dismissed."

Aetius paused for a moment, holding the young prince's angry glare. Then he turned away.

Without further word, Thorismund spun on his heel and stalked out of the tent into the rain, leaving the remaining advisors in the tent aghast.

There was a long silence, broken only by the pounding of rain on the sodden canvas. Finally, Carpilio spoke up.

"Flavius—do you realize what you have done? If the Visigoths leave, we will be down to half strength."

"Worse than that," Aetius replied, expressionless. "We are down to half strength already, with our casualties. Ask our young body counter here."

Antony winced. "Not quite half strength, sir, but the situation is serious."

"And with that I disagree," Aetius interjected before anyone else could say a word. "The main body of the Visigoths will not leave until morning. But the Huns are departing at this very moment."

"This is a game of timing I do not like," Carpilio muttered.

"And what would you have me do?"

"I?" Carpilio looked startled. "I'll tell you what I would have you do. I would . . . well—"

"I will save you the trouble of deciding," interrupted Aetius. "Even at half strength I will stand and face down the Huns, as will every Roman in this camp. Those men, sitting exhausted in the mud outside their tents—they're bandaging their wounds, and they're having a cup of Gallic wine to celebrate the Huns' retreat, but if the Huns return tomorrow, every one of those men will stand up and fight to his death. Would you officers—"

He gestured at the men standing around him at the central table, "—would you officers, warm and fed and unburdened by injury, would you do any less than those men?"

They all stared at him silently.

"Would you hesitate to stand firm? Would you betray their trust?"

They dropped their gaze. "By God, we wouldn't," growled the old senator fiercely.

"Then, game of timing or not, this is the game I play," Aetius said menacingly, "because it is the only game I *can* play. And you will either stand with me, wholeheartedly, or you will be declared an enemy of Rome, and I will fish my drunken guards out from whatever dice game they've fallen into and have you arrested—tribune, scout, or senator. Is that clear?"

The officers stared at him nervously but said nothing. Aetius went on.

"In the morning we will celebrate the Huns' withdrawal, or we will do battle again. At half strength, if necessary. Florentius and Senator, you stay. The rest of you, get some sleep."

The men shuffled out. Outside, in the camp, the celebration continued and became steadily more raucous, but inside the still tent only a single sound could be heard.

Aetius was dismayed, but not surprised, to hear Turgrid's labored breathing become even more ragged than before.

II

In the Hunnish camp, the clamor was indescribable, as soldiers loudly stowed their gear, officers shouted orders to bring about the wagons, and always and everywhere was the thunder of passing hoofbeats. The night was as dark as a cauldron, with the pouring rain turning the ground to a quagmire, yet every man was awake and moving. On the far side of the vast encampment, in his squarely built tent of greased leather, scarcely larger than that used by the army's junior officers, Attila furiously donned his battle armor, rage darkening his face. Muttering angrily to himself, he stalked about the cramped enclosure, seizing his gear from corners and thrusting aside the fumbling hands of the slow-moving squire who attempted to help him dress. It was the third squire he had suffered this day. The other two, like his horses, had been lost to battle.

There was a hiss at the tent entrance, and the boy jumped, then walked to the door and lifted the flap. After a short whispered conversation, the squire dropped the flap down and returned to Attila, who was adjusting a shoulder strap on his armor. Nervously the boy broke the silence.

"*Cur,* General Orestes has assembled the five hundred guards outside the camp—they await your orders."

Attila grunted. "I take it General Turgrid has still not been found?"

"No, *Cur.* Perhaps he lies dead or wounded on the battlefield."

"Perhaps. I have searched, and I have used wolves, but in this accursed rain we can no more find an individual man than we can a dirty coin in a mud hole. A fine time for him to trot off on his own to seek glory in battle. If that is what he did."

The squire reflected for a moment. "You will continue to search?"

"I can delay no longer. The night is well under way. Come—let us finish."

He strapped his cuirass and settled his helmet, then quickly inspected his battle sword. Frowning, he wiped it on his goatskin leggings and slid it fiercely into its sheath. He then strode to the rough camp table, the only piece of furniture in the tent, apart from a low wooden stool. He paused before a fine polished bone-and-ebony case, of a delicacy and fineness that were incongruous in the rustic camp setting. Carefully opening the lid, he removed the contents—the ancient, crumbling Sword of the Dynasty. He held it up to the torch sconce on the tent center post, inspecting it minutely in the flickering light, then carefully slid it into a second sheath on his back, near the arrow quiver.

The squire's curiosity overcame his nervousness at the great man's presence.

"You will take both swords, *Cur*?" he murmured.

Attila nodded and grunted. "This one"—he touched the plainly dressed, newer sword—"is a blade for battle, like any other. If I break it, I'll pick up another from the ground and continue to fight. It is forgettable. But this one"—and he gently reached behind his back to touch the hilt of the other—"is the sword that inspires my men. It represents our way of life—the blessing and watchfulness of the gods, the sword of our destiny. So long as I live, this blade stays with me."

Cinching his quiver strap tightly about his shoulder and adjusting his helmet once more, he stepped out of the tent and into the driving rain.

Before him was a scene that would have made a strong man weep. The vast army was preparing to march, to withdraw, though not out of defeat but rather out of pure momentum. For like a wooden ball thrown by a child against the stone walls of an alleyway it could not stop, but must continually move. If its forward progress was blocked it must turn another way and continue its inexorable, damnable movement. Tents were being struck and wadded into bundles, and wagons rolled past, loaded high with weaponry and gear. The king strode grim-faced through the chaos. Before him, activity ceased; men parted; horses and oxen were pulled to the side of the path to let him pass. Behind him the bustle resumed; the shouts and oaths again resounded. He strode, enveloped in a cocoon of angry silence, through the buzzing hive of activity to the farthest edge of the Hunnish encampment.

There, waiting for him in the darkness, in silence and in perfect alignment, were five hundred mounted warriors. No mere tribesmen these, they were hand-picked from the king's personal guard. Tough, hard-eyed veterans, armed to the teeth, horses pawing restlessly. They were not unreliable Ostrogoths, nor mere Vandal or Alamanni mercenaries. Every man was a Hun of noble family. Every man had fought with Attila for years, as their fathers had fought with his father, and their grandfathers with his grandfather. Every man was prepared to die for him. They watched in grim silence as Attila mounted the one remaining riderless horse.

"Where do we stand, Orestes?" he asked.

The Alaman kneed his horse and stepped forward from the rest.

"Half the army is breaking camp and preparing to move out," he said.

"I can see and hear that. My concern is with the other half."

"The other half is in battle position, my lord. They await only your signal."

Attila scanned the cohort of fighters before him. Motionless, they stared back, eyes flashing beneath the rims of their helmets, reflecting the distant lights of the camp, faces gleaming with rain. There was an occasional flash of white teeth in the darkness as here and there a man grinned fiercely. Attila took all this in with a single sweep of his gaze.

"The signal will be given from the Roman camp within four hours. Instruct the night watch to train their eyes there, to watch for the fire arrow."

"They have already been instructed, *Cur*."

Attila nodded in satisfaction; then raising his sword above his head, he shouted into the darkness.

"To Rome!"

A wordless bellow issued forth from the men, and all five hundred horses surged forward as if they were one being and disappeared into the darkness.

Despite the late hour, Aetius was still awake in his tent, poring over a map of the battlefield with Florentius and Carpilio, talking quietly. There was a persistent coughing in the background, so soft and regular as to almost form part of the background noise, like the steady pattering of the rain and the calling of the guards' watch, which men learn to ignore after a time and even to miss after it has ceased. It was only when the rain dwindled momentarily, engulfing the men in an unaccustomed silence, that the sound of the old Hun's suffering finally penetrated Aetius' thoughts. He stopped his contemplation of the map before him and strode over to Turgrid, whose eyes were open. The Hun sucked in air greedily, gasping for breath, floundering for air in his very bed, and a trickle of blood flowed from the corner of his mouth. With sinking heart, Aetius realized that these were the Hun's last moments of life.

The old man looked up, stretched out his hand, and

weakly grasped Aetius' sleeve. His mouth worked soundlessly.

"Calm, Turgrid, calm . . . calm," Aetius murmured, dropping onto the stool behind the Hun's cot. "You'll be fine in the morning, with a bit of rest. Sleep, old man."

Turgrid shook his head violently. "No. . . . Flavius, you must . . ."

"Don't try to talk. Just rest."

"Flavius . . ." Turgrid groaned. "You must keep . . . keep . . ."

Aetius smiled in understanding. "What, keep this?" He loosened his tunic and drew out the wolf tooth hanging by a leather thong about his neck. "Of course I'll keep it, old friend, always."

Turgrid's nostrils flared in agony and his voice quavered.

"No!" he protested. "No . . . Keep . . . eyes to the East. . . ."

With that, Turgrid gasped deeply and fell silent in mid-breath. He lay motionless on the cot but for the trickle of blood glimmering in the lamplight.

Carpilio, who had approached a moment before, reached over with his hand and closed the old man's eyes, which had rolled back and clouded over in death, pale as moonstone. Aetius stared at the old Hun, frozen, though not with an expression of sadness—rather, his eyes grew wide, almost as if startled.

" 'Eyes to the East,' " Carpilio repeated as he drew his hand back. "Poor old bastard. Still, he was a Hun. Can't say I'm sorry."

Florentius, who had also limped over, shrugged. "He meant well, but he was too late. Telling us to look to the East, to beware of the horde. But the horde is retreating now."

Aetius still sat staring at Turgrid's face, then finally looked up, a range of emotions flitting over his expression as a realization suddenly dawned upon him.

"No," Aetius said slowly. "That's not what he meant."

Florentius scoffed quietly. "Begging your pardon, sir, of course it's what he meant. But the East is no longer a threat to us."

"No!" Aetius repeated, more vehemently this time. "Eyes to the East—he came here to give me a warning. It means . . . It means, 'Watch your back!' "

He leaped up with a start, knocking over the stool, ignoring the dead man lying before him and his puzzled colleagues in the tent.

"Florentius!" he barked.

"Sir?"

"Has that supply column from Aurelius arrived in camp yet?"

Florentius retreated to the table and shuffled through several rain-soaked dispatches scattered about the surface. After a few seconds he found the correct one.

"It was due to arrive two hours ago, sir, but it has not. Probably delayed by the storm."

"The roads are still good—our scouts have been traveling at will, so it could not have been delayed by the storm." Aetius paused for a moment in thought. "I don't like it. They shouldn't have been delayed. There might be something happening behind our lines."

"Sir, that's impossible. It's a large baggage train, with guards and escorts. They are well equipped to defend themselves from all but the largest attacks. Surely the refugees could not have caused any damage—"

"I'm not thinking about the refugees," Aetius interrupted curtly. "Do you remember our discussion last night? How Attila was seeking not merely to win the battle, but to destroy our very civilization?"

"I remember," Florentius replied. "He has failed on both accounts."

"One does not give up such a goal so easily. Attila would not give up such a goal ever. Find the quartermaster general. Tell him to investigate the delay in the supply column, immediately."

"The quartermaster general?" Florentius repeated.

"Yes. Go now!"

"Sir," Florentius went on, "the quartermaster was killed in battle today."

"Killed!" Aetius exclaimed. "Then send his assistant."

"Also dead."

Aetius paced the inside perimeter of the tent in anger. "Damn it. Order the men to saddle up, Florentius. I'll go check on that supply column myself. Just a precaution. . . ."

"Saddle up the men—you mean your personal guard? You suspect mischief with a supply train, so you are *personally* going to ride out of camp at night with a squadron of guards to check, General?"

Aetius paused again in thought. "No, not my personal guard. The quartermaster's cavalry cohort who would normally have escorted the train had they not been in battle today. Five hundred men. Have them ready before the turn of the next watch."

"I will go with you as well."

Aetius looked down at the old man standing before him on one leg, trying to maintain his balance on the crutches, and smiled.

"You've served me well this day, old friend, and lost your leg for a second time. Ready the cohort for me, and then get some rest."

Florentius shook his head as he ducked out of the tent into the driving rain. "Five hundred men," he muttered. "For a supply train that's camped for the night."

III

The rain finally stopped, and with the brisk chill wind the sky began to clear. Thick moisture-laden clouds scudded rapidly across a full moon, causing rapid shifts in the light. From the hillock on which he and his men had stopped their horses Aetius could look across a forested valley and see the black moon shadows of the clouds as they raced across the earth, spotting the landscape with fluid and changing shades, gray, white, and black, as if the previous day's battle on the ground was now being taken up in the heavens. He gloomily wondered on whose side God was fighting tonight, then quickly put such thoughts out of his mind. He had just ridden ten miles in darkness, with five hundred men, who were now staring at him, waiting for his instructions.

Aetius peered at the stars through the shifting patches of clear sky. "Two hours still till sunrise. The light's too irregular to do anything until then." Then he forced himself to look back down and bit his lip to keep from weeping in his rage and frustration.

Before them was a scene of utter desolation. Smoldering supply wagons lay overturned on both sides of the road. Three hundred men lay dead, and there was silence all around, for even those who had been merely wounded and might have lived to see another rain-crossed night, had been executed where they fell, their throats hurriedly slit, their armor and valuables left intact. Wrecked supplies and provisions lay scattered about the ground. This was no raid by starving refugees, seeking supplies and plunder. This was outright murder.

Aetius' cavalrymen dismounted, but rather than spread out in formation to inspect the damage and look for survivors, they clustered closely together, looking warily about them. Even the animals remained spooked and jittery. Aetius beckoned for a torch, one of the few that still remained lit after the fast, rainy ride, and squatted to examine a set of tracks in the mud. The cohort's senior centurion, hurriedly appointed to the rank of tribune after the deaths of his superior officers, was aghast. He turned over a Roman corpse with his foot and recoiled as the head stayed where it was on the ground, even as the body rolled away.

"What happened here?" he exclaimed under his breath. The sound broke the silence like a blade sliding from a sheath in a close room, and several of the men standing nearby turned toward him, startled. "Who did this?"

Aetius stood and looked at him evenly, a hint of contempt on his face. "If you don't know, son, you don't deserve to be commanding a cohort."

The officer blinked in surprise for a moment, then persisted. "The Huns? But they're facing our army, executing a withdrawal. They're not ten miles *behind* our lines—"

With a hiss and a wet *thwack*, an arrowhead suddenly emerged from the man's throat, and he dropped to his knees gurgling blood. The moon disappeared behind a black cloud, throwing all into darkness.

"Heads down!" Aetius roared, heaving the lit torch away from him, but it was too late. The air was filled with the hissing of arrows, and as the troops dropped flat on their bellies into the mud, their ears rang with the screams of wounded men. Even as they lay in the filth, confused and terrified, the ground suddenly began shaking to the sound of hoofbeats that seemed to bear down on them in the darkness from all sides. Within moments, the black forms of galloping horsemen stormed out of the surrounding trees and swept into the supply camp they had just destroyed.

As the hissing of the volley of arrows became louder, Aetius realized there was no chance of escape and leaped back to his feet. "Stand and draw your weapons," he called out. "Forget the horses! Ground formation!"

The Roman cohort had been caught completely unawares, unable to move quickly in their stiff cavalry armor, while struggling to draw weapons at the same time. The terrified horses pulled away from their grounded riders and fled as the mounted Huns rampaged furiously through the destroyed convoy. In the darkness and confusion, the Roman detachment could do little to defend itself from the lightning attack—for the enemy seemed to be upon them from all sides, everywhere and yet nowhere they could be reached.

In a mist of anger and confusion, the Romans raised their shields high before their faces, forgoing visibility, for little could be seen in any case in the swiftly moving night shadows. All they could do was brace shields above their heads and against their shoulders, warding off the swords and axes raining down on them from the furious riders and shrinking from the arrows that swarmed through the air like angry hornets. The Huns, on their ponies, weaved in and around one another, dodging clumsy Roman blows with skill and lethal daring, seeing like cats in the darkness, striking like a pack of wolves at a flock of sheep. They seemed to be everywhere—cutting down Romans where they stood, smashing through upraised shields, unmercifully trampling everything in their path.

Through the grim slaughter, as eerily silent as his men in their focused killing, Attila stalked purposefully, on foot, sword held high. Reaching the very midst of the fighting, he leaped upon the side of an overturned supply wagon and bellowed, his full voice carrying to every living ear.

"Aetius!" he shouted. "Flavius Aetius is mine!"

The black clouds parted from the moon for a moment, revealing the carnage nearly as clearly as in the light of day, and with the light Attila spotted his quarry in the near distance. Aetius, too, was on foot, but facing away from him, preparing to defend himself against a Hunnish warrior bearing down on him at full gallop. The Hun's mouth was twisted in a grimace, and his battle-ax was held high. Aetius stood calmly at the ready, sword held with both hands in striking position.

Suddenly Attila dropped his sword and in a single fluid motion ripped the war bow from his back, drew an arrow from his quiver, fitted it to the string, and released. The grimace froze on the Hunnish rider's face, and with a grunt he dropped his ax, rolled from his horse, and came to a rest at Aetius' feet, the arrow protruding from his forehead. At this, all motion on the battlefield seemed to cease, and in silence the Hunnish horsemen drew up their mounts where they were, some standing atop the vanquished bodies of their Roman foes. The surviving Roman troops clustered in a tight circle, facing outward in desperation, at the Huns who surrounded them. Their shields were still raised before their faces, on arms so weary they shook, and their armor was bloodied and dented from the blows that had been raining down upon them in the darkness. In silence, Aetius looked at the dead Hun lying at his feet, eyes still open in surprise. He then slowly turned around.

Again a voice rang out, this time a cry of triumph rather than an order. "I said Flavius Aetius is mine!"

Attila stood poised, his bow discarded and again his battle sword drawn. The two men stared at each other for a moment, the Roman swaying in exhaustion, the Hun easily rocking forward and back on the balls of his feet. Nearby, Aetius' wolf Lucilla was crouching, a low snarl in her throat, readying herself for a pounce on Attila's wolf facing her.

Attila narrowed his eyes and smiled. "Thank you for 'rescuing' your supply column. You saved me the trouble of hunting you down in your camp."

Aetius stared at him. "You would have sneaked into my camp?"

Attila smiled. "You have a strange definition of

'sneaking.' When I give the signal, your camp will be annihilated."

Aetius glanced up quickly at the dark sky. There was not yet even a hint of the coming dawn. The wound on his arm burned intolerably and he felt he could barely stand, for sheer fatigue. Still, he must play for time.

"Impossible," Aetius said. "You're mad."

"While your men are drunk, celebrating my 'retreat'!"

Aetius glared. "We have a truce, until sunup. The Hunnish kings I have known would not have betrayed agreements. Rugila had honor."

Attila emitted a short, barking laugh. "Honor? How convenient. Romans pillage for a thousand years, but when they finally come under attack on their own soil, they plead *honor.* I gave you your chance, Flavius—you could have ruled Gaul; there would have been peace. Yet you refused, for 'honor's' sake, dragging us into war. Rome's honor is the world's destruction."

Aetius leaped at him, and Attila stepped forward to meet him. The two men battled furiously and wordlessly, in a series of lightning sword blows and parries of the Hunnish style. The Romans watched, agog at their commander's fury and skill, though the Huns looming over them on their horses never took their eyes off their captives. Beside the two leaders, their wolves tore at each other in a tight clinch, rolling through the gore, one atop the other, so quickly they could not be told apart. Snarling furiously, they snapped their jaws at each other's throats, and the skittish horses shied away.

With a lunge, the two men separated, unhurt but perspiring heavily, their chests heaving with exertion. They locked eyes on each other as the wolves battled furiously nearby.

"There is honor beyond emperors and armies," Aetius panted. "There is honor as a man—before God and . . . your own *people*!"

With the final word he leaped forward, fiercely and skillfully, but the Hun was too quick. Attila sidestepped and spun into a low wrestling stance. Aetius was thrown off-balance, and as Attila sensed an opportunity for a kill, he launched himself bodily into the air, throwing all his weight at his staggering opponent, knocking Aetius into the mud. The two men rolled for a moment before finally stopping. The surrounding troops, captors and prisoners, leaned forward to view the outcome of the combat, and perhaps of their own lives. What they saw made the Romans' blood run cold. There, among the blood and filth of mounds of men already dead, lay Aetius, Attila on top, serrated dagger held against the Roman's throat. For a moment, no sound could be heard but for the men's labored breathing. Then, the Hun's eyes fell on the wolf tooth dangling from Aetius's neck. Attila started in surprise.

"You captured the old man!"

With difficulty, Aetius shook his head. "He . . . repaid a favor. At least *he* had honor."

Attila snarled with rage and tightened the grip on the blade. "*This* is what I think of Roman honor . . ."

And then the world exploded.

With a deafening cry, hundreds of mounted men burst out of the forest. Romans and Huns alike froze in shock, and before they could react, the armored warriors were upon them, cutting down the Huns before they could drive their mounts to safety, trampling the foot-bound Romans as they dove frantically for cover. None knew whether the new attack was by friend or foe. In an instant, the air was again filled with the screams of angry and dying men, and all degenerated into a horrifying tumult.

At the moment of the attack, Attila started up in surprise, and as he did so Aetius rolled quickly to the side, evading the blade at his throat and throwing the Hun's weight off him. Both men leaped to their feet, but the Roman now had the momentum. Before Attila could react, Aetius executed a rapid feint, the one with which Attila himself had deceived him so many years before in their boyhood duel. Spinning rapidly on his feet, he maneuvered himself behind Attila, sword pointed firmly at his back.

Attila froze, and in that moment so, too, did every other combatant, when it became clear that the king's life hung in the balance. Huns lay dead and dying on the ground, their blood mingling with those of the Romans they had killed only moments before. Lucilla the wolf, bleeding from the ear and with a gaping, empty socket where her eye had been, crouched in front of Attila, snarling, ready to spring. The Hunnish wolf lay dead a few paces away. There was an awful moment of silence as all eyes fixed upon the two leaders.

Aetius spoke first, softly, almost inaudible to all but his captive.

"Turn around. Slowly."

Attila did so, chin high, eyes flashing fury.

"Now, drop your sword," Aetius continued.

Rather than obeying instantly, Attila slowly reached back with his free hand, to the arrow quiver on his back, and pulled out the ancient rusty sword, its broken blade pointed forward. He held both swords now, one in each hand.

"Which would you have me drop?" he hissed.

There was a long pause as Aetius looked from one blade to the other, sizing up the situation. Immediately he grasped the meaning of the two weapons. Without further hesitation, he nodded toward the standard-issue battle sword, its blade smeared with blood.

"That one only," he replied.

Attila dropped it in the mud and then lowered the hand holding the broken sword to his side. Before he could speak, a man strode forward, the leader of the attack party that had just arrived. He stepped up to Aetius' side, glaring at Attila.

"So this is the man who killed my father," Thorismund said.

Aetius nodded. "This is the man who commands the Hun army. Your father died in fair combat with the enemy."

"My father's blood calls," Thorismund snarled. "I will have my revenge!"

He drew his sword from its sheath and stepped toward Attila but then stopped abruptly as he felt a sword at his own back. Then all was silent as Thorismund slowly turned, eyed the sword, and followed it up the length of the blade to the hilt, the steady arm grasping it, and finally to Aetius' stern face.

"Now drop *your* sword, Prince," Aetius quietly ordered.

Thorismund's jaw clenched tightly and he paused for a moment, considering his options, but as his eyes flitted about him he saw he was surrounded by Aetius' men, all with weapons drawn. Grudgingly he dropped his blade beside that of Attila.

"Prince"—Aetius glanced at Thorismund—"you are no longer needed here. Continue on your way. Your kingdom awaits."

Still Thorismund did not move. Aetius turned on him in a fury.

"Go!"

Thorismund opened his mouth to protest, but seeing Aetius' expression, he strode away in silence. There was a brief bustle as he and the Visigoth escort mounted their horses, and then their fading gallop as they thundered off, continuing their journey to Tolosa.

Attila thrust out his chest defiantly.

"Now," he said in a commanding voice. "The stripling prince is gone. You may kill me yourself, Flavius."

Aetius shook his head slowly. "I will not. Go back to your men. They wait for you to lead them back east."

Attila stared at him with cold suspicion. "You would send back your mortal enemy?"

"A Hun does not forget a debt. And my debt has now been repaid."

"You are *not* a Hun!" Attila hissed. "You are a Roman, an enemy. Kill me!"

"No. You saved my life once. As I did Turgrid's. He said he would be my slave."

"That was rhetorical."

"Not to Turgrid," Aetius countered. "He lost his life. For rhetoric?"

Attila lunged for the point of the sword, but Aetius deftly flitted it away, then dropped his blade to his side. Attila glowered.

"If you are my slave," the Hun growled, a note of fury in his voice, "then do as I command you: Kill me!"

"That is how I would repay my debt? By killing you?"

"That is my will!" Attila spat.

Aetius paused, appraising the panting, desperate man before him.

"Then I renounce my debt and spurn my honor. A Roman is slave to no man."

"By releasing me, you spare my body, but kill my soul!"

Aetius shrugged and turned away. "I spare what I have the capacity to spare. Your soul is your own affair."

Not a sound could be heard, not a movement spied. Every man was frozen, listening to the extraordinary exchange. Finally, Attila broke the silence, stepping to where Lucilla lay in the mud, her head trembling in an agony of pain, her flanks heaving with exhaustion. He toed her with his foot and she snarled and snapped at him but did not have the strength to rise. Attila turned and glared at Aetius.

"Your wolf is dying," Attila pronounced. "She must be put out of her misery."

"So she shall," Aetius answered.

"And so you must do for me. I deserve at least the same honor as your animal."

Aetius laughed scornfully. "And so now it is *you* falling back on the plea for honor. So quickly your view changes when it is *you* on the other end of the blade."

Attila lunged once again for the sword, and again Aetius dodged it out of his reach.

"You used to be a Hun," Attila snarled. "You know this is our way. It is the Hunnish way!"

"It is not the way of Rome. . . ."

"I *spit* on the way of Rome! I would rather be dead, and my entire army dead with me, than live one day for the way of Rome, under the thumb of Rome!"

"All the more reason that you must live, then," Aetius said evenly, "as testimony to the power—and *honor*—of Rome."

Attila squeezed his eyes tightly closed for a moment, shutting out the unfathomable, the defeat of a dream, the disappointment of a million men in the field and countless millions more behind them. Then he opened them again and looked in silence at the sky. The full moon still played chase through scudding storm-laden clouds. It still created shifting shadows and white light that shone cool, not life-giving but rather lifeless and sterile, deadly and pale, and then disappeared into darkness. Nothing had changed. But something *had* changed, something immense, and the world would no longer be the same.

A flock of startled crows burst from the branches with a harsh cacophony. They flew into the empty sky, which was just beginning to lighten with pale dawn, and after circling for a moment they flapped away and disappeared into the distance, still screeching their mocking laughs.

A moment later, a squadron of horsemen thundered out of the clearing in the trees, taking the road that would lead them on the long northeasterly loop back to the Hunnish camp. Like Huns always, they were strong and they rode swiftly, and they carried themselves as determined warriors and bore the scars of fierce battles. But at the same time they were different; they were something they had not been even a few moments before, something they would now be for the rest of their lives.

For the first time, they were defeated men.

IV

Morning dawned brooding and gray, lending an ominous tone to the horrors of the previous day and the relief of the night before. The Roman troops no longer reveled. Rather, they deployed in wary formation at the crest of a low rise overlooking the battlefield. Before them black smoke still rose from the remains of smoldering wagons and puddles of oily flame left by the incendiary missiles. The men found it difficult even to look out over the plain, much less to stand in close ranks, and not be affected by the sheer scale of the destruction that had been wrought.

To the edge of the plain on the far horizon, thousands of bodies littered the field, horses and men, combatant and camp follower, mingling indiscriminately, lifeless and cold. Buzzards stalked about among the corpses, casting avid beady glances at the sheer quantity of pickings and squabbling with one another over individual victims, though surrounded by a hundred thousand others. Feral dogs scurried about, backs curved and tails between their legs, searching for meat but cowering lest they themselves be set upon by another.

Burn squads continued to move slowly through the field. The living, or at least those with sufficient life to raise a beckoning hand where they lay or to call a hoarse plea with a mud-caked tongue, had all been collected the night before. Now the squads picked up the dead and the near dead, with no particular care or tenderness. Exhaustion and despair had callused them, and men simply heaved their loads into stacks, like cordwood of flesh and blood.

Near one such stack, an elderly priest softly mumbled the prayers for the dead, slowly and sorrowfully forming the sign of the cross. Just as he finished, a burly soldier with a rag tied over his face roughly shouldered the old man aside, threw a bucket of flammable liquid over the corpses, and set them afire with a torch. Once again, columns of black smoke drifted with acrid stench over the field. The men standing in formation in ranks squinted into the distance, the older veterans with faces hard, the young recruits grateful in their minds for the distraction of the foul, greasy smoke that wafted over them, disguising the tears that rose to their eyes, which with the cover of the smoke they could allow to flow freely and without shame.

In the middle distance a huge, motley array traveled slowly along the rutted road—the thousands of horsemen and wagons of Attila's horde. The enormous column stretched to the horizon, though the rear ranks had still not even departed their camp, and the Romans stood silent, watching them move. Aetius and Carpilio sat their horses somewhat apart from the Roman troops but stared at the departing column with the same tired fascination as did their men.

"You have achieved a great victory," Carpilio said quietly. "You have saved the Western Empire. Your name will be remembered for all eternity."

Aetius shook his head ruefully. "There are still many other enemies."

"You are far too pessimistic, my son. With the Huns overcome, there are no other barbarians that can stand up to Rome's might. None would dare."

"Perhaps you are right," Aetius responded thoughtfully. "But not all Rome's enemies are outside its walls. As you well know."

Carpilio considered this for a moment and then shrugged. "Fortune has been kind to us. I leave it to her to hold us as safe in the court of the emperor as she has on the field against Attila."

"Then you put your life in untrustworthy hands, for Fortune is a very random goddess," Aetius replied. "Commit your boat to her winds and you sail wherever they blow, not just where you want. As for myself, I want nothing to do with her dangerous games. I rely on my own hands and my own lips, and if I fail it is for my own shortcomings, not the favors of Fortune."

Carpilio glanced at him with a wry smile. "And if our fickle goddess sides with Attila, in return for your neglect of her? Spurned women do not love *no* man—they love the enemy."

"That is her loss—for I know Attila spurns her as well. If ever a man trusted in his own abilities alone, it is Attila."

"All the more credit to you, then, for having defeated him. May poor Fortune bestow her scorned favors on me instead, for I welcome them with open arms. Come. To breakfast and then home. It is still a long journey. Your wife awaits. My grandchildren await."

Aetius smiled, for the first time in what seemed years. "And so they do. I am done here."

Spurring their horses, Aetius and Carpilio rode off, turning their backs on the Hunnish army in the distance.

On a low rise on the plain opposite the Romans' vantage point, another man, too, watched the progress of the departing column. Reining in his horse on the edge of the vast battlefield, Attila sat motionless and brooding, restlessly fingering a battle sword in his right hand. Gazing across the plain at the Roman formation, he squinted eagerly at the officers standing beneath each legion's standard, straining his eyes to recognize his adversary. Then, from the side of his vision, at the farthest edge of the Roman deployment, he made out two riders before they galloped out of his sight. One wore a Roman toga that shifted and trailed behind him in the breeze, and he slumped in his saddle like an old man unaccustomed to a warhorse between his thighs. But the other—from this distance, looking at the rider's posture and ease in the saddle, one could almost mistake him for a Hun. But Attila knew: The man was no Hun. His eyes focused on the man, and for that brief moment he felt weathered and worn, old beyond his years, and the west wind blowing through his long hair sang to him a song of defeat, rather than of ambition and promise. He was beaten, but he forced himself to ride erect in the saddle, and his expression remained defiant, his eyes calculating.

Suddenly he looked down. Something had touched his leg. There on the ground stood a small Hunnish boy, perhaps eight years old. Shaven knob, fox-head cape, miniature bow—all the trappings of Attila's squadron of cub warriors. The lad tugged on Attila's pant leg and looked up at him.

Attila reached down with his left hand to grasp the boy's arm and then hoisted him up to the horse. He propped him on the animal's back, just in front of his own legs.

The boy glanced to the side and saw the sword Attila gripped still in his right hand. He swiveled his head back and once again looked silently up at the king. Attila returned the boy's solemn gaze and then slowly reached back to the quiver on his shoulder and took out the broken, rusty Sword of the Huns. He gave it to the boy, who grasped it tightly in his right hand, just like the king. He then faced forward and cast the Roman enemy a fierce glare.

The king heeled his horse forward and, with the boy, began the long canter down the grassy hill, to join the column of wagons and horses winding down the road toward the eastern horizon.

AUTHOR'S POSTSCRIPT

In this age, when science seems able to assure us of all knowledge, from the intimacies of our genetics to the chronology of the nascent universe, it is surprising how little we know of the Huns, a people who nearly toppled Western civilization a millennium and a half ago. Like many nomadic, pastoral tribes, they left us no written records and precious little physical evidence of their passage. Indeed, even their very origins are subject to dispute, though most anthropologists are now converging on general agreement. The Huns seem to have first appeared on the steppe of what is now Mongolia or western Siberia and over the course of several generations moved gradually west, conquering or sweeping up other tribes in their path, mingling bloodlines and absorbing new customs. It was shortly after their arrival in the region of modern-day Hungary that Attila's ancestors first came to Rome's attention.

Yet even the Romans' knowledge of this strange people was vague. Their physical descriptions of the Huns sound accurate enough, if exaggerated, but their accounts of the Huns' customs often are mere repetitions of the most barbaric features of earlier eastern tribes, the Scythians and even the Amazons, whose own existence was probably mythical. Indeed, even information as basic as the year of Attila's birth is in question: A number of scholars claim it as recent as A.D. 406, while others (most

European) calculate it as early as A.D. 395 (the birth year of Aetius, which is the assumption I used). Thus, with so many gaps in our sources, a novelist seeking to write about the Huns from *inside* the Hunnish camp (as distinct from a story based on the "observations" of outsiders like Romans or Greeks) has his work cut out for him.

Of course, what I have written is a novel, not an academic study, and I did take some slight historical license with the known record, which the reader will, I hope, accept as inconsequential. The ancient Hunnish words included in my text may or may not be exact—some are transliterations of Hunnish terms into Greek or Latin by ancient travelers, while others are known words from ancient Mongol, Turkic, or Slavic that may have derived from the Hunnish or been borrowed by it. Words for certain familiar places, such as Rome and the Rhine River, have been rendered in modern English, as I felt that using their Latin names sounded jarring and pretentious. Units of measurement, such as yards or miles, are generally in the modern style, to avoid the unnecessary confusion that would occur with the use of archaic systems.

Attila's battle speech to his men took place on the eve of Châlons, though I split it and placed it partly on his crossing of the Rhine. My description of Plinthas' embassy to the Huns is actully a melding of several such meetings between the Eastern Romans and Attila's court. And Honoria's courier, Marcus, appears to have actually been a eunuch named Hyacinth, though that name's modern association with a tropical flower made it unsuitable and distracting for use in this novel. (Concerned readers will be relieved to know that Honoria eventually left prison, married a respected Roman senator named Herculanus, and apparently lived the remainder of her life uneventfully.)

Possibly the most significant license was not in what I included in this book but what I omitted. My focus was largely on the relationship between Aetius and Attila and the events leading up to the climactic Battle of Châlons, yet each man's individual story is much bigger than this. Major events in Attila's life that I was unable to depict include his devastating campaigns on the Danube and his aborted siege of Orleans just before Châlons, as well as his colorful life and death after the decisive battle. Omitted events involving Aetius include the struggle with his great political rival, Count Boniface, the Vandal invasion of Africa, and another possible boyhood stint as a hostage, this time among the Goths. Though fascinating in their own right, these events had to be sacrificed in order to keep the book to a reasonable length.

Of the ancient authors on this subject, Jordanes, a sixth-century Ostrogoth historian, is possibly the most useful. His *Getica,* the history of the Goths, was based on an earlier history, now lost, by the Roman politician and monk Cassiodorus, who lived within a generation of the Battle of Châlons and who very possibly knew or interviewed many of its participants. The *Mulomedicina* of the fifth-century Roman administrator Vegetius provides a lively description of the unusual Hunnish breed of horses, as well as their care and training. The Greek scribe Priscus provides a wonderfully detailed account of a dinner party he attended hosted by Attila, on which I closely modeled the dinner scene in the book. The *Consolatio Philosophiae,* by Boethius, a Roman nobleman who lived shortly after Aetius, is an interesting and moving effort to reconcile the ancient legacy of classical philosophy with Christianity. Indeed, my rendering of the tale of Orpheus, which some students of Greek mythology might find slightly odd, is taken directly from Boethius and is therefore presumably consistent with the version popular among Romans of Aetius' time. And Ammianus Marcellinus, in his *History of the Late Roman Empire,* provides indispensable information on Roman military tactics and weaponry in the last two centuries of the Western Empire, though he was often wildly inaccurate in describing the Huns (and was one of the earliest propagators of the false rumor of cooking meat in the saddle).

Readers interested in further information on the lives of Attila and Aetius would do well to consult Gibbon's *Decline and Fall of the Roman Empire*, E. A. Thompson's *The Huns*, and Otto J. Maenchen-Helfen's magisterial *The World of the Huns*, all of which are readily available.

ACKNOWLEDGMENTS

True gratitude is a rare and wonderful thing, the mirror image of true generosity, which is rarer still. After four novels' worth of importuning friends and family with requests for proofreading, for their historical expertise, for their editorial opinions, and for their patience with my impatience, I am pretty certain I know what true generosity is. Mark Usher has it in abundance, for his long-suffering attention to historical details and his dogged willingness to read my early drafts without squirming. Mir Bahmanyar, too, has copious amounts, for his multiple read-throughs, his constant availability to help me think through thorny plot issues, and his unswerving determination to keep the wolves alive. Alan Nevins not only has the sharp business mind and industry knowledge that one would expect from a top literary agent, but also has been blessed with a sense of unfailing optimism and cheerfulness about my prospects and is generous to me with those traits. And my editor, Pete Wolverton, not only has a drill sergeant's ability to hone in on precisely the weak point of a flabby manuscript but also affords me generous time and resources in aspects relating to the very fine production of my books.

The writing process involves its share of complaints and frustration, but it contains a great many rewards as well, and it is these—being able to work at home, to teach my children, to do what I love—that I dedicate to my family. To Eamon, whose computer and athletic prowess keeps me functioning and fit; to Isa, whose musical talent and spirituality keep me marveled and humbled; to my own personal Hun, Marie, whose exuberance and unconditional love keep my priorities properly grounded; and to my wife, Cristina, without whom all would indeed be very empty and gray. In my family I have seen true generosity. I can only hope that in me they are able to see true gratitude.

M.C.F.
September 2004